THE AUTHOR

Herbert George Wells was born in Bromley, Kent in 1866, the third son of an unsuccessful shopkeeper. At eighteen he left his job as a draper's apprentice and became a pupil teacher at Midhurst Grammar School, from where he won a scholarship to the Normal School of Science, South Kensington, and studied biology under T. H. Huxley. Although distracted by politics, writing and teaching he obtained a B.Sc. in 1890 and then lectured for the University Tutorial College until the success of his short stories allowed him to become a full-time writer. Idealistic and impatient, he flung himself into contemporary issues – free love, Fabianism, progressive education, scientific theory, 'world government', human rights. His personal life was equally restless: after an early marriage to his cousin Isabel in 1890 ended in divorce, he married a pupil, Amy Catherine Robbins, in 1895, and was later involved with a series of remarkable women including Amber Reeves, Elizabeth von Arnim, Rebecca West and Moura Budberg. He died in London in 1946.

H. G. Wells wrote over a hundred books, achieving unparalleled international fame for a British writer. His work ranged from the famous scientific fantasies like *The Time Machine* (1895) and realistic comedies like *Kipps* (1905) to provocative topical novels such as *Marriage* (1912), *Mr Britling Sees It Through* (1916), *The Autocracy of Mr Parham* (1932) and controversial or encyclopedic works like *A Modern Utopia* (1905) or *The Outline of History* (1920). He describes his own life in the two-volume *Experiment in Autobiography* (1934) and *H. G. Wells in Love*, unpublished until 1984.

The Hogarth Press also publishes *Mr Britling Sees It Through*, *Christina Alberta's Father*, *In the Days of the Comet*, *The Passionate Friends* and *The Wife of Sir Isaac Harman*.

MARRIAGE

H. G. Wells

'And the Poor Dears haven't the shadow of a doubt
they will live happily ever afterwards.'
From a Private Letter.

New Introduction by
Victoria Glendinning

THE HOGARTH PRESS
LONDON

Fraternally
to
Arnold Bennett

Published in 1986 by
The Hogarth Press
Chatto & Windus Ltd
40 William IV Street, London WC2N 4DF

First published in Great Britain by Macmillan 1912
Hogarth edition offset from Collins 1923 edition
Copyright the Executors of the Estate of H. G. Wells
New Introduction copyright © Victoria Glendinning 1986

ISBN 0 7012 0578 4

Printed in Finland by
Werner Söderström Oy

INTRODUCTION

There is a lot in this novel which will make women tear their hair out in fury; and yet it is enjoyable and absorbing. There is something candid, even touching, in the way H. G. Wells tries to come to grips with what goes wrong between men and women – failing dismally, you may think by the end, to transcend his male perspective and male egotism, but never failing in energy, commitment or entertainment value.

Marriage is one of a sequence of 'discussion' novels on the same topic – the relations between the sexes in a changing society – that Wells wrote when he was in his forties. He later called them his 'prig' novels. *Marriage* was published in 1912; he had recently emerged from a passionate affair with Amber Reeves, half his age, which had threatened his marriage, and was now engaged in a less serious liaison with the novelist Elizabeth von Arnim. His home life was more or less intact, and his second wife Jane, who was important to him in every way except sexually, tolerated his extramarital activities in the confidence that he would not leave her and their two children.

The early sex-and-society novels, of which *Marriage* is the third (following *Ann Veronica* and *The New Machiavelli*), are largely autobiographical, and the first two were considered scandalous by those in the know. The messages that come out of them are contradictory, since Wells had contradictory ideas of what he wanted women to be: chaste wives and mothers, passionate mistresses, frank comrades. What exercises him in this novel is how a marriage can stay alive, given the normative influence of conventional society, the differing needs and expectations of men and women, and the failure of passion to survive:

For this, indeed, is the truth of passionate love, that it works out its purpose and comes to an end. A day arrives in every marriage when the lovers must face each other, disillusioned, stripped of the last shred of excitement – undisguisedly themselves. And our two were married . . .

But that is halfway through the book. The beginning is the love story of 'our two'. Marjorie, an extremely pretty girl, studying science at Oxbridge, is in the bosom of her large family. Wells had a gift for social settings and the social comedy of bourgeois family life, and in the early chapters of 'pure story', wittily told, he hooks his readers in readiness for the serious discussions to come. In Marjorie's parents, moreover, he displays in action one model of marriage, and in the rich, wife-centred Jewish family, later on, we get another very different one.

Trafford, the modern man of science whom Marjorie will love, arrives on the carefully prepared scene literally like a *deus ex machina* – in an airplane: very dashing, very brilliant, irresistible. Before this we learn a lot about Marjorie. She is a modern girl, who has abandoned moral absolutes; she would like to have 'heaps of money'; she has 'an instinctive turn for decoration in costume and furniture' and 'an immense, tumultuous appetite for life'. She is quite capable of side-stepping her principles in order to have a London house and a position in society. She is therefore attractive, vital and venal: this is fine, except that as the story progresses it becomes clear that the author thinks of her as a 'typical' woman – rather than as a *type* of woman, which she certainly is. Wells makes it clear that the love between Marjorie and Trafford is the real thing, flame to flame; yet for all his own intense sexual experience, he writes sketchily about passion and gives Trafford some dreadful and unreal lines, as when he describes Marjorie to his doting mother: 'And she's tender. It's as if someone had taken tears, mother, and made a spirit out of them.'

Marjorie is a spirit with very earthly aspirations. She wants to have a nice home. She spends money – Trafford's money – lovingly on curtains, furniture and ornaments. He is a dedicated research scientist and finds that marriage erodes both his time for work and his bank account. There are some first-rate domestic scenes in the narrative, illustrating the gulf between their expectations of marriage so dramatically that anyone who has been married will recognise at least something in them. Through Trafford, Wells expresses his belief in the importance and primacy of science over both political and social life; through Marjorie, he expresses his belief in the limitations of the female vision. Marjorie, with her down-to-earth, wifely concerns, is unaware that 'she was destroying an essential thing in his life', his freedom to pursue ideas and do his research. He begins to despise her moral and intellectual standards – 'an agitated rat-bag' of unthought-out attitudes. Women, according to this novel, drag men down. 'She missed the high aim in him.'

Yet at times Trafford deplores his own intellectual selfishness; nor is Marjorie quite without insight. It is she who describes women in their society as 'neither pets nor partners, but something between the two'. She begins to comprehend the significance of the economic dependence of women: 'A woman gives herself to a man out of love, and remains clinging parasitically to him out of necessity. Was there no way of evading that necessity?' She feels that she is in 'a pleasant, high-class prison' – and so is he, except that he is so overworked and frustrated that it is no longer pleasant. He has too much to do – none of it, now, congenial – and she has too little. The passionate love affair has become an unhappy marriage.

Wells recycled characters, and even situations, in all his discussion novels. Minor characters such as the feminist writer Agatha Alimony and the novelist Wilkins (a caricature of Wells himself) recur in all of them. Others, particularly, 'advanced women', reappear under different names and hats. Wells had, as it were, a pack of cards which he shuffled shamelessly. There are more basic similarities between *Marriage* and the earlier *Ann Veronica*, which may point not so much to a failure in inventiveness as to a continuing set of obsessions.

In both *Ann Veronica* and *Marriage* the ravishingly pretty heroine is halfway through a science degree course and has a pompous and authoritarian father. In both books she is wooed by a ludicrous suitor at a party given by an influential titled lady, with the same sequence of results. In both books the man she loves is a gifted scientist who has to compromise between his passion for his work and his need to support his family; both books stress the need for thinking things out rationally when relations between lovers become strained, and both books canvass the idea of personal 'salvation'. Sexual happiness, for Wells, seems associated with being abroad and in the mountains; in both books the heights of bliss and harmony are reached on walking-tours in the Alps.

Ann Veronica ended with the girl-student and her scientist safely married after much dramatic strain and stress. The scientist, Capes, has written a commercially successful play, and Ann Veronica is happily pregnant. But will they be able to sustain their Alpine ecstasy, and not be overwhelmed by ordinary life and all the conventional dreariness against which their illicit early love had been a protest? *Marriage* can be seen as taking the argument on from this point, with a different cast of characters.

The once-subversive heroine of *Ann Veronica* makes a guest appearance in *Marriage*; she is now quiet Mrs Capes, 'a markedly correct and exclusive mother of daughters'. Her husband is successful as a playwright, and no longer a practising scientist. He 'has to' write plays, says Ann Veronica Capes, though 'it isn't what he cares to do'. Clearly their high hopes are forgotten, and they have become like any other conventional married couple.

This chance meeting between Mrs Capes and Marjorie, in *Marriage*, takes place just when the marriage between Marjorie and Trafford is at its lowest ebb. Trafford is on the point of going away by himself to 'think things out'. In order to save the marriage, he takes Marjorie with him. Just where they go, and what happens to them there, is such an astonishment to the reader that he may well wonder if he has not wandered by mistake into a different book altogether.

In the narrative part of this surprising section Wells is at his most boyish, even childlike, concocting an amazing adventure of a sort he himself had never had, in a distant location he had never seen; and even though it is ridiculous it is fun, like a good bad film. What is even more ridiculous is the desperate lengths to which the Traffords have to go, both physically and ideologically, in order to bring life back into their marriage. If the beneficial effects of their trial by ordeal were to wear off, what desperate remedy, one wonders, could they possibly try next?

But more infuriating than any of this are the conclusions about their marriage and about the relative positions of men and women to which they come during their adventure – conclusions which, for once, brought Wells the approval of the moral majority.

One contemporary review called *Marriage* 'a thrilling and inspiring book and one that can be placed on a puritan's family bookshelf ' – in contrast, the implication was, to its immediate predecessor, *The New Machiavelli*, which had ended subversively with a married man running away with his young mistress. Henry James, who had an ambivalent friendship with Wells (their aims and techniques as novelists could hardly have been more opposed), wrote in a letter to Wells that what interested him about *Marriage* was Wells's own reactions to his story, 'these attestations of your character and behaviour'. They are of interest to us also – and however much we may bristle at the rank male vanity and egotism, I would also agree with James that, for its time, Wells's writing was 'more convulsed with life and more brimming with blood than any it is given me nowadays to meet'. He is a minor Dickens in the vividness of his bizarre secondary characters, in his witty monitoring of motives and manners, and in the cinematic reality of his houses, gardens and interiors.

Rebecca West was not yet twenty when she reviewed *Marriage* in the *Freewoman*. She took a tough line. She mocked Wells, whom she had never met, about something on which he considered himself an expert and a progressive – sex:

Of course, he is the old maid among novelists, even the sex obsession that lay clotted on *Ann Veronica* and *The New Machiavelli* like cold white sauce was merely old maid's mania, the reaction towards the flesh of a mind too long absorbed in airships and colloids.

She poured contempt on the heroine Marjorie, calling her 'Our Lady of Loot', and complained how the author seemed to accept her financial incompetence and acquisitiveness as the normal condition of women. (As he probably did – Ann Veronica too was always in trouble over money.) Wells's first sin in *Marriage*, wrote Rebecca West, was his assumption that Marjorie was 'the normal woman'; his second was the suggestion that love and economics should be separated, by the provision of state subsidy. If furniture and fittings were automatically provided on marriage, the novel suggests, 'then every woman would be a princess to the man she loved'. But what would happen, Miss West asked, to the woman who did not marry but had to fend for herself? The economic position of women was one of her own pet subjects, as it was Wells's; she had already published articles about how 'the middle class woman will have to stop being a parasite'.

It was typical of Wells that while he thought seriously about the place of women in his ideal society, he was incapable of seeing them except in relation to men. In this sequence of novels he repeatedly made cruel and effective fun of independent women and militant feminists, caricaturing their ignorance of facts, feeble, muddled thinking, self-importance and – greatest sin of all, to him – their physical unattractiveness. He had reason when it came to characters like Aunt Plessington in *Marriage*, a smug do-gooder with a craving for importance, interfering with the 'defenceless lower classes'. But Wells/Trafford is equally scornful of the suffragist group that Marjorie joins in order to fill her time with something worthwhile; her friends talked 'a flood of rubbish'. It was 'a mistake to *mass* women. It brings out something silly . . . all hat and flutter.' Trafford, like Wells, nevertheless called himself a feminist. Perhaps what Wells wanted was for women to be sufficiently liberated to talk intelligently with men, and to go to bed with them enthusiastically, married or unmarried, but not so liberated as to put their own aspirations on a par with a man's, or to abandon the primary function of servicing men domestically and sexually.

Rebecca West was a feminist, and an independent, ardent

girl. Her provocative review of *Marriage* caused Wells to write to her and ask her to lunch with him and his wife. In view of its implications, it is ironic that it should have been this particular novel which brought about the first step in what was to be a stormy ten-year liaison.

Victoria Glendinning, London 1985

CONTENTS

BOOK THE FIRST
Marjorie Marries

CHAP.		PAGE
I.	A DAY WITH THE POPES	I
II.	THE TWO PROPOSALS OF MR. MAGNET	33
III.	THE MAN WHO FELL OUT OF THE SKY	77
IV.	CRISIS	113
V.	A TELEPHONE CALL	129

BOOK THE SECOND
Marjorie Married

I.	SETTLING DOWN	153
II.	THE CHILD OF THE AGES	177
III.	THE NEW PHASE	191

BOOK THE THIRD
Marjorie at Lonely Hut

I.	SUCCESSES	250
II.	TRAFFORD DECIDES TO GO	273
III.	THE PILGRIMAGE TO LONELY HUT	304
IV.	LONELY HUT	317
V.	THE TRAIL TO THE SEA	368

BOOK THE FIRST

MARJORIE MARRIES

CHAPTER THE FIRST

A DAY WITH THE POPES

§ 1

AN extremely pretty girl occupied a second-class compartment in one of those trains which percolate through the rural tranquillities of middle England from Ganford in Oxfordshire to Rumbold Junction in Kent. She was going to join her family at Buryhamstreet after a visit to some Gloucestershire friends. Her father, Mr. Pope, once a leader in the coach-building world and now by retirement a gentleman, had taken the Buryhamstreet vicarage furnished for two months (beginning on the fifteenth of July) at his maximum summer rental of seven guineas a week. His daughter was on her way to this retreat.

At first she had been an animated traveller, erect and keenly regardful of every detail upon the platforms of the stations at which her conveyance lingered, but the tedium of the journey and the warmth of the sunny afternoon had relaxed her pose by imperceptible degrees, and she sat now comfortably in the corner, with her neat toes upon the seat before her, ready to drop them primly at the first sign of a fellow-traveller. Her expression lapsed more and more towards an almost somnolent reverie. She wished she had not taken a second-class ticket, because then she might have afforded a cup of tea at Reading, and so fortified herself against this insinuating indolence.

She was travelling second class, instead of third as she ought to have done, through one of those lapses so inevitable to young people in her position. The two Carmel boys and a cousin, two greyhounds and a chow had come to see her off; they had made a brilliant and prosperous group on the platform and extorted the manifest admiration of two youthful porters, and it had been altogether too much for Marjorie Pope to admit it was the

family custom—except when her father's nerves had to
be considered—to go third class. So she had made a
hasty calculation—she knew her balance to a penny
because of the recent tipping—and found it would just
run to it. Fourpence remained—and there would be a
porter at Buryhamstreet !

Her mother had said : " You will have Ample." Well,
opinions of amplitude vary. With numerous details fresh
in her mind, Marjorie decided it would be wiser to avoid
financial discussion during her first few days at Buryhamstreet.

There was much in Marjorie's equipment in the key of
travelling second class at the sacrifice of afternoon tea.
There was, for example, a certain quiet goodness of style
about her clothes, though the skirt betrayed age, and an
entire absence of style about her luggage, which was all
in the compartment with her, and which consisted of a
distended hold-all, a very good tennis-racket in a stretcher,
a portmanteau of cheap white basketwork held together
by straps, and a very new, expensive-looking and meretricious dressing-bag of imitation morocco, which had been
one of her chief financial errors at Oxbridge. The collection
was eloquent indeed of incompatible standards. . . .

Marjorie had a chin that was small in size if resolute in
form, and a mouth that was not noticeably soft and weak
because it was conspicuously soft and pretty. Her nose
was delicately aquiline and very subtly and finely modelled,
and she looked out upon the world with steady, gray-blue
eyes beneath broad, level brows that contradicted in a
large measure the hint of weakness below. She had an
abundance of copper-red hair, which flowed back very
prettily from her broad, low forehead and over her delicate
ears, and she had that warm-tinted clear skin that goes
so well with reddish hair. She had a very dainty neck,
and the long slender lines of her body were full of the
promise of a riper beauty. She had the good open shoulders
of a tennis-player and a swimmer. Some day she was to
be a tall, ruddy, beautiful woman. She wore simple
clothes of silvery gray and soft green, and about her waist
was a belt of gray leather in which there now wilted two
creamy-petalled roses.

That was the visible Marjorie. Somewhere out of time
and space was an invisible Marjorie who looked out on the
world with those steady eyes, and smiled or drooped with
the soft red lips, and dreamt, and wondered, and desired.

§ 2

What a queer thing the invisible human being would appear if, by some discovery as yet inconceivable, some spiritual X-ray photography, we could flash it into sight ! Long ago I read a book called *Soul Shapes* that was full of ingenious ideas, but I doubt very much if the thing so revealed would have any shape, any abiding solid outline at all. It is something more fluctuating and discursive than that—at any rate, for every one young enough not to have set and hardened. Things come into it and become it, things drift out of it and cease to be it, things turn upside down in it and change and colour and dissolve, and grow and eddy about and blend into each other. One might figure it, I suppose, as a preposterous jumble animated by a will ; a floundering disconnectedness through which an old hump of impulse rises and thrusts unaccountably ; a river beast of purpose wallowing in a back eddy of mud and weeds and floating objects and creatures drowned. Now the sunshine of gladness makes it all vivid, now it is sombre and grimly insistent under the sky of some darkling mood, now an emotional gale sweeps across it and it is one confused agitation. . . .

And surely these invisible selves of men were never so jumbled, so crowded, complicated, and stirred about as they are at the present time. Once I am told they had a sort of order, were sphered in religious beliefs, crystal clear, were arranged in a cosmogony that fitted them as hand fits glove, were separated by definite standards of right and wrong which presented life as planned in all its essential aspects from the cradle to the grave. Things are so no longer. That sphere is broken for most of us ; even if it is tied about and mended again, it is burst like a seed case ; things have fallen out and things have fallen in. . . .

Can I convey in any measure how it was with Marjorie ?

What was her religion ?

In college forms and returns, and suchlike documents, she would describe herself as " Church of England." She had been baptized according to the usages of that body, but she had hitherto evaded confirmation into it, and although it is a large, wealthy, and powerful organisation with many minds to serve it, it had never succeeded in getting into her quick and apprehensive intelligence any lucid and persuasive conception of what it considered God

and the universe were up to with her. It had failed to
catch her attention and state itself to her. A number of
humorous and other writers, and the general trend of talk
around her, and perhaps her own shrewd little observation
of superficial things, had, on the other hand, created a
fairly definite belief in her that it wasn't as a matter of fact
up to very much at all, that what it said wasn't said with
that absolute honesty which is a logical necessity in every
religious authority, and that its hierarchy had all sorts of
political and social considerations confusing its treatment
of her immortal soul. . . .

Marjorie followed her father in abstaining from church.
He too professed himself " Church of England," but he
was, if we are to set aside merely superficial classifications,
an irascible atheist with a respect for usage and Good
Taste, and an abject fear of the disapproval of other gentlemen of his class. For the rest he secretly disliked clergymen
on account of the peculiarity of their collars, and a certain
influence they had with women. When Marjorie at the age
of fourteen had displayed a hankering after ecclesiastical
ceremony and emotional religion, he had declared : " We
don't want any of *that* nonsense," and sent her into the
country to a farm where there were young calves and a
bottle-fed lamb and kittens. At times her mother went
to church and displayed considerable orthodoxy and
punctilio, at times the good lady didn't, and at times she
thought in a broad-minded way that there was a Lot in
Christian Science, and subjected herself to the ministrations
of an American named Silas Root. But his ministrations
were too expensive for continuous use, and so the old faith
did not lose its hold upon the family altogether. . . .

At school Marjorie had been taught what I may best
describe as Muffled Christianity—a temperate and discreet
system designed primarily not to irritate parents, in which
the painful symbol of the crucifixion and the riddle of what
Salvation was to save her from, and, indeed, the coarser
aspects of religion generally, were entirely subordinate to
images of amiable perambulations, and a rich mist of finer
feelings. She had been shielded, not only from arguments
against her religion, but from arguments for it—the two
things go together—and I do not think it was particularly
her fault if she was now growing up like the great majority
of respectable English people, with her religious faculty, as
it were, artificially faded, and an acquired disposition to
regard any speculation of why she was, and whence and

whither, as rather foolish, not very important, and in the very worst possible taste.

And so, the crystal globe being broken which once held souls together, you may expect to find her a little dispersed and inconsistent in her motives, and with none of that assurance a simpler age possessed of the exact specification of goodness or badness, the exact delimitation of right and wrong. Indeed, she did not live in a world of right and wrong, or anything so stern ; " horrid " and " jolly " had replaced these archaic orientations. In a world where a mercantile gentility has conquered passion and God is neither blasphemed nor adored, there necessarily arises this generation of young people, a little perplexed, indeed, and with a sense of something missing, but feeling their way inevitably at last to the great releasing question, " Then why shouldn't we have a good time ? "

Yet there was something in Marjorie, as in most human beings, that demanded some general idea, some aim, to hold her life together. A girl upon the borders of her set at college was fond of the phrase " living for the moment," and Marjorie associated with it the speaker's lax mouth, sloe-like eyes, soft, quick-flushing, boneless face, and a habit of squawking and bouncing in a forced and graceless manner. Marjorie's natural disposition was to deal with life in a steadier spirit than that. Yet all sorts of powers and forces were at work in her, some exalted, some elvish, some vulgar, some subtle. She felt keenly and desired strongly, and in effect she came perhaps nearer the realisation of that offending phrase than its original exponent. She had a clean intensity of feeling that made her delight in a thousand various things, in sunlight and textures, and the vividly quick, accurate acts of animals, in landscape, and the beauty of other girls, in wit, and people's voices, and good strong reasoning, and the desire and skill of art. She had a clear, rapid memory that made her excel perhaps a little too easily at school and college, an eagerness of sympathetic interest that won people very quickly and led to disappointments, and a very strong sense of the primary importance of Miss Marjorie Pope in the world. And when any very definite dream of what she would like to be and what she would like to do, such as being the principal of a ladies' college, or the first woman member of Parliament, or the wife of a barbaric chief in Borneo, or a great explorer, or the wife of a millionaire and a great social leader, or George Sand, or Saint Teresa, had had

possession of her imagination for a few weeks, an entirely
contrasted and equally attractive dream would presently
arise beside it and compete with it and replace it. It
wasn't so much that she turned against the old one as that
she was attracted by the new, and she forgot the old dream
rather than abandoned it, simply because she was only one
person, and hadn't therefore the possibility of realising
both.

In certain types, Marjorie's impressionability aroused a
passion of proselytism. People of the most diverse kinds
sought to influence her, and they invariably did so. Quite
a number of people, including her mother and the principal
of her college, believed themselves to be the leading influence
in her life. And this was particularly the case with her
Aunt Plessington. Her Aunt Plessington was devoted to
social and political work of an austere and aggressive sort
(in which Mr. Plessington participated) ; she was childless,
and had a Movement of her own, the Good Habits Movement, a progressive movement of the utmost scope and
benevolence which aimed at extensive interferences with
the food and domestic intimacies of the more defenceless
lower classes by means ultimately of legislation, and she
had Marjorie up to see her, took her for long walks while
she influenced with earnestness and vigour, and at times
had an air of bequeathing her mantle, movement, and
everything, quite definitely to her " little Madge." She
spoke of training her niece to succeed her, and bought all
the novels of Mrs. Humphry Ward for her as they appeared,
in the hope of quickening in her that flame of politico-
social ambition, that insatiable craving for dinner-parties
with important guests, which is so distinctive of the more
influential variety of English womanhood. It was due
rather to her own habit of monologue than to any reserve
on the part of Marjorie that she entertained the belief that
her niece was entirely acquiescent in these projects. They
went into Marjorie's mind and passed. For nearly a week,
it is true, she had dramatised herself as the angel and
inspiration of some great modern statesman, but this had
been ousted by a far more insistent dream, begotten by a
picture she had seen in some exhibition, of a life of careless
savagery, whose central and constantly recurrent incident
was the riding of barebacked horses out of deep-shadowed
forest into a foamy sunlit sea—in a costume that
would certainly have struck Aunt Plessington as a
mistake.

If you could have seen Marjorie in her railway compartment, with the sunshine, sunshine mottled by the dirty
window, tangled in her hair and creeping to and fro over
her face as the train followed the curves of the line, you
would certainly have agreed with me that she was pretty,
and you might even have thought her beautiful. But it
was necessary to fall in love with Marjorie before you
could find her absolutely beautiful. You might have
speculated just what business was going on behind those
drowsily thoughtful eyes. If you are—as people say—
" Victorian," you might even have whispered " Day
Dreams " at the sight of her. . . .

She *was* dreaming, and in a sense she was thinking of
beautiful things. But only mediately. She was thinking how
very much she would enjoy spending freely and vigorously,
quite a considerable amount of money—Heaps of money.

You see, the Carmels, with whom she had just been
staying, were shockingly well off. They had two motor-
cars with them in the country, and the boys had the use
of the second one as though it was just an old bicycle.
Marjorie had had a cheap white dinner-dress, made the
year before by a Chelsea French girl, a happy find of her
mother's, and it was shapely and simple and not at all bad,
and she had worn her green beads and her Egyptian necklace of jade ; but Kitty Carmel and her sister had had a
new costume nearly every night, and pretty bracelets, and
rubies, big pearls, and woven gold, and half a score of
delightful and precious things for neck and hair. Everything in the place was bright and good and abundant, the
servants were easy and well-mannered, without a trace
of hurry or resentment, and one didn't have to be sharp
about the eggs and things at breakfast in the morning,
or go without. All through the day, and even when they
had gone to bathe from the smart little white and-green
shed on the upper lake, Marjorie had been made to feel
the insufficiency of her equipment. Kitty Carmel, being
twenty-one, possessed her own cheque-book and had
accounts running at half a dozen West End shops ; and
both sisters had furnished their own rooms according to
their taste, with a sense of obvious effect that had set
Marjorie speculating just how a room might be done by
a girl with a real eye for colour and a real brain behind it. . . .

The train slowed down for the seventeenth time.
Marjorie looked up and read " Buryhamstreet."

§ 3

Her reverie vanished, and by a complex but almost
instantaneous movement she had her basket off the rack
and the carriage door open. She became teeming anticipations. There, advancing in a string, were Daffy, her
elder sister, Theodore, her younger brother, and the dog
Toupee. Sydney and Rom hadn't come. Daffy was not
copper-red like her sister, but really quite coarsely red-
haired ; she was bigger than Marjorie, and with irregular
teeth instead of Marjorie's neat row ; she confessed them
in a broad simple smile of welcome. Theodore was hatless,
rustily fuzzy-headed, and now a wealth of quasi-humorous
gesture. The dog Toupee was straining at a leash, and
doing its best, in a yapping, confused manner, to welcome
the wrong people by getting its lead round their legs.

"Toupee !" cried Marjorie, waving the basket.
"Toupee !"

They all called it Toupee because it was like one, but
the name was forbidden in her father's hearing. Her
father had decided that the proper name for a family dog
in England is Towser, and did his utmost to suppress a
sobriquet that was at once unprecedented and not in the
best possible taste. Which was why the whole family, with
the exception of Mrs. Pope, of course, stuck to Toupee. . . .

Marjorie flashed a second's contrast with the Carmel
splendours.

"Hallo, old Daffy. What's it like ? " she asked, handing
out the basket as her sister came up.

"It's a lark," said Daffy. "Where's the dressing-bag ? "

"Thoddy," said Marjorie, following up the dressing-
bag with the hold-all. "Lend a hand."

"Stow it, Toupee," said Theodore, and caught the
hold-all in time.

In another moment Marjorie was out of the train, had
done the swift kissing proper to the occasion, and rolled
a hand over Toupee's head—Toupee, who, after a passionate
lunge at a particularly savoury drover from the next
compartment, was now frantically trying to indicate that
Marjorie was the one human being he had ever cared for.
Brother and sister were both sketching out the state of
affairs at Buryhamstreet Vicarage in rapid competitive
jerks, each eager to tell things first—and the whole party
moved confusedly towards the station exit. Things pelted
into Marjorie's mind.

" We've got an old donkey-cart. I thought we shouldn't get here—ever. . . . Madge, we can go up the church tower whenever we like, only old Daffy won't let me shin up the flagstaff. It's *perfectly* safe—you couldn't fall off if you tried. . . . Had positively to get out at the level crossing and *pull* him over. . . . There's a sort of moat in the garden. . . . You never saw such furniture, Madge ! And the study ! It's hung with texts, and stuffed with books about the Scarlet Woman. . . . Piano's rather good, it's a Broadwood. . . . The Dad's got a war on about the tennis-net. Oh, frightful ! You'll see. It won't keep up. He's had a letter kept waiting by *The Times* for a fortnight, and it's a terror at breakfast. Says the motor people have used influence to silence him. Says that's a game two can play at. . . . Old Sid got herself upset stuffing windfalls. Rather a sell for old Sid, considering how refined she's getting. . . ."

There was a brief lull as the party got into the waiting governess cart. Toupee, after a preliminary refusal to enter, made a determined attempt on the best seat, from which he would be able to bark in a persistent, official manner at anything that passed. That suppressed, and Theodore's proposal to drive refused, they were able to start, and attention was concentrated upon Daffy's negotiation of the station approach. Marjorie turned on her brother with a smile of warm affection.

" How are you, old Theodore ? "

" I'm all right, old Madge."

" Mummy ? "

" Every one's all right," said Theodore ; " if it wasn't for that damned infernal net——"

" Ssssh ! " cried both sisters together.

" *He* says it," said Theodore.

Both sisters conveyed a grave and relentless disapproval.

" Pretty bit of road," said Marjorie. " I like that little house at the corner."

A pause and the eyes of the sisters met.

" *He's* here," said Daffy.

Marjorie affected ignorance.

" Who's here ? "

" *Il vostro senior Miraculoso.*"

" Just as though a fellow couldn't understand your kiddy little Italian," said Theodore, pulling Toupee's ear.

" Oh, well, I thought he might be," said Marjorie, regardless of her brother.

" Oh ! " said Daffy. " I didn't know——"

Both sisters looked at each other, and then both glanced at Theodore. He met Marjorie's eyes with a grimace of profound solemnity.

" Little brothers," he said, " shouldn't know. Just as though they didn't ! Rot ! But let's change the subject, my dears, all the same. Lemme see. There are a new sort of flea on Toupee, Madge, that he gets from the hens."

" *Is* a new sort," corrected Daffy. " He's horrider than ever, Madge. He leaves his soap in soak now to make us think he has used it. This is the village High Street. Isn't it jolly ? "

" Corners don't *bite* people," said Theodore, with a critical eye to the driving.

Marjorie surveyed the High Street, while Daffy devoted a few moments to Theodore.

The particular success of the village was its brace of chestnut trees which, with that noble disregard of triteness which is one of the charms of villages the whole world over, shadowed the village smithy. On either side of the roadway between it and the paths was a careless width of vivid grass protected by white posts, which gave way to admit a generous access on either hand to a jolly public-house, leering over red blinds, and swinging a painted sign against its competitor. Several of the cottages had real thatch and most had porches ; they had creepers nailed to their faces, and their gardens, crowded now with flowers, marigolds, begonias, snapdragon, delphiniums, white fox-gloves, and monkshood, seemed almost too good to be true. The doctor's house was pleasantly Georgian, and the village shop, which was also a post and telegraph office, lay back with a slight air of repletion, keeping its bulging double shop-windows wide open in a manifest attempt not to fall asleep. Two score of shock-headed boys and pinafored girls were drilling upon a bald space of ground before the village school, and near by, the national emotion at the ever-memorable Diamond Jubilee of Queen Victoria had evoked an artistic drinking-fountain of gray stone. Beyond the subsequent green—there were the correctest geese thereon—the village narrowed almost to a normal road again, and then, recalling itself with a start, lifted a little to the churchyard wall about the gray and ample church.

" It's just like all the villages that ever were," said Marjorie, and gave a cry of delight when Daffy, pointing to the white gate between two elm trees that led to the vicarage, remarked : " That's us."

In confirmation of which statement, Sydney and Rom, the two sisters next in succession to Marjorie, and with a strong tendency to be twins in spite of the year between them, appeared in a state of vociferous incivility opening the way for the donkey-carriage. Sydney was Sydney, and Rom was just short for Romola—one of her mother's favourite heroines in fiction.

" Old Madge," they said ; and then throwing respect to the winds, " Old Gargoo ! " which was Marjorie's forbidden nickname, and short for gargoyle (though surely only Victorian Gothic ever produced a gargoyle that had the remotest right to be associated with the neat brightness of Marjorie's face).

She overlooked the offence, and the pseudo-twins boarded the cart from behind, whereupon the already overburthened donkey, being old and in a manner wise, quickened his pace for the house to get the whole thing over.

" It's really an avenue," said Daffy ; but Marjorie, with her mind strung up to the Carmel standards, couldn't agree. It was like calling a row of boy-scouts Potsdam grenadiers. The trees were at irregular distances, of various ages, and mostly on one side. Still it was a shady, pleasant approach.

And the vicarage was truly very interesting and amusing. To these Londoners accustomed to live in a state of compression, elbows practically touching, in a tall, narrow fore-and-aft stucco house, all window and staircase, in a despondent Brompton square, there was an effect of maundering freedom about the place, of enlargement almost to the pitch of adventure and sunlight to the pitch of intoxication. The house itself was long and low, as if a London house holidaying in the country had flung itself asprawl ; it had two disconnected and roomy staircases, and when it had exhausted itself completely as a house, it turned to the right and began again as rambling, empty stables, coach house, cart sheds, men's bedrooms up ladders, and outhouses of the most various kinds. On one hand was a neglected orchard, in the front of the house was a bald, worried-looking lawn area capable of simultaneous tennis and croquet, and at the other side a copious and confused vegetable and flower garden full of roses, honesty, hollyhocks, and suchlike herbaceous biennials

and perennials, lapsed at last into shrubbery, where a
sickle-shaped, weedy lagoon of uncertain aims, which had
evidently, as a rustic bridge and a weeping willow confessed,
aspired to be an " ornamental water," declined at last to
ducks.   And there was access to the church, and the key
of the church tower, and one went across the corner of the
lawn, and by a little iron gate into the churchyard to
decipher inscriptions, as if the tombs of all Buryhamstreet
were no more than a part of the accommodation relinquished
by the vicar's household.

Marjorie was hurried over the chief points of all this at
a breakneck pace by Sydney and Rom, and when Sydney
was called away to the horrors of practice—for Sydney in
spite of considerable reluctance was destined by her father
to be ," the musical one "—Rom developed a copious
affection, due apparently to some occult æsthetic influence
in Marjorie's silvery-gray and green, and led her into the
unlocked vestry, and there prayed in a whisper that she
might be given " one good hug, just *one* "—and so they
came out with their arms about each other very affectionately to visit the lagoon again.   And then Rom
remembered that Marjorie hadn't seen either the walnut-
tree in the orchard, or the hen with nine chicks. . . .

Somewhere among all these interests came tea and Mrs.
Pope.

Mrs. Pope kissed her daughter with an air of having
really wanted to kiss her half an hour ago, but of having
been distracted since.   She was a fine-featured, anxious-
looking little woman, with a close resemblance to all her
children, in spite of the fact that they were markedly
dissimilar one to the other, except only that they took
their ruddy colourings from their father.   She was dressed
in a neat blue dress that had perhaps been hurriedly chosen,
and her method of doing her hair was a manifest compromise between duty and pleasure.   She embarked at
once upon an exposition of the bedroom arrangements,
which evidently involved difficult issues.   Marjorie was to
share a room with Daffy—that was the gist of it—as the
only other available apartment, originally promised to
Marjorie, had been secured by Mr. Pope for what he called
his " matutinal ablutions, videlicet tub."

" Then when your Aunt Plessington comes, you won't
have to move," said Mrs. Pope with an air of a special
concession.   " Your father's looking forward to seeing
you, but he mustn't be disturbed just yet.   He's in the

vicar's study. He's had his tea in there. He's writing a letter to *The Times*, answering something they said in a leader, and also a private note calling attention to their delay in printing his previous communication, and he wants to be delicately ironical without being in any way offensive. He wants to hint without actually threatening that very probably he will go over to the *Spectator* altogether if they do not become more attentive. *The Times* used to print his letters punctually, but latterly these automobile people seem to have got hold of it. . . . He has the window on the lawn open, so that I think, perhaps, we'd better not stay out here—for fear our voices might disturb him."

" Better get right round the other side of the church," said Daffy.

" He'd hear far less of us if we went indoors," said Mrs. Pope.

§ 4

The vicarage seemed tight packed with human interest for Marjorie and her mother and sisters. Going over houses is one of the amusements proper to her sex, and she and all three sisters and her mother, as soon as they had finished an inaudible tea, went to see the bedroom she was to share with Daffy, and then examined, carefully and in order, the furniture and decoration of the other bedrooms, went through the rooms downstairs, always excepting and avoiding very carefully and closing as many doors as possible on, and hushing their voices whenever they approached, the study in which her father was being delicately ironical without being offensive to *The Times*. None of them had seen any of the vicarage people at all —Mr. Pope had come on a bicycle and managed all the negotiations—and it was curious to speculate about the individuals whose personalities pervaded the worn and faded furnishings of the place.

The Popes' keen-eyed inspection came at times, I think, dangerously near prying. The ideals of decoration and interests of the vanished family were so absolutely dissimilar to the London standards as to arouse a sort of astonished wonder in their minds. Some of the things they decided were perfectly hideous, some quaint, some were simply and weakly silly. Everything was different from Hartstone Square. Daffy was perhaps more inclined to contempt, and Mrs. Pope to refined amusement and witty appreciation than Marjorie. Marjorie felt there was something in these people that she didn't begin to understand, she needed some missing clue that would unlock the secret of their confused peculiarity. She was one of those people who have an almost instinctive turn for decoration in costume and furniture ; she had already had a taste of how to do things in arranging her rooms at Bennett College, Oxbridge, where also she was in great demand among the richer girls as an adviser. She knew what it was to try and fail as well as try and succeed, and these people, she felt, hadn't tried for anything she comprehended. She couldn't quite see why it was that there was at the same time an attempt at ornament and a disregard of beauty, she couldn't quite do as her mother did and dismiss it as an absurdity and have done with it. She couldn't understand, too, why everything should be as if it were faded and weakened from something originally bright and clear.

All the rooms were thick with queer little objects that indicated a quite beaver-like industry in the production of " work." There were embroidered covers for nearly every article on the wash-hand-stand, and mats of wool and crotchet wherever anything stood on anything ; there were " tidies " everywhere, and odd little brackets covered with gilded and varnished fir-cones and bearing framed photographs and little jars and all sorts of colourless, dusty little objects, and everywhere on the walls tacks sustained crossed fans with badly painted flowers or transfer pictures. There was a jar on the bedroom mantel covered with varnished postage stamps and containing gray-haired dried grasses. There seemed to be a moral element in all this, for in the room Sydney shared with Rom there was a decorative piece of lettering which declared that—

" Something attempted, something done,
Has earned a night's repose."

There were a great number of texts that set Marjorie's mind stirring dimly with intimations of a missed significance. Over her own bed, within the lattice of an Oxford frame, was the photograph of a picture of an extremely composed young woman in a trailing robe, clinging to the Rock of Ages in the midst of histrionically aggressive waves, and she had a feeling, rather than a thought, that perhaps for all the oddity of the presentation it did convey something acutely desirable, that she herself had had moods when she would have found something very comforting in just such

an impassioned grip. And on a framed, floriferous card,
these incomprehensible words :—

THY GRACE IS SUFFICIENT FOR ME.

seemed to be saying something to her tantalisingly just
outside her range of apprehension.

Did all these things light up somehow to those dis-
possessed people—from some angle she didn't attain ?
Were they living and moving realities when those others
were at home again ?

The drawing-room had no texts ; it was altogether
more pretentious and less haunted by the faint and faded
flavour of religion that pervaded the bedrooms. It had,
however, evidences of travel in Switzerland and the
Mediterranean. There was a piano in black and gold, a
little out of tune, and surmounted by a Benares brass jar,
enveloping a scarlet geranium in a pot. There was a
Japanese screen of gold wrought upon black, that screened
nothing. There was a framed chromo-lithograph of Jerusalem hot in the sunset, and another of Jerusalem cold
under a sub-tropical moon, and there were gourds, roses of
Jericho, sandalwood rosaries and kindred trash from the
Holy Land in no little profusion upon a whatnot. Such
books as the room had contained had been arranged as
symmetrically as possible about a large, pink-shaded lamp
upon the claret-coloured cloth of a round table, and were
to be replaced, Mrs. Pope said, at their departure. At
present they were piled on a side-table. The girls had been
through them all, and were ready with the choicer morsels
for Marjorie's amusement. There was *Black Beauty*, the
sympathetic story of a soundly Anglican horse, and a large
Bible extra-illustrated with photographs of every well-
known scriptural picture from Michael Angelo to Doré,
and a book of injunctions to young ladies upon their
behaviour and deportment that Rom and Sydney found
particularly entertaining. Marjorie discovered that Sydney
had picked up a new favourite phrase. " I'm afraid we're
all dreadfully cynical," said Sydney, several times.

A more advanced note was struck by a copy of *Aurora
Leigh*, richly underlined in pencil, but with exclamation
marks at some of the bolder passages. . . .

And presently, still avoiding the open study window
very elaborately, this little group of twentieth-century
people went again into the church—the church whose
foundations were laid in A.D. 912—foundations of rubble

and cement that included flat Roman bricks from a still
remoter basilica. Their voices dropped instinctively, as
they came into its shaded quiet from the exterior sunshine.
Marjorie went a little apart and sat in a pew that gave her
a glimpse of the one good stained-glass window. Rom
followed her, and perceiving her mood to be restful, sat
a yard away. Syd began a whispered dispute with her
mother whether it wasn't possible to try the organ, and
whether Theodore might not be bribed to blow. Daffy
discovered relics of a lepers' squint and a holy-water stoup,
and then went to scrutinise the lettering of the ten com-
mandments of the Mosaic law that shone black and red
on gold on either side of the I.H.S. monogram behind the
white-clothed communion-table that had once been the
altar. Upon a notice-board hung about the waist of the
portly pulpit were the numbers of hymns that had been
sung three days ago. The sound Protestantism of the vicar
had banished superfluous crosses from the building ; the
Bible reposed upon the wings of a great brass eagle ;
shining blue and crimson in the window, Saint Christopher
carried his Lord. What a harmonised synthesis of conflicts
a country church presents ! What invisible mysteries of
filiation spread between these ancient ornaments and
symbols and the new young minds from the whirlpool of
the town that looked upon them now with such bright,
keen eyes, wondering a little, feeling a little, missing so
much ?

It was all so very cool and quiet now—with something
of the immobile serenity of death.

§ 5

When Mr. Pope had finished his letter to *The Times*, he
got out of the window of the study, treading on a flower-bed
as he did so—he was the sort of man who treads on flower-
beds—partly with the purpose of reading his composition
aloud to as many members of his family as he could assemble
for the purpose, and so giving them a chance of appreciating
the nuances of his irony more fully than if they saw it just
in cold print without the advantage of his intonation, and
partly with the belated idea of welcoming Marjorie. The
lawn presented a rather discouraging desolation. Then
he became aware that the church tower frothed with his
daughters. In view of his need of an audience, he decided
after a brief doubt that their presence there was

unobjectionable, and waved his MS. amiably.   Marjorie
flapped a handkerchief in reply. . . .

The subsequent hour was just the sort of hour that
gave Mr. Pope an almost meteorological importance to his
family. He began with an amiability that had no fault,
except, perhaps, that it was a little forced after the epistolary strain in the study and his welcome to Marjorie
was more than cordial. "Well, little Madgecat ! " he said,
giving her an affectionate but sound and heavy thump
on the left shoulder-blade, "got a kiss for the old
daddy ? "

Marjorie submitted a cheek.

"That's right," said Mr. Pope ; "and now I just want
you all to advise me——"

He led the way to a group of wicker garden chairs.
"You're coming, Mummy ? " he said, and seated himself
comfortably and drew out a spectacle case, while his family
grouped itself dutifully. It made a charming little picture
of a Man and his Womankind. "I don't often flatter
myself," he said, "but this time I think I've been neat—
neat's the word for it."

He cleared his throat, put on his spectacles, and emitted
a long, flat preliminary note, rather like the sound of a
child's trumpet. "Er—' Dear Sir ! ' "

"Rom," said Mrs. Pope, "don't creak your chair."

"It's Daffy, mother," said Rom.

"Oh, *Rom* ! " said Daffy.

Mr. Pope paused, and looked with a warning eye over
his left spectacle-glass at Rom.

"Don't creak your chair, Rom," he said, "when your
mother tells you."

"I was *not* creaking my chair," said Rom.

"I heard it," said Mr. Pope, suavely.

"It was Daffy."

"Your mother does not think so," said Mr. Pope.

"Oh, all right ! I'll sit on the ground," said Rom,
crimson to the roots of her hair.

"Me too," said Daffy. "I'd rather."

Mr. Pope watched the transfer gravely. Then he
readjusted his glasses, cleared his throat again, trumpeted,
and began. "Er—' Dear Sir ! ' "

"Oughtn't it to be simply ' Sir,' father, for an editor ? "
said Marjorie.

"Perhaps I didn't explain, Marjorie," said her father,
with the calm of great self-restraint, and dabbing his left

hand on the manuscript in his right, " that this is a *private letter*—a private letter."

" I didn't understand," said Marjorie.

" It would have been evident as I went on," said Mr. Pope, and prepared to read again.

This time he was allowed to proceed, but the interruptions had ruffled him, and the gentle stresses that should have lifted the subtleties of his irony into prominence missed the words, and he had to go back and do his sentences again. Then Rom suddenly, horribly, uncontrollably, was seized with hiccups. At the second hiccup Mr. Pope paused, and looked very hard at his daughter with magnified eyes ; as he was about to resume, the third burst its way through the unhappy child's utmost effort.

Mr. Pope rose with an awful resignation. " That's enough," he said. He regarded the pseudo-twin vindictively. " You haven't the self-control of a child of six," he said. Then very touchingly to Mrs. Pope : " Mummy, shall we try a game of tennis with the New Generation ? "

" Can't you read it after supper ? " asked Mrs. Pope.

" It must go by the eight o'clock post," said Mr. Pope, putting the masterpiece into his breast pocket, the little masterpiece that would now perhaps never be read aloud to any human being. " Daffy, dear, do you mind going in for the rackets and balls ? "

The social atmosphere was now sultry, and overcast, and Mr. Pope's decision to spend the interval before Daffy returned in seeing whether he couldn't do something to the net, which was certainly very unsatisfactory, did not improve matters. Then, unhappily, Marjorie, who had got rather keen upon tennis at the Carmels', claimed her father's first two services as faults, contrary to the etiquette of the family. It happened that Mr. Pope had a really very good, hard, difficult, smart-looking serve, whose only defect was that it always went either too far or else into the net, and so a feeling had been fostered and established by his wife that, on the whole, it was advisable to regard the former variety as a legitimate extension of a father's authority. Naturally, therefore, Mr. Pope was nettled at Marjorie's ruling, and his irritation increased when his next two services to Daffy perished in the net. (" Damn that net ! Puts one's eye out.") Then Marjorie gave him an unexpected soft return which he somehow muffled, and then Daffy just dropped a return over the top of the net. (Love-game.) It was then Marjorie's turn to serve, which she did with a new twist acquired from the eldest Carmel boy that struck Mr. Pope as un-English. " Go on," he said concisely. " Fifteen-love."

She was gentle with her mother and they got their first rally, and when it was over Mr. Pope had to explain to Marjorie that if she returned right up into his corner of the court he would have to run backwards very fast and might fall over down the silly slope at that end. She would have to consider him and the court. One didn't get everything out of a game by playing merely to win. She said " All right, Daddy," rather off-handedly, and immediately served to him again, and he, taken a little unawares, hit the ball with the edge of his racket and sent it out, and then he changed rackets with Daffy—it seemed he had known all along she had taken his, but he had preferred to say nothing—uttered a word of advice to his wife just on her stroke, and she, failing to grasp his intention as quickly as she ought to have done, left the score forty-fifteen. He felt better when he returned Marjorie's serve, and then before she could control herself she repeated her new unpleasant trick of playing into the corner again, whereupon, leaping back with an agility that would have shamed many a younger man, Mr. Pope came upon disaster. He went spinning down the treacherous slope behind, twisted his ankle painfully and collapsed against the iron railings of the shrubbery. It was too much, and he lost control of himself. His daughters had one instant's glimpse of the linguistic possibilities of a strong man's agony. " I told her," he went on as if he had said nothing. " *Tennis !* "

For a second perhaps he seemed to hesitate upon a course of action. Then as if by a great effort he took his coat from the net-post and addressed himself houseward, incarnate Grand Dudgeon—limping.

" Had enough of it, Mummy," he said, and added some happily inaudible comment on Marjorie's new style of play.

The evening's exercise was at an end.

The three ladies regarded one another in silence for some moments.

" I will take in the rackets, dear," said Mrs. Pope.

" I think the other ball is at your end," said Daffy. . . .

The apparatus put away, Marjorie and her sister strolled thoughtfully away from the house.

" There's croquet here, too," said Daffy. " We've not had the things out yet ! " . . .

" He'll play, I suppose."

" He wants to play." . . .

" Of course," said Marjorie, after a long pause, " there's no *reasoning* with Dad ! "

§ 6

Character is one of England's noblest and most deliberate products, but some Englishmen have it to excess. Mr. Pope had.

He was one of that large and representative class which imparts a dignity to national commerce by inheriting big businesses from its ancestors. He was a coach-builder by birth, and a gentleman by education and training. He had been to City Merchant's and Cambridge.

Throughout the earlier half of the nineteenth century the Popes had been the princes of the coach-building world. Mr. Pope's great-grandfather had been a North London wheelwright of conspicuous dexterity and integrity, who had founded the family business ; his son, Mr. Pope's grandfather, had made that business the occupation of his life and brought it to the pinnacle of pre-eminence ; his son, who was Marjorie's grandfather, had displayed a lesser enthusiasm, left the house at the works for a home ten miles away and sent a second son into the Church. It was in the days of the third Pope that the business ceased to expand, and began to suffer severely from the competition of an enterprising person who had originally supplied the firm with varnish, gradually picked up the trade in most other materials and accessories needed in coach-building, and passed on by almost imperceptible stages to delivering the article complete—dispensing at last altogether with the intervention of Pope and Son—to the customer. Marjorie's father had succeeded in the fullness of time to the inheritance this insurgent had damaged.

Mr. Pope was a man of firm and resentful temper, with an admiration for Cato, Brutus, Cincinnatus, Cromwell, Washington, and the sterner heroes generally, and by nature a little ill-used and offended at things. He suffered from indigestion and extreme irritability. He found himself in control of a business where more flexible virtues were needed. The Popes based their fame on a heavy, proud type of vehicle, which the increasing luxury and triviality of the age tended to replace by lighter forms of carriage, carriages with diminutive and apologetic names. As these lighter forms were not only lighter but less expensive, Mr. Pope with a pathetic confidence in the loyalty of the better class of West End customer, determined to "make a stand" against them. He was the sort of man to whom making a stand is in itself a sombre joy. If he had had to choose his pose for a portrait, he would certainly have decided to have one foot advanced, the other planted like a British oak behind, the arms folded and the brows corrugated—making a stand.

Unhappily the stars in their courses and the general improvement of roads throughout the country fought against him. The lighter carriages, and especially the lighter carriages of that varnish-selling firm, which was now absorbing businesses right and left, prevailed over Mr. Pope's resistance. For crossing a mountain pass or fording a river, for driving over the scene of a recent earthquake or following a retreating army, for being run away with by frantic horses or crushing a personal enemy, there can be no doubt the Pope carriages remained to the very last the best possible ones and fully worth the inflexible price demanded. Unhappily all carriages in a civilisation essentially decadent are not subjected to these tests, and the manufactures of his rivals were not only much cheaper, but had a sort of meretricious smartness, a disingenuous elasticity, above all a levity, hateful indeed to the spirit of Mr. Pope yet attractive to the wanton customer. Business dwindled. Nevertheless the habitual element in the good-class customer did keep things going, albeit on a shrinking scale, until Mr. Pope came to the unfortunate decision that he would make a stand against automobiles. He regarded them as an intrusive nuisance which had to be seen only to be disowned by the landed gentry of England. Rather than build a car he said he would go out of business. He went out of business. Within five years of this determination he sold out the name, goodwill, and other vestiges of his concern to a mysterious buyer who turned out to be no more than an agent for these persistently expanding varnish-makers, and he retired with a genuine grievance upon the family accumulations—chiefly in Consols and Home Railways.

He refused, however, to regard his defeat as final, put great faith in the approaching exhaustion of the petrol supply, and talked in a manner that should have made the Automobile Association uneasy, of devoting the rest of his days to the purification of England from these aggressive mechanisms. "It was a mistake," he said, "to let them

in." He became more frequent at his excellent West End
club, and directed a certain portion of his capital to largely
indecisive but on the whole unprofitable speculations in
South African and South American enterprises.   He
mingled a little in affairs.   He was a tough conventional
speaker, rich in established phrases and never abashed by
hearing himself say commonplace things, and in addition
to his campaign against automobiles he found time to
engage also in quasi-political activities, taking chairs,
saying a few words and so on, cherishing a fluctuating hope
that his eloquence might ultimately win him an invitation
to contest a constituency in the interests of reaction and
the sounder elements in the Liberal party.

He had a public-spirited side, and he was particularly
attracted by that mass of modern legislative proposals
which aims at a more systematic control of the lives of
lower-class persons for their own good by their betters.
Indeed, in the first enthusiasm of his proprietorship of the
Pope works at East Purblow, he had organised one of
those benevolent industrial experiments that are now so
common.   He felt strongly against the drink evil, that is
to say, the unrestricted liberty of common people to drink
what they prefer, and he was acutely impressed by the fact
that working-class families do not spend their money in
the way that seems most desirable to upper middle-class
critics.   Accordingly he did his best to replace the dangerous
freedoms of money by that ideal of the social reformer,
Payment in Kind.   To use his invariable phrase, the East
Purblow experiment did " no mean service " to the cause
of social reform.   Unhappily it came to an end through
a prosecution under the Truck Act, that blot upon the
Statute Book, designed, it would appear, even deliberately
to vitiate man's benevolent control of his fellow man.
The lessons to be drawn from that experience, however,
grew if anything with the years.   He rarely spoke without
an allusion to it, and it was quite remarkable how readily
it could be adapted to illuminate a hundred different
issues in the hospitable columns of the *Spectator*. . . .

§ 7

At seven o'clock Marjorie found herself upstairs changing
into her apple-green frock.   She had had a good refreshing
wash in cold soft water, and it was pleasant to change into
thinner silk stockings and dainty satin slippers and let down

and at last brush her hair and dress loiteringly after the fatigues of her journey and the activities of her arrival. She looked out on the big church and the big trees behind it against the golden quiet of a summer evening with extreme approval.

" I suppose those birds are rooks," she said.

But Daffy had gone to see that the pseudo-twins had done themselves justice in their muslin frocks and pink sashes ; they were apt to be a little sketchy with their less accessible buttons.

Marjorie became aware of two gentlemen with her mother on the lawn below.

One was her almost affianced lover, Will Magnet, the humorous writer. She had been doing her best not to think about him all day, but now he became an unavoidable central fact. She regarded him with an almost perplexed scrutiny, and wondered vividly why she had been so excited and pleased by his attentions during the previous summer.

Mr. Magnet was one of those quiet, deliberately un-assuming people who do not even attempt to be beautiful. Not for him was it to pretend, but to prick the bladder of pretence. He was a fairish man of forty, pale, with a large protuberant, observant gray eye—I speak particularly of the left—and a face of quiet animation warily alert for the wit's opportunity. His nose and chin were pointed, and his lips thin and quaintly pressed together. He was dressed in gray, with a low-collared silken shirt showing a thin neck, and a flowing black tie, and he carried a gray felt hat in his joined hands behind his back. She could hear the insinuating cadences of his voice as he talked in her mother's ear. The other gentleman, silent on her mother's right, must, she knew, be Mr. Wintersloan, whom Mr. Magnet had proposed to bring over. His dress betrayed that modest gaiety of disposition becoming in an artist, and indeed he was one of Mr. Magnet's favourite illustrators. He was in a dark bluish-gray suit ; a black tie that was quite unusually broad went twice around his neck before succumbing to the bow, and his waistcoat appeared to be of some gaily-patterned orange silk. Marjorie's eyes returned to Mr. Magnet. Hitherto she had never had an opportunity of remarking that his hair was more than a little attenuated towards the crown. It was funny how his tie came out under his chin to the right.

What an odd thing men's dress had become ! she

thought. Why did they wear those ridiculous collars and ties ? Why didn't they always dress in flannels and look as fine and slender and active as the elder Carmel boy, for example ? Mr. Magnet couldn't be such an ill-shaped man. Why didn't every one dress to be just as beautiful and splendid as possible ?—instead of wearing queer things !

" Coming down ? " said Daffy, a vision of sulphur-yellow, appearing in the doorway.

" Let *them* go first," said Marjorie, with a finer sense of effect. " And Theodore. We don't want to make part of a comic entry with Theodore, Daffy."

Accordingly, the two sisters watched discreetly—they had to be wary on account of Mr. Magnet's increasingly frequent glances at the windows—and when at last all the rest of the family had appeared below, they decided their cue had come. Mr. Pope strolled into the group, with no trace of his recent debacle except a slight limp. He was wearing a jacket of damson-coloured velvet, which he affected in the country, and all traces of his Grand Dudgeon were gone. But then he rarely had Grand Dudgeon except in the sanctities of family life, and hardly ever when any other man was about.

" Well," his daughters heard him say, with a witty allusiveness that was difficult to follow, " so the Magnet has come to the Mountain again—eh ? "

" Come on, Madge," said Daffy, and the two sisters emerged harmoniously together from the house.

It would have been manifest to a meaner capacity than any present that evening that Mr. Magnet regarded Marjorie with a distinguished significance. He had two eyes, but he had that mysterious quality so frequently associated with a bluish-gray iris which gives the effect of looking hard with one large orb, a sort of gray searchlight effect, and he used this eye ray now to convey a respectful but firm admiration in the most unequivocal manner. He saluted Daffy courteously, and then allowed himself to retain Marjorie's hand for just a second longer than was necessary as he said—very simply—" I am very pleased indeed to meet you again—very."

A slight embarrassment fell between them.

" You are staying near here, Mr. Magnet ? "

" At the inn," said Mr. Magnet, and then, " I chose it because it would be near you."

His eye pressed upon her again for a moment.

" Is it comfortable ? " said Marjorie.

" So charmingly simple," said Mr. Magnet. " I love it."

A tinkling bell announced the preparedness of supper, and roused the others to the consciousness that they were silently watching Mr. Magnet and Marjorie.

" It's quite a simple farmhouse supper," said Mrs. Pope.

§ 8

There were ducks, green peas, and adolescent new potatoes for supper, and afterwards stewed fruit and cream and junket and cheese, bottled beer, Gilbey's Burgundy, and home-made lemonade. Mrs. Pope carved, because Mr. Pope splashed too much, and bones upset him and made him want to show up chicken in *The Times*. So he sat at the other end and rallied his guests while Mrs. Pope distributed the viands. He showed not a trace of his recent umbrage. Theodore sat between Daffy and his mother because of his table manners, and Marjorie was on her father's right hand and next to Mr. Wintersloan, while Mr. Magnet was in the middle of the table on the opposite side in a position convenient for looking at her. Both maids waited.

The presence of Magnet invariably stirred the latent humorist in Mr. Pope. He felt that he who talks to humorists should himself be humorous, and it was his private persuasion that with more attention he might have been, to use a favourite form of expression, " no mean jester." Quite a lot of little things of his were cherished as " Good " both by himself and, with occasional inaccuracies, by Mrs. Pope. He opened out now in a strain of rich allusiveness.

" What will you drink, Mr. Wintersloan ? " he said. " Wine of the country, yclept beer, red wine from France, or my wife's potent brew from the golden lemon ? "

Mr. Wintersloan thought he would take Burgundy. Mr. Magnet preferred beer.

> " I've heard there's iron in the Beer,
> And I believe it,"

misquoted Mr. Pope, and nodded as it were to the marker to score. " Daffy and Marjorie are still in the lemonade stage. Will you take a little Burgundy to-night, Mummy ? "

Mrs. Pope decided she would, and was inspired to ask Mr. Wintersloan if he had been in that part of the country before. Topography ensued. Mr. Wintersloan had a style

of his own, and spoke of the Buryhamstreet district as a
" pooty little country—pooty little hills, with a swirl in
them."

This pleased Daffy and Marjorie, and their eyes met for
a moment.

Then Mr. Magnet, with a ray full on Marjorie, said he
had always been fond of Surrey. " I think if ever I made
a home in the country I should like it to be here."

Mr. Wintersloan said Surrey would tire him, it was too
bossy and curly, too flocculent ; he would prefer to look
on broader, simpler lines, with just a sudden catch in the
breath in them—if you understand me ?

Marjorie did, and said so.

" A sob—such as you get at the break of a pinewood
on a hill."

This baffled Mr. Pope, but Marjorie took it. " Or the
short dry cough of a cliff," she said.

" Exactly," said Mr. Wintersloan, and having turned
a little deliberate close-lipped smile on her for a moment,
resumed his wing.

" So long as a landscape doesn't *sneeze*," said Mr. Magnet,
in that irresistible dry way of his, and Rom and Sydney,
at any rate, choked.

" Now is the hour when Landscapes yawn," mused Mr.
Pope, coming in all right at the end.

Then Mrs. Pope asked Mr. Wintersloan about his route
to Buryhamstreet, and then Mr. Pope asked Mr. Magnet
whether he was playing at a new work or working at a new
play.

Mr. Magnet said he was dreaming over a play. He
wanted to bring out the more serious side of his humour,
go a little deeper into things than he had hitherto done.

" Mingling smiles and tears," said Mr. Pope approvingly.

Mr. Magnet said very quietly that all true humour did that.

Then Mrs. Pope asked what the play was to be about,
and Mr. Magnet, who seemed disinclined to give an answer,
turned the subject by saying he had to prepare an address
on humour for the next dinner of the *Literati*. " It's to
be a humorist's dinner, and they've made me the guest
of the evening—by way of a joke to begin with," he said
with that dry smile again.

Mrs. Pope said he shouldn't say things like that. She
then said " Syd ! " quietly but sharply to Sydney, who
was making a disdainful, squinting face at Theodore,
and told the parlourmaid to clear the plates for sweets.

Mr. Magnet professed great horror of public speaking.   He said that whenever he rose to make an after-dinner speech all the ices he had ever eaten seemed to come out of the past and sit on his backbone.

The talk centred for a while on Mr. Magnet's address, and apropos of Tests of Humour Mr. Pope, who in his way was " no mean raconteur," related the story of the man who took the salad dressing with his hand, and when his host asked why he did that, replied : " Oh ! I thought it was spinach ! "

" Many people," added Mr. Pope, " wouldn't see the point of that.   And if they don't see the point they can't —and the more they try the less they do."

All four girls hoped secretly and not too confidently that their laughter had not sounded hollow.

And then for a time the men told stories as they came into their heads in an easy, irresponsible way.   Mr. Magnet spoke of the humour of the omnibus-driver who always dangled and twiddled his badge " by way of a joke " when he passed the conductor whose father had been hanged, and Mr. Pope, perhaps a little irrelevantly, told the story of the little boy who was asked his father's last words, and said, " mother was with him to the end," which particularly amused Mrs. Pope.   Mr. Wintersloan gave the story of the woman who was taking her son to the hospital with his head jammed into a saucepan, and explained to the other people in the omnibus : " You see, what makes it so annoying, it's me only saucepan ! "   Then they came back to the Sense of Humour with the dentist who shouted with laughter, and when asked the reason by his patient, choked out : " Wrong tooth ! " and then Mr. Pope reminded them of the heartless husband who, suddenly informed that his mother-in-law was dead, exclaimed : " Oh, don't make me laugh, please, I've got a split lip.   . . ."

§ 9

The conversation assumed a less anecdotal quality with the removal to the drawing-room.   On Mr. Magnet's initiative the gentlemen followed the ladies almost immediately, and it was Mr. Magnet who remembered that Marjorie could sing.

Both the elder sisters indeed had sweet clear voices, and they had learnt a number of those jolly songs the English made before the dull Hanoverians came.   Syd

accompanied, and Rom sat back in the low chair in the
corner and fell deeply in love with Mr. Wintersloan. The
three musicians in their green and sulphur-yellow and
white made a pretty group in the light of the shaded lamp
against the black-and-gold Broadwood, the tawdry screen,
its pattern thin glittering upon darkness, and the deep
shadows behind. Marjorie loved singing, and forgot herself
as she sang,—

> " I love, and he loves me again,
>   Yet dare I not tell who ;
> For if the nymphs should know my swain,
>   I fear they'd love him too,"

she sang, and Mr. Magnet could not conceal the intensity
of his admiration.

Mr. Pope had fallen into a pleasant musing ; several
other ripe old yarns, dear delicious old things, had come
into his mind that he felt he might presently recall when
this unavoidable display of accomplishments was overpast,
and it was with one of them almost on his lips that he
glanced across at his guest. He was surprised to see Mr.
Magnet's face transfigured. He was sitting forward,
looking up at Marjorie, and he had caught something of the
expression of those blessed boys who froth at the feet of an
Assumption. For an instant Mr. Pope did not understand.

Then he understood. It was Marjorie ! He had a
twinge of surprise, and glanced at his own daughter as
though he had never seen her before. He perceived in a
flash for the first time that this troublesome, clever, dis-
respectful child was tall and shapely and sweet and indeed
quite a beautiful young woman. He forgot his anecdotes.
His being was suffused with pride and responsibility and
the sense of virtue rewarded. He did not reflect for a
moment that Marjorie embodied in almost equal proportions the very best points in his mother and his mother-in-
law, and avoided his own more salient characteristics with
so neat a dexterity that from top to toe, except for the one
matter of colour, not only did she not resemble him but
she scarcely even alluded to him. He thought simply that
she was his daughter, that she derived from him, that her
beauty was his. She was the outcome of his meritorious
preparations. He recalled all the moments when he had
been kind and indulgent to her, all the bills he had paid
for her ; all the stresses and trials of the coach-building
collapse, all the fluctuations of his speculative adventures,

became things he had faced patiently and valiantly for her
sake. He forgot the endless times when he had been
viciously cross with her, all the times when he had pished
and tushed and sworn in her hearing. He had on provocation and in spite of her mother's protests slapped her pretty
vigorously, but such things are better forgotten ; nor did
he recall how bitterly he had opposed the college education
which had made her now so clear in eye and thought, nor
the frightful shindy, only three months since, about that
identical green dress in which she now stood delightful.
He forgot these petty details, as an idealist should. There
she was, his daughter. An immense benevolence irradiated
his soul—for Marjorie—for Magnet. His eyes were suffused
with a not ignoble tenderness. The man, he knew, was
worth at least thirty-five thousand pounds, a discussion of
investments had made that clear, and he must be making
at least five thousand a year ! A beautiful girl, a worthy
man ! A good fellow, a sound good fellow, a careful
fellow too—as these fellows went !

Old Daddy would lose his treasure, of course.

Well, a father must learn resignation, and he for one
would not stand in the way of his girl's happiness. A day
would come when, very beautifully and tenderly, he would
hand her over to Magnet, his favourite daughter to his
trusted friend. " Well, my boy, there's no one in all the
world——" he would begin.

It would be a touching parting. " Don't forget your
old father, Maggots," he would say. At such a moment
that quaint nickname would surely not be resented. . . .

He reflected how much he had always preferred Marjorie
to Daffy. She was brighter—more like him. Daffy was
unresponsive, with a touch of bitterness under her
tongue. . . .

He was already dreaming he was a widower, rather
infirm, the object of Magnet's and Marjorie's devoted care,
when the song ceased, and the wife he had for the purpose
of reverie just consigned so carelessly to the cemetery
proposed that they should have a little game that every
one could play at. A number of pencils and slips of paper
appeared in her hands. She did not want the girls to
exhaust their repertory on this first occasion—and besides,
Mr. Pope liked games in which one did things with pencils
and strips of paper. Mr. Magnet wished the singing to
go on, he said, but he was overruled.

So for a time every one played a little game in which

Mr. Pope was particularly proficient. Indeed, it was rare that any one won but Mr. Pope. It was called "The Great Departed," and it had such considerable educational value that all the children had to play at it whenever he wished.

It was played in this manner : one of the pseudo-twins opened a book and dabbed a finger on the page, and read out the letter immediately at the tip of her finger, then they all began to write as hard as they could, writing down the names of every great person they could think of, whose name began with that letter. At the end of five minutes Mr. Pope said Stop ! and then began to read his list out, beginning with the first name. Everybody who had that name crossed it out and scored one, and after his list was exhausted all the surviving names on the next list were read over in the same way, and so on. The names had to be the names of dead celebrated people, only one monarch of the same name of the same dynasty was allowed, and Mr. Pope adjudicated on all doubtful cases. It was great fun.

The first two games were won as usual by Mr. Pope, and then Mr. Wintersloan, who had been a little distraught in his manner, brightened up and scribbled furiously.

The letter was *D*, and after Mr. Pope had rehearsed a table of nine-and-twenty names, Mr. Wintersloan read out his list in that curious voice of his which suggested nothing so much as some mobile drink glucking out of the neck of a bottle held upside down.

" Dahl," he began.

" Who was Dahl ? " asked Mr. Pope.

" 'Vented dahlias," said Mr. Wintersloan, with a sigh. " Danton."

" Forgot him," said Mr. Pope.

" Davis."

" Davis ? "

" Davis Straits. Doe."

" Who ? "

" John Doe, Richard Roe."

" Legal fiction, I'm afraid," said Mr. Pope.

" Dam," said Mr. Wintersloan, and added after a slight pause : " Antony van."

Mr. Pope made an interrogative noise.

" Painter—eighteenth century—Dutch. Dam, Jan van, his son. Dam, Frederick van. Dam, Wilhelm van. Dam, Diedrich van. Dam, Wilhelmina, wood engraver, gifted woman. Diehl."

" Who ? "

" Painter—dead—famous. See Düsseldorf. It's all painters now—all guaranteed dead, all good men. Deeds of Norfolk, the aquarellist, Denton, Dibbs."

" Er ? " said Mr. Pope.

" The Warwick Claude, *you* know. Died 1823."

" Dickson, Dunting, John Dickery. Peter Dickery, William Dock—I beg your pardon ? "

Mr. Pope was making a protesting gesture, but Mr. Wintersloan's bearing was invincible, and he proceeded.

In the end he emerged triumphant with forty-nine names, mostly painters for whose fame he answered, but whose reputations were certainly new to every one else present. " I can go on like that," said Mr. Wintersloan, " with any letter," and turned that hard little smile full on Marjorie. " I didn't see how to do it at first. I just cast about. But I know a frightful lot of painters. No end. Shall we try again ? "

Marjorie glanced at her father. Mr. Wintersloan's methods were all too evident to her. A curious feeling pervaded the room that Mr. Pope didn't think Mr. Wintersloan's conduct honourable, and that he might even go some way towards saying so.

So Mrs. Pope became very brisk and stirring, and said she thought that now perhaps a charade would be more amusing. It didn't do to keep on at a game too long. She asked Rom and Daphne and Theodore and Mr. Wintersloan to go out, and they all agreed readily, particularly Rom. " Come on ! " said Rom to Mr. Wintersloan. Everybody else shifted into an audience-like group between the piano and the whatnot. Mr. Magnet sat at Marjorie's feet, while Syd played a kind of voluntary, and Mr. Pope leant back in his chair, with his brows knit and lips moving, trying to remember something.

The charade *was* very amusing. The word was Catarrh, and Mr. Wintersloan, as the patient in the last act being given gruel, surpassed even the children's very high expectations. Rom, as his nurse, couldn't keep her hands off him. Then the younger people kissed round and were packed off to bed, and the rest of the party went to the door upon the lawn and admired the night. It was a glorious summer night, deep blue, and rimmed warmly by the afterglow, moonless, and with a few big lamp-like stars above the black still shapes of trees.

Mrs. Pope said they would all accompany their guests

to the gate at the end of the avenue—in spite of the cock-chafers.

Mr. Pope's ankle, however, excused him ; the cordiality of his parting from Mr. Wintersloan seemed a trifle forced, and he limped thoughtfully and a little sombrely towards the study to see if he could find an Encyclopædia or some such book of reference that would give the names of the lesser lights of Dutch, Italian, and English painting during the last two centuries.

He felt that Mr. Wintersloan had established an extra-ordinary bad precedent.

§ 10

Marjorie discovered that she and Mr. Magnet had fallen a little behind the others. She would have quickened her pace, but Mr. Magnet stopped short and said : " Marjorie !

" When I saw you standing there and singing," said Mr. Magnet, and was short of breath for a moment.

Marjorie's natural gift for interruption failed her altogether.

" I felt I would rather be able to call you mine—than win an empire."

The pause seemed to lengthen between them, and Marjorie's remark when she made it at last struck her even as she made it as being but poorly conceived. She had some weak idea of being self-depreciatory.

" I think you had better win an empire, Mr. Magnet," she said meekly.

Then, before anything more was possible, they had come up to Daffy and Mr. Wintersloan and her mother at the gate. . . .

As they returned Mrs. Pope was loud in the praises of Will Magnet. She had a little clear-cut voice, very care-fully and very skilfully controlled, and she dilated on his modesty, his quiet helpfulness at table, his ready presence of mind. She pointed out instances of those admirable traits, incidents small in themselves but charming in their implications. When somebody wanted junket, he had made no fuss, he had just helped them to junket. " So modest and unassuming," said Mrs. Pope. " You'd never dream he was quite rich and famous. Yet every book he writes is translated into Russian and German and all sorts of languages. I suppose he's almost the greatest humorist we have. That play of his ; what is it called ?—*Our Owd*

Woman—has been performed nearly twelve hundred times !
I think that is the most wonderful of gifts. Think of the
people it has made happy."

The conversation was mainly monologue. Both Marjorie
and Daffy were unusually thoughtful.

§ 11

Marjorie ended the long day in a worldly mood.

" Penny for your thoughts," said Daffy abruptly,
brushing the long firelit rapids of her hair.

" Not for sale," said Marjorie, and roused herself. " I've
had a long day."

" It's always just the time I particularly wish I was
a man," she remarked after a brief return to meditation.
" Fancy, no hairpins, no brushing, no tie-up to get lost
about, no strings. I suppose they haven't got strings ? '

" They haven't," said Daffy with conviction.

She met Marjorie's interrogative eye. " Father would
swear at them," she explained. " He'd naturally tie
himself up—and we should hear of it."

" I didn't think of that," said Marjorie, and stuck out
her chin upon her fists. " Sound induction."

She forgot this transitory curiosity.

" Suppose one had a maid, Daffy—a real maid . . . a
maid who mended your things . . . did your hair while
you read. . . ."

" Oh ! here goes," and she stood up and grappled with
the task of undressing.

CHAPTER THE SECOND

THE TWO PROPOSALS OF MR. MAGNET

§ 1

IT was presently quite evident to Marjorie that Mr. Magnet
intended to propose marriage to her, and she did not even
know whether she wanted him to do so.

She had met him first the previous summer while she
had been staying with the Petley-Cresthams at High
Windower, and it had been evident that he found her
extremely attractive. She had never had a real grown
man at her feet before, and she had found it amazingly
entertaining. She had gone for a walk with him the

morning before she came away—a frank and ingenuous
proceeding that made Mrs. Petley-Crestham say the girl
knew what she was about, and she had certainly coquetted
with him in an extraordinary manner at golf-croquet.
After that Oxbridge had swallowed her up, and though he
had called once on her mother while Marjorie was in
London during the Christmas vacation, he hadn't seen her
again. He had written—which was exciting—a long,
friendly humorous letter about nothing in particular, with
an air of its being quite the correct thing for him to do,
and she had answered, and there had been other exchanges.
But all sorts of things had happened in the interval, and
Marjorie had let him get into quite a back place in her
thoughts—the fact that he was a member of her father's
club had seemed somehow to remove him from a great
range of possibilities—until a drift in her mother's talk
towards him and a letter from him with an indefinable
change in tone towards intimacy, had restored him to
importance. Now here he was in the foreground of her
world again, evidently more ardent than ever, and with a
portentous air of being about to do something decisive at
the very first opportunity. What was he going to do?
What had her mother been hinting at? And what, in
fact, did the whole thing amount to?

Marjorie was beginning to realise that this was going
to be a very serious affair indeed for her—and that she
was totally unprepared to meet it.

It had been very amusing, very amusing indeed, at the
Petley-Cresthams', but there were moments now when she
felt towards Mr. Magnet exactly as she would have felt if
he had been one of the Oxbridge tradesmen hovering
about her with a " little account," full of apparently
exaggerated items. . . .

Her thoughts and feelings were all in confusion about
this business. Her mind was full of scraps, every sort of
idea, every sort of attitude contributed something to that
Twentieth Century jumble. For example, and so far as
its value went among motives, it was by no means a trivial
consideration ; she wanted to be proposed to for its own
sake. Daffy had had a proposal last year, and although it
wasn't any sort of eligible proposal, still there it was, and
she had given herself tremendous airs. But Marjorie would
certainly have preferred some lighter kind of proposal
than that which now threatened her. She felt that behind
Mr. Magnet were sanctions ; that she wasn't free to deal

with this proposal as she liked. He was at Buryhamstreet almost with the air of being her parents' guest.

Less clear and more instinctive than her desire for a proposal was her inclination to see just all that Mr. Magnet was disposed to do, and hear all that he was disposed to say. She was curious. He didn't behave in the least as she had expected a lover to behave. But then none of the boys, the " others " with whom she had at times stretched a hand towards the hem of emotion, had ever done that. She had an obscure feeling that perhaps presently Mr. Magnet must light up, be stirred and stirring. Even now his voice changed very interestingly when he was alone with her. His breath seemed to go—as though something had pricked his lung. If it hadn't been for that new, disconcerting realisation of an official pressure behind him, I think she would have been quite ready to experiment extensively with his emotions. . . .

But she perceived as she lay awake next morning that she wasn't free for experiments any longer. What she might say or do now would be taken up very conclusively. And she had no idea what she wanted to say or do.

Marriage regarded in the abstract—that is to say with Mr. Magnet out of focus—was by no means an unattractive proposal to her. It was very much at the back of Marjorie's mind that after Oxbridge, unless she was prepared to face a very serious row indeed and go to teach in a school—and she didn't feel any call whatever to teach in a school—she would probably have to return to Hartstone Square and share Daffy's room again, and assist in the old collective, wearisome task of propitiating her father. The freedoms of Oxbridge had enlarged her imagination until that seemed an almost unendurably irksome prospect. She had tasted life as it could be in her father's absence, and she was beginning to realise just what an impossible person he was. Marriage was escape from all that ; it meant not only respectful parents but a house of her very own, furniture of her choice, great freedom of movement, an authority, an importance. She had seen what it meant to be a prosperously married young woman in the person of one or two resplendent old girls revisiting Bennett College, scattering invitations, offering protections and opportunities. . . .

Of course there is love.

Marjorie told herself, as she had been trained to tell herself, to be sensible, but something within her repeated : *there is love.*

Of course she liked Mr. Magnet. She really did like Mr.
Magnet very much. She had had her girlish dreams, had
fallen in love with pictures of men and actors and a music
master and a man who used to ride by as she went to
school ; but wasn't this desolating desire for self-abandonment rather silly ?—something that one left behind with
much else when it came to putting up one's hair and sensible
living, something to blush secretly about and hide from
every eye ?

Among other discrepant views that lived together in
her mind as cats and rats and parrots and squirrels and so
forth used to live together in those Happy Family cages
unseemly men in less well-regulated days were wont to
steer about our streets, was one instilled by quite a large
proportion of the novels she had read, that a girl was a sort
of self-giving prize for high moral worth. Mr. Magnet she
knew was good, was kind, was brave with that truer
courage, moral courage, which goes with his type of
physique ; he was modest, unassuming, well off, and
famous, and very much in love with her. His True Self, as
Mrs. Pope had pointed out several times, must be really
very beautiful, and in some odd way a line of Shakespeare
had washed up in her consciousness as being somehow
effectual on his behalf :—

"Love looks not with the eye but with the mind."

She felt she ought to look with the mind. Nice people
surely never looked in any other way. It seemed from
this angle almost her duty to love him. . . .

Perhaps she did love him, and mistook the symptoms.
She did her best to mistake the symptoms. But if she did
truly love him, would it seem so queer and important and
antagonistic as it did that his hair was rather thin upon
the crown of his head ?

She wished she hadn't looked down on him. . . .

Poor Marjorie ! She was doing her best to be sensible,
and she felt herself adrift above a clamorous abyss of feared
and forbidden thoughts. Down there she knew well enough
it wasn't thus that love must come. Deep in her soul, the
richest thing in her life indeed and the best thing she had
to give humanity, was a craving for beauty that at times
became almost intolerable, a craving for something other
than beauty and yet inseparably allied with it, a craving
for deep excitement, for a sort of glory in adventure, for
passion—for things akin to great music and heroic poems

and bannered traditions of romance. She had hidden away in her an immense tumultuous appetite for life, an immense tumultuous capacity for living. To be loved beautifully was surely the crown and climax of her being.

She did not dare to listen to these deeps, yet these insurgent voices filled her. Even while she drove her little crocodile of primly sensible thoughts to their sane appointed conclusion, her blood and nerves and all her being were protesting that Mr. Magnet would not do, that whatever other worthiness was in him, regarded as a lover he was preposterous and flat and foolish and middle-aged, and that it were better never to have lived than to put the treasure of her life to his meagre lips and into his hungry, unattractive arms. "The ugliness of it! The spiritless horror of it!" so dumbly and formlessly the rebel voices urged.

"One has to be sensible," said Marjorie to herself, suddenly putting down Shaw's book on Municipal Trading, which she imagined she had been reading. . . .

(Perhaps all marriage was horrid, and one had to get over it.)

That was rather what her mother had conveyed to her.

§ 2

Mr. Magnet made his first proposal in form three days later, after coming twice to tea and staying on to supper. He had played croquet with Mr. Pope, he had been beaten twelve times in spite of twinges in the sprained ankle—heroically borne—had had three victories lucidly explained away, and heard all the particulars of the East Purblow experiment three times over, first in relation to the new Labour Exchanges, then regarded at rather a different angle in relation to female betting, tally-men, and the sanctities of the home generally, and finally in a more exhaustive style, to show its full importance from every side and more particularly as demonstrating the gross injustice done to Mr. Pope by the neglect of its lessons, a neglect too systematic to be accidental, in the social reform literature of the time. Moreover, Mr. Magnet had been made to understand thoroughly how several later quasi-charitable attempts of a similar character had already become, or must inevitably become, unsatisfactory through their failure to follow exactly in the lines laid down by Mr. Pope.

Mr. Pope was really very anxious to be pleasant and agreeable to Mr. Magnet, and he could think of no surer way of doing so than by giving him an unrestrained intimacy of conversation that prevented anything more than momentary intercourse between his daughter and her admirer. And not only did Mr. Magnet find it difficult to get away from Mr. Pope without offence, but whenever by any chance Mr. Pope was detached for a moment Mr. Magnet discovered that Marjorie either wasn't to be seen, or if she was she wasn't to be isolated by any device he could contrive, before the unappeasable return of Mr. Pope.

Mr. Magnet did not get his chance therefore until Lady Petchworth's little gathering at Summerhay Park.

Lady Petchworth was Mrs. Pope's oldest friend, and one of those brighter influences which save our English countryside from lassitude. She had been more fortunate than Mrs. Pope, for while Mr. Pope with that aptitude for disadvantage natural to his temperament had, he said, been tied to a business that never gave him a chance, Lady Petchworth's husband had been a reckless investor of exceptional good-luck. In particular, led by a dream, he had put most of his money into a series of nitrate deposits in caves in Saghalien haunted by benevolent penguins, and had been rewarded beyond the dreams of avarice. His foresight had received the fitting reward of a knighthood, and Sir Thomas, after restoring the Parish Church at Summerhay in a costly and destructive manner, spent his declining years in an enviable contentment with Lady Petchworth and the world at large, and died long before infirmity made him really troublesome.

Good fortune had brought out Lady Petchworth's social aptitudes. Summerhay Park was everything that a clever woman, inspired by that gardening literature which has been so abundant in the opening years of the twentieth century, could make it. It had rosaries and rock gardens, sundials, and yew hedges, pools and ponds, lead figures and stone urns, box borderings and wilderness corners and hundreds and hundreds of feet of prematurely-aged red-brick wall with broad herbaceous borders ; the walks had primroses, primulas, and cowslips in a quite disingenuous abundance, and in spring the whole extent of the park was gay, here with thousands of this sort of daffodil just bursting out and here with thousands of that sort of narcissus just past its prime, and every patch ready to pass itself off in its naturalised way as the accidental native

flower of the field, if only it hadn't been for all the other
different varieties coming on or wilting-off in adjacent
patches. . . .

Her garden was only the beginning of Lady Petchworth's
activities. She had a model dairy, and all her poultry was
white, and so far as she was able to manage it she made
Summerhay a model village. She overflowed with activities,
it was astonishing in one so plump and blonde, and meeting
followed meeting in the artistic little red-brick and green-
stained timber village hall she had erected. Now it was
the National Theatre and now it was the National Mourning;
now it was the Break Up of the Poor Law, and now the
Majority Report, now the Mothers' Union, and now
Socialism, and now Individualism, but always something
progressive and beneficial. She did her best to revive the
old village life, and brought her very considerable powers
of compulsion to make the men dance in simple old Morris
dances, dressed up in costumes they secretly abominated,
and to induce the mothers to dress their children in art-
coloured smocks instead of the prints and blue serge frocks
they preferred. She did not despair, she said, of creating
a spontaneous peasant art movement in the district
springing from the people and expressing the people, but
so far it had been necessary to import not only instructors
and material, but workers to keep the thing going, so
sluggish had the spontaneity of our English countryside
become.

Her little gatherings were quite distinctive of her. They
were a sort of garden party extending from midday to six
or seven ; there would be a nucleus of house guests, and
the highways and byways on every hand would be raided
to supply persons and interests. She had told her friend
to " bring the girls over for the day," and flung an invitation
to Mr. Pope, who had at once excused himself on the score
of his ankle. Mr. Pope was one of those men who shun
social gatherings—ostensibly because of a sterling simplicity
of taste, but really because his intolerable egotism made
him feel slighted and neglected on these occasions. He
told his wife he would be far happier with a book at home,
exhorted her not to be late, and was seen composing
himself to read the *Vicar of Wakefield*—whenever they
published a new book Mr. Pope pretended to read an old
one—as the hired wagonette took the rest of his family—
Theodore very unhappy in buff silk and a wide Stuart
collar—down the avenue.

They found a long lunch table laid on the lawn beneath the chestnuts, and in full view of the poppies and forget-me-nots around the stone obelisk, a butler and three men servants with brass buttons and red and white striped waistcoats gave dignity to the scene, and beyond, on the terrace, amidst abundance of deck-chairs, cane chairs, rugs, and cushions, a miscellaneous and increasing company seethed under Lady Petchworth's plump but entertaining hand. There were, of course, Mr. Magnet and his friend Mr. Wintersloan—Lady Petchworth had been given to understand how the land lay ; and there was Mr. Bunford Paradise, the musician, who was doing his best to teach a sullen holiday class in the village schoolroom to sing the artless old folk-songs of Surrey again, in spite of the invincible persuasion of everybody in the class that the songs were rather indelicate and extremely silly ; there were the Rev. Jopling Baynes, and two Cambridge undergraduates in flannels, and a Doctor something or other from London. There was also the Hon. Charles Muskett, Lord Pottinger's cousin and estate agent, in tweeds and very helpful. The ladies included Mrs. Raff, the well-known fashion writer in a wonderful costume, the anonymous doctor's wife, three or four neighbouring mothers with an undistinguished daughter or so, and two quiet-mannered middle-aged ladies, whose names Marjorie could not catch, and whom Lady Petchworth, in that well-controlled voice of hers, addressed as Kate and Julia, and seemed on the whole disposed to treat as humorous. There was also Fräulein Schmidt in charge of Lady Petchworth's three tall and already abundant children, Prunella, Prudence, and Mary, and a young, newly-married couple of cousins, who addressed each other in soft undertones and sat apart. These were the chief items that became distinctive in Marjorie's survey ; but there were a number of other people who seemed to come and go, split up, fuse, change their appearance slightly, and behave in the way inadequately apprehended people do behave on these occasions.

Marjorie very speedily found her disposition to take a detached and amused view of the entertainment in conflict with more urgent demands. From the outset Mr. Magnet loomed upon her—he loomed nearer and nearer. He turned his eye upon her as she came up to the wealthy expanse of Lady Petchworth's presence, like some sort of obsolescent ironclad turning a dull-gray, respectful, loving searchlight upon a fugitive torpedo boat, and thereafter he seemed to her to be looking at her without intermission, relentlessly, and urging himself towards her. She wished he wouldn't. She hadn't at all thought he would on this occasion.

At first she relied upon her natural powers of evasion, and the presence of a large company. Then gradually it became apparent that Lady Petchworth and her mother, yes—and the party generally, and the gardens and the weather and the stars in their courses were of a mind to co-operate in giving opportunity for Mr. Magnet's unmistakable intentions.

And Marjorie, with that instability of her sex which has been a theme for masculine humour in all ages, suddenly and with an extraordinary violence didn't want to make up her mind about Mr. Magnet. She didn't want to accept him ; and as distinctly she didn't want to refuse him. She didn't even want to be thought about as making up her mind about him—which was, so to speak, an enlargement of her previous indisposition. She didn't even want to seem to avoid him, or to be thinking about him, or aware of his existence.

After the greeting of Lady Petchworth she had succeeded very clumsily in not seeing Mr. Magnet, and had addressed herself to Mr. Wintersloan, who was standing a little apart, looking under his hand, with one eye shut, at the view between the tree stems towards Buryhamstreet. He told her that he thought he had found something "pooty" that hadn't been done, and she did her best to share his artistic interests with a vivid sense of Mr. Magnet's tentative incessant approach behind her.

He joined them, and she made a desperate attempt to entangle Mr. Wintersloan in a three-cornered talk in vain. He turned away at the first possible opportunity, and left her to an embarrassed and eloquently silent *tête-à-tête*. Mr. Magnet's professional wit had deserted him. " It's nice to see you again," he said, after an immense interval. " Shall we go and look at the aviary ? "

" I hate to see birds in cages," said Marjorie, " and it's frightfully jolly just here. Do you think Mr. Wintersloan will paint this ? He does paint, doesn't he ? "

" I know him best in black and white," said Mr. Magnet.

Marjorie embarked on entirely insincere praises of Mr. Wintersloan's manner and personal effect ; Magnet replied tepidly, with an air of reserving himself to grapple with the first conversational opportunity.

" It's a splendid day for tennis," said Marjorie. ' I think I shall play tennis all the afternoon."

" I don't play well enough for this publicity."

" It's glorious exercise," said Marjorie. " Almost as good as dancing," and she decided to stick to that resolution. " I never lose a chance of tennis if I can help it."

She glanced round and detected a widening space between themselves and the next adjacent group.

" They're looking at the goldfish," she said. " Let us join them."

Every one moved away as they came up to the little round pond, but then Marjorie had luck, and captured Prunella, and got her to hold hands and talk, until Fräulein Schmidt called the child away. And then Marjorie forced Mr. Magnet to introduce her to Mr. Bunford Paradise. She had a bright idea of sitting between Prunella and Mary at the lunch table, but a higher providence had assigned her to a seat at the end between Julia—or was it Kate ?—and Mr. Magnet. However, one of the undergraduates was opposite, and she saved herself from undertones by talking across to him boldly about Newnham, though she hadn't an idea of his name or college. From that she came to tennis. To her inflamed imagination he behaved as if she was under a Taboo, but she was desperate, and had pledged him and his friend to a foursome before the meal was over.

" Don't *you* play ? " said the undergraduate to Mr. Magnet.

" Very little," said Mr. Magnet. " Very little——"

At the end of an hour she was conspicuously and publicly shepherded from the tennis court by Mrs. Pope.

" Other people want to play," said her mother in a clear little undertone.

Mr. Magnet fielded her neatly as she came off the court.

" You play tennis like—a wild bird," he said, taking possession of her.

Only Marjorie's entire freedom from Irish blood saved him from a vindictive repartee.

§ 3

" Shall we go and look at the aviary ? " said Mr. Magnet, reverting to a favourite idea of his, and then remembered she did not like to see caged birds.

" Perhaps we might see the Water Garden ? " he said.

" The Water Garden is really very delightful indeed—anyhow. You ought to see that."

On the spur of the moment Marjorie could think of no objection to the Water Garden, and he led her off.

" I often think of that jolly walk we had last summer," said Mr. Magnet, " and how you talked about your work at Oxbridge."

Marjorie fell into a sudden rapture of admiration for a butterfly.

Twice more was Mr. Magnet baffled, and then they came to the little pool of water-lilies with its miniature cascade of escape at the head and source of the Water Garden. " One of Lady Petchworth's great successes," said Mr. Magnet.

" I suppose the lotus is like the water-lily," said Marjorie, with no hope of staving off the inevitable——

She stood very still by the little pool, and in spite of her pensive regard of the floating blossoms, stiffly and intensely aware of his relentless regard.

" Marjorie," came his voice at last, strangely softened. " There is something I want to say to you."

She made no reply.

" Ever since we met last summer——"

A clear cold little resolution not to stand this had established itself in Marjorie's mind. If she must decide, she *would* decide. He had brought it upon himself.

" Marjorie," said Mr. Magnet, " I love you."

She lifted a clear unhesitating eye to his face. " I'm sorry, Mr. Magnet," she said.

" I wanted to ask you to marry me," he said.

" I'm sorry, Mr. Magnet," she repeated.

They looked at one another. She felt a sort of scared exultation at having done it ; her mother might say what she liked.

" I love you very much," he said, at a loss.

" I'm sorry," she repeated obstinately.

" I thought you cared for me a little."

She left that unanswered. She had a curious feeling that there was no getting away from this splashing, babbling pool, that she was fixed there until Mr. Magnet chose to release her, and that he didn't mean to release her yet. In which case she would go on refusing.

" I'm disappointed," he said.

Marjorie could only think that she was sorry again, but as she had already said that three times, she remained awkwardly silent.

" Is it because——" he began and stopped.

" It isn't because of anything. Please let's go back to
the others, Mr. Magnet. I'm sorry if I'm disappointing."

And by a great effort she turned about.

Mr. Magnet remained regarding her—I can only compare
it to the searching preliminary gaze of an artistic photo-
grapher. For a crucial minute in his life Marjorie hated
him. " I don't understand," he said at last.

Then with a sort of naturalness that ought to have touched
her he said : " Is it possible, Marjorie—that I might hope ?
—that I have been inopportune ? "

She answered at once with absolute conviction.

" I don't think so, Mr. Magnet. "

" I'm sorry," he said, " to have bothered you."

" *I'm* sorry," said Marjorie.

A long silence followed.

" I'm sorry too," he said.

They said no more, but began to retrace their steps.
It was over. Abruptly, Mr. Magnet's bearing had become
despondent—conspicuously despondent. " I had hoped,"
he said, and sighed.

With a thrill of horror Marjorie perceived he meant to
look rejected, let every one see he had been rejected—after
encouragement.

What would they think ? How would they look ? What
conceivably might they not say ? Something of the importance of the thing she had done, became manifest to
her. She felt first intimations of regret. They would all
be watching, Mother, Daffy, Lady Petchworth. She
would reappear with this victim visibly suffering beside
her. What could she say to straighten his back and lift
his chin ? She could think of nothing. Ahead at the end
of the shaded path she could see the copious white form,
the agitated fair wig and red sunshade of Lady
Petchworth——

§ 4

Mrs. Pope's eye was relentless ; nothing seemed hidden
from it ; nothing indeed was hidden from it ; Mr. Magnet's
back was diagrammatic. Marjorie was a little flushed
and bright-eyed, and professed herself eager, with an unnatural enthusiasm, to play golf-croquet. It was eloquently
significant that Mr. Magnet did not share her eagerness,
declined to play, and yet when she had started with the

Rev. Jopling Baynes as partner, stood regarding the game with a sort of tender melancholy from the shade of the big chestnut-tree.

Mrs. Pope joined him unobtrusively.

" You're not playing, Mr. Magnet," she remarked.

" I'm a looker-on this time," he said with a sigh.

" Marjorie's winning, I think," said Mrs. Pope.

He made no answer for some seconds.

" She looks so charming in that blue dress," he remarked at last, and sighed from the lowest deeps.

" That bird's-egg blue suits her," said Mrs. Pope, ignoring the sigh. " She's clever in her girlish way, she chooses all her own dresses—colours, material, everything."

(And also, though Mrs. Pope had not remarked it, she concealed her bills.)

There came a still longer interval, which Mrs. Pope ended with the slightest of shivers. She perceived Mr. Magnet was heavy for sympathy and ripe to confide. " I think," she said, " it's a little cool here. Shall we walk to the Water Garden, and see if there are any white lilies ? ."

" There are," said Mr. Magnet sorrowfully, " and they are very beautiful *quite* beautiful."

He turned to the path along which he had so recently led Marjorie.

He glanced back as they went along between Lady Petchworth's herbaceous border and the poppy beds. " She's so full of life," he said, with a sigh in his voice.

Mrs. Pope knew she must keep silent.

" I asked her to marry me this afternoon," Mr. Magnet blurted out. " I couldn't help it."

Mrs. Pope made her silence very impressive.

" I know I ought not to have done so without consulting you "—he went on lamely ; " I'm very much in love with her. It's—it's done no harm."

Mrs. Pope's voice was soft and low. " I had no idea, Mr. Magnet. . . . You know she is very young. Twenty. A mother——"

" I know," said Magnet. " I can quite understand. But I've done no harm. She refused me. I shall go away to-morrow. Go right away for ever. . . . I'm sorry."

Another long silence.

" To me, of course, she's just a child," Mrs. Pope said at last. " She *is* only a child, Mr. Magnet. She could have had no idea that anything of the sort was in your mind——"

Her words floated away into the stillness.

For a time they said no more. The lilies came into sight, dreaming under a rich green shade on a limpid pool of brown water, water that slept and brimmed over, as it were, unconsciously into a cool splash and ripple of escape.

" How beautiful ! " cried Mrs. Pope, for a moment genuine.

" I spoke to her here," said Mr. Magnet.

The fountains of his confidence were unloosed.

" Now I've spoken to you about it, Mrs. Pope," he said, " I can tell you just how I—oh, it's the only word—adore her. She seems so sweet and easy—so graceful——"

Mrs. Pope turned on him abruptly, and grasped his hands ; she was deeply moved. " I can't tell you," she said, " what it means to a mother to hear such things——"

Words failed her, and for some moments they engaged in a mutual pressure.

" Ah ! " said Mr. Magnet, and had a queer wish it was the mother he had to deal with.

" Are you sure, Mr. Magnet," Mrs. Pope went on as their emotions subsided, " that she really meant what she said ? Girls are very strange creatures——"

" She seems so clear and positive."

" Her manner is always clear and positive."

" Yes. I know."

" I know she *has* cared for you."

" No ! "

" A mother sees. When your name used to be mentioned—— But these are not things to talk about. There is something—something sacred——"

" Yes," he said. " Yes. Only—— Of course, one thing——"

Mrs. Pope seemed lost in the contemplation of water-lilies.

" I wondered," said Mr. Magnet, and paused again. Then almost breathlessly, " I wondered if there should be perhaps—some one else ? "

She shook her head slowly. " I should know," she said.

" Are you sure ? "

" I know I should know."

" Perhaps recently ? "

" I am sure I should know. A mother's intuition——"

Memories possessed her for awhile. " A girl of twenty is a mass of contradictions. I can remember myself as if it was yesterday. Often one says no, or yes—out of sheer nervousness. . . . I am sure there is no other attachment——"

It occurred to her that she had said enough. " What a dignity that old goldfish has ! " she remarked. " He waves his tail—as if he were a beadle waving little boys out of church."

§ 5

Mrs. Pope astonished Marjorie by saying nothing about the all too obvious event of the day for some time, but her manner to her second daughter on their way home was strangely gentle. It was as if she had realised for the first time that regret and unhappiness might come into that young life. After supper, however, she spoke. They had all gone out just before the children went to bed to look for the new moon ; Daffy was showing the pseudo-twins the old moon in the new moon's arms, and Marjorie found herself standing by her mother's side. " I hope, dear," said Mrs. Pope, " that it's all for the best—and that you've done wisely, dear."

Marjorie was astonished and moved by her mother's tone.

" It's so difficult to know what *is* for the best," Mrs. Pope went on.

" I had to do—as I did," said Marjorie.

" I only hope you may never find you have made a Great Mistake, dear. He cares for you very, very much."

" Oh ! we see it now ! " cried Rom, " we see it now ! Mummy have you seen it ? Like a little old round ghost being nursed ! "

When Marjorie said " Good-night," Mrs. Pope kissed her with an unaccustomed effusion.

It occurred to Marjorie that after all her mother had no selfish end to serve in this affair.

§ 6

The idea that perhaps after all she had made a Great Mistake, the Mistake of her Life it might be, was quite firmly established in its place among all the other ideas in Marjorie's mind by the time she had dressed next morning. Subsequent events greatly intensified this persuasion. A pair of new stockings she had trusted sprang a bad hole as she put them on. She found two unmistakable bills from Oxbridge beside her plate, and her father was " horrid " at breakfast.

Her father, it appeared, had bought the ordinary shares of a Cuban railway very extensively, on the distinct

understanding that they would improve. In a decent
universe, with a proper respect for meritorious gentlemen,
these shares would have improved accordingly, but the
weather had seen fit to shatter the wisdom of Mr. Pope
altogether. The sugar crop had collapsed, the bears were
at work, and every morning now saw his nominal capital
diminished by a dozen pounds or so. I do not know what
Mr. Pope would have done if he had not had his family to
help him bear his trouble. As it was he relieved his tension
by sending Theodore from the table for dropping a knife,
telling Rom when she turned the plate round to pick the
largest banana that she hadn't the self-respect of a child
of five, and remarking sharply from behind *The Times* when
Daffy asked Marjorie if she was going to sketch : " Oh,
for God's sake don't *whisper* ! " Then when Mrs. Pope
came round the table and tried to take his coffee cup softly
to refill it without troubling him, he snatched at it,
wrenched it roughly out of her hand, and said with his
mouth full, and strangely in the manner of a snarling
beast : " No' ready yet. Half foo'."

Marjorie wanted to know why every one didn't get up
and leave the room. She glanced at her mother and came
near to speaking.

And very soon she would have to come home and live
in the midst of this again—indefinitely !

After breakfast she went to the tumbledown summer-
house by the duckpond, and contemplated the bills she had
not dared to open at table. One was boots, nearly three
pounds, the other books, over seven. " I *know* that's
wrong," said Marjorie, and rested her chin on her hand,
knitted her brows and tried to remember the details of
orders and deliveries. . . .

Marjorie had fallen into the net prepared for our sons
and daughters by the delicate modesty of the Oxbridge
authorities in money matters, and she was, for her circumstances, rather heavily in debt. But I must admit that in
Marjorie's nature the Oxbridge conditions had found an
eager and adventurous streak that rendered her particularly
apt to these temptations.

I doubt if reticence is really a virtue in a teacher. But
this is a fearful world, and the majority of those who instruct
our youth have the painful sensitiveness of the cloistered
soul to this spirit of terror in things. The young need
particularly to be told truthfully and fully all we know of
three fundamental things ; the first of which is God, the

next their duty towards their neighbours in the matter of
work and money, and the third Sex. These things, and
the adequate why of them, and some sort of adequate how,
make all that matters in education. But all three are
obscure and deeply moving topics, topics for which the
donnish mind has a kind of special ineptitude, and which
it evades with the utmost skill and delicacy. The middle
part of this evaded triad was now being taken up in
Marjorie's case by the Oxbridge tradespeople.

The Oxbridge shopkeeper is peculiar among shopkeepers
in the fact that he has to do very largely with shy and
immature customers with an extreme and distinctive
ignorance of most commercial things. They are for the
most part short of cash, but with vague and often large
probabilities of credit behind them, for most people, even
quite straitened people, will pull their sons and daughters
out of altogether unreasonable debts at the end of their
university career ; and so the Oxbridge shopkeeper becomes
a sort of propagandist of the charms and advantages of
insolvency. Alone among retailers he dislikes the sight of
cash, declines it, affects to regard it as a coarse ignorant
truncation of a budding relationship, begs to be permitted
to wait. So the youngsters just up from home discovers that
money may stay in the pocket, be used for cab and train
fares and light refreshments ; all the rest may be had for
the asking. Marjorie, with her innate hunger for good
fine things, with her quite insufficient pocket-money, and
the irregular habits of expenditure a spasmodically financed,
hard-up home is apt to engender, fell very readily into this
new, delightful custom of having it put down (whatever
it happened to be). She had all sorts of things put down.
She and the elder Carmel girl used to go shopping together,
having things put down. She brightened her rooms with
colour-prints and engravings, got herself pretty and becoming clothes, acquired a fitted dressing-bag already noted
in this story, and one or two other trifles of the sort, revised
her footwear, created a very nice little book-shelf, and
although at times she felt a little astonished and scared at
herself, resolutely refused to estimate the total of accumulated debt she had attained. Indeed until the bills came in
it was impossible to do that, because, following the splendid
example of the Carmel girl, she hadn't even inquired the
price of quite a number of things.

She didn't dare think now of the total. She lied even
to herself about that. She had fixed on fifty pounds as the

unendurable maximum. " It is less than fifty pounds,"
she said, and added : " *must* be." But something in her
below the threshold of consciousness knew that it was more.

And now she was in her third year, and the Oxbridge
tradesman, generally satisfied with the dimensions of her
account, and no longer anxious to see it grow, was displaying the less obsequious side of his character. He wrote
remarks at the bottom of his account, remarks about
settlement, about having a bill to meet, about having
something to go on with. He asked her to give the matter
her " early attention." She had a disagreeable persuasion
that if she wanted many more things anywhere she would
have to pay ready money for them. She was particularly
short of stockings. She had overlooked stockings recently.

Daffy, unfortunately, was also short of stockings.

And now, back with her family again, everything con-
spired to remind Marjorie of the old stringent habits from
which she had had so delightful an interlude. She saw
Daffy eye her possessions, reflect. This morning something of the awfulness of her position came to her. . . .

At Oxbridge she had made rather a joke of her debts.

" I'd *swear* I haven't had three pairs of house shoes,"
said Marjorie. " But what can one do ? "

And about the whole position the question was, " What
can one do ? "

She proceeded with tense nervous movements to tear
these two distasteful demands into very minute pieces.
Then she collected them all together in the hollow of her
hand, and buried them in the loose mould in a corner of
the summer-house.

" Madge," said Theodore, appearing in the sunshine of
the doorway. " Aunt Plessington's coming ! She's sent
a wire. Some one's got to meet her by the twelve-forty
train."

§ 7

Aunt Plessington's descent was due to her sudden
discovery that Buryhamstreet was in close proximity to
Summerhay Park, indeed only three miles away. She had
promised a lecture on her movement for Lady Petchworth's village room in Summerhay, and she found that
with a slight readjustment of dates she could combine this
engagement with her promised visit to her husband's sister,
and an evening or so of influence for her little Madge. So
she had sent Hubert to telegraph at once, and " here,"

she said triumphantly on the platform, after a hard kiss at Marjorie's cheek, " we are again."

There, at any rate, she was, and Uncle Hubert was up the platform seeing after the luggage, in his small, anxious way.

Aunt Plessington was a tall, lean woman, with firm features, a high colour, and a bright eye, who wore hats to show she despised them, and carefully dishevelled hair. Her dress was always good, but extremely old and grubby, and she commanded respect chiefly by her voice. Her voice was the true governing-class voice, a strangulated contralto, abundant and authoritative ; it made everything she said clear and important, so that if she said it was a fine morning it was like leaded print in *The Times*, and she had over her large front teeth lips that closed quietly and with a slight effort after her speeches, as if the words she spoke tasted well and left a peaceful, secure sensation in the mouth.

Uncle Hubert was a less distinguished figure, and just a little reminiscent of the small attached husbands one finds among the lower crustacea ; he was much shorter and rounder than his wife, and if he had been left to himself, he would probably have been comfortably fat in his quiet little way. But Aunt Plessington had made him a Haigite, which is one of the fiercer kinds of hygienist, just in the nick of time. He had round shoulders, a large nose, and glasses that made him look astonished—and she said he had a great gift for practical things, and made him see after everything in that line while she did the lecturing. His directions to the porter finished, he came up to his niece. "Hallo, Marjorie ! " he said, in a peculiar voice that sounded as though his mouth was full (though, of course, poor dear, it wasn't), " how's the First Class ? "

" A second's good enough for me, Uncle Hubert," said Marjorie, and asked if they would rather walk or go in the donkey-cart, which was waiting outside with Daffy. Aunt Plessington, with an air of great *bonhomie*, said she'd ride in the donkey-cart, and they did. But no psuedo-twins or Theodore came to meet this arrival, as both uncle and aunt had a way of asking how the lessons were getting on that they found extremely disagreeable. Also, their Aunt measured them, and incited them with loud encouraging noises to grow one against the other in an urgent, disturbing fashion.

Aunt Plessington's being was consumed by thoughts of getting on. She was like Bernard Shaw's life force, and she really did not seem to think there was anything in existence but shoving. She had no idea what a lark life can be, and occasionally how beautiful it can be, when you do not shove, if only, which becomes increasingly hard each year, you can get away from the shovers. She was one of an energetic family of eight sisters who had maintained themselves against a mutual pressure by the use of their elbows from the cradle. They had all married against each other, all sorts of people ; two had driven their husbands into bishoprics and made quite typical bishop's wives, one got a leading barrister, one a high War Office official, and one a rich Jew, and Aunt Plessington, after spending some years in just missing a rich and only slightly demented baronet, had pounced—it's the only word for it—on Uncle Hubert. "A woman is nothing without a husband," she said, and took him. He was a fairly comfortable Oxford Don in his furtive way, and bringing him out and using him as a basis, she specialised in intellectual philanthropy and evolved her Movement. It was quite remarkable how rapidly she overhauled her sisters again.

What the Movement was, varied considerably from time to time, but it was always aggressively beneficial towards the lower strata of the community. Among its central ideas was her belief that these lower strata can no more be trusted to eat than they can to drink, and that the licensing monopoly which has made the poor man's beer thick, lukewarm and discreditable, and so greatly minimised its consumption, should be extended to the solid side of his dietary. She wanted to place considerable restrictions upon the sale of all sorts of meat, upon groceries and the less hygienic and more palatable forms of bread (which do not sufficiently stimulate the coatings of the stomach), to increase the present difficulties in the way of tobacco purchasers, and to put an end to that wanton and deleterious consumption of sweets which has so bad an effect upon the enamel of the teeth of the younger generation. Closely interwoven with these proposals was an adoption of the principle of the East Purblow Experiment, the principle of Payment in Kind. She was quite in agreement with Mr. Pope that poor people, when they had money, frittered it away, and so she proposed very extensive changes in the Truck Act, which could enable employers, under suitable safeguards, and with the advice of a small body of spinster inspectors, to supply hygienic housing, approved clothing of a moral and wholesome sort, various forms of insurance, edifying rations, cuisine, medical aid and educational facilities as circumstances seemed to justify in lieu of the wages the employees handled so ill. . . .

As no people in England will ever admit they belong to the lower strata of society, Aunt Plessington's Movement attracted adherents from every class in the community.

She now, as they drove slowly to the vicarage, recounted to Marjorie—she had the utmost contempt for Daffy because of her irregular teeth and a general lack of progressive activity—the steady growth of the Movement, and the increasing respect shown for her and Hubert in the world of politico-social reform. Some of the meetings she had addressed had been quite full, various people had made various remarks about her, hostile for the most part and yet insidiously flattering, and everybody seemed quite glad to come to the little dinners she gave in order, she said, to gather social support for her reforms. She had been staying with the Mastersteins, who were keenly interested, and after she had polished off Lady Petchworth she was to visit Lady Rosenbaum. It was all going on swimmingly, these newer English gentry were eager to learn all she had to teach in the art of breaking in the Anglo-Saxon villagers, and now, how was Marjorie going on, and what was *she* going to do in the world ?

Marjorie said she was working for her final.

" And what then ? " asked Aunt Plessington.

" Not very clear, aunt, yet."

" Looking round for something to take up ? "

" Yes, aunt."

" Well, you've time yet. And it's just as well to see how the land lies before you begin. It saves going back. You'll have to come up to London with me for a little while, and see things, and be seen a little."

" I should love to."

" I'll give you a good time," said Aunt Plessington, nodding promisingly. " Theodore getting on at school ? "

" He's had his remove."

" And how's Sydney getting on with the music ? "

" Excellently."

" And Rom. Rom getting on ? "

Marjorie indicated a more restrained success.

" And what's Daffy doing ? "

" Oh ! *get* on ! " said Daffy, and suddenly whacked the donkey rather hard. " I beg your pardon, aunt ? "

" I asked what *you* were up to, Daffy ? "

" Dusting, aunt—and the virtues," said Daffy.

" You ought to find something better than that."

" Father tells me a lot about the East Purblow Experiment," said Daffy, after a perceptible interval.

" Ah ! " cried Aunt Plessington with a loud encouraging note, but evidently making the best of it, " *that's* better. Sociological observation."

" Yes, aunt," said Daffy, and negotiated a corner with exceptional care.

§ 8

Mrs. Pope, who had an instinctive disposition to pad when Aunt Plessington was about, had secured the presence at lunch of Mr. Magnet (who was after all staying on in Buryhamstreet) and the Rev. Jopling Baynes. Aunt Plessington liked to meet the clergy, and would always if she could win them over to an interest in the Movement. She opened the meal with a brisk attack upon him. " Come, Mr. Baynes," she said, " what do your people eat here ? Hubert and I are making a study of the gluttonous side of village life, and we find that no one knows so much of that as the vicar—not even the doctor."

The reverend Jopling Baynes was a clergyman of the evasive type with a quite distinguished voice. He pursed his lips and made his eyes round. " Well, Mrs. Plessington," he said and fingered his glass, " it's the usual dietary. The usual dietary."

" Too much and too rich, badly cooked and eaten too fast," said Aunt Plessington. " And what do you think is the remedy ? "

" We make an Effort," said the Rev. Jopling Baynes, " we make an Effort. A Hint here, a Word there."

" Nothing organised ? "

" Nu," said the Rev. Jopling Baynes, and shook his head with a kind of resignation.

" We are going to alter all that," said Aunt Plessington briskly, and went on to expound the Movement and the diverse way in which it might be possible to control and improve the domestic expenditure of the working classes.

The Rev. Jopling Baynes listened sympathetically across the table and tried to satisfy a healthy appetite with as abstemious an air as possible while he did so. Aunt Plessington passed rapidly from general principles to a sketch of the success of the movement, and Hubert, who had hitherto been busy with his lunch, became audible from behind the exceptionally large floral trophy that concealed him from his wife, bubbling confirmatory details. She was very bright and convincing as she told of this prominent man met and subdued, that leading antagonist confuted, and how the Bishops were coming in. She made it clear in her swift way that an intelligent cleric resolved to get on in this world *en route* for a better one hereafter, might do worse than take up her Movement. And this touched in, she turned her mind to Mr. Magnet.

(That floral trophy, I should explain, by the way, was exceptionally large because of Mrs. Pope's firm conviction that Aunt Plessington starved her husband. Accordingly she masked him, and so was able to heap second and third helpings upon his plate without Aunt Plessington discovering his lapse. The avidity with which Hubert ate confirmed her worst suspicions and evinced, so far as anything ever did evince, his gratitude.)

" Well, Mr. Magnet," she said, " I wish I had your sense of humour."

" I wish you had," said Mr. Magnet.

" I should write tracts," said Aunt Plessington.

" I knew it was good for something," said Mr. Magnet, and Daffy laughed in a tentative way.

" I mean it," said Aunt Plessington brightly. " Think if we had a Dickens—and you are the nearest man alive to Dickens—on the side of social reform to-day ! "

Mr. Magnet's light manner deserted him. " We do what we can, Mrs. Plessington," he said.

" How much more might be done," said Aunt Plessington, " if humour could be organised."

" Hear, hear ! " said Mr. Pope.

" If all the humorists of England could be induced to laugh at something together."

" They do—at times," said Mr. Magnet, but the atmosphere was too serious for his light touch.

" They could laugh it out of existence," said Aunt Plessington.

It was evident Mr. Magnet was struck by the idea.

" Of course," he said, " in *Punch*, to which I happen to be an obscure occasional contributor——"

Mrs. Pope was understood to protest that he should not say such things.

" We *do* remember just what we can do either in the

way of advertising or injury. I don't think you'll find us
up against any really *solid* institutions."

" But do you think, Mr. Magnet, you are sufficiently
kind to the New ? " Aunt Plessington persisted.

" I think we are all grateful to *Punch*," said the Rev.
Jopling Baynes suddenly and sonorously, " for its steady
determination to direct our mirth into the proper channels.
I do not think that any one can accuse its editor of being
unmindful of his great responsibilities——"

Marjorie found it a very interesting conversation.

She always met her aunt again with a renewal of a kind
of admiration. That loud authoritative rudeness, that
bold thrusting forward of the Movement until it became
the sole criterion of worth or success, this annihilation by
disregard of all that Aunt Plessington wasn't and didn't
and couldn't, always in the intervals seemed too good to
be true. Of course this really was the way people got on
and made a mark, but she felt it must be almost as trying
to the nerves as aeronautics. Suppose, somewhere up there
your engine stopped ! How Aunt Plessington dominated
the table ! Marjorie tried not to catch Daffy's eye. Daffy
was unostentatiously keeping things going, watching the
mustard, rescuing the butter, restraining Theodore, and I
am afraid not listening very carefully to Aunt Plessington.
The children were marvellously silent and jumpily well-
behaved, and Mr. Pope, in a very unusual state of subdued
amiability, sat at the end of the table with the East Purblow
Experiment on the tip of his tongue. He liked Aunt
Plessington, and she was good for him. They had the
same inherent distrust of the intelligence and good intentions of their fellow-creatures, and she had the knack of
making him feel that he too was getting on, that she was
saying things on his behalf in influential quarters, and in
spite of the almost universal conspiracy (based on jealousy)
to ignore his stern old-world virtues, he might still be able
to battle his way to the floor of the House of Commons and
there deliver himself before he died of a few sorely needed
home-truths about motor-cars, decadence and frivolity
generally. . . .

§ 9

After lunch Aunt Plessington took her little Madge for
an energetic walk, and showed herself far more observant
than the egotism of her conversation at that meal might

have led one to suppose. Or perhaps she was only better informed. Aunt Plessington loved a good hard walk in the afternoon ; and if she could get any one else to accompany her, then Hubert stayed at home, and curled up into a ball on a sofa somewhere, and took a little siesta that made him all the brighter for the intellectual activities of the evening. The thought of a young life, new, untarnished, just at the outset, just addressing itself to the task of getting on, always stimulated her mind extremely, and she talked to Marjorie with a very real and effectual desire to help her to the utmost of her ability.

She talked of a start in life, and the sort of start she had had. She showed how many people who began with great advantages did not shove sufficiently, and so dropped out of things and weren't seen and mentioned. She defended herself for marrying Hubert, and showed what a clever shoving thing it had been to do. It startled people a little, and made them realise that here was a woman who wanted something more in a man than a handsome organ-grinder. She made it clear that she thought a clever marriage, if not a startlingly brilliant one, the first duty of a girl. It was a girl's normal gambit. She branched off to the things single women might do, in order to justify this view. She did not think single women could do very much. They might perhaps shove as suffragettes, but even there a husband helped tremendously—if only by refusing to bail you out. She ran over the cases of a number of prominent single women.

"And what," said Aunt Plessington, "do they all amount to ? A girl is so hampered and an old maid is so neglected," said Aunt Plessington.

She paused.

"Why don't you hurry up and marry Mr. Magnet, Marjorie ? " she said, with her most brilliant flash.

"It takes two to make a marriage, aunt," said Marjorie after a slight hesitation.

"My dear child ! he worships the ground you tread on ! " said Aunt Plessington.

"He's rather—grown up," said Marjorie.

"Not a bit of it. He's not forty. He's just the age."

"I'm afraid it's a little impossible."

"Impossible ? "

"You see I've refused him, aunt."

"Naturally—the first time ! But I wouldn't send him packing the second."

There was an interval.

Marjorie decided on a blunt question. " Do you really think, aunt, I should do well to marry Mr. Magnet ? "

" He'd give you everything a clever woman needs," said Aunt Plessington. " Everything."

With swift capable touches she indicated the sort of life the future Mrs. Magnet might enjoy. " He's evidently a man who wants helping to a position," she said. " Of course his farces and things, I'm told, make no end of money, but he's just a crude gift by himself. Money like that is nothing. With a clever wife he might be all sorts of things. Without one he'll just subside—you know the sort of thing this sort of man does. A rather eccentric humorous house in the country, golf, croquet, horse-riding, rose-growing, queer hats."

" Isn't that rather what he would like to do, aunt ? " said Marjorie.

" That's not *our* business, Madge," said Aunt Plessington with humorous emphasis.

She began to sketch out a different and altogether smarter future for the fortunate humorist. There would be a house in a good central position in London where Marjorie would have bright successful lunches and dinners, very unpretending and very good, and tempt the clever smart with the lure of the interestingly clever; there would be a bright little country cottage in some pretty accessible place to which Aunt and Uncle Plessington and able and influential people generally could be invited for gaily recreative and yet extremely talkative and helpful week-ends. Both places could be made centres of intrigue ; conspiracies for getting on and helping and exchanging help could be organised, people could be warned against people whose getting-on was undesirable. In the midst of it all, dressed with all the natural wit she had and an en-larging experience, would be Marjorie, shining like a rising planet. It wouldn't be long, if she did things well, before she had permanent officials and young cabinet ministers mingling with her salad of writers and humorists and the Plessington connection.

" Then," said Aunt Plessington, with a joyous lift in her voice, " you'll begin to *weed* a little."

For a time the girl's mind resisted her.

But Marjorie was of the impressionable sex at an im-pressionable age, and there was something overwhelming in the undeviating conviction of her aunt, in the clear

assurance of her voice, that this life which interested her
was the real life, the only possible successful life.   The
world reformed itself in Marjorie's fluent mind, until it
was all a scheme of influence and effort and ambition and
triumphs.   Dinner parties and receptions, men wearing
orders, cabinet ministers more than a little in love asking
her advice, beautiful robes, a great blaze of lights ; why
she might be, said Aunt Plessington, rising to enthusiasm,
" another Marcella."   The life was not without its adventurous side ; it wasn't in any way dull.   Aunt Plessington
to illustrate that point told amusing anecdotes of how two
almost impudent invitations on her part had succeeded,
and how she had once scored off her elder sister by getting
a coveted celebrity through their close family resemblance.
" After accepting he couldn't very well refuse because I
wasn't somebody else," she ended gleefully.   " So he came
—and stayed as long as anybody."

What else was there for Marjorie to contemplate ?   If
she didn't take this by no means unattractive line, what
was the alternative ?   Some sort of employment after a
battle with her father, a parsimonious life, and even then
the Oxbridge tradesmen and their immortal bills. . . .

Aunt Plessington was so intent upon her theme that she
heeded nothing of the delightful little flowers she trampled
underfoot across the down, nor the jolly squirrel with an
artistic temperament who saw fit to give an uninvited
opinion upon her personal appearance from the security
of a beech-tree in the wood.   But Marjorie, noting quite a
number of such things with the corner of her mind, and
being now well under the Plessington sway, wished she had
more concentration. . . .

In the evening after supper the customary games were
suspended, and Mr. and Mrs. Plessington talked about
getting on, and work and efficiency generally, and explained
how So-and-so had spoilt his chances in life, and why So-
and-so was sure to achieve nothing, and how this man ate
too much and that man drank too much, and on the
contrary what promising and capable people the latest
adherents of and subscribers to the Movement were, until
two glasses of hot water came—Aunt Plessington had been
told it was good for her digestion, and she thought it just
as well that Hubert should have some too—and it was time
for every one to go to bed.

§ 10

Next morning an atmosphere of getting on and strenu-
osity generally prevailed throughout the vicarage. The
Plessingtons were preparing a memorandum on their movement for the *Reformer's Year Book*, every word was of
importance and might win or lose adherents and subscribers, and they secured the undisturbed possession of the
drawing-room, from which the higher notes of Aunt
Plessington's voice explaining the whole thing to Hubert,
who had to write it out, reached, a spur to effort, into every
part of the house.

Their influence touched every one.

Marjorie, struck by the idea that she was not perhaps
getting on at Oxbridge so fast as she ought to do, went into
the summer-house with Marshall's *Principles of Economics*,
read for two hours, and did not think about her bills for
more than a quarter of the time. Rom, who had already
got up early and read through about a third of *Aurora
Leigh*, now set herself with dogged determination to finish
that great poem. Syd practised an extra ten minutes—for
Aunt Plessington didn't mind practice so long as there
wasn't a tune. Mrs. Pope went into the kitchen and made
a long-needed fuss about the waste of rice. Mr. Pope
began the pamphlet he had had in contemplation for some
time upon the advantages to public order of Payment in
Kind. Theodore, who had washed behind his ears and
laced his boots in all the holes, went into the yard before
breakfast and hit a tennis-ball against the wall and back,
five hundred and twenty-two times—a record. He would
have resumed this after breakfast, but his father came
round the corner of the house with a pen in his mouth,
and asked him indistinctly, but fiercely, what the *devil* he
was doing. So he went away, and after a fretful interval
set himself to revise his Latin irregular verbs. By twelve
he had done wonders.

Later in the day the widening circle of aggressive
urgency reached the kitchen, and at two the cook gave
notice in order, she said, to better herself.

Lunch, unconscious of this impending shadow, was
characterised by a virtuous cheerfulness, and Aunt Plessington told in detail how her seven-and-twenty nephews and
nieces, the children of her various sisters, were all getting
on. On the whole, they were not getting on so brilliantly
as they might have done (which indeed is apt to be the

case with the children of people who have loved not well but too wisely), and it was borne in upon the mind of the respectfully listening Marjorie that, to borrow an easy colloquialism of her aunt's, she might " take the shine out of the lot of them " with a very little zeal and effort—and of course, Mr. Magnet.

The lecture in the evening at Summerhay was a great success.

The chair was taken by the Rev. Jopling Baynes, Lady Petchworth was enthroned behind the table. Hubert was in charge of his wife's notes—if notes should be needed— and Mr. Pope, expectant of an invitation at the end to say a few words about the East Purblow Experiment, also occupied a chair on the platform. Lady Petchworth, with her abundant soft blond hair, brightly blond still in spite of her fifty-five years, her delicate features, her plump hands, her numerous chins and her entirely inaudible voice, made a pleasing contrast with Aunt Plessington's resolute personality. She had perhaps an even greater assurance of authority, but it was a quiet assurance ; you felt that she knew that if she spoke in her sleep she would be obeyed, that it was quite unnecessary to make herself heard. The two women, indeed, the one so assertive, the other so established, were at the opposite poles of authoritative British womanhood, and harmonised charmingly. The little room struck the note of a well-regulated brightness at every point, it had been decorated in a Keltic but entirely respectful style by one of Lady Petchworth's artistic discoveries, it was lit by paraffin lamps that smelt hardly at all, and it was gay with colour prints illustrating the growth of the British Empire from the Battle of Ethandune to the surrender of Cronje. The hall was fairly full. Few could afford to absent themselves from these brightening occasions, but there was a tendency on the part of the younger and the less thoughtful section of the village manhood to accumulate at the extreme back and rumble in what appeared to be a slightly ironical spirit, so far as it had any spirit, with its feet.

The Rev. Jopling Baynes opened proceedings with a few well-chosen remarks, in which he complimented every one present either singly or collectively according to their rank and importance, and then Aunt Plessington came forward to the centre of the platform amidst a hectic flush of applause, and said " Haw ! " in a loud, clear, ringing tone.

She spoke without resorting to the notes in Hubert's

little fist, very freely and easily. Her strangulated contralto went into every corner of the room and positively
seemed to look for and challenge inattentive auditors.
She had come over, she said, and she had been very glad
to come over and talk to them that night, because it
meant not only seeing them but meeting her very dear
delightful friend Lady Petchworth (loud applause) and
staying for a day or so with her brother-in-law Mr. Pope
(unsupported outburst of applause from Mr. Magnet), to
whom she and social reform generally owed so much. She
had come to talk to them that night about the National
Good Habits Movement, which was attracting so much
attention and which bore so closely on our National Life
and Character ; she happened to be—here Aunt Plessington
smiled as she spoke—a humble person connected with that
movement, just a mere woman connected with it ; she was
going to explain to them as well as she could in her
womanly way and in the time at her disposal just what it
was and just what it was for, and just what means it
adopted and just what ends it had in view. Well, they all
knew what Habits were, and that there were Good Habits
and Bad Habits, and she supposed that the difference between a good man and a bad man was just that the good
man had good habits and the bad one had bad habits.
Everybody she supposed wanted to get on. If a man had
good habits he got on, and if he had bad habits he didn't
get on, and she supposed it was the same with a country,
if its people had good habits they got on, and if its people
had bad habits they didn't get on. For her own part she
and her husband (Hubert gave a little self-conscious jump)
had always cultivated good habits, and she had to thank
him with all her heart for his help in doing so. (Applause
from the front seats.) Now, the whole idea of her movement
was to ask, how can we raise the standard of the national
habits ? how can we get rid of bad habits and cultivate
good ones ? . . . (Here there was a slight interruption due
to some one being suddenly pushed off the end of a form
at the back, and coming to the floor with audible violence,
after which a choked and obstructed tittering continued
intermittently for some time.)

Some of her audience, she remarked, had not yet acquired
the habit of sitting still.

(Laughter, and a coarse vulgar voice : " Good old Billy
Punt ! ")

Well, to resume, she and her husband had made a special

and careful study of habits; they had consulted all sorts
of people and collected all sorts of statistics, in fact they
had devoted themselves to this question, and the conclusion
to which they came was this, that Good Habits were
acquired by Training and Bad Habits came from neglect
and carelessness and leaving people, who weren't fit for
such freedom, to run about and do just whatever they liked.
And so, she went on with a note of complete demonstration,
the problem resolved itself into the question of how far
they could get more Training into the national life, and
how they could check extravagant and unruly and wasteful
and unwise ways of living. (Hear, hear ! from Mr. Pope.)
And this was the problem she and her husband had set
themselves to solve.

(Scuffle, and a boy's voice at the back, saying : " Oh,
shut it, Nuts ! SHUT it ! ")

Well, she and her husband had worked the thing out,
and they had come to the conclusion that what was the
matter with the great mass of English people was first that
they had rather too much loose money, and secondly that
they had rather too much loose time. (A voice : " What
O ! " and the Rev. Jopling Baynes suddenly extended his
neck, knitted his brows, and became observant of the
interrupter.) She did not say they had too much money
(a second voice : " Not 'Arf ! "), but too much *loose* money.
She did not say they had too much time, but too much
loose time, that is to say, they had money and time they
did not know how to spend properly. And so they got into
mischief. A great number of people in this country, she
maintained, and this was especially true of the lower classes,
did not know how to spend either money or time ; they
bought themselves wasteful things and injurious things,
and they frittered away their hours in all sorts of foolish,
unprofitable ways. And, after the most careful and
scientific study of this problem, she and her husband had
come to the conclusion that two main principles must
underlie any remedial measures that were attempted, the
first of which was the Principle of Payment in Kind, which
had already had so interesting a trial at the great carriage
works of East Purblow, and the second, the Principle of
Continuous Occupation, which had been recognised long
ago in popular wisdom by that admirable proverb—or
rather quotation—she believed it was a quotation, though
she gave, she feared, very little time to poetry (" Better
employed," from Mr. Pope)—

." Satan finds some mischief still
For idle hands to do."

(Irrepressible outbreak of wild and sustained applause
from the back seats, and in a sudden lull a female voice
asking in a flattened, thwarted tone : " Ain't there to be
no lantern then ? ")

The lecturer went on to explain what was meant by
either member of what perhaps they would permit her to
call this double-barrelled social remedy.

It was an admirable piece of lucid exposition. Slowly
the picture of a better, happier, more disciplined England
grew upon the minds of the meeting. First she showed
the new sort of employer her movement would evoke, an
employer paternal, philanthropic, vaguely responsible for
the social order of all his dependants. (Lady Petchworth
was seen to nod her head slowly at this.) Only in the last
resort, and when he was satisfied that his worker and his
worker's family were properly housed, hygienically clothed
and fed, attending suitable courses of instruction and free
from any vicious inclinations, would he pay wages in cash.
In the discharge of the duties of payment he would have
the assistance of expert advice, and the stimulus of voluntary inspectors of his own class. He would be the natural
clan-master, the captain and leader, adviser and caretaker
of his banded employees. Responsibility would stimulate
him, and if responsibility did not stimulate him, inspectors
(both men and women inspectors) would. The worker, on
the other hand, would be enormously more healthy and
efficient under the new régime. His home, designed by
qualified and officially recognised architects, would be
prettier as well as more convenient and elevating to his
taste, his children admirably trained and dressed in the new
and more beautiful clothing with which Lady Petchworth
(applause) had done so much to make them familiar, his
vital statistics compared with current results would be
astonishingly good, his mind free from any anxiety but the
proper anxiety of a man in his position, to get his work
done properly and earn recognition from those competent
and duly authorised to judge it. Of all this she spoke with
the inspiring note of absolute conviction. All this would
follow Payment in Kind and Continuous Occupation as the
day follows sunrise. And there would always—and here
Aunt Plessington's voice seemed to brighten—be something
for the worker to get on with, something for him to do :

lectures, classes, reading-rooms, improving entertainments.
His time would be filled. The proper authorities would see
that it was filled—and filled in the right way. Never for
a moment need he be bored. He would never have an
excuse for being bored. That was the second great idea,
the complementary idea to the first. "And here it is,"
she said, turning a large encouraging smile on Lady Petchworth, "that the work of a National Theatre, instructive,
stimulating, well regulated, and morally sustaining, would
come in." He wouldn't, of course, be *compelled* to go, but
there would be his seat, part of his payment in kind, and
the public-house would be shut, most other temptations
would be removed. . . .

The lecture reached its end at last with only one other
interruption. Some would-be humorist suddenly inquired,
apropos of nothing : " What's the fare to America, Billy ? "
and a voice, presumably Billy's, answered him : " More'n
you'll ev 'av in *you*' pocket."

The Rev. Jopling Baynes, before he called upon Mr.
Pope for his promised utterance about East Purblow, could
not refrain from pointing out how silly " in every sense of
the word " these wanton interruptions were. What, he
asked, had English social reform to do with the fare to
America ?—and having roused the meeting to an alert
silence by the length of his pause, answered in a voice
of ringing contempt : " Nothing—*whatsoever*." Then Mr.
Pope made his few remarks about East Purblow with the
ease and finish that comes from long practice ; much, he
said, had to be omitted " in view of " the restricted time
at his disposal, but he did not grudge that, the time had
been better filled. (" No, no," from Aunt Plessington.)
Yes, yes,—by the lucid and delightful lecture they had all
enjoyed, and he not least among them. (Applause.) . . .

§ 11

They came out into a luminous blue night, with a
crescent young moon high overhead. It was so fine that
the Popes and the Plessingtons and Mr. Magnet declined
Lady Petchworth's proffered car, and walked back to
Buryhamstreet across the park through a sleeping pallid
cornfield, and along by the edge of the pine woods. Mr.
Pope would have liked to walk with Mr. Magnet and explain
all that the pressure on his time had caused him to omit
from his speech, and why it was he had seen fit to omit

this part and include that. Some occult power, however, baffled this intention, and he found himself going home in the company of his brother-in-law and Daffy, with Aunt Plessington and his wife like a barrier between him and his desire. Marjorie, on the other hand, found Mr. Magnet's proximity inevitable. They fell a little behind and were together again for the first time since her refusal.

He behaved, she thought, with very great restraint, and indeed he left her a little doubtful on that occasion whether he had not decided to take her decision as final. He talked chiefly about the lecture, which had impressed him very deeply. Mrs. Plessington, he said, was so splendid —made him feel trivial. He felt stirred up by her, wanted to help in this social work, this picking up of helpless people from the muddle in which they wallowed.

He seemed not only extraordinarily modest but extraordinarily gentle that night, and the warm moonshine gave emphatic lights. She felt the profound change in her feelings towards him that had followed her rejection of him. It had cleared away the oppression from him. She had no longer any sense of entanglement and pursuit, and all the virtues his courtship had obscured shone clear again. He was kindly, he was patient—and she felt something about him a woman is said always to respect, he gave her an impression of ability. After all, he could banish the trouble that crushed and overwhelmed her with a movement of his little finger. Of all her load of debt he could earn the payment in a day.

" Your aunt goes to-morrow ? " he said.

Marjorie admitted it.

" I wish I could talk to her more. She's so inspiring."

" You know of our little excursion for Friday ? " he asked after a pause.

She had not heard. Friday was Theodore's birthday ; she knew it only too well because she had had to part with her stamp collection—which very luckily had chanced to get packed and come to Buryhamstreet—to meet its demand. Mr. Magnet explained he had thought it might be fun to give a picnic in honour of the anniversary.

" How jolly of you ! " said Marjorie.

" There's a pretty bit of river between Wamping and Friston Hanger—I've wanted you to see it for a long time, and Friston Hanger church has the prettiest view. The tower gets the bend of the river."

He told her all he meant to do as if he submitted his

plans for her approval. They would drive to Wamping and get a very comfortable little steam-launch one could hire there. Wintersloan was coming down again ; an idle day of this kind just suited his temperament. Theodore would like it, wouldn't he ?

" Theodore will think he is King of Surrey ! "

" I'll have a rod and line if he wants to fish. I don't want to forget anything. I want it to be *his* day really and truly."

The slightest touch upon the pathetic note ? She could not tell.

But that evening brought Marjorie nearer to loving Magnet than she had ever been. Before she went to sleep that night she had decided he was quite a tolerable person again ; she had been too nervous and unjust with him. After all, his urgency and awkwardness had been just a part of his sincerity. Perhaps the faint doubt whether he would make his request again gave the zest of uncertainty to his devotion. Of course, she told herself, he would ask again. And then the blissful air of limitless means she might breathe. The blessed release. . . .

She was suddenly fast asleep.

§ 12

Friday was after all not so much Theodore's day as Mr· Magnet's.

Until she found herself committed there was no shadow of doubt in Marjorie's mind of what she meant to do. " Before I see you again," said Aunt Plessington at the parting kiss, " I hope you'll have something to tell me." She might have been Hymen thinly disguised as an aunt, waving from the departing train. She continued by vigorous gestures and unstinted display of teeth and a fluttering handkerchief to encourage Marjorie to marry Mr. Magnet until the curve of the cutting hid her from view. . . .

Fortune favoured Mr. Magnet with a beautiful day, and the excursion was bright and successful from the outset. It was done well, and what perhaps was more calculated to impress Marjorie, it was done with lavish generosity. From the outset she turned a smiling countenance upon her host. She did her utmost to suppress a reviving irrational qualm in her being, to maintain clearly and simply her over-night decision, that he should propose again and that she should accept him.

Yet the festival was just a little dreamlike in its quality to her perceptions. She found she could not focus clearly on its details.

Two wagonettes came from Wamping; there was room for everybody and to spare, and Wamping revealed itself a pleasant small country town with stocks under the market hall, and just that tint of green paint and that loafing touch the presence of a boating river gives.

The launch was brilliantly smart with abundant crimson cushions and a tasselled awning, and away to the left was a fine old bridge that dated in its essentials from Plantagenet times.

They started with much whistling and circling, and went away up river under overhanging trees that sometimes swished the funnel, splashing the meadow path and making the reeds and bulrushes dance with their wash. They went through a reluctant lock, steamed up a long reach, they passed the queerly painted Potwell Inn with its picturesque group of poplars and its absurd new notice-board of " Omlets." . . . Theodore was five stone of active happiness; he and the pseudo-twins, strictly under his orders as the universal etiquette of birthday prescribes, clambered round and round the boat, clutching the awning rail and hanging over the water in an entirely secure and perilous-looking manner. No one, unless his father happened to be upset by something, would check him, he knew, on this auspicious day. Mr. Magnet sat with the gray eye on Marjorie and listened a little abstractedly to Mr. Pope, who was telling very fully what he would say if the Liberal party were to ask his advice at the present juncture. Mrs. Pope attended discreetly, and Daffy and Marjorie, with a less restrained interest, to Mr. Wintersloan, who showed them how to make faces out of a fist tied up in a pocket-handkerchief, how to ventriloquise, how to conjure with halfpence—which he did very amusingly— and what the buttons on a man's sleeve were for ; Theodore clambering at his back discovered what he was at, and by right of birthday made him do all the faces and tricks over again. Then Mr. Wintersloan told stories of all the rivers along which, he said, he had travelled in steamboats ; the Rhine, the Danube, the Hoogly and the Fall River, and particularly how he had been bitten by a very young crocodile. " It's the smell of the oil brings it all back to me," he said. " And the kind of sway it gives you."

He made sinuous movements of his hand, and looked at Marjorie with that wooden yet expressive smile.

Friston Hanger proved to be even better than Wamping. It had a character of its own because it was built very largely of a warm buff-coloured local rock instead of the usual brick, and the outhouses at least of the little inn at which they landed were thatched. Most of the cottages had casement windows with diamond panes, and the streets were cobbled and very up and down hill. The place ran to high walls richly suggestive of hidden gardens, overhung by big trees and pierced by secretive important-looking doors. And over it all rose an unusually big church, with a tall buttressed tower surmounted by a lantern of pierced stone.

" We'll go through the town and look at the ruins of the old castle beyond the church," said Mr. Magnet to Marjorie, " and then I want you to see the view from the church tower."

And as they went through the street, he called her attention again to the church tower in a voice that seemed to her to be inexplicably charged with significance. " I want you to go up there," he said.

" How about something to eat, Mr. Magnet ? " remarked Theodore suddenly, and everybody felt a little surprised when Mr. Magnet answered : " Who wants things to eat on your birthday, Theodore ? "

But they saw the joke of that when they reached the castle ruins and found in the old tilting yard, with its ivy-covered arch framing a view of the town and stream, a table spread with a white cloth that shone in the sunshine, glittering with glass and silver and gay with a bowl of salad and flowers and cold pies and a jug of claret-cup and an ice pail—a silver pail ! containing two promising-looking bottles—in the charge of two real live waiters, in evening dress as waiters should be, but with straw hats to protect them from the sun and weather. " Oh ! " cried Mrs. Pope, " what a *splendid* idea, Mr. Magnet," when the destination of the feast was perfectly clear, and even Theodore seemed a little overawed—almost as if he felt his birthday was being carried too far and might provoke a judgment later. Manifestly Mr. Magnet must have ordered this in London, and have had it sent down, waiters and all ! Theodore knew he was a very wonderful little boy in spite of the acute criticism of four devoted sisters, and Mr. Magnet had noticed him before at times, but this was, well, rather immense ! " Look at the pie-crusts, old man ! " And on the pie-crusts, and on the icing of the cake, their munificent host had caused to be done in little raised letters of dough and chocolate the word " Theodore."

" Oh, *Mr*. Magnet ! " said Marjorie—his eye so obviously invited her to say something. Mr. Pope tried a nebulous joke about " groaning boards of Frisky Hanger," and only Mr. Wintersloan restrained his astonishment and admiration. " You could have got those chaps in livery," he said —unheeded. The lunch was as a matter of fact his idea ; he had refused to come unless it was provided, and he had somehow counted on blue coats, brass buttons, and yellow waistcoats—but everybody else of course ascribed the whole invention to Mr. Magnet.

" Well," said Mr. Pope, with a fine air of epigram, " the only thing I can say is—to eat it," and prepared to sit down.

" Melon," cried Mr. Magnet to the waiters, " we'll begin with the melon. Have you ever tried melon with pepper and salt, Mrs. Pope ? "

" You put salt in everything," admired Mr. Pope. " Salt from those attics of yours—Attic salt."

" Or there's ginger ! " said Mr. Magnet, after a whisper from the waiter.

Mr. Pope said something classical about " ginger hot in the mouth."

" Some of these days," said Mr. Wintersloan, " when I have exhausted all other sensations, I mean to try melon and mustard."

Rom made a wonderful face at him.

" I can think of worse things than that," said Mr. Wintersloan with a hard brightness.

" Not till after lunch, Mr. Wintersloan ! " said Rom heartily.

" The claret cup's all right for Theodore, Mrs. Pope," said Magnet. " It's a special twelve-year-old brand." (He thought of everything !)

" Mummy," said Mr. Pope, " you'd better carve this pie, I think."

" I want very much," said Mr. Magnet in Marjorie's ear and very confidentially, " to show you the view from the church tower. I think—it will appeal to you."

" Rom ! " said Theodore, uncontrollably, in a tremendous stage whisper, " there's peaches ! . . . *There !* on the hamper ! "

" Champagne, ma'am ? " said the waiter suddenly in
Mrs. Pope's ear, wiping ice-water from the bottle.

(But what could it have cost him ?)

§ 13

Marjorie would have preferred that Mr. Magnet should
not have decided with such relentless determination to
make his second proposal on the church tower.   His
purpose was luminously clear to her from the beginning
of lunch onward, and she could feel her nerves going under
the strain of that long expectation.   She tried to pull
herself together, tried not to think about it, tried to be
amused by the high spirits and nonsense of Mr. Wintersloan
and Syd and Rom and Theodore ; but Mr. Magnet was
very pervasive, and her mother didn't ever look at her,
looked past her and away from her and all round her, in a
profoundly observant manner.   Marjorie felt chiefly anxious
to get to the top of that predestinate tower and have the
whole thing over, and it was with a start that she was just
able to prevent one of the assiduous waiters filling her glass
with champagne for the third time.

There was a little awkwardness in dispersing after lunch.
Mr. Pope, his heart warmed by the champagne and mellowed
by a subsequent excellent cigar, wanted very much to
crack what he called a " post-prandial jest " or so with
the great humorist, while Theodore also, deeply impressed
with the discovery that there was more in Mr. Magnet
than he had supposed, displayed a strong disposition to
attach himself more closely than he had hitherto done to
this remarkable person, and study his quiet but enormous
possibilities with greater attention.   Mrs. Pope with a
still alertness did her best to get people adjusted, but Syd
and Rom had conceived a base and unnatural desire to
subjugate the affections of the youngest waiter, and wouldn't
listen to her proposal that they should take Theodore
away into the town ;   Mr. Wintersloan displayed extraordinary cunning and resource in evading a *tête-à-tête* with
Mr. Pope that would have released Mr. Magnet.   Now
Mrs. Pope came to think of it, Mr. Wintersloan never
had had the delights of a good talk with Mr. Pope, he
knew practically nothing about the East Purblow Experiment except for what Mr. Magnet might have retailed to
him, and she was very greatly puzzled to account for his
almost manifest reluctance to go into things thoroughly.

Daffy remained on hand, available but useless, and Mrs. Pope, smiling at the landscape and a prey to Management within, was suddenly inspired to take her eldest daughter into her confidence. "Daffy," she said, with a guileful finger extended and pointing to the lower sky as though she was pointing out the less obvious and more atmospheric beauties of Surrey, "get Theodore away from Mr. Magnet if you can. He wants to talk to Marjorie."

Daffy looked round. "Shall I call him?" she said.

"No," said Mrs. Pope, "do it—just—quietly."

"I'll try," said Daffy and stared at her task, and Mrs. Pope, feeling that this might or might not succeed but that anyhow she had done what she could, strolled across to her husband and laid a connubial touch upon his shoulder. "All the young people," she said, "are burning to climb the church tower. I never *can* understand this activity after lunch."

"Not me," said Mr. Pope. "Eh, Magnet?"

"*I'm* game," said Theodore. "Come along, Mr. Magnet."

"I think," said Mr. Magnet, looking at Marjorie, "I shall go up. I want to show Marjorie the view."

"We'll stay here, Mummy, eh?" said Mr. Pope, with a quite unusual geniality, and suddenly put his arm round Mrs. Pope's waist. Her motherly eye sought Daffy's, and indicated her mission. "I'll come with you, Theodore," said Daffy. "There isn't room for every one at once up that tower."

"I'll go with Mr. Magnet," said Theodore, relying firmly on the privileges of the day. . . .

For a time they played for position, with the intentions of Mr. Magnet showing more and more starkly through the moves of the game. At last Theodore was lured down a side street by the sight of a huge dummy fish dangling outside a tackle and bait shop, and Mr. Magnet and Marjorie, already with a dreadful feeling of complicity, made a movement so rapid it seemed to her almost a bolt for the church tower. Whatever Mr. Magnet desired to say, and whatever elasticity his mind had once possessed with regard to it, there can be no doubt that it had now become so rigid as to be sayable only in that one precise position, and in the exact order he had determined upon. But when at last they got to that high serenity, Mr. Magnet was far too hot and far too much out of breath to say anything at all for a time except an almost explosive gust or so of approbation of the scenery. "Shor' breath!" he said,

" win'ey stairs always—that 'fect on me—buful sceny—
Suwy—like it always."

Marjorie found herself violently disposed to laugh ; indeed
she had never before been so near the verge of hysterics.

" It's a perfectly lovely view," she said. " No wonder
you wanted me to see it."

" Naturally," said Mr. Magnet, " wanted you to see it."

Marjorie, with a skill her mother might have envied,
wriggled into a half-sitting position in an embrasure and
concentrated herself upon the broad wooded undulations
that went about the horizon, and Mr. Magnet mopped his
face with surreptitious gestures, and took deep restoring
breaths.

" I've always wanted to bring you here," he said, " ever
since I found it in the spring."

" It was very kind of you, Mr. Magnet," said Marjorie.

" You see," he explained, " whenever I see anything
fine or rich or splendid or beautiful now, I seem to want
it for you."   His voice quickened as though he were
repeating something that had been long in his mind. " I
wish I could give you all this country. I wish I could
put all that is beautiful in the world at your feet."

He watched the effect of this upon her for a moment.

" Marjorie," he said, " did you really mean what you
told me the other day, that there was indeed no hope for
me ? I have a sort of feeling I bothered you that day,
that perhaps you didn't mean all——"

He stopped short.

" I don't think I knew what I meant," said Marjorie,
and Magnet gave a queer sound of relief at her words.
" I don't think I know what I mean now. I don't think
I can say I love you, Mr. Magnet. I would if I could. I
like you very much indeed, I think you are awfully kind,
you're more kind and generous than any one I have ever
known. . . ."

Saying he was kind and generous made her through
some obscure association of ideas feel that he must have
understanding. She had an impulse to put her whole
case before him frankly. " I wonder," she said, " if you
can understand what it is to be a girl ? "

Then she saw the absurdity of her idea, of any such
miracle of sympathy. He was entirely concentrated upon
the appeal he had come prepared to make.

" Marjorie," he said, " I don't ask you to love me yet.
All I ask is that you shouldn't decide *not* to love me."

Marjorie became aware of Theodore, hotly followed by
Daffy, in the churchyard below. " I *know* he's up there,"
Theodore was manifestly saying.

Marjorie faced her lover gravely.

"Mr. Magnet," she said, "I will certainly promise you that."

" I would rather be your servant, rather live for your
happiness, than do anything else in all the world," said
Mr. Magnet. " If you would trust your life to me, if you
would deign——" He paused to recover his thread.
" If you would deign to let me make life what it should
be for you, take every care from your shoulders, face
every responsibility——"

Marjorie felt she had to hurry. She could almost feel
the feet of Theodore coming up that tower.

" Mr. Magnet," she said, " you don't understand. You
don't realise what I am. You don't know how unworthy
I am—what a mere ignorant child——"

" Let me be judge of that ! " cried Mr. Magnet.

They paused almost like two actors who listen for the
prompter. It was only too obvious that both were aware
of a little medley of imperfectly subdued noises below.
Theodore had got to the ladder that made the last part
of the ascent, and there Daffy had collared him. " *My*
birthday," said Theodore. " Come down ! You *shan't*
go up there ! " said Daffy. " You *mustn't*, Theodore ! "
" Why not ? " There was something like a scuffle, and
whispers. Then it would seem Theodore went—reluctantly
and with protests. But the conflict receded.

" Marjorie ! " said Mr. Magnet, as though there had
been no pause, " if you would consent only to make an
experiment, if you would try to love me. Suppose you
tried an engagement. I do not care how long I waited. . . ."
He paused. " Will you try ? " he urged upon her
distressed silence.

She felt as though she forced the word. " *Yes !* " she
said in a very low voice.

Then it seemed to her that Mr. Magnet leapt upon her.
She felt herself pulled almost roughly from the embrasure,
and he had kissed her. She struggled in his embrace.
" Mr. Magnet ! " she said. He lifted her face and kissed
her lips. " Marjorie ! " he said, and she had partly
released herself.

" Oh, *don't* kiss me," she cried, " don't kiss me yet ! "

" But a kiss ! "

" I don't like it."

" I beg your pardon ! " he said.   " I forgot—— But you. . . . You. . . . I couldn't help it."

She was suddenly wildly sorry for what she had done. She felt she was going to cry, to behave absurdly.

" I want to go down," she said.

" Marjorie, you have made me the happiest of men ! All my life, all my strength I will spend in showing you that you have made no mistake in trusting me——"

" Yes," she said, " yes," and wondered what she could say or do.   It seemed to him that her shrinking pose was the most tenderly modest thing he had ever seen.

" Oh, my dear ! " he said, and restrained himself and took her passive hand and kissed it.

" I want to go down to them ! " she insisted.

He paused on the topmost rungs of the ladder, looking unspeakable things at her.   Then he turned to go down, and for the second time in her life she saw that incipient thinness. . . .

" I am sure you will never be sorry," he said. . . .

They found Mr. and Mrs. Pope in the churchyard.   Mr. Pope was reading with amusement for the third time an epitaph that had caught his fancy,—

> "Lands ever bright, days ever fair,
>   And yet we weep that *he* is there,"

he read.   " You know, that's really Good.   That ought to be printed somewhere."

Mrs. Pope glanced sharply at her daughter's white face, and found an enigma.   Then she looked at Mr. Magnet.

There was no mistake about Mr. Magnet.   Marjorie had accepted him, whatever else she had felt or done.

§ 14

Marjorie's feelings for the rest of the day are only to be accounted for on the supposition that she was over-wrought.   She had a preposterous reaction.   She had done this thing with her eyes open after days of delibera-tion, and now she felt as though she was caught in a trap. The clearest thing in her mind was that Mr. Magnet had taken hold of her and kissed her, kissed her on the lips, and that presently he would do it again.   And also she was asking herself with futile reiteration why she had got into debt at Oxbridge ?   Why had she got into debt ?   For such silly little things, too !

Nothing definite was said in her hearing about the engagement, but everybody seemed to understand. Mr. Pope was the most demonstrative; he took occasion to rap her hard upon the back, his face crinkled with a resolute kindliness. " Ah ! " he said, " sly Maggots ! "

He also administered several resounding blows to Magnet's shoulder-blades, and irradiated the party with a glow of benevolent waggery. Marjorie submitted without an answer to these paternal intimations. Mrs. Pope did no more than watch her daughter. Invisible but overwhelming forces were busy in bringing Marjorie and her glowing lover alone together again. It happened at last, as he was departing ; she was almost to her inflamed imagination thrust out upon him, had to take him to the gate ; and there in the shadow of the trees he kissed her " good-night " with passionate effusion.

" Madge," he said, " Madge ! "

She made no answer. She submitted passively to his embrace, and then suddenly and dexterously disengaged herself from him, ran in, and without saying good-night to any one went to her room to bed.

Mr. Pope was greatly amused by this departure from the customary routine of life, and noted it archly.

When Daffy came up Marjorie was ostentatiously going to sleep. . . .

As she herself was dropping off Daffy became aware of an odd sound, somehow familiar, and yet surprising and disconcerting.

Suddenly, wide awake again, she started up. Yes, there was no mistake about it ! And yet it was very odd.

" Madge, what's up ? "

No answer.

" I say ! you aren't crying, Madge, are you ? "

Then after a long interval : " *Madge !* "

An answer came in a muffled voice, almost as if Marjorie had something in her mouth. " Oh, shut it, old Daffy."

" But, Madge ? " said Daffy after reflection.

" Shut it. *Do* shut it ! Leave me alone, I say ! Can't you leave me alone ? Oh ! "—and for a moment she let her sobs have way with her—" Daffy, don't worry me. Old Daffy ! *Please !* "

Daffy sat up for a long time in the stifled silence that ensued, and then like a sensible sister gave it up, and composed herself again to slumber. . . .

Outside, watching the window in a state of nebulous

ecstasy, was Mr. Magnet, moonlit and dewy. It was a high serene night with a growing moon and a scattered company of major stars, and if no choir of nightingales sang there was at least a very active nightjar. " More than I hoped," whispered Mr. Magnet, " more than I dared to hope." He was very sleepy, but it seemed to him improper to go to bed on such a night—on such an occasion.

CHAPTER THE THIRD

THE MAN WHO FELL OUT OF THE SKY

§ 1

FOR the next week Marjorie became more nearly introspective than she had ever been in her life before. She began to doubt her hitherto unshaken conviction that she was a single, consistent human being. She found such discords and discrepancies between mood and mood, between the conviction of this hour and the feeling of that, that it seemed to her she was rather a collection of samples of emotion and attitude than anything so simple as an individual.

For example, there can be no denying there was one Marjorie in the bundle who was immensely set up by the fact that she was engaged, and going to be at no very remote date mistress of a London house. She was profoundly Plessingtonian, and quite the vulgarest of the lot. The new status she had attained and the possibly beautiful house and the probably successful dinner-parties and the arrangement and importance of it was the substance of this creature's thought. She designed some queenly dresses. This was the Marjorie most in evidence when it came to talking with her mother and Daphne. I am afraid she patronised Daphne, and ignored the fact that Daphne, who had begun with a resolute magnanimity, was becoming annoyed and resentful.

And she thought of things she might buy, and the jolly feeling of putting them about and making fine effects with them. One thing, she told Daphne, she had clearly resolved upon : the house should be always full and brimming over with beautiful flowers. " I've always wished mother would have more flowers—and not keep them so long when she has them. . . ."

Another Marjorie in the confusion of her mind was doing her sincerest, narrow best to appreciate and feel grateful for and return the devotion of Mr. Magnet. This Marjorie accepted and even elaborated his views, laid stress on his voluntary subjection, harped upon his goodness, brought her to kiss him.

" I don't deserve all this love," this side of Marjorie told Magnet. " But I mean to learn to love you——"

" My dear one ! " cried Magnet, and pressed her hand. . . .

A third Marjorie among the many was an altogether acuter and less agreeable person. She was a sprite of pure criticism, and in spite of the utmost efforts to suppress her, she declared night and day in the inner confidences of Marjorie's soul that she did not believe in Mr. Magnet's old devotion at all. She was anti-Magnet, a persistent insurgent. She was dreadfully unsettling. It was surely this Marjorie that wouldn't let the fact of his baldness alone, and who discovered and insisted upon a curious unbeautiful flatness in his voice whenever he was doing his best to speak from the heart. And as for this devotion, what did it amount to ? A persistent, unimaginative besetting of Marjorie, a growing air of ownership, an expansive, indulgent, smiling disposition to thwart and control. And he was always touching her ! Whenever he came near her she would wince at the freedoms a large, kind hand might take with her elbow or wrist, at a possible sudden, clumsy, pat at some erring strand of hair.

Then there was an appraising satisfaction in his eye.

On the third day of their engagement he began, quite abruptly, to call her " Magsy." " We'll end this scandal of a Girl Pope," he said. " Magsy Magnet, you'll be—M.M. No women M.P.'s for *us*, Magsy. . . ."

She became acutely critical of his intellectual quality. She listened with a new alertness to the conversations at the dinner-table, the bouts of wit with her father. She carried off utterances and witticisms for maturer reflection. She was amazed to find how little they could withstand the tests and acids of her mind. So many things, such wide and interesting fields, he did not so much think about as cover with a large enveloping shallowness. . . .

He came strolling round the vicarage into the garden one morning about eleven, though she had not expected him until lunch-time ; and she was sitting with her feet tucked up on the aged but still practicable garden-seat

reading Shaw's *Common Sense of Municipal Trading*. He
came and leant over the back of the seat, and she looked
up, said "Good-morning. Isn't it perfectly lovely?"
and indicated by a book still open that her interest in it
remained alive.

"What's the book, Magsy?" he asked, took it out of
her slightly resisting hand, closed it, and read the title.
"Um," he said; "isn't this a bit stiff for little women's
brains?"

All the rebel Marjories were up in arms at that.

"Dreadful word, 'Municipal.' I *don't* like it." He
shook his head with a grimace of humorous distaste.

"I suppose women have as good brains as men," said
Marjorie, "if it comes to that."

"Better," said Magnet. "That's why they shouldn't
trouble about horrid things like Municipal and Trading.
. . . On a day like this!"

"Don't you think this sort of thing is interesting?"

"Oh!" he said, and flourished the book. "Come!
And besides—*Shaw!*"

"He makes a very good case."

"But he's such a—mountebank."

"Does that matter? He isn't a mountebank there."

"He's not sincere. I doubt if you had a serious book
on Municipal Trading, Magsy, whether you'd make head
or tail of it. It's a stiff subject. Shaw just gets his chance
for a smart thing or so. . . . I'd rather you read a good
novel."

He really had the air of taking her reading in hand.

"You think I ought not to read an intelligent book."

"I think we ought to leave those things to the people
who understand."

"But we ought to understand."

He smiled wisely. "There's a lot of things *you* have
to understand," he said, "nearer home than this."

Marjorie was ablaze now. "What a silly thing to say!"
she cried, with an undergraduate's freedom. "Really,
you are talking nonsense! I read that book because it
interests me. If I didn't, I should read something else.
Do you mean to suggest that I'm reading like a child, who
holds a book upside down?"

She was so plainly angry that he was taken aback.
"I don't mean to suggest——" he began, and turned to
greet the welcome presence, the interrogative eye of
Mrs. Pope.

" Here we are ! " he said, " having a quarrel ! "

" Marjorie ! " said Mrs. Pope.

" Oh, it's serious ! " said Mr. Magnet, and added with a gleam : " It's about Municipal Trading ! "

Mrs. Pope knew the wicked little flicker in Marjorie's eye better than Mr. Magnet. She had known it from the nursery, and yet she had never quite mastered its meaning. She had never yet realised it was Marjorie, she had always regarded it as something Marjorie, some other Marjorie, ought to keep under control. So now she adopted a pacificatory tone.

" Oh ! lovers' quarrels," she said, floating over the occasion. " Lovers' quarrels. You mustn't ask *me* to interfere ! "

Marjorie, already a little ashamed of her heat, thought for an instant she ought to stand that, and then decided abruptly with a return to choler that she would not do so. She stood up, and held out her hand for her book.

" Mr. Magnet," she said to her mother with remarkable force and freedom as she took it, " has been talking un-utterable nonsense. I don't call that a lovers' quarrel—anyhow."

Then, confronted with a double astonishment, and having no more to say, she picked up her skirt quite un-necessarily, and walked with a heavenward chin indoors.

" I'm afraid," explained Mr. Magnet, " I was a little too free with one of Magsy's favourite authors."

" Which is the favourite author now ? " asked Mrs. Pope, after a reflective pause, with a mother's indulgent smile.

" Shaw." He raised his amused eyebrows. " It's just the age, I suppose."

" She's frightfully loyal while it lasts," said Mrs. Pope. " No one dare say a word against them."

" I think it's adorable of her," said Mr. Magnet—with an answering loyalty and gusto.

§ 2

The aviation accident occurred while Mrs. Pope, her two eldest daughters, and Mr. Magnet were playing golf-croquet upon the vicarage lawn. It was a serene, hot afternoon, a little too hot to take a game seriously, and the four little figures moved slowly over the green and grouped and dispersed as the game required. Mr. Magnet was very fond of golf-croquet, he displayed a whimsical humour and much invention at this game, it was not too exacting physically ; and he could make his ball jump into the air in the absurdest manner. Occasionally he won a laugh from Marjorie or Daffy. No one else was in sight ; the pseudo-twins and Theodore and Toupee were in the barn, and Mr. Pope was six miles away at Wamping, lying prone, nibbling grass blades and watching a county cricket match, as every good Englishman, who knows what is expected of him, loves to do. . . . Click went ball and mallet, and then after a long interval, click. It seemed incredible that anything could possibly happen before tea.

But this is no longer the world it was. Suddenly this tranquil scene was slashed and rent by the sound and vision of a monoplane tearing across the heavens.

A purring and popping arrested Mr. Magnet in mid jest, and the monster came sliding up the sky over the trees beside the church to the east, already near enough to look big, a great stiff shape, big buff sails stayed with glittering wire, and with two odd little wheels beneath its body. It drove up the sky, rising with a sort of upward heaving, until the croquet players could see the driver and a passenger perched behind him quite clearly. It passed a little to the right of the church tower and only a few yards above the level of the flagstaff, there wasn't fifty feet of clearance altogether, and as it did so Marjorie could see both driver and passenger making hasty movements. It became immense and overshadowing, and every one stood rigid as it swept across the sun above the vicarage chimneys. Then it seemed to drop twenty feet or so abruptly, and then both the men cried out as it drove straight for the line of poplars between the shrubbery and the meadow. " Oh, oh, OH ! " cried Mrs. Pope and Daffy. Evidently the aviator was trying to turn sharply ; the huge thing banked, but not enough, and came about and slipped away until its wing was slashing into the tree-tops with a thrilling swish of leaves and the snapping of branches and stays.

" Run ! " cried Magnet, and danced about the lawn, and the three ladies rushed sideways as the whole affair slouched down on them. It came on its edge, hesitated whether to turn over as a whole, then crumpled, and amidst a volley of smashing and snapping came to rest amidst ploughed-up turf, a clamorous stench of petrol, and a cloud of dust and blue smoke within twenty yards of them. The

two men had jumped to clear the engine, had fallen headlong, and were now both covered by the fabric of the
shattered wing.

It was all too spectacular for word or speech until the
thing lay still. Even then the croquet players stood
passive for awhile waiting for something to happen. It
took some seconds to reconcile their minds to this sudden
loss of initiative in a monster that had been so recently
and threateningly full of go. It seemed quite a long time
before it came into Marjorie's head that she ought perhaps
to act in some way. She saw a tall young man wriggling
on all fours from underneath the wreckage of fabric. He
stared at her rather blankly. She went forward with a
vague idea of helping him. He stood up, swayed doubtfully on his legs, turned, and became energetic, struggling
mysteriously with the edge of the left wing. He gasped
and turned fierce blue eyes over his shoulder.

" Help me to hold the confounded thing up ! " he cried,
with a touch of irritation in his voice at her attitude.

Marjorie at once seized the edge of the plane and pushed.
The second man, in a peculiar button-shaped head-dress,
was lying crumpled up underneath, his ear and cheek were
bright with blood, and there was a streak of blood on the
ground near his head.

" That's right. Can you hold it if I use only one hand ? "

Marjorie gasped " Yes," with a terrific weight as it
seemed suddenly on her wrists.

" Right O," and the tall young man had thrust himself
backwards under the plane until it rested on his back, and
collared the prostrate man. " Keep it up ! " he said fiercely
when Marjorie threatened to give way. He seemed to
assume that she was there to obey orders, and with much
grunting and effort he had dragged his companion clear of
the wreckage.

The man's face was a mass of blood, and he was sicken-
ingly inert to his companion's lugging.

" Let it go," said the tall young man, and Marjorie
thanked heaven as the broken wing flapped down again.

She came helpfully to his side, and became aware of
Daffy and her mother a few paces off. Magnet—it astonished
her—was retreating hastily. But he had to go away because
the sight of blood upset him—so much that it was always
wiser for him to go away.

" Is he hurt ? " cried Mrs. Pope.

" We both are," said the tall young man, and then, as

though these other people didn't matter and he and Marjorie were old friends, he said : " Can we turn him over ? "

" I think so," said Marjorie, grasped the damaged man's shoulder and got him over skilfully.

" Will you get some water ? " said the tall young man to Daffy and Mrs. Pope, in a way that sent Daffy off at once for a pail.

" He wants water," she said to the parlour-maid who was hurrying out of the house.

The tall young man had gone down on his knees by his companion, releasing his neck, and making a hasty first examination of his condition. " The pneumatic cap must have saved his head," he said, throwing the thing aside. " Lucky he had it. He can't be badly hurt. Just rubbed his face along the ground. Silly thing to have come as we did." .

He felt the heart, and tried the flexibility of an arm.

" *That's* all right," he said.

He became judicial and absorbed over the problems of his friend's side. " Um," he remarked. He knelt back and regarded Marjorie for the first time. " Thundering smash," he said. His face relaxed into an agreeable smile. " He only bought it last week."

" Is he hurt ? "

" Rib, I think—or two ribs perhaps. Stunned rather. All *this*—just his nose."

He regarded Marjorie and Marjorie him for a brief space. He became aware of Mrs. Pope on his right hand. Then at a clank behind, he turned round to see Daphne advancing with a pail of water. The two servants were now on the spot, and the odd-job man, and the old lady who did out the church, and Magnet hovered doubtfully in the distance. Suddenly with shouts and barks of sympathetic glee the pseudo-twins, Theodore and Toupee, shot out of the house. New thoughts were stirring in the young aviator. He rose, wincing a little as he did so. " I'm afraid I'm a little rude," he said.

" I do hope your friend isn't hurt," said Mrs. Pope, feeling the duty of a hostess.

" He's not hurt *much*—so far as I can see. Haven't we made rather a mess of your lawn ? "

" Oh, not at all ! " said Mrs. Pope.

" We have. If that is your gardener over there, it would be nice if he kept back the people who seem to be hesitating beyond those trees. There will be more presently.

I'm afraid I must throw myself on your hands." He broke into a chuckle for a moment. " I have, you know. Is it possible to get a doctor ? My friend's not hurt so very much, but still he wants expert handling. He's Sir Rupert Solomonson, from "—he jerked his head back—" over beyond Tunbridge Wells. My name's Trafford."

" I'm Mrs. Pope, and these are my daughters."

Trafford bowed. " We just took the thing out for a lark," he said.

Marjorie had been regarding the prostrate man. His mouth was a little open, and he showed beautiful teeth. Apart from the dry blood upon him he was not an ill-looking man. He was manifestly a Jew, a square-rigged Jew (you have remarked, of course, that there are square-rigged Jews, whose noses are within bounds, and fore-and-aft Jews, whose noses aren't), with not so much a bullet-head as a round-shot, cropped like the head of a Capuchin monkey. Suddenly she was down and had his head on her knee, with a quick movement that caught Trafford's eye. " He's better," she said. " His eyelids flickered. Daffy, bring the water."

She had felt a queer little repugnance at first with this helpless man, but now that professional nurse who lurks in the composition of so many women, was uppermost. " Give me your handkerchief," she said to Trafford, and with Daffy kneeling beside her and also interested, and Mrs. Pope a belated but more experienced and authoritative third, Sir Rupert was soon getting the best of attention.

" Wathall . . ." said Sir Rupert suddenly, and tried again : "Wathall." A third effort gave "Wathall about, eh?"

" If we could get him into the shade," said Marjorie.

" Woosh," cried Sir Rupert. " Weeeooo ! "

" That's all right," said Trafford. "It's only a rib or two."

" Eeeeeyoooo ! " said Sir Rupert.

" Exactly. We're going to carry you out of the glare."

" Don't touch me," said Sir Rupert. " Gooo."

It took some little persuasion before Sir Rupert would consent to be moved, and even then he was for a time—oh ! crusty. But presently Trafford and the two girls had got him into the shade of a large bush close to where in a circle of rugs and cushions the tea-things lay prepared. There they camped. The helpful odd-job man was ordered to stave off intruders from the village ; water, towels, pillows were forthcoming. Mr. Magnet reappeared as tentative assistance, and Solomonson became articulate and brave and said he'd nothing but a stitch in his side. In his present position he wasn't at all uncomfortable. Only he didn't want any one near him. He enforced that by an appealing smile. The twins, invited to fetch the doctor, declined, proffering Theodore. They had conceived juvenile passions for the tall young man, and did not want to leave him. He certainly had a very nice face. So Theodore, after walking twice round the wreckage, tore himself away and departed on Rom's bicycle. Inquiry centred on Solomonson for a time. His face, hair, and neck were wet but no longer bloody, and he professed perfect comfort so long as he wasn't moved, and no one came too near him. He was very clear about that, though perfectly polite, and scrutinised their faces to see if they were equally clear. Satisfied upon this point he closed his eyes and spoke no more. He looked then like a Capuchin monkey lost in pride. There came a pause. Every one was conscious of having risen to an emergency and behaved well under unusual circumstances. The young man's eye rested on the adjacent tea-things, lacking nothing but the coronation of the teapot.

"Why not," he remarked, "have tea?"

"If you think your friend——" began Mrs. Pope.

"Oh! *he's* all right. Aren't you, Solomonson? There's nothing more now until the doctor."

"Only want to be left alone," said Solomonson, and closed his heavy eyelids again.

Mrs. Pope told the maids, with an air of dismissal, to get tea.

"We can keep an eye on him," said Trafford.

Marjorie surveyed her first patient with a pretty unconscious mixture of maternal gravity and girlish interest, and the twins, to avoid too openly gloating upon the good looks of Trafford, chose places and secured cushions round the tea-things, calculating to the best of their ability how they might secure the closest proximity to him. Mr. Magnet and Toupee had gone to stare at the monoplane; they were presently joined by the odd-job man in an interrogative mood. " Pretty complete smash, sir! " said the odd-job man, and then perceiving heads over the hedge by the churchyard, turned back to his duty of sentinel. Daffy thought of the need of more cups and plates and went into get them, and Mrs. Pope remarked that she did hope Sir Rupert was not badly hurt. . . .

" Extraordinary all this is," remarked Mr. Trafford. " Now, here we were after lunch, twenty miles away—

smoking cigars and with no more idea of having tea with
you than—I was going to say—flying. But that's out of
date now. Then we just thought we'd try the thing. . . .
Like a dream."

He addressed himself to Marjorie : " I never feel that
life is quite real until about three days after things have
happened. Never. Two hours ago I had not the slightest
intention of ever flying again."

" But haven't you flown before ? " asked Mrs. Pope.

" Not much. I did a little at Sheppey, but it's so hard
for a poor man to get his hands on a machine. And here
was Solomonson, with this thing in his hangar, eating its
head off. ' Let's take it out,' I said, ' and go once round
the park. And here we are. . . . I thought it wasn't wise
for him to come. . . ."

Sir Rupert, without opening his eyes, was understood
to assent.

" Do you know," said Trafford, " the sight of your tea
makes me feel frightfully hungry."

" I don't think the engine's damaged ? " he said cheerfully,
" do you ? " as Magnet joined them. " The ailerons are
in splinters, and the left wing's not much better. But
that's about all except the wheels. One falls so much
lighter than you might suppose—from the smash. . . .
Lucky it didn't turn over. Then, you know, the engine
comes on the top of you, and you're done."

§ 3

The doctor arrived after tea, with a bag and a stethoscope
in a small coffin-like box, and the Popes and Mr. Magnet
withdrew while Sir Rupert was carefully sounded, tested,
scrutinised, questioned, watched, and examined in every
way known to medical science. The outcome of the
conference was presently communicated to the Popes by
Mr. Trafford and the doctor. Sir Rupert was not very
seriously injured, but he was suffering from concussion and
shock, two of his ribs were broken and his wrist sprained,
unless perhaps one of the small bones was displaced. He
ought to be bandaged up and put to bed. . . .

" Couldn't we——" said Mrs. Pope, but the doctor
assured her his own house was quite the best place. There
Sir Rupert could stay for some days. At present the
cross-country journey over the Downs or by the South-
Eastern Railway would be needlessly trying and painful.

He would with the Popes' permission lie quietly where he was for an hour or so, and then the doctor would come with a couple of men and a carrying bed he had, and take him off to his own house. There he would be, as Mr. Trafford said, " as right as ninepence," and Mr. Trafford could put up either at the Red Lion with Mr. Magnet or in the little cottage next door to the doctor. (Mr. Trafford elected for the latter as closer to his friend.) As for the smashed aeroplane, telegrams would be sent at once to Sir Rupert's engineers at Chesilbury, and they would have all that cleared away by midday to-morrow. . . .

The doctor departed ; Sir Rupert, after stimulants, closed his eyes, and Mr. Trafford seated himself at the tea-things for some more cake, as though introduction by aeroplane was the most regular thing in the world.

He had very pleasant and easy manners, an entire absence of self-consciousness, and a quick talkative dis-position that made him very rapidly at home with every-body. He described all the sensations of flight, his early lessons and experiments, and in the utmost detail the events of the afternoon that had led to this disastrous adventure. He made his suggestion of " trying the thing " seem the most natural impulse in the world. The bulk of the conversation fell on him ; Mr. Magnet, save for the intervention of one or two jests, was quietly observant ; the rest were well disposed to listen. And as Mr. Trafford talked his eye rested ever and again on Marjorie with the faintest touch of scrutiny and perplexity, and she, too, found a curious little persuasion growing up in her mind that some-where, somehow, she and he had met and had talked rather earnestly. But how and where eluded her altogether. . . .

They had sat for an hour—the men from the doctor's seemed never coming—when Mr. Pope returned un-expectedly from his cricket match, which had ended a little prematurely in a rot on an over-dry wicket. He was full of particulars of the day's play, and how Wiper had got a most amazing catch and held it, though he fell ; how Jenks had deliberately bowled at a man's head, he believed, and little Gibbs thrown a man out from slip. He was burning to tell all this in the utmost detail to Magnet and his family, so that they might at least share the retrospect of his pleasure. He had thought out rather a good pun on Wiper, and he was naturally a little thwarted to find all this good, rich talk crowded out by a more engrossing topic.

At the sight of a stranger grouped in a popular manner beside the tea-things, he displayed a slight acerbity, which was, if anything, increased by the discovery of a prostrate person with large brown eyes and an expression of Oriental patience and disdain, in the shade of a bush near by. At first he seemed scarcely to grasp Mrs. Pope's explanations, and regarded Sir Rupert with an expression that bordered on malevolence. Then, when his attention was directed to the smashed machine upon the lawn, he broke out into a loud indignant : " Good God ! What next ? "

He walked towards the wreckage, disregarding Mr. Trafford beside him. " A man can't go away from his house for an hour ! " he complained.

" I can assure you we did all we could to prevent it," said Trafford.

" Ought never to have had it to prevent," said Mr. Pope. " Is your friend hurt ? "

" A rib—and shock," said Trafford.

" Well—he deserves it," said Mr. Pope. " Rather than launch myself into the air in one of those infernal things I'd be stood against a wall and shot."

" Tastes differ, of course," said Trafford, with unruffled urbanity.

" You'll have all this cleared away," said Mr. Pope.

" Mechanics—oh ! a complete break-down party—are speeding to us in fast motors," said Trafford. " Thanks to the kindness of your domestic in taking a telegram for me."

" Hope they won't kill any one," said Mr. Pope, and just for a moment the conversation hung fire. " And your friend ? " he asked.

" He goes in the next ten minutes—well, whenever the litter comes from the doctor's. Poor old Solomonson ! "

" Solomonson ? "

" Sir Rupert."

" Oh ! " said Mr. Pope. " Is that the Pigmentation Solomonson ? "

" I believe he does do some beastly company of that sort," said Trafford. " Isn't it amazing we didn't smash our engine ? "

Sir Rupert Solomonson was indeed a familiar name to Mr. Pope. He had organised the exploitation of a number of pigment and by-product patents, and the ordinary and deferred shares of his syndicate had risen to so high a price as to fill Mr. Pope with the utmost confidence in their future ; indeed he had bought considerably, withdrawing capital to do so from an Argentine railway whose stock had awakened his distaste and a sort of moral aversion by slumping heavily after a bad wheat and linseed harvest. This discovery did much to mitigate his first asperity, his next remark to Trafford was almost neutral, and he was even asking Sir Rupert whether he could do anything to make him comfortable, when the doctor returned with a litter, borne by four hastily compiled bearers.

§ 4

Some brightness seemed to vanish when the buoyant Mr. Trafford, still undauntedly cheerful, limped off after his more injured friend, and disappeared through the gate. Marjorie found herself in a world whose remaining manhood declined to see anything but extreme annoyance in this gay, exciting rupture of the afternoon. " Good God ! " said Mr. Pope. " What next ? What next ? "

" Registration, I hope," said Mr. Magnet,—" and relegation to the desert of Sahara."

" One good thing about it," said Mr. Pope—" it all wastes petrol. And when the petrol supply gives out— they're done."

" Certainly we might all have been killed ! " said Mrs. Pope, feeling she had to bear her witness against their visitors, and added : " If we hadn't moved out of the way, that is."

There was a simultaneous movement towards the shattered apparatus, about which a small contingent of villagers, who had availed themselves of the withdrawal of the sentinel, had now assembled.

" Look at it ! " said Mr. Pope, with bitter hostility. " Look at it ! "

Every one had anticipated his command.

" They'll never come to anything," said Mr. Pope, after a pause of silent hatred.

" But they *have* come to something," said Marjorie.

" They've come to smash ! " said Mr. Magnet, with the true humorist's air.

" But consider the impudence of this invasion, the wild —objectionableness of it ! "

" They're nasty things," said Mr. Magnet. " Nasty things ! "

A curious spirit of opposition stirred in Marjorie. It seemed to her that men who play golf-croquet and watch

cricket matches have no business to contemn men who
risk their lives in the air. She sought for some controversial opening.

" Isn't the engine rather wonderful ? " she remarked.

Mr. Magnet regarded the engine with his head a little
one one side. " It's the usual sort," he said.

" There weren't engines like that twenty years ago."

" There weren't people like *you* twenty years ago," said
Mr. Magnet, smiling wisely and kindly, and turned his
back on the thing.

Mr. Pope followed suit. He was filled with the bitter
thought that he would never now be able to tell the history
of the remarkable match he had witnessed. It was all
spoilt for him—spoilt for ever. Everything was disturbed
and put out.

" They've left us our tennis lawn," he said, with a not
unnatural resentment passing to invitation. " What do
you say, Magnet ? Now you've begun the game you must
keep it up ? "

" If Marjorie, or Mrs. Pope, or Daffy . . .? " said Magnet.

Mrs. Pope declared the house required her. And so
with the gravest apprehensions, and an insincere compli-
ment to their father's energy, Daffy and Marjorie made up
a foursome for that healthy and invigorating game. But
that evening Mr. Pope got his serve well into the bay of the
sagging net almost at once, and with Marjorie in the background taking anything he left her, he won quite easily,
and everything became pleasant again. Magnet gloated
upon Marjorie and served her like a missionary giving
Bibles to heathen children, he seemed always looking at
her instead of the ball, and except for a slight disposition
on the part of Daffy to slash, nothing could have been more
delightful. And at supper Mr. Pope, rather crushing his
wife's attempt to recapitulate the more characteristic
sayings and doings of Sir Rupert and his friend, did after
all succeed in giving every one a very good idea indeed of
the more remarkable incidents of the cricket match at
Wamping, and made the pun he had been accustomed to
use upon the name of Wiper in a new and improved form.
A general talk about cricket and the Immense Good of
cricket followed. Mr. Pope said he would make cricket-
playing compulsory for every English boy.

Every one, it seemed to Marjorie, was forgetting that
dark shape athwart the lawn, and all the immense implication of its presence, with a deliberate and irrational skill,

and she noted that the usual move towards the garden at the end of the evening was not made.

§ 5

In the night time Marjorie had a dream that she was flying about in the world on a monoplane with Mr. Trafford as a passenger.

Then Mr. Trafford disappeared, and she was flying about alone with a curious uneasy feeling that in a minute or so she would be unable any longer to manage the machine. Then her father and Mr. Magnet appeared very far below, walking about and disapproving of her. Mr. Magnet was shaking his head very, very sagely, and saying: "Rather a stiff job for little Marjorie," and her father was saying she would be steadier when she married. And then, she wasn't clear how, the engine refused to work until her bills were paid, and she began to fall and fall and fall towards Mr. Magnet. She tried frantically to pay her bills. She was falling down the fronts of skyscrapers and precipices—and Mr. Magnet was waiting for her below with a quiet kindly smile that grew wider and wider and wider. . . .

She woke up palpitating.

§ 6

Next morning a curious restlessness came upon Marjorie. Conceivably it was due to the absence of Magnet, who had gone to London to deliver his long promised address on The Characteristics of English Humour to the *Literati* Club. Conceivably she missed his attentions. But it crystallised out in the early afternoon into the oddest form, a powerful craving to go to the little town of Pensting, five miles off, on the other side of Buryhamstreet, to buy silk shoelaces.

She decided to go in the donkey-cart. She communicated her intention to her mother, but she did not communicate an equally definite intention to be reminded suddenly of Sir Rupert Solomonson as she was passing the surgery, and make an inquiry on the spur of the moment—it wouldn't surely be anything but a kindly and justifiable impulse to do that. She might see Mr. Trafford perhaps, but there was no particular harm in that.

It is also to be remarked that finding Theodore a little

disposed to encumber her vehicle with his presence she
expressed her delight at being released from the need of
going, and abandoned the whole expedition to him—
knowing as she did perfectly well that if Theodore hated
anything more than navigating the donkey-cart alone, it
was going unprotected into a shop to buy articles of feminine
apparel—until he chucked the whole project and went
fishing—if one can call it fishing when there are no fish and
the fisherman knows it—in the decadent ornamental water.

And it is also to be remarked that as Marjorie approached
the surgery she was seized with an absurd and powerful
shyness, so that not only did she not call at the surgery,
she did not even look at the surgery, she gazed almost
rigidly straight ahead, telling herself, however, that she
merely deferred that kindly impulse until she had bought
her laces.   And so it happened that about half a mile
beyond the end of Buryhamstreet she came round a corner
upon Trafford, and by a singular fatality he also was driving
a donkey, or, rather, was tracing a fan-like pattern on the
road with a donkey's hoofs.   It was a very similar donkey
to Marjorie's, but the vehicle was a governess cart, and
much smarter than Marjorie's turn-out.   His ingenuous
face displayed great animation at the sight of her, and as
she drew alongside he hailed her with an almost unnatural
ease of manner.

"Hallo ! " he cried.   " I'm taking the air.   You seem
to be able to drive donkeys forward.   How do you do it ?
I can't.   Never done anything so dangerous in my life
before.   I've just been missed by two motor-cars, and hung
for a terrible minute with my left wheel on the very verge
of an unfathomable ditch.   I could hear the little ducklings
far, far below, and bits of mould dropping.   I tried to count
before the splash.   Aren't you—*white* ? "

" But why are you doing it ? "

" One must do something.   I'm bandaged up and can't
walk.   It hurt my leg more than I knew—your doctor
says.   Solomonson won't talk of anything but how he
feels, and *I* don't care a rap how he feels.   So I got this
thing and came out with it."

Marjorie made her inquiries.   There came a little pause.

" Some day no one will believe that men were ever so
foolish as to trust themselves to draught animals," he
remarked.   " Hallo !   Look out !   The horror of it ! "

A large oil van—a huge drum on wheels—motor-driven,
had come round the corner, and after a preliminary and

quite insufficient hoot, bore down upon them, and, missing Trafford as it seemed by a miracle, swept past. Both drivers did wonderful things with whips and reins, and found themselves alone in the road again, with their wheels locked and an indefinite future.

"I leave the situation to you," said Trafford. "Or shall we just sit and talk until the next motor-car kills us?"

"We ought to make an effort," said Marjorie cheerfully, and descended to lead the two beasts.

Assisted by an elderly hedger, who had been taking a disregarded interest in them for some time, she separated the wheels and got the two donkeys abreast. The old hedger's opinion of their safety on the king's highway was expressed by his action rather than his words ; he directed the beasts towards a shady lane that opened at right angles to the road. He stood by their bridles while Marjorie resumed her seat.

"It seems to me clearly a case for compromise," said Trafford. "You want to go that way, I want to go that way. Let us both go *this* way. It is by such arrangements that civilisation becomes possible."

He dismissed the hedger generously and resumed his reins.

"Shall we race?" he asked.

"With your leg?" she inquired.

"No ; with the donkeys. I say, this *is* rather a lark. At first I thought it was both dangerous and dull. But things have changed. I am in beastly high spirits. I feel there will be a cry before night ; but still, I am—— I wanted the companionship of an unbroken person. It's so jolly to meet you again."

"Again?"

"After the year before last."

"After the year before last?"

"You didn't know," said Trafford, "I had met you before? How aggressive I must have seemed! Well, *I* wasn't quite clear. I spent the greater part of last night —my ankle being foolish in the small hours—in trying to remember how and where."

"I don't remember," said Marjorie.

"I remembered you very distinctly, and some things I thought about you, but not where it had happened. Then in the night I got it. It *is* a puzzle, isn't it? You see, I was wearing a black gown, and I had been out of the sunlight for some months—and my eye, I remember it acutely, was bandaged. I'm usually bandaged somewhere.

"I was a King in Babylon
And you were a Christian slave"

—I mean a candidate."

Marjorie remembered suddenly. "You're Professor Trafford."

"Not in this atmosphere. But I am at the Romeike College. And as soon as I recalled examining you I remembered it—minutely. You were intelligent, though unsound—about cryo-hydrates it was. Ah, you remember me now. As most young women are correct by rote and unintelligent in such questions, and as it doesn't matter a rap about anything of that sort, whether you are correct or not, as long as the mental gesture is right——" He paused for a moment, as though tired of his sentence. "I remembered you."

He proceeded in his easy and detached manner, that seemed to make every topic possible, to tell her his first impressions of her, and show how very distinctly indeed he remembered her.

"You set me philosophising. I'd never examined a girl's school before, and I was suddenly struck by the spectacle of the fifty of you. What's going to become of them all?"

"I thought," he went on, "how bright you were, and how keen and eager you were—*you*, I mean, in particular —and just how certain it was your brightness and eagerness would be swallowed up by some silly ordinariness or other—stuffy marriage or stuffy domestic duties. The old, old story—done over again with a sort of threadbare baldness. (Nothing to say against it if it's done well.) I got quite sentimental and pathetic about life's breach of faith with women. Odd, isn't it, how one's mind runs on? But that's what I thought. It's all come back to me.'

Marjorie's bright, clear eye came round to him. "I don't see very much wrong with the lot of women," she reflected. "Things are different nowadays. Anyhow——"

She paused.

"You don't want to be a man?"

"*No!*"

She was emphatic.

"Some of us cut more sharply at life than you think," he said, plumbing her unspoken sense.

She had never met a man before who understood just how a girl can feel the slow obtuseness of his sex. It was almost as if he had found her out at something.

" Oh," she said, " perhaps you do," and looked at him
with an increased interest.

" I'm half feminine, I believe," he said. " For instance,
I've got just a woman's joy in textures and little significant
shapes. I know how you feel about that. I can spend
hours, even now, in crystal gazing—I don't mean to see
some silly revelation of some silly person's proceedings
somewhere, but just for the things themselves. I wonder
if you have ever been in the Natural History Museum at
South Kensington, and looked at Ruskin's crystal collection ? I saw it when I was a boy, and it became—I can't
help the word—an obsession. The inclusions like moss and
like trees, and all sorts of fantastic things, and the cleavages
and enclosures with little bubbles, and the lights and
shimmer—— What were we talking about ? Oh, about
the keen way your feminine perceptions cut into things.
And yet somehow I was throwing contempt on the feminine
intelligence. I don't do justice to the order of my thoughts.
Never mind. We've lost the thread. But I wish you knew
my mother."

He went on while Marjorie **was** still considering the
proper response to this.

" You see, I'm her only son and she brought me up, and
we know each other—oh ! very well. She helps with my
work. She understands nearly all of it. She makes
suggestions. And to this day I don't know if she's the
most original or the most parasitic of creatures. And
that's the way with all women and girls, it seems to me.
You're as critical as light, and as undiscriminating. . . .
I say, do I strike you as talking nonsense ? "

" Not a bit," said Marjorie. " But you do go rather fast."

" I know," he admitted. " But somehow you excite
me. I've been with Solomonson a week, and he's dull at
all times. It was that made me take out that monoplane
of his. But it did him no good."

He paused.

" They told me after the exam," said Marjorie, " you
knew more about crystallography—than any one."

" Does that strike you as a dull subject ? "

" No," said Marjorie, in a tone that invited justifications.

" It isn't. I think—naturally, that the world one goes
into when one studies molecular physics is quite the most
beautiful of Wonderlands. . . . I can assure you I work
sometimes like a man who is exploring a magic palace. . . .
Do you know anything of molecular physics ? "

" You examined me," said Marjorie.

" The sense one has of exquisite and wonderful rhythms
—just beyond sound and sight ! And there's a taunting
suggestion of its being all there, displayed and confessed,
if only one were quick enough to see it. Why, for instance,
when you change the composition of a felspar almost
imperceptibly, do the angles change ? What's the correspondence between the altered angle and the substituted
atom ? Why does this bit of clear stuff swing the ray of
light so much out of its path, and that swing it more ?
Then what happens when crystals gutter down and go into
solution.   The endless launching of innumerable little
craft.   Think what a clear solution must be if only one
had ultramicroscopic eyes and could see into it, see the
extraordinary patternings, the swimming circling constellations. And then the path of a ray of polarised light beating
through it ! It takes me like music. Do you know anything of the effects of polarised light, the sight of a slice of
olivine-gabbro for instance between crossed Nicols ? "

" I've seen some rock sections," said Marjorie.   " I
forget the names of the rocks."

" The colours ? "

" Oh, yes, the colours."

" Is there anything else so rich and beautiful in all the
world ? And every different mineral and every variety of
that mineral has a different palette of colours, a different
scheme of harmonies—and is telling you something."

" If only you understood."

" Exactly. All the ordinary stuff of life—you know—
the carts and motor-cars and dusty roads and—cinder
sifting, seems so blank to me—with that persuasion of
swing and subtlety beneath it all. As if the whole world
was fire and crystal and aquiver—with some sort of cotton
wrappers thrown over it. . . ."

" Dust sheets," said Marjorie. " I know."

" Or like a diamond painted over ! "

" With that sort of gray paint, very full of body—that
lasts."

" Yes."   He smiled at her.   " I can't help apologetics.
Most people think a professor of science is just——"

" A professor of science."

" Yes. Something all pedantries and phrases. I want
to clear my character. As though it is foolish to follow
a vortex ring into a vacuum, and wise to whack at a dirty
golf ball on a suburban railway bank. Oh, their golf !

Under high heaven ! . . . You don't play golf, do you, by any chance ? "

" Only the woman's part," said Marjorie.

" And they despise us," he said. " Solomonson can hardly hide how he despises us. Nothing is more wonderful than the way these people go on despising us who do research, who have this fever of curiosity, who won't be content with—what did you call those wrappers ? "

" Dust sheets."

" Yes, dust sheets. What a life ! Swaddling bands, dust sheets and a shroud ! You know, research and discovery aren't nearly so difficult as people think—if only you have the courage to say a thing or try a thing now and then that it isn't usual to say or try. And after all——" he went off at a tangent, " these confounded ordinary people aren't justified in their contempt. We keep on throwing them things over our shoulders, electric bells, telephones, Marconigrams. Look at the beautiful electric trams that come towering down the London streets at nightfall, ships of light in full sail ! Twenty years ago they were as impossible as immortality. We conquer the seas for these—golfers, put arms in their hands that will certainly blow them all to bits if ever the idiots go to war with them, come sailing out of the air on them——"

He caught Marjorie's eye and stopped.

" *Falling* out of the air on them," corrected Marjorie very softly.

" That was only an accident," said Mr. Trafford. . . .

So they began a conversation in the lane where the trees met overhead that went on and went on like a devious path in a shady wood, and touched upon all manner of things. . . .

§ 7

In the end quite a number of people were aggrieved by this dialogue, in the lane that led nowhither. . . .

Sir Rupert Solomonson was the first to complain. Trafford had been away " three mortal hours." No one had come near him, not a soul, and there hadn't been even a passing car to cheer his ear.

Sir Rupert admitted he had to be quiet. " But not so *damned* quiet."

" I'd have been glad," said Sir Rupert, " if a hen had laid an egg and clucked a bit. You might have thought

there had been a Resurrection or somethin', and cleared
off everybody. Lord ! it was deadly. I'd have sung out
myself if it hadn't been for these infernal ribs. . . ."

Mrs. Pope came upon the affair quite by accident.

" Well, Marjorie," she said, as she poured tea for the
family, " did you get your laces ? "

" Never got there, Mummy," said Marjorie, and paused
fatally.

" Didn't get there ! " said Mr. Pope. " That's worse
than Theodore ! Wouldn't the donkey go, poor dear ? "

There was nothing to colour about, and yet Marjorie
felt the warm flow in neck and cheek and brow. She
threw extraordinary quantities of candour into her manner.
" I had a romantic adventure," she said rather quietly.
" I was going to tell you."

(Sensation.)

" You see, it was like this," said Marjorie. " I ran
against Mr. Trafford. . . ."

She drank tea, and pulled herself together for a lively
description of the wheel-locking and the subsequent conversation, a bright ridiculous account which made the
affair happen by implication on the high road and not in a
by-way, and was adorned with every facetious ornament
that seemed likely to get a laugh from the children. But
she talked rather fast, and she felt she forced the fun a
little. However, it amused the children all right, and
Theodore created a diversion by choking with his tea.
From first to last Marjorie was extremely careful to avoid
the affectionate scrutiny of her mother's eye. And had
this lasted the *whole* afternoon ? asked Mrs. Pope. Oh,
they'd talked for half an hour, said Marjorie, or more,
and had driven back very slowly together. " He did all
the talking. You saw what he was yesterday. And the
donkeys seemed too happy together to tear them away."

" But what was it all about ? " asked Daffy, curious.

" He asked after you, Daffy, most affectionately," said
Marjorie, and added, " several times." (Though Trafford
had, as a matter of fact, displayed a quite remarkable
disregard of all her family.)

" And," she went on, getting a plausible idea at last, " he
explained all about aeroplanes. And all that sort of thing.
Has Daddy gone to Wamping for some more cricket ? . . ."

(But none of this was lost on Mrs. Pope.)

§ 8

Mr. Magnet's return next day was heralded by nearly two-thirds of a column in *The Times*.

The lecture on the Characteristics of Humour had evidently been quite a serious affair, and a very imposing list of humorists and of prominent people associated with their industry had accepted the hospitality of the Literati.

Marjorie ran her eyes over the Chairman's flattering introduction, then with a queer faint flavour of hostility, she reached her destined husband's utterance. She seemed to hear the flat, full tones of his voice as she read, and automatically the desiccated sentences of the reporter filled out again into those rich, quietly deliberate unfoldings of sound that were already too familiar to her ear.

Mr. Magnet had begun with modest disavowals. " There was a story, he said,"—so the report began—" whose hallowed antiquity ought to protect it from further exploitation, but he was tempted to repeat it because it offered certain analogies to the present situation. There were three characters in the story, a bluebottle and two Scotsmen. (Laughter.) The bluebottle buzzed on the pane, otherwise a profound silence reigned. This was broken by one of the Scotsmen trying to locate the bluebottle with zoological exactitude. Said this Scotsman : ' Sandy, I am thinking if yon fly is a birdie or a beastie.' The other replied : ' Man, don't spoil good whisky with religious conversation.' (Laughter.) He was tempted, Mr. Magnet resumed, to ask himself and them why it was that they should spoil the after-effects of a most excellent and admirably served dinner by an academic discussion on British humour. At first he was pained by the thought that they proposed to temper their hospitality with a demand for a speech. A closer inspection showed that he was to introduce a debate and that others were to speak, and that was a new element in their hospitality. Further, he was permitted to choose the subject so that he could bring their speeches within the range of his comprehension. (Laughter.) His was an easy task. He could make it easier ; the best thing to do would be to say nothing at all. (Laughter.) "

For a space the reporter seemed to have omitted largely —perhaps he was changing places with his relief—and the next sentence showed Mr. Magnet engaged as it were in revising a *hortus siccus* of jokes. " There was the humour

of facts and situations," he was saying, " or that humour
of expression for which there was no human responsibility,
as in the case of Irish humour ; he spoke of the humour of
the soil which found its noblest utterance in the bull.
Humour depended largely on contrast.   There was a
humour of form and expression which had many local
varieties.   American humour had been characterised by
exaggeration, the suppression of some link in the chain of
argument or narrative, and a wealth of simile and metaphor
which had been justly defined as the poetry of a pioneer
race." . . .

Marjorie's attention slipped its anchor, and caught
lower down upon : " In England there was a near kinship
between laughter and tears ; their mental relations were
as close as their physical.   Abroad this did not appear to
be the case.   It was different in France.   But perhaps on
the whole it would be better to leave the humour of France
and what some people still unhappily chose to regard as
matters open to controversy—he referred to choice of
subject—out of their discussion altogether.   (' Hear, hear,'
and cheers.) " . . .

Attention wandered again.   Then she remarked :—it
reminded her in some mysterious way of a dropped hairpin
—" It was noticeable that the pun to a great extent had
become *démodé*. . . ."

At this point the flight of Marjorie's eyes down the
column was arrested by her father's hand gently but firmly
taking possession of *The Times*.   She yielded it without
reluctance, turned to the breakfast table, and never
resumed her study of the social relaxations of humorists. . . .

Indeed she forgot it.   Her mind was in a state of extreme
perplexity.   She didn't know what to make of herself or
anything or anybody.   Her mind was full of Trafford and
all that he had said and done and all that he might have
said and done, and it was entirely characteristic that she
could not think of Magnet in any way at all except as a
bar-like shadow that lay across all her memories and all
the bright possibilities of this engaging person.

She thought particularly of the mobile animation of his
face, the keen flash of enthusiasm in his thoughts and
expressions. . . .

It was perhaps more characteristic of her time than of
her that she did not think she was dealing so much with a
moral problem as an embarrassment, and that she hadn't
as yet felt the first stirrings of self-reproach for the series

of disingenuous proceedings that had rendered the yesterday's encounter possible. But she was restless, wildly restless, as a bird whose nest is taken. She could abide nowhere. She fretted through the morning, avoided Daffy in a marked manner, and inflicted a stinging and only partially-merited rebuke upon Theodore for slouching, humping and—of all trite grievances !—not washing behind his ears. As if any chap washed behind his ears ! She thought tennis with the pseudo-twins might assuage her, but she broke off after losing two sets ; and then she went into the garden to get fresh flowers, and picked a large bunch and left them on the piano until her mother reminded her of them. She tried a little Shaw. She struggled with an insane wish to walk through the wood behind the village and have an accidental meeting with some one who couldn't possibly appear but whom it would be quite adorable to meet. Anyhow, she conquered that.

She had a curious and rather morbid indisposition to go after lunch to the station and meet Mr. Magnet as her mother wished her to do, in order to bring him straight to the vicarage to early tea, but here again reason prevailed and she went.

Mr. Magnet arrived by the 2.27, and to Marjorie's eye his alighting presence had an effect of being not so much covered with laurels as distended by them. His face seemed whiter and larger than ever. He waved a great handful of newspapers.

" Hallo, Magsy ! " he said. " They've given me a thumping Press. I'm nearer swelled head than I've ever been, so mind how you touch me ! "

" We'll take it down at croquet," said Marjorie.

" They've cleared that thing away ? "

" And made up the lawn like a billiard table," she said.

" That makes for skill," he said waggishly. " I shall save my head after all."

For a moment he seemed to loom towards kissing her, but she averted this danger by a business-like concern for his bag. He entrusted this to a porter, and reverted to the triumph of over-night so soon as they were clear of the station. He was overflowing with kindliness towards his fellow-humorists, who had appeared in force and very generously at the banquet, and had said the most charming things—some of which were in one report and some in another, and some the reporters had missed altogether . . . some of the kindliest.

" It's a pleasant feeling to think that a lot of good fellows think you are a good fellow," said Mr. Magnet.

He became solicitous for her. How had she got on while he was away ? She asked him how one was likely to get on at Buryhamstreet ; monoplanes didn't fall every day, and as she said that it occurred to her she was behaving meanly. But he was going on to his next topic before she could qualify.

" I've got something in my pocket," he remarked, and playfully : " Guess."

She did, but she wouldn't. She had a curious sinking of the heart.

" I want you to see it before any one else," he said. " Then if you don't like it, it can go back. It's a sapphire."

He was feeling nervously in his pockets, and then the little box was in her hand.

She hesitated to open it. It made everything so dreadfully concrete. And this time the sense of meanness was altogether acuter. He'd bought this in London ; he brought it down, hoping for her approval. Yes, it was—horrid. But what was she to do ? "

" It's—awfully pretty," she said, with the glittering symbol in her hand, and indeed he had gone to one of those artistic women who are reviving and improving upon the rich old Roman designs. " It's so beautifully made."

" I'm so glad you like it. You really *do* like it ? "

" I don't deserve it."

" Oh ! But you *do* like it ? "

" Enormously."

" Ah ! I spent an hour in choosing it."

She could see him. She felt as though she had picked his pocket.

" Only I don't deserve it, Mr. Magnet. Indeed I don't. I feel I am taking it on false pretences."

" Nonsense, Magsy. Nonsense ! Slip it on your finger, girl."

" But I don't," she insisted.

He took the box from her, pocketed it and seized her hand. She drew it away from him.

" No ! " she said. " I feel like a cheat. You know, I don't—I'm sure I don't love——"

" I'll love enough for two," he said, and got her hand again. " No ! " he said at her gesture, " you'll wear it. Why shouldn't you ? "

And so Marjorie came back along the vicarage avenue

with his ring upon her hand. And Mr. Pope was evidently very glad to see him. . . .

The family was still seated at tea upon rugs and wraps, and still discussing humorists at play, when Professor Trafford appeared, leaning on a large stick and limping, but resolute, by the church gate. " Pish ! " said Mr. Pope. Marjorie tried not to reveal a certain dismay, there was dumb, rich approval in Daphne's eyes, and the pleasure of Theodore and the pseudo-twins was only too scandalously evident. " Hoo-Ray ! " said Theodore, with ill-concealed relief.

Mrs. Pope was the incarnate invocation of tact as Trafford drew near.

" I hope," he said, with obvious insincerity, " I don't invade you. But Solomonson is frightfully concerned and anxious about your lawn, and whether his men cleared it up properly and put things right." His eye went about the party and rested on Marjorie. " How are you ? " he said, in a friendly voice.

" Well, we seem to have got our croquet lawn back," said Mr. Pope. " And our nerves are recovering. How is Sir Rupert ? "

" A little fractious," said Trafford, with the ghost of a smile.

" You'll take some tea ? " said Mrs. Pope in the pause that followed.

" Thank you," said Trafford, and sat down instantly.

" I saw your jolly address in the *Standard*," he said to Magnet. " I haven't read anything so amusing for some time."

" Rom, dear," said Mrs. Pope, " will you take the pot in and get some fresh tea ? "

Mr. Trafford addressed himself to the flattery of Magnet with considerable skill. He had detected a lurking hostility in the eyes of the two gentlemen that counselled him to propitiate them if he meant to maintain his footing in the vicarage, and now he talked to them almost exclusively and ignored the ladies modestly but politely in the way that seems natural and proper in a British middle-class house of the better sort. But as he talked chiefly of the improvement of motor machinery that had recently been shown at the Engineering Exhibition, he did not make that headway with Marjorie's father that he had perhaps anticipated. Mr. Pope fumed quietly for a time, and then suddenly spoke out.

" I'm no lover of machines," he said abruptly, slashing across Mr. Trafford's description. " All our troubles began with villainous saltpetre. I'm an old-fashioned man with a nose—and a neck, and I don't want the one offended or the other broken. No, don't ask me to be interested in your valves and cylinders. What do you say, Magnet ? It starts machinery in my head to hear about them. . . ."

On such occasions as this when Mr. Pope spoke out, his horror of an anti-climax or any sort of contradiction was apt to bring the utterance to a culmination not always to be distinguished from a flight. And now he rose to his feet as he delivered himself.

" Who's for a game of tennis ? " he said, " in this last uncontaminated patch of air ? I and Marjorie will give you a match, Daffy—if Magnet isn't too tired to join you."

Daffy looked at Marjorie for an instant.

" We'll want you, Theodore, to look after the balls in the potatoes," said Mr. Pope, lest that ingenuous mind should be corrupted behind his back. . . .

Mrs. Pope found herself left to entertain a slightly disgruntled Trafford. Rom and Syd hovered on the offchance of notice, at the corner of the croquet lawn nearest the teathings. Mrs. Pope had already determined to make certain little matters clearer than they appeared to be to this agreeable but superfluous person, and she was greatly assisted by his opening upon the subject of her daughters. " Jolly tennis looks," he said.

" Don't they ? " said Mrs. Pope. " I think it is such a graceful game for a girl."

Mr. Trafford glanced at Mrs. Pope's face, but her expression was impenetrable.

" They both like it and play it so well," she said. " Their father is so skilful and interested in games. Marjorie tells me you were her examiner a year or so ago."

" Yes. She stuck in my memory—her work stood out."

" Of course she is clever," said Mrs. Pope, " or we shouldn't have sent her to Oxbridge. There she's doing quite well—quite well. Every one says so. I don't know, of course, if Mr. Magnet will let her finish there."

" Mr. Magnet ? "

" She's just engaged to him. Of course she's frightfully excited about it, and naturally he wants her to come away and marry. There's very little excuse for a long engagement. No."

Her voice died in a musical little note, and she seemed

to be scrutinising the tennis with an absorbed interest.
" They've got new balls," she said, as if to herself.

Trafford had rolled over, and she fancied she detected
a change in his voice when it came. " Isn't it rather a
waste not to finish a university career ? " he said.

" Oh, it wouldn't be wasted. Of course a girl like that
will be hand and glove with her husband. She'll be able
to help him with the scientific side of his jokes and all
that. I sometimes wish it had been Daffy who had gone
to college, though. I sometimes think we've sacrificed
Daffy a little. She's not the bright quickness of Marjorie,
but there's something quietly solid about her mind—something *stable*. Perhaps I don't want her to go away from
me. . . . Mr. Magnet is doing wonders at the net. He's
just begun to play—to please Marjorie. Don't you think
he's a dreadfully amusing man, Mr. Trafford ? He says
such *quiet* things."

§ 9

The effect of this *éclaircissement* upon Mr. Trafford was
not what it should have been. Properly he ought to have
realised at once that Marjorie was for ever beyond his
aspirations, and if he found it too difficult to regard her
with equanimity, then he ought to have shunned her
presence. But instead, after his first shock of incredulous
astonishment, his spirit rose in a rebellion against arranged
facts that was as un-English as it was ungentlemanly.
He went back to Solomonson with a mood of thoughtful
depression giving place to a growing passion of indignation.
He presented it to himself in a generalised and altruistic
form. " What the deuce is the good of all this talk of
Eugenics," he asked himself aloud, " if they are going to
hand over that shining girl to that beastly little area sneak ?"

He called Mr. Magnet a " beastly little area sneak "!

Nothing could show more clearly just how much he had
contrived to fall in love with Marjorie during his brief
sojourn in Buryhamstreet and the acuteness of his disappointment, and nothing could be more eloquent of his
forcible and undisciplined temperament. And out of the
ten thousand possible abusive epithets with which his
mind was no doubt stored, this one, I think, had come
into his head because of the alert watchfulness with which
Mr. Magnet followed a conversation,' as he waited his
chance for some neat but brilliant flash of comment. . . .

Trafford, like Marjorie, was another of those undisciplined young people our age has produced in such significant quantity. He was just six-and-twenty, but the facts that he was big of build, had as an only child associated much with grown-up people, and was already a conspicuous success in the world of microchemical research, had given him the self-reliance and assurance of a much older man. He had still to come his croppers and learn most of the important lessons in life, and, so far, he wasn't aware of it. He was naturally clean-minded, very busy and interested in his work, and on remarkably friendly and confidential terms with his mother, who kept house for him, and though he had had several small love disturbances, this was the first occasion that anything of the kind had ploughed deep into his feelings and desires.

Trafford's father had died early in life. He had been a brilliant pathologist, one of that splendid group of scientific investigators in the middle Victorian period which shines ever more brightly as our criticism dims their associated splendours, and he had died before he was thirty through a momentary slip of the scalpel. His wife—she had been his wife for five years—found his child and his memory and the quality of the life he had made about her too satisfying for the risks of a second marriage, and she had brought up her son with a passionate belief in the high mission of research and the supreme duty of seeking out and expressing truth finely. And here he was, calling Mr. Magnet a " beastly little area sneak."

The situation perplexed him. Marjorie perplexed him. It was, had he known it, the beginning for him of a lifetime of problems and perplexities. He was absolutely certain she didn't love Magnet. Why, then, had she agreed to marry him ? Such pressures and temptations as he could see about her seemed light to him in comparison with such an undertaking.

Were they greater than he supposed ?

His method of coming to the issue of that problem was entirely original. He presented himself next afternoon with the air of an invited guest, drove Mr. Pope, who was suffering from liver, to expostulatory sulking in the study, and expressed a passionate craving for golf-croquet, in spite of Mrs. Pope's extreme solicitude for his still bandaged ankle. He was partnered with Daffy, and for a long time he sought speech with Marjorie in vain. At last she was isolated in a corner of the lawn, and with the thinnest

pretence of inadvertence, in spite of Daffy's despairing cry
of " She plays next ! " he laid up within two yards of her.
He walked across to her as she addressed herself to her
ball, and speaking in an incredulous tone and with the air
of a comment on the game, he said : " I say, are you
engaged to that chap Magnet ? "

Marjorie was amazed, but remarkably not offended.
Something in his tone set her trembling. She forgot to
play, and stood with her mallet hanging in her hand.

" Punish him ! " came the voice of Magnet from afar.

" Yes," she said faintly.

His remark came low and clear. It had a note of angry
protest. " *Why* ? "

Marjorie, by way of answer, hit her ball so that it
jumped and missed his, ricochetted across the lawn and
out of the ground on the farther side.

" I'm sorry if I've annoyed you," said Trafford, as
Marjorie went after her ball, and Daffy thanked heaven
aloud for the respite.

They came together no more for a time, and Trafford,
observant with every sense, found no clue to the riddle of
her grave, intent bearing. She played very badly, and
with unusual care and deliberation. He felt he had made
a mess of things altogether, and suddenly found his leg was
too painful to go on. " Partner," he asked, " will you play
out my ball for me ? I can't go on. I shall have to go."

Marjorie surveyed him, while Daffy and Magnet expressed solicitude. He turned to go, mallet in hand, and
found Marjorie following him.

" Is that the heavier mallet ? " she asked, and stood
before him looking into his eyes and weighing a mallet in
either hand.

" Mr. Trafford, you're one of the worst examiners I've
ever met," she said.

He looked puzzled.

" I don't know *why*," said Marjorie. " I wonder as much
as you. But I am " ; and seeing the light dawning in his
eyes, she turned about, and went back to the debacle of
her game.

§ 10

After that Mr. Trafford had one clear desire in his being
which ruled all his other desires. He wanted a long, frank,
unembarrassed and uninterrupted conversation with Marjorie. He had a very strong impression that Marjorie

wanted exactly the same thing. For a week he besieged
the situation in vain. After the fourth day Solomonson
was only kept in Buryhamstreet by sheer will-power,
exerted with a brutality that threatened to end that
friendship abruptly. He went home on the sixth day in
his largest car, but Trafford stayed on beyond the limits
of decency to perform some incomprehensible service that
he spoke of as " clearing up."

" I want," he said, " to clear up."

" But what *is* there to clear up, my dear boy ? "

" Solomonson, you're a pampered plutocrat," said
Trafford, as though everything was explained.

" I don't see any sense in it at all," said Solomonson,
and regarded his friend aslant with thick, black eyebrows
raised.

" I'm going to stay," said Trafford.

And Solomonson said one of those unhappy and entirely
disregarded things that ought never to be said.

" There's some girl in this," said Solomonson.

" Your bedroom's always waiting for you at Riplings,"
he said, when at last he was going off. . . .

It was Trafford's conviction that Marjorie also wanted,
with an almost equal eagerness, the same opportunity for
speech and explanations that he desired, and this sustained
him in a series of unjustifiable intrusions upon the seclusion
of the Popes. But although the manner of Mr. and Mrs.
Pope did change considerably for the better after his next
visit, it was extraordinary how impossible it seemed for him
and Marjorie to achieve their common end of an encounter.

Always something intervened.

In the first place, Mrs. Pope's disposition to optimism
had got the better of her earlier discretions, and a casual
glance at Daphne's face when their visitor reappeared
started quite a new thread of interpretations in her mind.
She had taken the opportunity of hinting at this when Mr.
Pope asked over his shirt-stud that night, " What the devil
that—that chauffeur chap meant by always calling in the
afternoon."

" Now that Will Magnet monopolises Marjorie," she
said, after a little pause and a rustle or so, " I don't see
why Daffy shouldn't have a little company of her own age."

Mr. Pope turned round and stared at her. " I didn't
think of that," he said. " But anyhow, I don't like the
fellow."

" He seems to be rather clever," said Mrs. Pope, " though

THE MAN WHO FELL OUT OF THE SKY

he certainly talks too much. And after all it was Sir
Rupert's aeroplane. *He* was only driving it to oblige."

" He'll think twice before he drives another," said Mr.
Pope, wrenching off his collar. . . .

Once Mrs. Pope had turned her imagination in this more
and more agreeable direction, she was rather disposed, I
am afraid, to let it bolt with her. And it was a deflection
that certainly fell in very harmoniously with certain secret
speculations of Daphne's. Trafford, too, being quite
unused to any sort of social furtiveness, did perhaps, in
order to divert attention from his preoccupation with
Marjorie, attend more markedly to Daphne than he would
otherwise have done. And so presently he found Daphne
almost continuously on his hands. So far as she was
concerned, he might have told her the entire history of his
life, and every secret he had in the world, without let or
hindrance. Mrs. Pope, too, showed a growing appreciation
of his company, became sympathetic and confidential in a
way that invited confidence, and threw a lot of light on
her family history and Daffy's character. She had found
Daffy a wonderful study, she said. Mr. Pope, too, seemed
partly reconciled to him. The idea that, after all, both
motor-cars and monoplane were Sir Rupert's, and not
Trafford's, had produced a reaction in the latter gentleman's favour. Moreover, it had occurred to him that
Trafford's accident had perhaps disposed him towards a
more thoughtful view of mechanical traction, and that this
tendency would be greatly helped by a little genial chaff.
So that he ceased to go indoors when Trafford was there,
and hung about meditating and delivering sly digs at this
new victim of his ripe, old-fashioned humour.

Nor did it help Trafford in his quest for Marjorie and a
free, outspoken delivery that the pseudo-twins considered
him a person of very considerable charm, and that Theodore,
though indisposed to " suck up " to him publicly—I write
here in Theodorese—did so desire intimate and solitary
communion with him, more particularly in view of the
chances of an adventitious aeroplane ride that seemed to
hang about him—as to stalk him persistently—hovering
on the verge of groups, playing a waiting game with a
tennis ball and an old racket, strolling artlessly towards
the gate of the avenue when the time seemed ripening for
his appearance or departure.

On the other hand, Marjorie was greatly entangled by
Magnet.

Magnet was naturally an attentive lover; he was full
of small encumbering services, and it made him none the
less assiduous to perceive that Marjorie seemed to find no
sort of pleasure in all the little things he did. He seemed
to think that if picking the very best rose he could find for
her did not cause a very perceptible brightening in her,
then it was all the more necessary quietly to force her
racket from her hand and carry it for her, or help her
ineffectually to cross a foot-wide ditch, or offer to read her
in a rich, abundant, well-modulated voice, some choice
passage from *The Forest Lovers* of Mr. Maurice Hewlett.
And behind these devotions there was a streak of jealousy.
He knew as if by instinct that it was not wise to leave
these two handsome young people together; he had a
queer little disagreeable sensation whenever they spoke to
one another or looked at one another. Whenever Trafford
and Marjorie found themselves in a group, there was
Magnet in the midst of them. He knew the value of his
Marjorie, and did not mean to lose her. . . .

Being jointly baffled in this way was oddly stimulating
to Marjorie's and Trafford's mutual predisposition. If you
really want to throw people together, the thing to do—
thank God for Ireland !—is to keep them apart. By the
fourth day of this emotional incubation, Marjorie was
thinking of Trafford to the exclusion of all her reading ;
and Trafford was lying awake at nights—oh, for half an
hour and more—thinking of bold, decisive ways of getting at
Marjorie, and bold, decisive things to say to her when he did.

(But why she should be engaged to Magnet continued,
nevertheless, to puzzle him extremely. It was a puzzle
to which no complete solution was ever to be forthcoming. . . .)

§ 11

At last that opportunity came. Marjorie had come with
her mother into the village, and while Mrs. Pope made some
purchases at the general shop she walked on to speak to
Mrs. Blythe the washerwoman. Trafford suddenly emerged
from the Red Lion with a soda siphon under each arm.
She came forward smiling.

" I say," he said forthwith, " I want to talk with you—
badly."

" And I," she said unhesitatingly, " with you."

" How can we ? "

" There's always people about. It's absurd."

" We'll have to meet."

" Yes."

" I have to go away to-morrow. I ought to have gone two days ago. Where *can* we meet ? "

She had it all prepared.

" Listen," she said. " There is a path runs from our shrubbery through a little wood to a stile on the main road." He nodded. " Either I will be there at three or about half-past five or—there's one more chance. While father and Mr. Magnet are smoking at nine. . . . I might get away."

" Couldn't I write ? "

" No. Impossible."

" I've no end of things to say. . . ."

Mrs. Pope appeared outside her shop, and Trafford gesticulated a greeting with the siphons. " All right," he said to Marjorie. " I'm shopping," he cried as Mrs. Pope approached.

§ 12

All through the day Marjorie desired to go to Trafford and could not do so. It was some minutes past nine when at last with a swift rustle of skirts that sounded louder than all the world to her, she crossed the dimly-lit hall between dining-room and drawing-room and came into the dreamland of moonlight upon the lawn. She had told her mother she was going upstairs ; at any moment she might be missed, but she would have fled now to Trafford if an army pursued her. Her heart seemed beating in her throat, and every fibre of her being was aquiver. She flitted past the dining-room window like a ghost, she did not dare to glance aside at the smokers within, and round the lawn to the shrubbery, and so under a blackness of trees to the gate where he stood waiting. And there he was, dim and mysterious and wonderful, holding the gate open for her, and she was breathless and speechless and near sobbing. She stood before him for a moment, her face moonlit and laced with the shadows of little twigs, and then his arms came out to her.

" My darling," he said, " oh, my darling ! "

They had no doubt of one another or of anything in the world. They clung together ; their lips came together fresh and untainted as those first lovers' in the garden.

" I will die for you," he said ; " I will give all the world for you. . . ."

They had thought all through the day of a hundred statements and explanations they would make when this moment came, and never a word of it all was uttered. All their anticipations of a highly-strung eventful conversation vanished, phrases of the most striking sort went like phantom leaves before a gale. He held her and she clung to him between laughing and sobbing, and both were swiftly and conclusively assured their lives must never separate again.

§ 13

Marjorie never knew whether it was a moment or an age before her father came upon them. He had decided to take a turn in the garden when Magnet could no longer restrain himself from joining the ladies, and he chanced to be stick in hand because that was his habit after twilight. So it was he found them. She heard his voice falling through love and moonlight like something that comes out of an immense distance.

" Good God ! " he cried, " what next ! "

But he still hadn't realised the worst.

" Daffy," he said, " what in the name of goodness——? "

Marjorie put her hands before her face too late.

" Good Lord ! " he cried, with a rising inflection, " it's Madge ! "

Trafford found the situation difficult. " I should explain——"

But Mr. Pope was giving himself up to a towering rage. " You damned scoundrel ! " he said. " What the devil are you doing ? " He seized Marjorie by the arm and drew her towards him. " My poor misguided girl ! " he said, and suddenly she was tensely alive, a little cry of horror in her throat, for her father, at a loss for words and full of heroic rage, had suddenly swung his stick with passionate force, and struck at Trafford's face. She heard the thud, saw Trafford wince and stiffen. For a perfectly horrible moment it seemed to her these men, their faces queerly distorted by the shadows of the branches in the slanting moonlight, might fight. Then she heard Trafford's voice, sounding cool and hard, and she knew that he would do nothing of the kind. In that instant if there had remained anything to win in Marjorie it was altogether won. " I asked your daughter to meet me here," he said.

" Be off with you, sir ! " cried Mr. Pope. " Don't tempt me further, sir," and swung his stick again. But now the

force had gone out of him. Trafford stood with a hand
out ready for him, and watched his face.

" I asked your daughter to meet me here, and she
came. I am prepared to give you any explanation——"

" If you come near this place again——"

For some moments Marjorie's heart had been held still,
now it was beating violently. She felt this scene must end.
" Mr. Trafford," she said, " will you go ? Go now. Nothing
shall keep us apart ! "

Mr. Pope turned on her. " Silence, girl ! " he said.

" I shall come to you to-morrow," said Trafford.

" Yes," said Marjorie, " to-morrow."

" Marjorie ! " said Mr. Pope, " *will* you go indoors ? "

" I have done nothing——"

" Be off, sir."

" I have done nothing——"

" Will you be off, sir ? And you, Marjorie—will you go
indoors ? "

He came round upon her, and after one still moment of
regard for Trafford—and she looked very beautiful in the
moonlight with her hair a little disordered and her face alight
—she turned to precede her father through the shrubbery.

Mr. Pope hesitated whether he should remain with Trafford.
A perfectly motionless man is very disconcerting.

" Be off, sir," he said over his shoulder, lowered through
a threatening second, and followed her.

But Trafford remained stiffly with a tingling temple
down which a little thread of blood was running, until
their retreating footsteps had died down into that confused
stirring of little sounds which makes the stillness of an
English wood at night.

Then he roused himself with a profound sigh, and put a
hand to his cut and bruised cheek.

" *Well !* " he said.

CHAPTER THE FOURTH

CRISIS

§ 1

CRISIS prevailed in Buryhamstreet that night. On half a
dozen sleepless pillows souls communed with the darkness,
and two at least of those pillows were wet with tears.

Not one of those wakeful heads was perfectly clear

about the origins and bearings of the trouble ; not even
Mr. Pope felt absolutely sure of himself. It had come as
things come to people nowadays, because they will not
think things out, much less talk things out, and are therefore in a hopeless tangle of values that tightens sooner or
later to a knot. . . .

What an uncharted perplexity, for example, was the
mind of that excellent woman Mrs. Pope !

Poor lady ! she hadn't a stable thing in her head. It
is remarkable that some queer streak in her composition
sympathised with Marjorie's passion for Trafford. But
she thought it such a pity ! She fought that sympathy
down as if it were a wicked thing. And she fought too
against other ideas that rose out of the deeps and did not
so much come into her mind as cluster at the threshold,
the idea that Marjorie was in effect grown up, a dozen queer
criticisms of Magnet, and a dozen subtle doubts whether
after all Marjorie was going to be happy with him as she
assured herself the girl would be. (So far as any one knew,
Trafford might be an excellent match !) And behind these
would-be invaders of her guarded mind prowled even
worse ones, doubts, horrible disloyal doubts, about the
wisdom and kindness of Mr. Pope.

Quite early in life Mrs. Pope had realised that it is
necessary to be very careful with one's thoughts. They
lead to trouble. She had clipped the wings of her own
mind therefore so successfully that all her conclusions had
become evasions, all her decisions compromises. Her
profoundest working conviction was a belief that nothing
in the world was of value but " tact," and that the art of
living was to " tide things over." But here it seemed
almost beyond her strength to achieve any sort of tiding
over. . . .

(Why *couldn't* Mr. Pope lie quiet ?)

Whatever she said or did had to be fitted to the exigencies
of Mr. Pope.

Availing himself of the privileges of matrimony, her
husband, so soon as Mr. Magnet had gone and they were
upstairs together, had explained the situation with vivid
simplicity, and had gone on at considerable length and with
great vivacity to enlarge upon his daughter's behaviour.
He ascribed this moral disaster—he presented it as a moral
disaster of absolutely calamitous dimensions—entirely to
Mrs. Pope's faults and negligences. Warming with his
theme he had employed a number of homely expressions

rarely heard by decent women except in these sacred intimacies, to express the deep indignation of a strong man moved to unbridled speech by the wickedness of those near and dear to him. Still warming, he raised his voice and at last shouted out his more forcible meanings, until she feared the servants and children might hear, waved a clenched fist at imaginary Traffords and scoundrels generally, and at last, giving way to his outraged virtue, smote and kicked blameless articles of furniture in a manner deeply impressive to the feminine intelligence.

Finally he sat down in the little arm-chair between her and the cupboard where she was accustomed to hang up her clothes, stuck out his legs very stiffly across the room, and despaired of his family in an obtrusive and impregnable silence for an enormous time.

All of which awakened a deep sense of guilt and unworthiness in Mrs. Pope's mind, and prevented her going to bed, but did not help her in the slightest degree to grasp the difficulties of the situation. . . .

She would have lain awake anyhow, but she was greatly helped in this by Mr. Pope's restlessness. He was now turning over from left to right or from right to left at intervals of from four to seven minutes, and such remarks as " Damned scoundrel ! Get out of this ! " or " *My* daughter and degrade yourself in this way ! " or " Never let me see your face again ! " " Plight your troth to one man, and fling yourself shamelessly—I repeat it, Marjorie, shamelessly—into the arms of another ! " kept Mrs. Pope closely in touch with the general trend of his thoughts.

She tried to get together her plans and perceptions rather as though she swept up dead leaves on a gusty day. She knew that the management of the whole situation rested finally on her, and that whatever she did or did not do, or whatever arose to thwart her arrangements, its entire tale of responsibility would ultimately fall upon her shoulders. She wondered what was to be done with Marjorie, with Mr. Magnet ? Need he know ? Could that situation be saved ? Everything at present was raw in her mind. Except for her husband's informal communications she did not even know what had appeared, what Daffy had seen, what Magnet thought of Marjorie's failure to bid him good-night. For example, had Mr. Magnet noticed Mr. Pope's profound disturbance ? She had to be ready to put a face on things before morning, and it seemed impossible she could do so. In times of crisis, as every

woman knows, it is always necessary to misrepresent everything to everybody, but how she was to dovetail her
misrepresentations, get the best effect from them, extract
a working system of rights and wrongs from them, she could
not imagine. . . .

(Oh ! she did so wish Mr. Pope would lie quiet.)

But he had no doubts of what became *him*. He had to
maintain a splendid and irrational rage—at any cost—to
anybody.

§ 2

A few yards away, a wakeful Marjorie confronted a
joyless universe. She had a baffling realisation that her
life was in a hopeless mess, that she really had behaved
disgracefully, and that she couldn't for a moment understand how it had happened. She had intended to make
quite sure of Trafford—and then put things straight.

Only her father had spoilt everything.

She regarded her father that night with a want of
natural affection terrible to record. Why had he come
just when he had, just as he had ? Why had he been so
violent, so impossible ?

Of course, she had had no business to be there. . . .

She examined her character with a new unprecedented
detachment. Wasn't she, after all, rather a mean human
being ? It had never occurred to her before to ask such
a question. Now she asked it with only too clear a sense
of the answer. She tried to trace how these multiplying
threads of meanness had first come into the fabric of a life
she had supposed herself to be weaving in extremely
bright, honourable, and adventurous colours. She ought,
of course, never to have accepted Magnet. . . .

She faced the disagreeable word ; was she a liar ?

At any rate, she told lies.

And she'd behaved with extraordinary meanness to
Daphne. She realised that now. She had known, as
precisely as if she had been told, how Daphne felt about
Trafford, and she'd never given her an inkling of her own
relations. She hadn't for a moment thought of Daphne.
No wonder Daphne was sombre and bitter. Whatever she
knew, she knew enough. She had heard Trafford's name
in urgent whispers on the landing. " I suppose you
couldn't leave him alone," Daffy had said, after a long,
hostile silence. That was all. Just a sentence without
prelude or answer flung across the bedroom, revealing a

perfect understanding—deeps of angry disillusionment. Marjorie had stared and gasped, and made no answer.

Would she ever see him again ? After this horror of rowdy intervention ? She didn't deserve to ; she didn't deserve anything. . . . Oh, the tangle of it all ! The tangle of it all ! And those bills at Oxbridge ! She was just dragging Trafford down into her own miserable morass of a life.

Her thoughts would take a new turn. " I love him," she whispered soundlessly. " I would die for him. I would like to die under his feet—and him not know it."

Her mind hung on that for a long time. " Not know it until afterwards," she corrected.

She liked to be exact, even in despair. . . .

And then in her memory he was struck again, and stood stiff and still. She wanted to kneel to him, imagined herself kneeling. . . .

And so on, quite inconclusively, round and round through the interminable night hours.

§ 3

The young man in the village was, if possible, more perplexed, round eyed and generally inconclusive than any one else in this series of nocturnal disturbances. He spent long intervals sitting on his window-sill regarding a world that was scented with nightstock, and seemed to be woven of moonshine and gossamer. Being an inexpert and infrequent soliloquist, his only audible comment on his difficulties was the repetition in varying intonations of his fervent, unalterable conviction that he was damned. But behind this simple verbal mask was a great fury of mental activity.

He had something of Marjorie's amazement at the position of affairs.

He had never properly realised that it was possible for any one to regard Marjorie as a daughter, to order her about and resent the research for her society as criminal. It was a new light in his world. Some day he was to learn the meaning of fatherhood, but in these night watches he regarded it as a hideous survival of mediæval darknesses.

" Of course," he said, entirely ignoring the actual quality of their conversation, " she had to explain about the Magnet affair. Can't one—converse ? "

He reflected through great intervals.

" I *will* see her ! Why on earth shouldn't I see her ? "

" I suppose they can't lock her up ! "

For a time he contemplated a writ of habeas corpus. He saw reason to regret the gaps in his legal knowledge.

" Can any one get a writ of habeas corpus for any one —it doesn't matter whom "—more especially if you are a young man of six-and-twenty, anxious to exchange a few richly charged words with a girl of twenty who is engaged to some one else ?

The night had no answer.

It was nearly dawn when he came to the entirely unadvisable conclusion—I use his own words—to go and have it out with the old ruffian. He would sit down and ask him what he meant by it all—and reason with him. If he started flourishing that stick again, it would have to be taken away.

And having composed a peroration upon the institution of the family of a character which he fondly supposed to be extraordinarily tolerant, reasonable, and convincing, but which was indeed calculated to madden Mr. Pope to frenzy, Mr. Trafford went very peacefully to sleep.

§ 4

Came dawn, with a noise of birds and afterwards a little sleep, and then day, and heavy eyes opened again, and the sound of frying and the smell of coffee recalled our actors to the stage. Mrs. Pope was past her worst despair ; always the morning brings courage and a clearer grasp of things, and she could face the world with plans shaped subconsciously during those last healing moments of slumber.

Breakfast was difficult, but not impossible. Mr. Pope loomed like a thundercloud, but Marjorie pleaded a headache very wisely, and was taken a sympathetic cup of tea. The pseudo-twins scented trouble, but Theodore was heedless and over-full of an entertaining noise made by a moorhen as it dived in the ornamental water that morning. You could make it practically *sotto voce*, and it amused Syd. He seemed to think *The Times* opaque to such small sounds, and learnt better only to be dismissed underfed and ignominiously from the table to meditate upon the imperfections of his soul in the schoolroom. There for a time he was silent, and then presently became audible again, playing with a ball and, presumably, Marjorie's tennis racket.

Directly she could disentangle herself from breakfast, Mrs. Pope, with all her plans acute, went up to the girls' room. She found her daughter dressing in a leisurely and meditative manner. She shut the door almost confidentially. "Marjorie," she said, "I want you to tell me all about this."

"I thought I heard father telling you," said Marjorie.

"He was too indignant," said Mrs. Pope, "to explain clearly. You see, Marjorie"—she paused before her effort —"he knows things—about this Professor Trafford."

"What things?" asked Marjorie, turning sharply.

"I don't know, my dear—and I can't imagine."

She looked out of the window, aware of Marjorie's entirely distrustful scrutiny.

"I don't believe it," said Marjorie.

"Don't believe what, dear?"

"Whatever he says."

"I wish I didn't," said Mrs. Pope, and turned. "Oh, Madge," she cried, "you cannot imagine how all this distresses me! I cannot—I cannot conceive how you came to be in such a position! Surely honour——! Think of Mr. Magnet, how good and patient he has been! You don't know that man. You don't know all he is, and all that it means to a girl. He is good and honourable and —pure. He is kindness itself. It seemed to me that you were to be so happy—rich, honoured."

She was overcome by a rush of emotion ; she turned to the bed and sat down.

"*There!*" she said desolately. "It's all ruined, shattered, gone."

Marjorie tried not to feel that her mother was right.

"If father hadn't interfered," she said weakly.

"Oh, don't, my dear, speak so coldly of your father! You don't know what he has to put up with. You don't know his troubles and anxieties—all this wretched business." She paused, and her face became portentous. "Marjorie, do you know if these railways go on as they are going he may have to *eat into his capital* this year. Just think of that, and the worry he has! And this last shame and anxiety!"

Her voice broke again. Marjorie listened with an expression that was almost sullen.

"But what is it," she asked, "that father knows about Mr. Trafford?"

"I don't know, dear. I don't know. But it's something that matters—that makes it all different."

" Well, may I speak to Mr. Trafford before he leaves Buryhamstreet ? "

" My dear ! Never see him, dear—never think of him again ! Your father would not dream—— Some day, Marjorie, you will rejoice—you will want to thank your father on your bended knees that he saved you from the clutches of this man. . . ."

" I won't believe anything about Mr. Trafford," she said slowly, " until I know——"

She left the sentence incomplete.

She made her declaration abruptly. " I love Mr. Trafford," she said, with a catch in her voice, " and I don't love Mr. Magnet."

Mrs. Pope received this like one who is suddenly stabbed. She sat still as if overwhelmed, one hand pressed to her side and her eyes closed. Then she said, as if she gasped involuntarily,—

" It's too dreadful ! Marjorie," she said, " I want to ask you to do something. After all, a mother has *some* claim. Will you wait just a little ? Will you promise me to do nothing—nothing, I mean, to commit you—until your father has been able to make inquiries ? Don't *see* him for a little while. Very soon you'll be one-and-twenty, and then perhaps things may be different. If he cares for you, and you for him, a little separation won't matter . . . until your father has inquired . . ."

" Mother," said Marjorie, " I can't——"

Mrs. Pope drew in the air sharply between her teeth, as if in agony.

" But, mother—— Mother, I *must* let Mr. Trafford know that I'm not to see him. I *can't* suddenly cease . . . If I could see him once——"

" Don't ! " said Mrs. Pope in a hollow voice.

Marjorie began weeping. " He'd not understand," she said. " If I might just speak to him ! "

" Not alone, Marjorie."

Marjorie stood still. " Well—before you."

Mrs. Pope conceded the point. " And then, Marjorie——" she said.

" I'd keep my word, mother," said Marjorie, and began to sob in a manner she felt to be absurdly childish —" until—until I am one-and-twenty. I'd promise that."

Mrs. Pope did a brief calculation. " Marjorie," she said, " it's only your happiness I think of."

" I know," said Marjorie, and added in low voice, " and father."

" My dear, you don't understand your father. . . . I believe—I do firmly believe—if anything happened to any of you girls—anything bad—he would kill himself. . . . And I know he means that you aren't to go about so much as you used to do, unless we have the most definite promises. Of course, your father's ideas aren't always my ideas, Marjorie ; but it's your duty—— You know how hasty he is and—quick. Just as you know how good and generous and kind he is "—she caught Marjorie's eye, and added a little lamely—" at bottom." . . . She thought. " I think I could get him to let you say just one word with Mr. Trafford. It would be very difficult, but——"

She paused for a few seconds, and seemed to be thinking deeply.

" Marjorie," she said. " Mr. Magnet must never know anything of this."

" But, mother—— ! "

" Nothing ! "

" I can't go on with my engagement ! "

Mrs. Pope shook her head inscrutably.

" But how *can* I, mother ? "

" You need not tell him *why*, Marjorie."

" But——"

" Just think how it would humiliate and distress him ! You *can't* Marjorie. You must find some excuse—oh, any excuse ! But not the truth—not the truth, Marjorie. It would be too dreadful."

Marjorie thought. " Look here, mother, I *may* see Mr. Trafford again ? I *may* really speak to him ? "

" Haven't I promised ? "

" Then, I'll do as you say," said Marjorie.

§ 5

Mrs. Pope found her husband seated at the desk in the ultra-Protestant study, meditating gloomily.

" I've been talking to her," she said. " She's in a state of terrible distress."

" She ought to be," said Mr. Pope.

" Philip, you don't understand Marjorie."

" I don't."

" You think she was kissing that man."

" Well, she was."

" You can think *that* of her ! "

Mr. Pope turned his chair to her. " But I *saw* ! "

Mrs. Pope shook her head. " She wasn't ; she was struggling to get away from him. She told me so herself. I've been into it with her. You don't understand, Philip. A man like that has a sort of fascination for a girl. He dazzles her. It's the way with girls. But you're quite mistaken. . . . Quite. It's a sort of hypnotism. She'll grow out of it. Of course, she *loves* Mr. Magnet. She does indeed. I've not a doubt of it. But——"

" You're *sure* she wasn't kissing him ? "

" Positive."

" Then why didn't she say so ? "

" A girl's so complex. You didn't give her a chance. She's fearfully ashamed of herself—fearfully ; but it's just because she *is* ashamed that she won't admit it."

" I'll make her admit it."

" You ought to have had all boys," said Mrs. Pope. " Oh ! she'll admit it some day—readily enough. But I believe a girl of her spirit would rather *die* than begin explaining. You can't expect it of her. Really you can't."

He grunted and shook his head slowly from side to side. She sat down in the arm-chair beside the desk.

" I want to know just exactly what we are to do about the girl, Philip. I can't bear to think of her—up there."

" How ? " he asked. " Up there ? "

" Yes," she answered, with that skilful inconsecutiveness of hers, and let a brief silence touch his imagination. " Do you think that man means to come here again ? " she asked.

" Chuck him out if he does," asid Mr. Pope grimly.

She pressed her lips together firmly. She seemed to be weighing things painfully. " I wouldn't," she said at last.

" What do you mean ? " asked Mr. Pope.

" I do not want you to make an open quarrel with Mr. Trafford."

" *Not* quarrel ! "

" Not an open one," said Mrs. Pope. " Of course I know how nice it would be if you *could* use a horsewhip, dear. There's such a lot of things—if we could only just slash. But—it won't help. Get him to go away. She's consented never to see him again—practically. She's ready to tell him so herself. Part them against their will —oh ! and the thing may go on for no end of time. But treat it as it ought to be treated—— She'll be very tragic for a week or so, and then she'll forget him like a dream.

He *is* a dream—a girl's dream. . . . If only we leave it alone, she'll leave it alone."

§ 6

Things were getting straight, Mrs. Pope felt. She had now merely to add a few touches to the tranquillisation of Daphne, and the misdirection of the twins' curiosity. These touches accomplished, it seemed that everything was done. After a brief reflection, she dismissed the idea of putting things to Theodore. She ran over the possibilities of the servants eavesdropping, and found them negligible. Yes, everything was done—everything. And yet. . . .

The queer string in her nature between religiosity and superstition began to vibrate. She hesitated. Then she slipped upstairs, fastened the door, fell on her knees beside the bed and put the whole thing as acceptably as possible to Heaven in a silent, simple, but lucid explanatory prayer. . . .

She came out of her chamber brighter and braver than she had been for eighteen long hours. She could now, she felt, await the developments that threatened with the serenity of one who is prepared at every point. She went almost happily to the kitchen, only about forty-five minutes behind her usual time, to order the day's meals and see with her own eyes that economies prevailed. And it seemed to her, on the whole, consoling, and at any rate a distraction, when the cook informed her that after all she *had* meant to give notice on the day of Aunt Plessington's visit.

§ 7

The unsuspecting Magnet, fatigued but happy—for three hours of solid humorous writing (omitting every unpleasant suggestion and mingling in the most acceptable and saleable proportions smiles and tears) had added its quota to the intellectual heritage of England—made a simple light lunch cooked in homely village-inn fashion, lit a well-merited cigar, and turned his steps towards the vicarage. He was preceded at some distance along the avenuesque drive by the back of Mr. Trafford, which he made no attempt to overtake.

Mr. Trafford was admitted and disappeared, and a minute afterwards Magnet reached the door.

Mrs. Pope appeared radiant—about the weather. A rather tiresome man had just called upon Mr. Pope about business matters, she said, and he might be detained five or ten minutes. Marjorie and Daffy were upstairs—resting. They had been disturbed by bats in the night.

" Isn't it charmingly rural ? " said Mrs. Pope. " *Bats !* " She talked about bats and the fear she had of their getting in her hair, and as she talked she led the way brightly but firmly as far as possible out of earshot of the windows of the ultra-Protestant study in which Mr. Pope was now (she did so hope temperately) interviewing Mr. Trafford.

§ 8

Directly Mr. Trafford had reached the front door it had opened for him, and closed behind him at once. He had found himself with Mrs. Pope. " You wish to see my husband ? " she had said, and had led him to the study forthwith. She had returned at once to intercept Mr. Magnet. . . .

Trafford found Mr. Pope seated sternly at the centre of the writing-desk, regarding him with a threatening brow.

" Well, sir," said Mr. Pope, breaking the silence, " you have come to offer some explanation——"

While awaiting this encounter Mr. Pope had not been insensitive to the tactical and scenic possibilities of the occasion. In fact, he had spent the latter half of the morning in intermittent preparations, arranging desk, books, hassocks in advantageous positions, and not even neglecting such small details as the stamp tray, the articles of interest from Jerusalem, and the rock-crystal cenotaph, which he had exhibited in such a manner as was most calculated to damp, chill and subjugate an antagonist in the exposed area towards the window. He had also arranged the chairs in a highly favourable pattern.

Mr. Trafford was greatly taken aback by Mr. Pope's juridical manner and by this form of address, and he was further put out by Mr. Pope saying with a regal gesture to the best illuminated and most isolated chair : " Be seated, sir."

Mr. Trafford's exordium vanished from his mind, he was at a loss for words until spurred to speech by Mr. Pope's almost truculent : " Well ? "

" I am in love, sir, with your daughter."

" I am not aware of it," said Mr. Pope, and lifted and

dropped the paper-weight. "My daughter, sir, is engaged to marry Mr. Magnet. If you had approached me in a proper fashion before presuming to attempt—to attempt"—his voice thickened with indignation—"liberties with her, you would have been duly informed of her position —and every one would have been saved "—he lifted the paper-weight—" everything that has happened." (Bump.)

Mr. Trafford had to adjust himself to the unexpected elements in this encounter. "Oh ! " he said.

"Yes," said Mr. Pope, and there was a distinct interval.

"Is your daughter in love with Mr. Magnet ? " asked Mr. Trafford in an almost colloquial tone.

Mr. Pope smiled gravely. "I presume so, sir."

"She never gave me that impression, anyhow," said the young man.

"It was neither her duty to give nor yours to receive that impression," said Mr. Pope.

Again Mr. Trafford was at a loss.

"Have you come here, sir, merely to bandy words ? " asked Mr. Pope, drumming with ten fingers on the table.

Mr. Trafford thrust his hands into his pockets and assumed a fictitious pose of ease. He had never found any one in his life before quite so provocative of colloquialism as Mr. Pope.

"Look here, sir, this is all very well," he began, "but why can't I fall in love with your daughter ? I'm a Doctor of Science and all that sort of thing. I've a perfectly decent outlook. My father was rather a swell in his science. I'm an entirely decent and respectable person."

"I beg to differ," said Mr. Pope.

"But I am."

"Again," said Mr. Pope, with great patience, and a slight forward bowing of the head, "I beg to differ."

"Well—differ. But all the same——"

He paused and began again, and for a time they argued to no purpose. They generalised about the position of an engaged girl and the rights and privileges of a father. Then Mr. Pope, " to cut all this short," told him frankly he wasn't wanted, his daughter did not want him, nobody wanted him ; he was an invader, he had to be got rid of —" if possible by peaceful means." Trafford disputed these propositions, and asked to see Marjorie. Mr. Pope had been leading up to this, and at once closed with that request.

"She is as anxious as any one to end this intolerable

siege," he said. He went to the door and called for Marjorie, who appeared with conspicuous promptitude. She was in a dress of green linen that made her seem very cool as well as very dignified to Trafford ; she was tense with restrained excitement, and either—for these things shade into each other—entirely without a disposition to act her part or acting with consummate ability. Trafford rose at the sight of her, and remained standing. Mr. Pope closed the door and walked back to the desk. " Mr. Trafford has to be told," he said, " that you don't want him in Buryhamstreet." He arrested Marjorie's forward movement towards Trafford by a gesture of the hand, seated himself, and resumed his drumming on the table. " Well ? " he said.

" I don't think you ought to stay in Buryhamstreet, Mr. Trafford," said Marjorie.

" You don't want me to ? "

" It will only cause trouble—and scenes."

" You want me to go ? "

" Away from here."

" You really mean that ? "

Marjorie did not answer for a little time ; she seemed to be weighing the exact force of all she was going to say.

" Mr. Trafford," she answered, " everything I've ever said to you—everything—I've *meant*, more than I've ever meant anything. Everything ! "

A little flush of colour came into Trafford's cheeks. He regarded Marjorie with a brightening eye.

" Oh, well," he said, " I don't understand. But I'm entirely in your hands, of course."

Marjorie's pose and expression altered. For an instant she was a miracle of instinctive expression, she shone at him, she conveyed herself to him, she assured him. Her eyes met his, she stood warmly flushed and quite unconquered—visibly, magnificently *his*. She poured into him just that riotous pride and admiration that gives a man altogether to a woman. . . . Then it seemed as if a light passed, and she was just an everyday Marjorie standing there:

" I'll do anything you want to," said Trafford.

" Then I want you to go."

" Ah ! " said Mr. Pope.

" Yes," said Trafford, with his eyes on her self-possession.

" I've promised not to write or send to you, or think more than I can help of you, until I'm twenty-one—nearly two months from now."

" And then ? "

" I don't know. How can I ? "

" You hear, sir ? " from Mr. Pope, in the pause of mutual scrutiny that followed.

" One question," said Mr. Trafford.

" You've surely asked enough, sir," said Mr. Pope.

" Are you still engaged to Magnet ? "

" Sir ! "

" Please, father ! " said Marjorie, with unusual daring and in her mother's voice. " Mr. Trafford, after what I've told you—you must leave that to me."

" She *is* engaged to Mr. Magnet," said Mr. Pope. " Tell him outright, Marjorie. Make it clear."

" I think I understand," said Trafford, with his eyes on Marjorie.

" I've not seen Mr. Magnet since last night," said Marjorie. " And so—naturally—I'm still engaged to him."

" Precisely ! " said Mr. Pope, and turned with a face of harsh interrogation to his importunate caller. Mr. Trafford seemed disposed for further questions. " I don't think we need detain you, Madge," said Mr. Pope, over his shoulder.

The two young people stood facing one another for a moment, and I am afraid that they were both extremely happy and satisfied with each other. It was all right, they were quite sure—all right. Their lips were almost smiling. Then Marjorie made an entirely dignified exit. She closed the door very softly, and Mr. Pope turned to his visitor again with a bleak politeness. " I hope that satisfies you," he said.

" There is nothing more to be said at present, I admit," said Mr. Trafford.

" Nothing," said Mr. Pope.

Both gentlemen bowed. Mr. Pope rose ceremoniously, and Mr. Trafford walked doorward. He had a sense of latent absurdities in these tremendous attitudes. They passed through the hall—processionally. But just at the end some lower strain in Mr. Trafford's nature touched the fine dignity of the occasion with an inappropriate remark.

" Good-bye, sir," said Mr. Pope, holding the house-door wide.

" Good-bye, sir," said Mr. Trafford, and then added with a note of untimely intimacy in his voice, and an inexcusable levity upon his lips : " You know—there's

nobody—no man in the world—I'd sooner have for a
father-in-law than you."

Mr. Pope, caught unprepared on the spur of the moment,
bowed in a cold and distant manner, and then almost
immediately closed the door to save himself from
violence. . . .

From first to last neither gentleman had made the
slightest allusion to a considerable bruise upon Mr.
Trafford's left cheek, and a large abrasion above his ear.

§ 9

That afternoon Marjorie began her difficult task of
getting disengaged from Mr. Magnet. It was difficult
because she was pledged not to tell him of the one thing
that made this line of action not only explicable, but
necessary. Magnet, perplexed and disconcerted, and
secretly sustained by her mother's glancing side-lights on
the feminine character and the instability of " girlish
whims," remained at Buryhamstreet until the family
returned to Hartstone Square. The engagement was ended
—formally—but in such a manner that Magnet was left
a rather pathetic and invincibly assiduous besieger. He
lavished little presents upon both sisters, he devised little
treats for the entire family, he enriched Theodore beyond
the dreams of avarice, and he discussed his love and
admiration for Marjorie, and the perplexities and delicacies
of the situation, not only with Mrs. Pope but with Daphne.
At first he had thought very little of Daphne, but now he
was beginning to experience the subtle pleasures of a
confidential friendship. She understood, he felt ; it was
quite wonderful how she understood. He found Daffy
much richer in response than Marjorie, and far less disconcerting in reply. . . .

Mr. Pope, for all Marjorie's submission to his wishes,
developed a Grand Dudgeon of exceptionally fine proportions when he heard of the breach of the engagement.
He ceased to speak to his daughter or admit himself aware
of her existence, and the Grand Dudgeon's blighting shadow
threw a chill over the life of every one in the house. He
made it clear that the Grand Dudgeon would only be lifted
by Marjorie's re-engagement to Magnet, and that whatever
blight or inconvenience fell on the others was due entirely
to Marjorie's wicked obstinacy. Using Mrs. Pope as an
intermediary, he also conveyed to Marjorie his decision

to be no longer burthened with the charges of her education at Oxbridge, and he made it seem extremely doubtful whether he should remember her approaching twenty-first birthday.

Marjorie received the news of her severance from Oxbridge, Mrs. Pope thought, with a certain hardness.

"I thought he would do that," said Marjorie. "He's always wanted to do that," and said no more.

CHAPTER THE FIFTH

A TELEPHONE CALL

§ 1

TRAFFORD went back to Solomonson for a day or so, and then to London, to resume the experimental work of the research he had in hand. But he was so much in love with Marjorie that for some days it was a very dazed mind that fumbled with the apparatus—arranged it and rearranged it, and fell into day-dreams that gave the utmost concern to Durgan the bottle-washer.

"He's not going straight at things," said Durgan the bottle-washer to his wife. "He usually goes so straight at things it's a pleasure to watch it. He told me he was going down into Kent to think everything out." Mr. Durgan paused impressively, and spoke with a sigh of perplexity. "He hasn't . . ."

But later Durgan was able to report that Trafford had pulled himself together. The work was moving.

"I was worried for a bit," said Mr. Durgan. "But I *think* it's all right again. I *believe* it's all right again."

§ 2

Trafford was one of those rare scientific men who really ought to be engaged in scientific research.

He could never leave an accepted formula alone. His mind was like some insatiable corrosive, that ate into all the hidden inequalities and plastered weaknesses of accepted theories, and bit its way through every plausibility of appearance. He was extraordinarily fertile in exasperating alternative hypotheses. His invention of destructive test experiments was as happy as the respectful irony with which he brought them into contact with the generalisations they doomed. He was already, at six-and-twenty, hated, abused, obstructed, and respected. He was still outside the Royal Society, of course, and the editors of the scientific periodicals admired his papers greatly, and delayed publication ; but it was fairly certain that that pressure of foreign criticism and competition which prevents English scientific men of good family and social position from maintaining any such national standards as we are able to do in art, literature, and politics, would finally carry him in. And since he had a small professorship worth three hundred a year, which gave him the command of a sufficient research laboratory and the services of Mr. Durgan, a private income of nearly three hundred more, a devoted mother to keep house for him, and an invincible faith in Truth, he had every prospect of winning in his particular struggle to inflict more Truth, new lucidities, and fresh powers upon this fractious and unreasonable universe.

In the world of science now, even more than in the world of literature and political thought, the thing that is alive struggles, half suffocated, amidst a copious production of things born dead. The endowment of research, the organisation of scientific progress, the creation of salaried posts, and the assignment of honours, has attracted to this field just that type of man which is least gifted to penetrate and discover, and least able to admit its own defect or the quality of a superior. Such men are producing great, bulky masses of imitative research, futile inquiries, and monstrous entanglements of technicality about their subjects ; and it is to their instinctive antagonism to the idea of a " gift " in such things that we owe the preposterous conception of a training for research, the manufacture of mental blinkers that is to say, to avoid what is the very soul of brilliant inquiry—applicable discursiveness. The trained investigator is quite the absurdest figure in the farce of contemporary intellectual life ; he is like a bath-chair perpetually starting to cross the Himalayas by virtue of a licence to do so. For such enterprises one must have wings. Organisation and genius are antipathetic. The vivid and creative mind, by virtue of its qualities, is a spasmodic and adventurous mind ; it resents blinkers, and the mere implication that it can be driven in harness to the unexpected. It demands freedom. It resents regular attendance from ten to four and punctualities in general and all those paralysing minor tests of conduct that are vitally important to the imagination of the authoritative dull. Consequently, it is being eliminated from its legitimate field, and it is only here and there among the younger men that such a figure as Trafford gives any promise of a renewal of that enthusiasm, that intellectual enterprise, which was distinctive of the great age of scientific advance.

Trafford was the only son of his parents. His father had been a young surgeon, more attracted by knowledge than practice, who had been killed by a scratch of the scalpel in an investigation upon ulcerative processes, at the age of twenty-nine. Trafford at that time was three years old, so that he had not the least memory of his father ; but his mother, by a thousand almost unpremeditated touches, had built up a figure for him and a tradition that was shaping his life. She had loved her husband passionately, and when he died her love burnt up like a flame released, and made a god of the good she had known with him. She was then a very beautiful and active-minded woman of thirty, and she did her best to reconstruct her life ; but she could find nothing so living in the world as the clear courage, the essential simplicity, and tender memories of the man she had lost. And she was the more devoted to him that he had had little weaknesses of temper and bearing, and that an outrageous campaign had been waged against him that did not cease with his death. He had, in some medical periodical, published drawings of a dead dog clamped to display a deformity, and these had been seized upon by a group of anti-vivisection fanatics as the representation of a vivisection. A libel action had been pending when he died ; but there is no protection of the dead from libel. That monstrous lie met her on pamphlet cover, on hoardings, in sensational appeals ; it seemed immortal, and she would have suffered the pains of a dozen suttees if she could have done so, to show the world how the power and tenderness of this alleged tormentor of helpless beasts had gripped one woman's heart. It counted enormously in her decision to remain a widow and concentrate her life upon her son.

She watched his growth with a care and passionate subtlety that even at six-and-twenty he was still far from suspecting. She dreaded his becoming a mother's pet ; she sent him away to school and fretted through long terms alone, that he might be made into a man. She interested herself in literary work and social affairs lest she should press upon him unduly. She listened for the crude expression of growing thought in him with an intensity that was almost anguish. She was too intelligent to dream of forming his mind, he browsed on every doctrine to find his own, but she did desire most passionately, she prayed, she prayed in the darkness of sleepless nights, that the views, the breadths, the spacious emotions which had ennobled her husband in her eyes should rise again in him.

There were years of doubt and waiting. He was a good boy and a bad boy, now brilliant, now touching, now disappointing, now gloriously reassuring, and now heartrending as only the children of our blood can be. He had errors and bad moments, lapses into sheer naughtiness, phases of indolence, attacks of contagious vulgarity. But more and more surely she saw him for his father's son ; she traced the same great curiosities, the same keen dauntless questioning ; whatever incidents might disturb and perplex her, his intellectual growth went on strong and clear and increasing like some sacred flame that is carried in procession, halting perhaps and swaying a little but keeping on, over the heads of a tumultuous crowd.

He went from his school to the Royal College of Science, thence to successes at Cambridge, and thence to Berlin. He travelled a little in Asia Minor and Persia, had a journey to America, and then came back to her and London, sunburnt, moustached, manly, and a little strange. When he had been a boy she had thought his very soul pellucid, it had clouded opaquely against her scrutiny as he passed into adolescence. Then through the period of visits and departures, travel together, separations, he grew into something detached and admirable, a man curiously reminiscent of his father, unexpectedly different. She ceased to feel what he was feeling in his mind, had to watch him, infer, guess, speculate about him. She desired for him and dreaded for him with an undying tenderness, but she no longer had any assurance that she could interfere to help him. He had his father's trick of falling into thought. Her brown eyes would watch him across the flowers and delicate glass and silver of her dinner table when he dined at home with her. Sometimes he seemed to forget she existed, sometimes he delighted in her, talked to amuse her, petted her ; sometimes, and then it was she was happiest, he talked of plays and books with her, discussed general questions, spoke even of that broadly conceived scheme of work which engaged so much of his imagination. She knew that it was distinguished and powerful work. Old friends of her husband spoke of it to her, praised its inspired directness, its beautiful simplicity. Since the days of Wollaston, they say, no one had been so witty an experimenter, no one had got more out of mere scraps of apparatus or contrived more ingenious simplifications.

When he had accepted the minor professorship which gave him a footing in the world of responsible scientific men, she had taken a house in a quiet street in Chelsea which necessitated a daily walk to his laboratory. It was a little old Georgian house with worn and graceful rooms, a dignified front door and a fine gateway of Sussex ironwork much painted and eaten away. She arranged it with great care ; she had kept most of her furniture, and his study had his father's bureau, and the selfsame agate paper-weight that had pressed the unfinished paper he left when he died. She was a woman of persistent friendships, and there came to her, old connections of those early times trailing fresher and younger people in their wake, sons, daughters, nephews, disciples ; her son brought home all sorts of interesting men, and it was remarkable to her that, amidst the talk and discussion at her table, she discovered aspects of her son and often quite intimate aspects she would never have seen with him alone.

She would not let herself believe that this Indian summer of her life could last for ever. He was no passionless devotee of research, for all his silence and restraints. She had seen him kindle with anger at obstacles and absurdities, and quicken in the presence of beauty. She knew how readily and richly he responded to beauty. Things happened to have run smoothly with him so far, that was all. " Of course," she said, " he must fall in love. It cannot be long before he falls in love."

Once or twice that had seemed to happen, and then it had come to nothing. . . .

She knew that sooner or later this completion of his possibilities must come, that the present steadfastness of purpose was a phase in which forces gathered, that love must sweep into his life as a deep and passionate disturbance. She wondered where it would take him, whether it would leave him enriched or devastated. She saw at times how young he was ; she had, as I suppose most older people have about their juniors, the profoundest doubt whether he was wise enough yet to be trusted with a thing

so good as himself. He had flashes of high-spirited indis-
cretion, and at times a wildfire of humour flared in his
talk. So far that had done no worse for him that make an
enemy or so in scientific circles. But she had no idea of
the limits of his excitability. She would watch him and
fear for him—she knew the wreckage love can make—and
also she desired that he should lose nothing that life and
his nature could give him.

§ 3

In the two months of separation that ensued before
Marjorie was one-and-twenty, Trafford's mind went
through some remarkable phases. At first the excitement
of his passion for Marjorie obscured everything else, then
with his return to London and his laboratory the immense
inertia of habit and slowly developed purposes, the complex
yet convergent system of ideas and problems to which so
much of his life had been given, began to reassert itself.
His love was vivid and intense, a light in his imagination,
a fever in his blood ; but it was a new thing ; it had not
crept into the flesh and bones of his being, it was away there
in Surrey ; the streets of London, his home, the white-
walled chamber with its skylight and high windows and
charts of constants, in which his apparatus was arranged,
had no suggestion of her. She was outside—an adventure—a perplexing incommensurable with all these
things.

He had left Buryhamstreet with Marjorie riotously in
possession of his mind. He could think of nothing but
Marjorie in the train, and how she had shone at him in the
study, and how her voice had sounded when she spoke,
and how she stood and moved, and the shape and sensation
of her hands, and how it had felt to hold her for those
brief moments in the wood and press lips and body to his,
and how her face had gleamed in the laced shadows of the
moonlight, soft and wonderful.

In fact, he thought of Marjorie.

He thought she was splendid, courageous, wise by
instinct. He had no doubt of her or that she was to be
his—when the weeks of waiting had passed by. She was
his, and he was Marjorie's ; that had been settled from the
beginning of the world. It didn't occur to him that anything had happened to alter his life or any of his arrangements in any way, except that they were altogether altered

—as the world is altered without displacement when the sun pours up in the east. He was glorified—and everything was glorified.

He wondered how they would meet again, and dreamt a thousand impossible and stirring dreams, but he dreamt them as dreams.

At first, to Durgan's infinite distress, he thought of her all day, and then, as the old familiar interests grappled him again, he thought of her in the morning and the evening and as he walked between his home and the laboratory and at all sorts of incidental times—and even when the close-locked riddles of his research held the foreground and focus of his thought, he still seemed to be thinking of her as a radiant background to ions and molecules and atoms and interwoven systems of eddies and quivering oscillations deep down in the very heart of matter.

And always he thought of her as something of the summer. The rich decays of autumn came, the Chelsea roads were littered with variegated leaves that were presently wet and dirty and slippery, the twilight crept down into the day towards five o'clock and four, but in his memory of her the leaves were green, the evenings were long, the warm quiet of rural Surrey in high August filled the air. So that it was with a kind of amazement he found her in London and in November close at hand. He was called to the college telephone one day from a conversation with a proposed research student. It was a middle-aged woman bachelor anxious for the D.Sc., who wished to occupy the farther bunch in the laboratory ; but she had no mental fire, and his mind was busy with excuses and discouragements.

He had no thought of Marjorie when she answered, and for an instant he did not recognise her voice.

" Yes, I'm Mr. Trafford." . . .

" Who is it ? " he reiterated, with a note of irascibility. *Who ?* "

The little voice laughed. "Why! I'm Marjorie!" it said.

Then she was back in his life like a lantern suddenly become visible in a wood at midnight.

It was like meeting her as a china figure, neat and perfect and two inches high. It was her voice, very clear and very bright, and quite characteristic, as though he was hearing it through the wrong end of a telescope. It was her voice, clear as a bell ; confident without a shadow.

" It's *me* ! Marjorie ! I'm twenty-one to-day ! "

It was like a little arrow of exquisite light shot into the very heart of his life.

He laughed back. "Are you for meeting me then, Marjorie?"

§ 4

They met in Kensington Gardens with an air of being clandestine and defiant. It was one of those days of amber sunlight, soft air, and tender beauty with which London relieves the tragic glooms of the year's decline. There were still a residue of warm-tinted leaves in puffs and clusters upon the tree branches, a boat or two ruffled the blue Serpentine, and the waterfowl gave colour and animation to the selvage of the water. The sedges were still a greenish yellow.

The two met shyly. They were both a little unfamiliar to each other. Trafford was black-coated, silk-hatted, umbrella'd, a decorous young professor in the place of the cheerful aeronaut who had fallen so gaily out of the sky. Marjorie had a new tailor-made dress of russet-green, and a little cloth toque ruled and disciplined the hair he had known as a ruddy confusion. . . . They had dreamt, I think, of extended arms and a wild rush to embrace one another. Instead, they shook hands.

"And so," said Trafford, "we meet again!"

"I don't see why we shouldn't meet!" said Marjorie.

There was a slight pause.

"Let's have two of those jolly little green chairs," said Trafford. . . .

They walked across the grass towards the chairs he had indicated, and both were full of the momentous things they were finding it impossible to say.

"There ought to be squirrels here, as there are in New York," he said at last.

They sat down. There was a moment's silence, and then Trafford's spirit rose in rebellion and he plunged at this —this stranger beside him.

"Look here," he said, "do you still love me, Marjorie?"

She looked up into his face with eyes in which surprise and scrutiny passed into something altogether beautiful. "I love you—altogether," she said in a steady, low voice.

And suddenly she was no longer a stranger, but the girl who had flitted to his arms, breathless, unhesitating, through the dusk. His blood quickened. He made an

awkward gesture as though he arrested an impulse to touch her. " My sweetheart," he said. " My dear one ! "
" Marjorie's face flashed responses. " It's you," he said.
" Me," she answered.
" Do you remember ? "
" Everything ! "
" My dear ! "
" I want to tell you things," said Marjorie. " What are we to do ? " . . .

He tried afterwards to retrace that conversation. He was chiefly ashamed of his scientific preoccupations during that London interval. He had thought of a thousand things ; Marjorie had thought of nothing else but love and him. Her happy assurance, her absolute confidence that his desires would march with hers, reproached and confuted every adverse thought in him as though it was a treachery to love. He had that sense which I suppose comes at times to every man, of entire unworthiness for the straight, unhesitating decision, the clear simplicity of a woman's passion. He had dreamt vaguely, unsubstantially, the while he had arranged his pressures and temperatures and infinitesimal ingredients, and worked with gonimeter and trial models and the new calculating machine he had contrived for his research. But she had thought clearly, definitely, fully—of nothing but coming to him. She had thought out everything that bore upon that ; reasons for precipitance, reasons for delay, she had weighed the rewards of conformity against the glamour of romance. It became more and more clear to him as they talked, that she was determined to elope with him, to go to Italy, and there have an extraordinarily picturesque and beautiful time. Her definiteness shamed his poverty of anticipation. Her enthusiasm carried him with her. Of course it was so that things must be done. . . .

When at last they parted under the multiplying lamps of the November twilight, he turned his face eastward. He was afraid of his mother's eyes—he scarcely knew why. He walked along Kensington Gore, and the clustering confused lights of street and house, white and golden and orange and pale lilac, the moving lamps and shining glitter of the traffic, the luminous interiors of ominbuses, the reflection of carriage and hoarding, the fading daylight overhead, the phantom trees to the left, the deepening shadows and blacknesses among the houses on his right, the bobbing heads of wayfarers, were just for him the stir

and hue and texture of fairyland. All the world was fairyland. He went to his club and dined there, and divided the
evening between geography, as it is condensed in Baedecker
and Murray on North Italy, Italian Switzerland and the
Italian Riviera, and a study of the marriage laws as they
are expounded in *Whitaker's Almanack*, the *Encyclopædia
Britannica*, and other convenient works of reference. He
replaced the books as he used them, and went at last from
the library into the smoking-room, but seeing a man who
might talk to him there, he went out at once into the
streets, and fetched a wide compass by Baker Street,
Oxford Street, and Hyde Park, home.

He was a little astonished at himself and everything.

But it was going to be—splendid.

(What poor things words can be !)

§ 5

He found his mother still up. She had been re-reading
The Old Wives' Tale, and she sat before a ruddy fire in the
shadow beyond the lit circle of a green-shaded electric
light, thinking, with the book put aside. In the dimness
above was his father's portrait. " Time you were in bed,
mother," he said reprovingly, and kissed her eyebrow and
stood above her. " What's the book ? " he asked, and
picked it up and put it down, forgotten. Their eyes met.
She perceived he had something to say ; she did not know
what. " Where have you been ? " she asked.

He told her, and they lapsed into silence. She asked
another question and he answered her, and the indifferent
conversation ended again. The silence lengthened. Then
he plunged : " I wonder, mother, if it would put you out
very much if I brought home a wife to you ? "

So it had come to this—and she had not seen it coming.
She looked into the glowing recesses of the fire before her
and controlled her voice by an effort. " I'd be glad for
you to do it, dear—if you loved her," she said very quietly.
He stared down at her for a moment ; then he knelt down
beside her and took her hand and kissed it. " *My dear*,"
she whispered softly, stroking his head, and her tears came
streaming. For a time they said no more.

Presently he put coal on the fire, and then sitting on the
hearthrug at her feet and looking away from her into the
flames—in an attitude that took her back to his boyhood
—he began to tell her brokenly and awkwardly of Marjorie.

" It's so hard, mother, to explain these things," he began.
" One doesn't half understand the things that are happening
to one. I want to make you in love with her, dear, just as
I am. And I don't see how I can."

" Perhaps I shall understand, my dear. Perhaps I shall
understand better than you think."

" She's such a beautiful thing—with something about
her———. You know these steel blades you can bend back
to the hilt—and they're steel ! And she's tender. It's
as if some one had taken tears, mother, and made a spirit
out of them———"

She caressed and stroked his hand. " My dear," she
said, " I know."

" And a sort of dancing daring in her eyes."

" Yes," she said. " But tell me where she comes from,
and how you met her—and all the circumstantial things
that a sensible old woman can understand."

He kissed her hand and sat down beside her, with his
shoulder against the arm of her chair, his fingers interlaced
about his knee. She could not keep her touch from his
hair, and she tried to force back the thought in her mind
that all these talks must end, that very soon indeed they
would end. And she was glad, full of pride and joy, too,
that her son was a lover after her heart, a clean and simple
lover as his father had been before him. He loved this
unknown Marjorie, finely, sweetly, bravely, even as she
herself could have desired to have been loved. She told
herself she did not care very greatly even if this Marjorie
should prove unworthy. So long as her son was not
unworthy.

He pieced his story together. He gave her a picture of
the Popes, Marjorie in her family like a jewel in an ugly
setting, so it seemed to him, and the queer dull rage of her
father and all that they meant to do. She tried to grasp
his perplexities and advise, but chiefly she was filled with
the thought that he was in love. If he wanted a girl he
should have her, and if he had to take her by force, well,
wasn't it his right ? She set small store upon the Popes
that night—or any circumstances. And since she herself
had married on the slightest of security, she was concerned
very little that this great adventure was to be attempted
on an income of a few hundreds a year. It was outside
her philosophy that a wife should be anything but glad to
tramp the roads if need be with the man who loved her.
He sketched out valiant plans, was for taking Marjorie

away in the teeth of all opposition and bringing her back
to London. It would have to be done decently, of course,
but it would have, he thought, to be done. Mrs. Trafford
found the prospect perfect ; never before had he sounded
and looked so like that dim figure which hung still and
sympathetic above them. Ever and again she glanced up
at her husband's quiet face. . . .

On one point she was very clear with him.

" You'll live with us, mother ? " he said abruptly.

" Not with you. As near as you like. But one house,
one woman. . . . I'll have a little flat of my own—for you
both to come to me."

" Oh, nonsense, mother ! You'll have to be with us.
Living alone, indeed ! "

" My dear, I'd *prefer* a flat of my own. You don't
understand—everything. It will be better for all of us
like that."

There came a little pause between them, and then her
hand was on his head again. " Oh, my dear," she said,
" I want you to be happy. And life can be difficult. I
won't give a chance—for things to go wrong. You're
hers, dear, and you've got to be hers—be each other's
altogether. I've watched so many people. And that's
the best, the very best you can have. There's just the
lovers—the real enduring lovers ; and the uncompleted
people who've failed to find it." . . .

§ 6

Trafford's second meeting with Marjorie, which, by the
bye, happened on the afternoon of the following day,
brought them near to conclusive decisions. The stiffness of
their first encounter in London had altogether vanished.
She was at her prettiest and in the highest spirits—and she
didn't care for anything else in the world. A gauzy silk
scarf which she had bought and not paid for that day
floated atmospherically about her straight, trim body ; her
hair had caught the infection of insurrection and was
waving rebelliously about her ears. As he drew near her
his grave discretion passed from him as clouds pass from a
hillside. She smiled radiantly. He held out both his
hands for both of hers, and never did a maiden come so
near and yet not get a public and shameless kissing.

One could as soon describe music as tell their conversation. It was a matter of tones and feelings. But the idea

of flight together, of the bright awakening in unfamiliar
sunshine with none to come between them, had gripped
them both. A certain sober gravity of discussion only
masked that deeper inebrity. It would be easy for them
to get away; he had no lectures until February ; he could,
he said, make arrangements, leave his research. She
dreaded disputation. She was for a simple disappearance,
notes on pincushions and defiantly apologetic letters from
Boulogne, but his mother's atmosphere had been a gentler
one than her home's, with a more powerful disposition to
dignity. He still couldn't understand that cantankerous
egotism of Pope was indeed the essential man ; it seemed
to him a crust of bad manners that reason ought to
pierce.

The difference in their atmospheres came out in their
talk—in his desire for a handsome and dignified wedding—
though the very heavens protested—and her resolve to
cut clear of every one, to achieve a sort of jail delivery of
her life, make a new beginning altogether, with the minimum of friction and the maximum of surprise. Unused to
fighting, he was magnificently prepared to fight ; she, with
her intimate knowledge of chronic domestic conflict, was
for the evasion of all the bickerings, scoldings, and misrepresentations his challenge would occasion. He thought
in his innocence a case could be stated and discussed ; but,
no family discussion she had ever heard had even touched
the realities of the issue that occasioned it.

" I don't like this underhand preparation," he said.

" Nor I," she echoed. " But what can one do ? "

" Well, oughtn't I to go to your father and give him
a chance ? Why shouldn't I ? It's—the dignified way."

" It won't be dignified for father," said Marjorie, " anyhow."

" But what right has he to object ? "

" He isn't going to discuss his rights with you. He *will*
object."

" But *why* ? "

" Oh ! because he's started that way. He hit you. I
haven't forgotten it. Well, if he goes back on that now——
He'd rather die than go back on it. You see, he's ashamed
in his heart. It would be like confessing himself wrong
not to keep it up that you're the sort of man one hits. He
just hates you because he hit you. I haven't been his
daughter for twenty-one years for nothing."

" I'm thinking of us," said Trafford. " I don't see we

oughtn't to go to him just because he's likely to be—unreasonable."

"My dear, do as you please. He'll forbid and shout, and hit tables until things break. Suppose he locks me up ! "

"Oh, Habeas Corpus, and my strong right arm ! He's much more likely to turn you out of doors."

"Not if he thinks the other will annoy you more. I'll have to bear a storm."

"Not for long."

"He'll bully mother till she cries over me. But do as you please. She'll come and she'll beg me—— Do as you please. Perhaps I'm a coward. I'd far rather I could slip away."

Trafford thought for a moment. "I'd far rather you could," he answered, in a voice that spoke of inflexible determinations.

They turned to the things they meant to do. "*Italy !* " she whispered. "*Italy !* " Her face was alight with her burning expectation of beauty, of love, of the new heaven and the new earth that lay before them. The intensity of that desire blazing through her seemed to shame his dull discretions. He had to cling to his resolution, lest it should vanish in that contagious intoxication.

"You understand I shall come to your father," he said, as they drew near the gate where it seemed discreet for them to part.

"It will make it harder to get away," she said, with no apparent despondency. "It won't stop us. Oh ! do as you please."

She seemed to dismiss the question, and stood hand-in-hand with him in a state of glowing gravity. She wouldn't see him again for four-and-twenty hours. Then a thought came into her head—a point of great practical moment.

"Oh ! " she said, "of course, you won't tell father you've seen me."

She met his eye. "Really you mustn't," she said. "You see—he'll make a row with mother for not having watched me better. I don't know what he isn't likely to do. It isn't myself—— This is a confidential communication—all this. No one in this world knows I am meeting you. If you *must* go to him, go to him."

"For myself ? "

She nodded, with her open eyes on his—eyes that looked now very blue and very grave, and her lips a little apart.

She surprised him a little, but even this sudden weakness seemed adorable.

" All right," he said.

" You don't think that I'm shirking——— ? " she asked, a little too eagerly.

" You know your father best," he answered. " I'll tell you all he says and all the terror of him here to-morrow afternoon."

§ 7

In the stillness of the night Trafford found himself thinking over Marjorie; it was a new form of mental exercise which was destined to play a large part in his existence for many subsequent years. There had come a shadow on his confidence in her. She was a glorious person; she had a kind of fire behind her and in her—shining through her, like the lights in a fire-opal, but——— He wished she had not made him promise to conceal their meeting and their close co-operation from her father. Why did she do that? It would spoil his case with her father, and it could forward things for them in no conceivable way. And from that, in some manner too subtle to trace, he found his mind wandering to another problem, which was destined to reappear with a slowly dwindling importance very often in this procedure of thinking over Marjorie in the small hours. It was the riddle—it never came to him in the daytime, but only in those intercalary and detachedly critical periods of thought—why exactly had she engaged herself to Magnet? Why had she? He couldn't imagine himself, in Marjorie's position, doing anything of the sort. Marjorie had ways of her own; she was different. . . . Well, anyhow, she was splendid and loving and full of courage. . . . He had got no further than this when at last he fell asleep.

§ 8

Trafford's little attempt to regularise his position was as creditable to him as it was inevitably futile. He sought out 29 Hartstone Square in the morning on his way to his laboratory, and he found it one of a great row of stucco houses each with a portico and a dining-room window on the ground floor, and each with a railed area from which troglodytic servants peeped. Collectively the terrace might claim a certain ugly dignity of restraint, there was none of your Queen Anne nonsense of art or beauty about it, and the narrow height, the subterranean kitchens of each constituent house, told of a steep relentless staircase and the days before the pampering of the lower classes began. The houses formed a square, as if the British square so famous at Waterloo for its dogged resistance to all the forces of the universe had immortalised itself in buildings, and they stared upon a severely railed garden of hardy shrubs and gravel to which the tenants had the inestimable privilege of access. They did not use it much, that was their affair, but at any rate they had keys and a nice sense of rights assured, and at least it kept other people out.

Trafford turned out of a busy high-road full of the mixed exhilarating traffic of our time, and came along a quiet street into this place, and it seemed to him he had come into a corner of defence and retreat, into an atmosphere of obstinate and unteachable resistances. But this illusion of convervatism in its last ditch was dispelled altogether in Mr. Pope's portico. Youth flashed out of these solemnities like a dart shot from a cave. Trafford was raising his hand to the solid brass knocker when abruptly it was snatched from his fingers, the door was flung open, and a small boy with a number of dirty books in a strap flew out and hit him with projectile violence.

" Blow ! " said the young gentleman, recoiling, and Trafford recovering said : " Hallo, Theodore ! "

" Lord ! " said Theodore, breathless, " it's you ! *What* a lark ! Your name's never mentioned—nohow. What *did* you do ? . . . Wish I could stop and see it ! I'm ten minutes late. *Ave atque vale.* So long ! "

He vanished with incredible velocity. And Mr. Trafford was alone in possession of the open doorway except for Toupee, who after a violent outbreak of hostility altered his mind and cringed to his feet in abject and affectionate propitiation. A pseudo-twin appeared, said " Hallo ! " and vanished, and then he had an instant's vision of Mr. Pope, newspaper in hand, appearing from the dining-room. His expression of surprise changed to malevolence, and he darted back into the room from which he had emerged. Trafford decided to take the advice of a small brass plate on his left hand, and " ring also."

A housemaid came out of the bowels of the earth very promptly and ushered him up two flights of stairs into what was manifestly Mr. Pope's study.

It was a narrow, rather dark room lit by two crimson-curtained windows, and with a gas fire before which Mr. Pope's walking boots were warming for the day. The apartment revealed to Trafford's cursory inspection many of the stigmata of an Englishman of active intelligence and literary tastes. There in the bookcase were the collected works of Scott, a good large illustrated Shakespeare in numerous volumes, and a complete set of bound *Punches* from the beginning. A pile of back numbers of *The Times* stood on a cane stool in a corner, and in a little bookcase handy for the occupier of the desk were Whitaker, Wisden, and an old peerage. The desk bore traces of recent epistolary activity, and was littered with the printed matter of Aunt Plessington's movements. Two or three recent issues of the *Financial Review of Reviews* were also visible. About the room hung steel engravings apparently of defunct judges or at any rate of exceedingly grim individuals, and over the mantel were trophies of athletic prowess, a bat witnessing that Mr. Pope had once captained the second eleven at Harrogby.

Mr. Pope entered with a stern expression and a sentence prepared. "Well, sir," he said with a note of ironical affability, "to what may I ascribe this—intrusion?"

Mr. Trafford was about to reply when Mr. Pope interrupted. "Will you be seated?" he said, and turned his desk chair about for himself, and occupying it, crossed his legs and pressed the finger-tips of his two hands together. "Well, sir?" he said.

Trafford remained standing astraddle over the boots before the gas fire.

"Look here, sir," he said; "I am in love with your daughter. She's one-and-twenty, and I want to see her—and in fact——" He found it hard to express himself. He could think only of a phrase that sounded ridiculous. "I want—in fact—to pay my addresses to her."

"Well, sir, I don't want you to do so. That is too mild. I object strongly—very strongly. My daughter has been engaged to a very distinguished and able man, and I hope very shortly to hear that that engagement—— Practically it is still going on. I don't want you to intrude upon my daughter further."

"But look here, sir. There's a certain justice—I mean a certain reasonableness——"

Mr. Pope held out an arresting hand. "I don't wish it. Let that be enough."

"Of course it isn't enough. I'm in love with her—and she with me. I'm an entirely reputable and decent person——"

"May I be allowed to judge what is or is not suitable companionship for my daughter ?—and what may or may not be the present state of her affections ? "

"Well, that's rather the point we are discussing. After all, Marjorie isn't a baby. I want to do all this—this affair openly and properly if I can, but, you know, I mean to marry Marjorie—anyhow."

"There are two people to consult in that matter."

"I'll take the risk of that."

"Permit me to differ."

A feeling of helplessness came over Trafford. The curious irritation Mr. Pope always roused in him began to get the better of him. His face flushed hotly. "Oh, really ! really ! this is—this is nonsense ! " he cried. " I never heard anything so childish and pointless as your objection——"

"Be careful, sir ! " cried Mr. Pope, " be careful ! "

"I'm going to marry Marjorie."

"If she marries you, sir, she shall never darken my doors again ! "

"If you had a thing against me ! "

"*Haven't* I ? "

"What have you ? "

There was a quite perceptible pause before Pope fired his shot.

"Does any decent man want the name of Trafford associated with his daughter. Trafford ! Look at the hoardings, sir ! "

A sudden blaze of anger lit Trafford. "My God ! " he cried, and clenched his fists and seemed for a moment ready to fall upon the man before him. Then he controlled himself by a violent effort. "You believe in that libel on my dead father ? " he said, with white lips.

"Has it ever been answered ? "

"A hundred times. And anyhow !—Confound it ! I don't believe—*you* believe it. You've raked it up—as an excuse ! You want an excuse for your infernal domestic tyranny ! That's the truth of it. You can't bear a creature in your household to have a will or preference of her own. I tell you, sir, you are intolerable—intolerable ! "

He was shouting, and Pope was standing now and shouting too. "Leave my house, sir. Get out of my house, sir. You come here to insult me, sir ! "

A sudden horror of himself and Pope seized the younger man. He stiffened and became silent. Never in his life before had he been in a bawling quarrel. He was amazed and ashamed.

"Leave my house!" cried Pope, with an imperious gesture towards the door.

Trafford made an absurd effort to save the situation. "I am sorry, sir, I lost my temper. I had no business to abuse you——"

"You've said enough."

"I apologise for that. I've done what I could to manage things decently.

"Will you go, sir?" threatened Mr. Pope.

"I'm sorry I came," said Trafford.

Mr. Pope took his stand with folded arms and an expression of weary patience.

"I did what I could," said Trafford at the door.

The staircase and passage were deserted. The whole house seemed to have caught from Mr. Pope that same quality of seeing him out. . . .

"Confound it!" said Trafford in the street. "How on earth did all this happen?" . . .

He turned eastward, and then realised that work would be impossible that day. He changed his direction for Kensington Gardens, and in the flower-bordered walk near the Albert Memorial he sat down on a chair, and lugged at his moustache and wondered. He was extraordinarily perplexed, as well as ashamed and enraged by this uproar. How had it begun? Of course, he had been stupidly abusive, but the insult to his father had been unendurable. Did a man of Pope's sort quite honestly believe that stuff? If he didn't, he deserved kicking. If he did, of course he was entitled to have it cleared up. But then he wouldn't listen! Was there any case for the man at all? Had he, Trafford, really put the thing so that Pope would listen? He couldn't remember. What was it he had said in reply to Pope? What was it exactly that Pope had said?

It was already vague; it was a confused memory of headlong words and answers; what wasn't vague, what rang in his ears still, was the hoarse discord of two shouting voices.

Could Marjorie have heard?

§ 9

So Marjorie carried her point. She wasn't to be married
tamely after the common fashion which trails home and
all one's beginnings into the new life. She was to be eloped
with, romantically and splendidly, into a glorious new
world. She walked on shining clouds, and if she felt some
remorse, it was a very tender and satisfactory remorse,
and with a clear conviction below it that in the end she
would be forgiven.

They made all their arrangements elaborately and carefully. Trafford got a licence to marry her; she was to
have a new outfit from top to toe to go away with on that
eventful day. It accumulated in the shop, and they
marked the clothes $M.T.$ She was watched, she imagined,
but as her father did not know she had seen Trafford,
nothing had been said to her, and no attempt was made to
prohibit her going out and coming in. Trafford entered
into the conspiracy with a keen interest, a certain amusement, and a queer little feeling of distaste. He hated to
hide any act of his from any human being. The very soul
of scientific work, you see, is publication. But Marjorie
seemed to justify all things, and when his soul turned
against furtiveness, he reminded it that the alternative
was bawling.

One eventful afternoon he went to the college, and
Marjorie slipped round by his arrangement to have tea
with Mrs. Trafford. . . .

He returned about seven in a state of nervous apprehension; came upstairs two steps at a time, and stopped
breathless on the landing. He gulped as he came in, and
his eyes were painfully eager. " She's been ? " he asked.

But Marjorie had won Mrs. Trafford.

" She's been," she answered. " Yes, she's all right,
my dear."

" Oh, mother ! " he said.

" She's a beautiful creature, dear—and such a child !
Oh ! such a child ! And God bless you, dear, God bless
you. . . .

" I think all young people are children. I want to take
you both in my arms and save you. . . . I'm talking
nonsense, dear."

He kissed her, and she clung to him as if he were something too precious to release.

§ 10

The elopement was a little complicated by a surprise manœuvre of Mrs. Pope's. She was more alive to the quality of the situation, poor lady ! than her daughter suspected ; she was watching, dreading, perhaps even furtively sympathising and trying to arrange—oh ! trying dreadfully to arrange. She had an instinctive understanding of the deep blue quiet in Marjorie's eyes, and the girl's unusual tenderness with Daffy and the children. She peeped under the blind as Marjorie went out, noted the care in her dress, watched her face as she returned, never plumbed her with a question for fear of the answer. She did not dare to breathe a hint of her suspicions to her husband, but she felt things were adrift in swift, smooth water, and her soul cried out for delay. So presently there came a letter from Cousin Susan Pendexter at Plymouth. The weather was beautiful, Marjorie must come at once, pack up and come and snatch the last best glow of the dying autumn away there in the west. Marjorie's jerry-built excuses, her manifest chagrin and reluctance confirmed her mother's worst suspicions.

She submitted and went, and Mrs. Pope and Syd saw her off.

I do not like to tell how a week later Marjorie explained herself and her dressing-bag and a few small articles back to London from Plymouth. Suffice it that she lied desperately and elaborately. Her mother had never achieved such miracles of misstatement, and she added a vigour that was all her own. It is easier to sympathise with her than exonerate her. She was in a state of intense impatience, and—what is strange—extraordinarily afraid that something would separate her from her lover if she did not secure him. She was in a fever of determination. She could not eat or sleep or attend to anything whatever ; she was occupied altogether with the thought of assuring herself to Trafford. He towered in her waking vision over town and land and sea.

He didn't hear the lies she told ; he only knew she was magnificently coming back to him. He met her at Paddington, a white-faced, tired, splendidly resolute girl, and they went to the waiting registrar's forthwith.

She bore herself with the intentness and dignity of one who is taking the cardinal step in life. They kissed as though it was a symbol, and were keenly business-like

about cabs and luggage and trains. At last they were
alone in the train together. They stared at one another.

" We've done it, Mrs. Trafford ! " said Trafford.

She snapped like an over-taut string, crumpled, clung
to him, and without a word was weeping passionately in
his arms.

It surprised him that she could weep as she did, and
still more to see her as she walked by his side along the
Folkestone pier, altogether recovered, erect, a little flushed
and excited like a child. She seemed to miss nothing.
" Oh, smell the sea ! " she said. " Look at the lights !
Listen to the swish of the water below." She watched the
luggage spinning on the wire rope of the giant crane, and
he watched her face and thought how beautiful she was.
He wondered why her eyes could sometimes be so blue
and sometimes dark as night.

The boat cleared the pier and turned about and headed
for France. They walked the upper deck together and
stood side by side, she very close to him.

" I've never crossed the sea before," she said.

" Old England," she whispered. " It's like leaving a
nest. A little row of lights and that's all the world I've
ever known, shrunken to that already."

Presently they went forward and peered into the night.

" Look ! " she said. " *Italy !* There's sunshine and all
sorts of beautiful things ahead. Warm sunshine, wonderful
old ruins, green lizards. . . ." She paused and whispered
almost noiselessly : " *love*——"

They pressed against each other.

" And yet isn't it strange ? All you can see is darkness,
and clouds—and big waves that hiss as they come near. . . ."

§ 11

Italy gave all her best to welcome them. It was a late
year, a golden autumn, with skies of such blue as Marjorie
had never seen before. They stayed at first in a pretty
little Italian hotel with a garden on the lake, and later
they walked over Salvatore to Morcote and by boat to
Ponte Tresa, and thence they had the most wonderful and
beautiful tramp in the world to Luino, over the hills by
Castelrotto. To the left of them all day was a broad
valley with low-lying villages swimming in a luminous
mist, to the right were purple mountains. They passed
through paved streets with houses the colour of flesh and

ivory, with balconies hung with corn and gourds, with tall church campaniles rising high, and great archways giving upon the blue lowlands ; they tramped along avenues of sweet chestnut and between stretches of exuberant vineyard, in which men and women were gathering grapes—purple grapes, a hatful for a soldo, that rasped the tongue. Everything was strange and wonderful to Marjorie's eyes ; now it would be a wayside shrine and now a yoke of softgoing, dewlapped oxen, now a chapel hung about with *ex votos*, and now some unfamiliar cultivation—or a gipsyeyed child—or a scorpion that scuttled in the dust. The very names of the villages were like jewels to her, Varasca, Croglio, Ronca, Sesia, Monteggio. They walked, or sat by the wayside and talked, or rested at the friendly table of some kindly albergo. A woman as beautiful as Ceres, with a white neck all open, made them an omelet, and then fetched her baby from its cradle to nurse it while she talked to them as they made their meal. And afterwards she filled their pockets with roasted chestnuts, and sent them with melodious good wishes upon their way. And always high over all against the translucent blue hung the white shape of Monte Rosa, that warmed in colour as the evening came.

Marjorie's head was swimming with happiness and beauty, and with every fresh delight she recurred again to the crowning marvel of this clean-limbed man beside her, who smiled and carried all her luggage in a huge rucksack that did not seem to exist for him, and watched her and caressed her—and was hers, *hers* !

At Baveno there were letters. They sat at a little table outside a café and read them, suddenly mindful of England again. Incipient forgiveness showed through Mrs. Pope's reproaches, and there was also a simple, tender love-letter (there is no other word for it) from old Mrs. Trafford to her son.

From Baveno they set off up Monte Mottarone—whence one may see the Alps from Visto to Ortler Spitz—trusting to find the inn still open, and if it was closed to get down to Orta somehow before night. Or, at the worst, sleep upon the mountain-side.

(Monte Mottarone ! Just for a moment taste the sweet Italian name upon your lips.) These were the days before the funicular from Stresa, when one trudged up a rude path through the chestnuts and walnuts.

As they ascended the long windings through the woods,

they met an old poet and his wife, coming down from sunset and sunrise. There was a word or two about the inn, and they went upon their way. The old man turned ever and again to look at them.

"Adorable young people," he said. "Adorable happy young people. . . .

"Did you notice, dear, how she held that dainty little chin of hers ? . . .

"Pride is such a good thing, my dear, clear, straight pride like theirs—and they were both so proud ! . . .

"Isn't it good, dear, to think that once you and I may have looked like that to some passer-by. I wish I could bless them—sweet, swift young things ! I wish, dear, it was possible for old men to bless young people without seeming to set up for saints. . . ."

BOOK THE SECOND
MARJORIE MARRIED

CHAPTER THE FIRST

SETTLING DOWN

§ I

IT was in a boat among reeds upon the lake of Orta that Trafford first became familiarised with the idea that Marjorie was capable of debt.

"Oh, I ought to have told you," she began, apropos of nothing.

Her explanation was airy ; she had let the thing slip out of her mind for a time. But there were various debts to Oxbridge tradespeople. How much ? Well, rather a lot. Of course, the tradespeople were rather enticing when first one went up—— How much, anyhow ?

"Oh, about fifty pounds," said Marjorie, after her manner. "Not *more*. I've not kept all the bills ; and some haven't come in. You know how slow they are."

"These things *will* happen," said Trafford, though, as a matter of fact, nothing of the sort had happened in his case. "However, you'll be able to pay as soon as you get home, and get them all off your mind."

"I think fifty pounds will clear me," said Marjorie, clinging to her long-established total, "if you'll let me have that."

"Oh, we don't do things like that," said Trafford. "I'm arranging that my current account will be a sort of joint account, and your signature will be as good as mine—for the purpose of drawing, at least. You'll have your own cheque-book——"

"I don't understand, quite," said Marjorie.

"You'll have your own cheque-book and write cheques as you want them. That seems the simplest way to me."

"Of course," said Marjorie. "But isn't this—rather unusual ? Father always used to allowance mother."

"It's the only decent way according to my ideas," said

Trafford. "A man shouldn't marry when he can't trust."

"Of course not," said Marjorie. Something between fear and compunction wrung her. "Do you think you'd better ? " she asked, very earnestly.

"Better ? "

"Do this."

"Why not ? "

"It's—it's so generous."

He didn't answer. He took up an oar and began to push out from among the reeds with something of the shy awkwardness of a boy who becomes apprehensive of thanks. He stole a glance at her presently and caught her expression—there was something very solemn and intent in her eyes—and he thought what a grave, fine thing his Marjorie could be.

But, indeed, her state of mind was quite exceptionally confused. She was disconcerted—and horribly afraid of herself.

"Do you mean that I can spend what I like ? " asked Marjorie.

"Just as I may," he said.

"I wonder," said Marjorie again, "if I'd better ? "

She was tingling with delight at this freedom, and she knew she was not fit for its responsibility. She just came short of a passionate refusal of his proposal. He was still so new to her, and things were so wonderful, or I think she would have made that refusal.

"You've got to," said Trafford, and ended the matter.

So Marjorie was silent—making good resolutions.

§ 2

Perhaps some day it may be possible to tell in English again, in the language of Shakespeare and Herrick, of the passion, the tenderness, the beauty, and the delightful familiarisations of a happy honeymoon ; suffice it now, in this delicate period, to record only how our two young lovers found one day that neither had a name for the other. He said she could be nothing better than Marjorie to him ; and she, after a number of unsuccessful experiments, settled down to the old schoolboy nickname made out of his initials, R.A.G.

"Dick," she said, "is too bird-like and boy-like. Andrew I can't abide. Godwin gives one no chances for current use. Rag you must be. Mag and Rag—poor innocents! Old Rag!"

"Mag," he said, "has its drawbacks. The street-boy in London says, 'Shut your mag.' No, I think I shall stick to Marjorie. . . ."

All honeymoons must end at last, so back they came to London, still very bright and happy. And then Marjorie, whose eyes had changed from flashing stones to darkly shining pools of blue, but whose soul had still perhaps to find its depths, set herself to the business of decorating and furnishing the little house Mrs. Trafford had found for them within ten minutes of her own. Meanwhile they lived in lodgings.

There can be no denying that Marjorie began her furnishing with severely virtuous intentions. She was very particular to ask Trafford several times what he thought she might spend upon the enterprise. He had already a bedroom and a study equipped, and he threw out three hundred pounds as his conception of an acceptable figure.

"Very well," said Marjorie, with a note of great precision, "now I shall know," and straightway that sum took a place in her imagination that was at once definitive and protective, just as her estimate of fifty pounds for her Oxbridge debts had always been. She assured herself she was going to do things, and she assured herself she was doing things, on three hundred pounds. At times the astonishment of two or three school friends, who joined her in her shopping, stirred her to a momentary surprise at the way she was managing to keep things within that limit, and following a financial method that had, after all, in spite of some momentary and already nearly forgotten distresses, worked very well at Oxbridge, she refrained from any additions until all the accounts had come to hand.

It was an immense excitement shopping to make a home. There was in her composition a strain of constructive artistry with such concrete things, a strain that had hitherto famished. She was making a beautiful, secure little home for Trafford, for herself, for possibilities—remote perhaps, but already touching her imagination with the anticipation of warm, new, wonderful delights. There should be simplicity indeed in this home, but no bareness, no harshness, never an ugliness nor a discord. She had always loved colour in the skies, in the landscape, in the texture of stuffs and garments; now out of the chaotic skein of countless shops she could choose and pick and mingle her threads in a glow of feminine self-expression.

On three hundred pounds, that is to say—as a maximum. The house she had to deal with was, like Mrs. Trafford's, old and rather small ; it was partly to its lack of bedroom accommodation, but much more to the invasion of the street by the back premises of Messrs. Siddons & Thrale, the great Chelsea outfitters, that the lowness of the rent was due which brought it within the means of Trafford. Marjorie knew very clearly that her father would say her husband had taken her to live in a noisy slum, and that made her all the keener to ensure that every good point in the interior told to its utmost, and that whatever was to be accessible to her family should glow with a refined but warm prosperity. The room downstairs was shapely, and by ripping off the papered canvas of the previous occupier, some very dilapidated but admirably proportioned panelling was brought to light. The dining-room and study door on the ground floor, by a happy accident, were of mahogany, with really very beautiful brass furnishings ; and the dining-room window upon the minute but by no means offensive paved garden behind, was curved and had a little shallow balcony of ironwork, half covered by a devitalised but leafy grape-vine. Moreover, the previous occupier had equipped the place with electric light and a bath-room of almost American splendour on the landing, glass-shelved, white-tiled, and white-painted, so that it was a delight to go into.

Marjorie's mind leapt very rapidly to the possibilities of this little establishment. The panelling must be done and done well, anyhow ; that would be no more than a wise economy, seeing it might at any time help them to re-let ; it would be painted white, of course, and thus set the key for a clean brightness of colour throughout. The furniture would stand out against the softly shining white, and its line and proportions must be therefore the primary qualities to consider as she bought it. The study was much narrower than the dining-room, and so the passage, which the agent called the hall, was much broader and more commodious behind the happily wide staircase than in front, and she was able to banish out of the sight of the chance visitor all that litter of hat-stand and umbrella-stand, letters, boxes arriving and parcels to post, which had always offended her eye at home. At home there had been often the most unsightly things visible, one of

Theo's awful caps, or his school books, and not infrequently her father's well-worn and all too fatally comfortable house slippers. A good effect at first is half the victory of a well-done house, and Marjorie accomplished another of her real economies here by carpeting hall and staircase with a fine-toned, rich-feeling and rather high-priced blue carpet, held down by very thick brass stair-rods. She hung up four well-chosen steel engravings, put a single Chippendale chair in the hall, and a dark old Dutch clock that had turned out to be only five pounds when she had expected the shopman to say eleven or twelve, on the half-landing. That was all. Round the corner by the study door was a mahogany slab, and the litter all went upon a capacious but very simple dark-stained hat-stand and table that were out of the picture entirely until you reached the stairs.

Her dining-room was difficult for some time. She had equipped that with a dark oak Welsh dresser made very bright with a dessert service that was, in view of its extremely decorative quality, remarkably cheap, and with some very pretty silver-topped glass bottles and flasks. This dresser and a number of simple but shapely facsimiles of old chairs, stood out against a nearly primrose paper, very faintly patterned, and a dark blue carpet with a margin of dead black-stained wood. Over the mantel was a German colour-print of waves full of sunlight breaking under cliffs, and between this and the window were dark bookshelves and a few bright-coloured books. On the wall, black-framed, were four very good Japanese prints, rich in greenish-blues and bluish-grays that answered the floor, and the window curtains took up some of the colours of the German print. But something was needed towards the window, she felt, to balance the warmly shining plates upon the dresser. The deep rose-red of the cherries that adorned them was too isolated, usurped too dominating a value. And while this was weighing upon her mind she saw in a window in Regent Street a number of Bokhara hangings very nobly displayed. They were splendid pieces of needlework, particularly glorious in their crimsons and reds, and suddenly it came to her that it was just one of these, one that had great ruby flowers upon it with dead-blue interlacings, that was needed to weld her gay-coloured scheme together. She hesitated, went halfway to Piccadilly Circus, turned back and asked the prices. The prices were towering prices, ten, fifteen, eighteen guineas, and when at last the shopman produced one with all the charm of

colour she sought at eight, it seemed like ten guineas
snatched back as they dropped from her hands. And still
hesitating, she had three that pleased her most sent home,
" on approval," before she decided finally to purchase one
of them. But the trial was conclusive. And then, struck
with a sudden idea, she carried off a long narrow one she
had had no idea of buying before into the little study
behind. Suppose, she thought, instead of hanging two
curtains as anybody else would do in that window, she ran
this glory of rich colour across from one side on a great
rod of brass.

She was giving the study the very best of her attention.
After she had lapsed in some other part of the house from
the standards of rigid economy she had set up, she would
as it were restore the balance by adding something to the
gracefully dignified arrangement of this den he was to use.
And the brass rod of the Bokhara hanging that was to do
instead of curtains released her mind somehow to the
purchase of certain old candlesticks she had hitherto
resisted. They were to stand, bored to carry candle
electric lights, on either corner of the low bookcase that
faced the window. They were very heavy, very shapely
candlesticks, and they cost thirty-five shillings. They
looked remarkably well when they were put up, except that
a sort of hollowness appeared between them and clamoured
for a delightful old brass-footed workbox she had seen in
a shop in Baker Street. Inquiry confirmed her quick impression that this was a genuine piece (of quite exceptional
genuineness) and that the price—they asked five pounds
ten and came down to five guineas—was in accordance
with this. It was a little difficult (in spite of the silent
hunger between the candlesticks) to reconcile this particular
article with her dominating idea of an austerely restrained
expenditure, until she hit on the device of calling it a hors-
d'œuvre, and regarding it not as furniture but as a present
from herself to Trafford that happened to fall in very
agreeably with the process of house furnishing. She
decided she would some day economise its cost out of her
dress allowance. The bookcase on which it stood was a
happy discovery in Kensington, just five feet high, and
with beautiful oval glass fronts, and its capacity was
supplemented and any excess in its price at least morally
compensated by a very tall, narrow, distinguished-looking
set of open shelves that had been made for some special
corner in another house, and which anyhow were really

and truly dirt cheap. The desk combined grace and good
proportions to an admirable extent, the fender of pierced
brass looked as if it had always lived in immediate contact
with the shapely old white marble fireplace, and the two
arm-chairs were marvels of dignified comfort. By the fireplace were a banner-shaped needlework fire-screen, a white
sheepskin hearthrug, a little patch-and-powder table
adapted to carry books, and a green-shaded lamp, grouped
in a common inaudible demand for a reader in slippers.
Trafford, when at last the apartment was ready for his
inspection, surveyed these arrangements with a kind of
dazzled admiration.

" By Jove ! " he said. " How little people know of the
homes of the Poor ! "

Marjorie was so delighted with his approval that she
determined to show Mrs. Trafford next day how prettily
at least her son was going to live. The good lady came
and admired everything, and particular the Bokhara
hangings. She did not seem to appraise, but something
set Marjorie talking rather nervously of a bargain-hunter's
good fortune. Mrs. Trafford glanced at the candlesticks
and the low bookcase, and returned to the glowing piece
of needlework that formed the symmetrical window curtain
in the study. She took it in her hand, and whispered,
" Beautiful ! "

" But aren't these rather good ? " asked Mrs. Trafford.

Marjorie answered, after a little pause. " They're not
too good for *him*," she said.

§ 3

And now these young people had to resume life in London
in earnest. The orchestral accompaniment of the world
at large began to mingle with their hitherto unsustained
duet. It had been inaudible in Italy. In Chelsea it had
sounded, faintly perhaps but distinctly, from their very
first inspection of the little house. A drawing-room speaks
of callers, a dining-room of lunches and dinners. It had
swayed Marjorie from the front door inward.

During their honeymoon they had been gloriously unconscious of comment. Now Marjorie began to show
herself keenly sensitive to the advent of a score of personalities, and very anxious to show just how completely
successful in every sense her romantic disobedience had
been. She knew she had been approved of, admired,

condemned, sneered at, thoroughly discussed. She felt it
her first duty to Trafford, to all who had approved of her
flight, to every one, herself included, to make this marriage
obviously, indisputably, a success, a success not only by
her own standards, but by the standards of any one soever
who chose to sit in judgment on her.

There was Trafford. She felt she had to extort the
admission from every one that he was the handsomest,
finest, ablest, most promising and most delightful man a
prominent humorist was ever jilted for. She wanted them
to understand clearly just all that Trafford was—and that
involved, she speedily found in practice, making them
believe a very great deal that as yet Trafford wasn't. She
found it practically impossible not to anticipate his election
to the Royal Society and the probability of a more important professorship. She felt that anyhow he was an
F.R.S. in the sight of God. . . .

It was almost equally difficult not to indicate a larger
income than facts justified.

It was entirely in Marjorie's vein in those early days
that she would want to win on every score and by every
standard of reckoning. If Marjorie had been a general she
would have counted no victory complete if the struggle
was not sustained and desperate, and if it left the enemy
with a single gun or flag, or herself with so much as a man
killed or wounded. The people she wanted to impress
varied very widely. She wanted to impress the Carmel
girls, and the Carmel girls, she knew, with their racial
trick of acute appraisement, were only to be won by the
very highest quality all round. They had, she knew, two
standards of quality, cost and distinction. As far as
possible, she would give them distinction. But whenever
she hesitated over something on the verge of cheapness the
thought of those impending judgments tipped the balance.
The Carmel girls were just two influential representatives
of a host. She wanted to impress quite a number of other
school and college friends. There were various shy, plastic-
spirited, emotional creatures, of course, for the most part,
with no confidence in their own appearance, who would be
impressed quite adequately enough by Trafford's good
looks and witty manner and easy temper. They might
perhaps fall in love with him and become slavish to her
after the way of their kind, and anyhow they would be
provided for, but there were plenty of others of a harder
texture whose tests would be more difficult to satisfy.

There were girls who were the daughters of prominent men, who must be made to understand that Trafford was prominent, girls who were well connected, who must be made to realise the subtle excellence of Trafford's blood. As she thought of Constance Graham, for example, or Ottiline Winchelsea, she felt the strongest disposition to thicken the by no means well-authenticated strands that linked Trafford with the Traffords of Trafford-over-Lea. She went about the house dreaming a little apprehensively of these coming calls, and the pitiless light of criticism they would bring to bear, not indeed upon her happiness—that was assured—but upon her success.

The social side of the position would have to be strained to the utmost, Marjorie felt, with Aunt Plessington. The thought of Aunt Plessington made her peculiarly apprehensive. Aunt Plessington had to the fullest extent that contempt for merely artistic or scientific people which sits so gracefully upon the administrative English. You see, people of that sort do not get on in the sense that a young lawyer or barrister gets on. They do not make steps; they boast and quarrel and are jealous perhaps, but that steady patient shove upward seems beyond their intelligence. The energies God manifestly gave them for shoving, they dissipate in the creation of weak beautiful things and unremunerative theories, or in the establishment of views sometimes diametrically opposed to the ideas of influential people. And they are " queer "—socially. They just moon about doing this so-called " work " of theirs, and even when the judgment of eccentric people forces a kind of reputation upon them—Heaven knows why !—they make no public or social use of it. It seemed to Aunt Plessington that the artist and the scientific man were dealt with very neatly and justly in the Parable of the Buried Talent. Moreover, their private lives were often scandalous, they married for love instead of interest, often quite disadvantageously, and their relationships had all the instability that is natural upon such a foundation. And, after all, what good were they ? She had never met an artist or a prominent imaginative writer or scientific man that she had not been able to subdue in a minute or so by flat contradiction, and if necessary slightly raising her voice. They had little or no influence even upon their own public appointments. . . .

The thought of the invasion of her agreeable little backstreet establishment by this Britannic system of judgments

filled Marjorie's heart with secret terrors. She felt she had
to grapple with an overcome Aunt Plessington, or be for
ever fallen—at least, so far as that amiable lady's report
went, and she knew it went pretty far. She wandered
about the house trying to imagine herself Aunt Plessington.
Immediately she felt the gravest doubts whether the
whole thing wasn't too graceful and pretty. A rich and
rather massive ugliness, of course, would have been the
thing to fetch Aunt Plessington. Happily, it was Aunt
Plessington's habit to veil her eyes with her voice. She
might not see very much.

The subjugation of Aunt Plessington was difficult, but
not altogether hopeless, Marjorie felt, provided her rejection
of Magnet had not been taken as an act of personal ingratitude. There was a case on her side. She was discovering, for example, that Trafford had a really very
considerable range of acquaintance among quite distinguished people ; big figures like Evesham and MacHaldo,
for example, were intelligently interested in the trend of
his work. She felt this gave her a basis for Plessingtonian
justifications. She could produce those people—as one
shows one's loot. She could imply. " Oh, Love and all
that nonsense ! Certainly not ! *This* is what I did it for."
With skill and care and good luck, and a word here and
there in edgeways, she believed she might be able to represent the whole adventure as the well-calculated opening
of a campaign on soundly Plessingtonian lines. Her
marriage to Trafford, she tried to persuade herself, might
be presented as something almost as brilliant and startling
as her aunt's swoop upon her undistinguished uncle.

She might pretend that all along she had seen her way
to things, to coveted dinner-tables and the familiarity of
coveted guests, to bringing people together and contriving
arrangements, to influence and prominence, to culmina-
tions and intrigues impossible in the comparatively specialised world of a successful humorist and playwright, and so
at last to those high freedoms of authoritative and if
necessary offensive utterance in a strangulated contralto,
and from a position of secure eminence, which is the goal
of all virtuously ambitious Englishwomen of the governing
classes—that is to say, of all virtuously ambitious Englishwomen. . . .

§ 4

And while such turbid solicitudes as these were flowing
in again from the London world to which she had returned,
and fouling the bright, romantic clearness of Marjorie's
life, Trafford, in his ampler, less detailed way was also
troubled about their coming re-entry into society. He,
too, had his old associations.

For example, he was by no means confident of the
favourable judgments of his mother upon Marjorie's circle
of school and college friends, whom he gathered from
Marjorie's talk were destined to play a large part in this
new phase of his life. She had given him very ample
particulars of some of them ; and he found them interesting
rather than richly attractive personalities. It is to be
noted that while he thought always of Marjorie as a
beautiful, grown-up woman, and his mate and equal, he
was still disposed to regard her intimate friends as school-
girls of an advanced and aggressive type. . . .

Then that large circle of distinguished acquaintances
which Marjorie saw so easily and amply utilised for the
subjugation of Aunt Plessington didn't present itself quite
in that service to Trafford's private thoughts. He hadn't
that certitude of command over them, nor that confidence
in their unhesitating approval of all he said and did. Just
as Marjorie wished him to shine in the heavens over all
her people, so, in regard to his associates, he was extraordinarily anxious that they should realise, and realise
from the outset without qualification or hesitation, how
beautiful, brave, and delightful she was. And you know
he had already begun to be aware of an evasive feeling in
his mind that at times she did not altogether do herself
justice—he scarcely knew as yet how or why. . . .

She was very young. . . .

One or two individuals stood out in his imagination,
representatives and symbols of the rest. Particularly
there was that old giant, Sir Roderick Dover, who had been,
until recently, the Professor of Physics in the great Oxford
laboratories. Dover and Trafford had one of those warm
friendships which spring up at times between a rich-minded
man whose greatness is assured and a young man of
brilliant promise. It was all the more affectionate because
Dover had been a friend of Trafford's father. These two
and a group of other careless-minded, able, distinguished,
and uninfluential men at the Winton Club affected the end

of the smoking-room near the conservatory in the hours
after lunch, and shared the joys of good talk and fine jesting about the big fireplace there. Under Dover's broad
influence they talked more ideas and less gossip than is
usual with English club men. Twaddle about appointments, about reputations, topics from the morning's papers,
London architecture, and the commerce in " good stories "
took refuge at the other end in the window bays or by the
farther fireplace. Trafford only began to realise on his
return to London how large a share this intermittent
perennial conversation had contributed to the atmosphere
of his existence. Amidst the romantic circumstances of
his flight with Marjorie he had forgotten the part these
men played in his life and thoughts. Now he was enormously exercised in the search for a reconciliation between
these, he felt, incommensurable factors.

He was afraid of what might be Sir Roderick's unspoken
judgment on Marjorie and the house she had made—
though what was there to be afraid of ? He was still more
afraid—and this was even more remarkable—of the clear
little judgments—hard as loose, small diamonds in a bed—
that he thought Marjorie might pronounce on Sir Roderick.
He had never disguised from himself that Sir Roderick was
fat—nobody who came within a hundred yards of him
could be under any illusion about that—and that he drank
a good deal, ate with a cosmic spaciousness, loved a cigar,
and talked and laughed with a freedom that sometimes
drove delicate-minded new members into the corners
remotest from the historical fireplace. Trafford knew
himself quite definitely that there was a joy in Dover's
laugh and voice, a beauty in his face (that was somehow
mixed up with his healthy corpulence), and a breadth, a
charity, a leonine courage in his mind (that was somehow
mixed up with his careless freedom of speech) that made
him an altogether satisfactory person.

But supposing Marjorie didn't see any of that !

Still, he was on the verge of bringing Sir Roderick home
when a talk at the club one day postponed that introduction
of the two extremes of Trafford's existence for quite a
considerable time.

Those were the days of the first enthusiasms of the
militant suffrage movement, and the occasional smashing
of a Downing Street window or an assault upon a minister
kept the question of woman's distinctive intelligence and
character persistently before the public. Godley Buzard,

the feminist novelist, had been the guest of some member to lunch, and the occasion was too provocative for any one about Dover's fireplace to avoid the topic. Buzard's presence, perhaps, drove Dover into an extreme position on the other side ; he forgot Trafford's new-wedded condition, and handled this great argument, an argument which has scarcely progressed since its beginning in the days of Plato and Aristophanes, with the freedoms of an ancient Greek and the explicitness of a modern scientific man.

He opened almost apropos of nothing. " Women," he said, " are inferior—and you can't get away from it."

" You can deny it," said Buzard.

" In the face of the facts," said Sir Roderick. " To begin with, they're several inches shorter, several pounds lighter ; they've less physical strength in foot-pounds."

" More endurance," said Buzard.

" Less sensitiveness merely. All those are demonstrable things—amenable to figures and apparatus. Then they stand nervous tensions worse, the breaking-point comes sooner. They have weaker inhibitions, and inhibition is the test of a creature's position in the mental scale."

He maintained that in the face of Buzard's animated protest. Buzard glanced at their moral qualities. " More moral ! " cried Dover, " more self-restraint ! Not a bit of it ! Their desires and passions are weaker even than their controls ; that's all. Weaken restraints and they show their quality. A drunken woman is far worse than a drunken man. And as for their biological significance——"

" They are the species," said Buzard, " and we are the accidents."

" They are the stolen and we are the individualised branches. They are the stem and we are the fruits. Surely it's better to exist than just transmit existence. And that's a woman's business, though we've fooled and petted most of 'em into forgetting it. . . ."

He proceeded to an attack on the intellectual quality of women. He scoffed at the woman artist, at feminine research, at what he called the joke of feminine philosophy. Buzard broke in with some sentences of reply. He alleged the lack of feminine opportunity, inferior education.

" You don't or won't understand me," said Dover. " It isn't a matter of education or opportunity, or simply that they're of inferior capacity ; it lies deeper than that. They don't *want* to do these things. They're different."

" Precisely," ejaculated Buzard, as if he claimed a score.

" They don't care for these things. They don't care for
art or philosophy, or literature or anything except the
things that touch them directly. That's their peculiar
difference. Hunger they understand, and comfort, and
personal vanity and desire, furs and chocolate and husbands,
and the extreme importance conferred upon them by
having babies at infrequent intervals. But philosophy or
beauty for its own sake, or dreams ! Lord ! no ! The
Mahometans know they haven't souls, and they say it.
We know, and keep it up that they have. Haven't all we
scientific men had 'em in our laboratories working ; don't
we know the papers they turn out ? Every sane man of
five-and-forty knows something of the disillusionment of
the feminine dream, but we who've had the beautiful
creatures under us, weighing rather badly, handling rather
weakly, invariably missing every fine detail and all the
implications of our researches, never flashing, never leaping,
never being even thoroughly bad—we're specialists in the
subject. At the present time there are far more educated
young women than educated young men available for
research work—and who wants them ? Oh, the young
professors who've still got ideals perhaps. And in they
come, and if they're dull, they just voluminously do nothing,
and if they're bright, they either marry your demonstrator
or get him into a mess. And the work—— ? It's nothing
to them. No woman ever painted for the love of painting,
or sang for the sounds she made, or philosophised for the
sake of wisdom as men do——"

Buzard intervened with instances. Dover would have
none of them. He displayed astonishing and distinctive knowledge. " Madame Curie," clamoured Buzard,
" Madame Curie."

" There was Curie," said Dover. " No woman alone
has done such things. I don't say women aren't clever,"
he insisted. " They're too clever. Give them a man's
track or a man's intention marked and defined, they'll ape
him to the life——"

Buzard renewed his protests, talking at the same time
as Dover, and was understood to say that women had to
care for something greater than art or philosophy. They
were custodians of life, the future of the race——

" And that's my crowning disappointment," cried
Dover. " If there was one thing in which you might
think women would show a sense of some divine purpose in
life, it is in the matter of children—and they show about

as much care in that matter, oh !—as rabbits. Yes,
rabbits ! I stick to it. Look at the things a nice girl will
marry ; look at the men's children she'll consent to bring
into the world. Cheerfully ! Proudly ! For the sake of
the home and the clothes. Nasty little beasts they'll breed
without turning a hair. All about us we see girls and
women marrying ugly men, dull and stupid men, ill-
tempered dyspeptic wrecks, sickly young fools, human rats
—*rats* ! "

" No, no ! " cried Trafford to Dover.

Buzard's voice clamoured that all would be different
when women had the vote.

" If ever we get a decent care for Eugenics, it will come
from men," said a white-faced little man on the sofa
beside Trafford, in the confidential tone of one who tells
a secret.

" Doing it cheerfully ! " insisted Dover.

Trafford in mid-protest was suddenly stricken into
silence by a memory. It was as if the past had thrown a
stone at the back of his head and hit it smartly. He
nipped his sentence in the bud. He left the case for women
to Buzard. . . .

He revived that memory again on his way home. It
had been in his mind overlaid by a multitude of newer,
fresher things, but now he took it out and looked at it.
It was queer, it was really very queer, to think that once
upon a time, not so very long ago, Marjorie had been
prepared to marry Magnet. Of course she had hated it.
but still . . .

There is much to be discovered about life, even by a
brilliant and rising young Professor of Physics. . . .

Presently Dover, fingering the little glass of yellow
chartreuse he had hitherto forgotten in the heat of controversy, took a more personal turn.

" Don't we know," he said, and made the limpid amber
vanish in his pause—" don't we know we've got to manage
and control 'em—just as we've got to keep 'em and stand
the racket of their misbehaviour ? Don't our instincts
tell us ? Doesn't something tell us all that if we let a
woman loose with our honour and trust, some other man
will get hold of her ? We've tried it long enough now,
this theory that a woman's a partner and an equal ; we've
tried it long enough to see some of the results, and does it
work ? Does it ? A woman's a prize, a possession, a
responsibility, something to take care of and be careful

about. . . . You chaps, if you'll forgive me, you advanced chaps, seem to want to have the women take care of you. You seem always to want to force decisions on them, make them answerable for things that you ought to decide and answer for. . . . If one could, if one could! If ! . . . But they're not helps—that's a dream—they're distractions, gratifications, anxieties, dangers, undertakings. . . .

Buzard got in his one effective blow at this point. " That's why you've never married, Sir Roderick ? " he threw out.

The big man was checked for a moment. Trafford wondered what memory lit that instant's pause. " I've had my science," said Dover.

§ 5

Mrs. Pope was, of course, among the first to visit the new home so soon as it was open to inspection. She arrived, looking very bright and neat in a new bonnet and some new black furs that suited her, bearing up bravely but obviously in a state of dispersed and miscellaneous emotion. . . .

In many ways Marjorie's marriage had been a great relief to her mother. Particularly it had been a financial relief. Marjorie had been the most expensive child of her family, and her cessation had led to increments both of Mrs. Pope's and Daphne's all too restricted allowances. Mrs. Pope had been able, therefore, to relapse from the orthodox Anglicanism into which poverty had driven her, and indulge for an hour weekly in the consolations of Higher Thought. These exercises in emancipated religiosity occurred at the house of Mr. Silas Root, and were greatly valued by a large circle of clients. Essentially they were orgies of vacuity, and they cost six guineas for seven hours. They did her no end of good. All through the precious weekly hour she sat with him in a silent twilight, very, very still and feeling—oh ! " higher " than anything, and when she came out she wore an inane smile on her face, and was prepared not to worry, to lie with facility, and to take the easiest way in every eventuality in an entirely satisfactory and exalted manner. Moreover, he was " treating " her investments. Acting upon his advice, and doing the whole thing quietly with the idea of preparing a pleasant surprise for her husband, she had sold out of certain Home Railway debentures and invested in a company for working the auriferous waste which is so abundant in the drainage of Philadelphia, a company whose shareholders were chiefly higher-thought disciples, and whose profits therefore would inevitably be greatly enhanced by their concerted mental action. It was to the prospective profits in this that she owed the new black furs she was wearing.

The furs and the bonnet and the previous day's treatment she had had, all helped to brace her up on Marjorie's doorstep for a complex and difficult situation, and to carry her through the first tensions of her call. She was so much to pieces as it was that she could not help feeling how much more to pieces she might have been—but for the grace of Silas Root. She knew she ought to have very strong feelings about Trafford, though it was not really clear to her what feelings she ought to have. On the whole, she was inclined to believe she was experiencing moral disapproval mixed up with a pathetic and rather hopeless appeal for the welfare of the tender life that had entrusted itself so recklessly to these brutal and discreditable hands, though indeed if she had really dared to look inside her mind her chief discovery would have been a keenly jealous appreciation of Trafford's good looks and generous temper, and a feeling of injustice as between her own lot and Marjorie's. However, going on her assumed basis she managed to be very pale, concise, and tight-lipped at any mention of her son-in-law, and to put a fervour of helpless devotion into her embraces of her daughter. She surveyed the house with a pained constrained expression, as though she tried in vain to conceal from herself that it was all slightly improper, and even such objects as the Bokhara hangings failed to extort more than an insincere, " Oh, very nice, dear—*very* nice."

In the bedroom, she spoke about Mr. Pope. " He was dreadfully upset," she said. " His first thought was to come after you both with a pistol. If—if *he* hadn't married you——"

" But, dear Mummy, of *course* we meant to marry ! We married right away."

" Yes, dear, of course. But if he hadn't——"

She paused, and Marjorie, with a momentary flush of indignation in her cheeks, did not urge her to conclude her explanation.

" He's *wounded*," said Mrs. Pope. " Some day, perhaps, he'll come round—you were always his favourite daughter."

"I know," said Marjorie concisely, with a faint flavour of cynicism in her voice.

"I'm afraid, dear, at present—he will do nothing for you."

"I don't think Rag would like him to," said Marjorie, with an unreal serenity ; "*ever*."

"For a time I'm afraid he'll refuse to see you. He just wants to forget——. Everything."

"Poor old Dad! I wish he wouldn't put himself out like this. Still, I won't bother him, Mummy, if you mean that."

Then suddenly into Mrs. Pope's unsystematic, unstable mind, started perhaps by the ring in her daughter's voice, there came a wave of affectionate feeling. That she had somehow to be hostile and unsympathetic to Marjorie, that she had to pretend that Trafford was wicked and disgusting, and not be happy in the jolly hope and happiness of this bright little house, cut her with a keen swift pain. She didn't know clearly why she was taking this coldly hostile attitude, or why she went on doing so, but the sense of that necessity hurt her none the less. She put out her hands upon her daughter's shoulders and whimpered : "Oh, my dear ! I do wish things weren't so difficult —so very difficult."

The whimper changed by some inner force of its own to honest sobs and tears.

Marjorie passed through a flash of amazement to a sudden understanding of her mother's case. "Poor dear Mummy," she said. "Oh ! poor dear Mummy. It's a shame of us ! "

She put her arms about her mother and held her for awhile.

"It *is* a shame," said her mother in a muffled voice, trying to keep hold of this elusive thing that had somehow both wounded her and won her daughter back. But her poor grasp slipped again. "I knew you'd come to see it," she said, dabbing with her handkerchief at her eyes. "I knew you would." And then with the habitual loyalty of years resuming its sway : "He's always been so good to you." . . .

But Mrs. Pope had something more definite to say to Marjorie, and came to it at last with a tactful offhandedness. Marjorie communicated it to Trafford about an hour later on his return from the laboratory. "I say," she said, "old Daffy's engaged to Magnet ! "

She paused, and with just the faintest trace of resentment in her voice, "She can have him, as far as I'm concerned."

"He didn't wait long," said Trafford tactlessly.

"No," said Marjorie; "he didn't wait long. . . . Of course, she got him on the rebound." . . .

§ 6

Mrs. Pope was only a day or so ahead of a cloud of callers. The Carmel girls followed close upon her, tall figures of black fur, with costly-looking muffs and a rich glitter at neck and wrist. Marjorie displayed her house, talking fluently about other things, and watching for effects. The Carmel girls ran their swift dark eyes over her appointments, glanced quickly from side to side of her rooms, saw only too certainly that the house was narrow and small——. But did they see that it was clever? They saw, at any rate, that she meant it to be clever, and with true Oriental politeness said as much urgently and extravagantly. Then there were the Rambord girls and their mother, an unobservant lot who chattered about the ice at Prince's; then Constance Graham came with a thoroughbred but very dirty aunt; and then Ottiline Winchelsea with an American minor poet, who wanted a view of mountains from the windows at the back, and said the bathroom ought to be done in pink. Then Lady Solomonson came; an extremely expensive-looking fair lady with an affectation of cynicism, a keen intelligence, acutely apt conversation, and a queer effect of thinking of something else all the time she was talking. She missed nothing. . . .

Hardly anybody failed to appreciate the charm and decision of Marjorie's use of those Bokhara embroideries. They would have been cheap at double the price.

§ 7

And then our two young people went out to their first dinner-parties together. They began with Trafford's rich friend Solomonson, who had played so large and so passive a part in their first meeting. He had behaved with a sort of magnanimous triumph over the marriage. He made it almost his personal affair, as though he had brought it about. "I knew there was a girl in it," he insisted, "and you told me there wasn't. O-a-ah! And you kept me in that smell of disinfectant and things—what a chap that doctor was for spilling stuff !—for six blessed days ! . . ."

Marjorie achieved a dress at once simple and good with

great facility by not asking the price until it was all over.
(There is no half-success with dinner-dresses, either the
thing is a success and inestimable, or not worth having at
any price at all.)   It was blue with a thread of gold, and
she had a necklace of bluish moonstones, gold-set, and her
hair ceased to be copper and became golden, and her eyes
unfathomable blue.   She was radiant with health and
happiness, no one else there had her clear freshness, and
her manner was as restrained and dignified and ready as a
proud young wife can be.   Every one seemed to like her
and respect her and be interested in her, and Trafford
kissed her flushed cheek in the hansom as they came home
again and crowned her happiness.   It had been quite a
large party, and really much more splendid and brilliant
than anything she had ever seen before.   There had been
one old gentleman with a coloured button and another
with a ribbon ; there had been a countess with historical
pearls, and half a dozen other people one might fairly call
distinguished.   The house was tremendous in its way,
spacious, rich, glowing with lights, abounding in vistas and
fine remote backgrounds.   In the midst of it all she had
a sudden thrill at the memory that less than a year ago
she had been ignominiously dismissed from the dinner-table
by her father for a hiccup. . . .

A few days after Aunt Plessington suddenly asked the
Traffords to one of her less important but still interesting
gatherings ; not one of those that swayed the world perhaps, but one which Marjorie was given to understand
achieved important subordinate wagging.   Aunt Plessington had not called, she explained in her note, because of
the urgent demands the Movement made upon her time ;
it was her wonderful hard-breathing way never to call on
any one, and it added tremendously to her reputation ;
none the less it appeared—though here the scrawl became
illegible—she meant to shove and steer her dear niece upward at a tremendous pace.   They were even asked to come a
little early so that she might make Trafford's acquaintance.

The dress was duly admired, and then Aunt Plessington
—assuming the hearthrug and forgetting the little matter
of their career—explained quite Napoleonic and wonderful
things she was going to do with her Movement, fresh
principles, fresh applications, a big committee of all the
" names "—they were easy to get if you didn't bother
them to do things—a new and more attractive title, " Payment in Kind " was to give way to " Reality of Reward,"

and she herself was going to have her hair bleached bright
white (which would set off her eyes and colour and the
general geniality of appearance due to her projecting
teeth), and so greatly increase her " platform efficiency."
Hubert, she said, was toiling away hard at the detail of
these new endeavours. He would be down in a few minutes'
time. Marjorie, she said, ought to speak at their meetings.
It would help both the Traffords to get on if Marjorie cut
a dash at the outset, and there was no such dash to be cut
as speaking at Aunt Plessington's meetings. It was
catching on ; all next season it was sure to be the thing.
So many promising girls allowed themselves to be submerged altogether in marriage for a time, and when they
emerged every one had forgotten the promise of their
debut. She had an air of rescuing Marjorie from an impending fate by disabusing Trafford from injurious
prepossessions. . . .

Presently the guests began to drop in, a vegetarian
health specialist, a rising young woman factory inspector,
a phrenologist who was being induced to put great talents
to better uses under Aunt Plessington's influence, his
dumb, obscure, but inevitable wife, a colonial bishop, a
baroness with a taste rather than a capacity for intellectual
society, a wealthy jam and pickle manufacturer and his
wife, who had subscribed largely to the funds of the Movement and wanted to meet the lady of title, and the editor
of the Movement's organ, *Upward and On*, a young gentleman of abundant hair and cadaverous silences, whom
Aunt Plessington patted on the shoulder and spoke of as
" one of our discoveries." And then Uncle Hubert came
down, looking ruffled and overworked, with his ready-made
dress-tie—he was one of those men who can never master
the art of tying a bow—very much askew. The conversation turned chiefly on the Movement ; if it strayed Aunt
Plessington reached out her voice after it and brought it
back in a masterful manner.

Through soup and fish Marjorie occupied herself with
the inflexible rigour of the young editor, who had brought
her down. When she could give her attention to the
general conversation she discovered her husband a little
flushed and tackling her aunt with an expression of quiet
determination. The phrenologist and the vegetarian
health specialist were regarding him with amazement, the
jam and pickle manufacturer's wife was evidently deeply
shocked. He was refusing to believe in the value of the

Movement, and Aunt Plessington was manifestly losing her temper.

"I don't see, Mrs. Plessington," he was saying, "that all this amounts to more than a kind of Glorious District Visiting. That is how I see it. You want to attack people in their homes—before they cry out to you. You want to compel them by this Payment in Kind of yours to do what you want them to do instead of trying to make them want to do it. Now, I think your business is to make them want to do it. You may perhaps increase the amount of milk in babies, and the amount of whitewash in cottages and slums by your methods—I don't dispute the promise of your statistics—but you're going to do it at a cost of human self-respect that's out of all proportion——"

Uncle Hubert's voice, with that thick utterance that always suggested a mouthful of plums, came booming down the table. "All these arguments," he said, "have been answered along ago."

"No doubt," said Trafford, with a faint asperity. "But tell me the answers."

"It's ridiculous," said Aunt Plessington, "to talk of the self-respect of the kind of people—oh! the very dregs!"

"It's just because the plant is delicate that you've got to handle it carefully," said Trafford.

"Here's Miss Gant," said Aunt Plessington, "*she* knows the strata we are discussing. She'll tell you they have positively *no* self-respect—none at all."

"*My* people," said Miss Gant, as if in conclusive testimony, "actually conspire with their employers to defeat me."

"I don't see the absence of self-respect in that," said Trafford.

"But all their interests——"

"I'm thinking of their pride." . . .

The discussion lasted to the end of dinner and made no headway. As soon as the ladies were in the drawing-room, Aunt Plessington, a little flushed from the conflict, turned on Marjorie and said, "I *like* your husband. He's wrong-headed, but he's young, and he's certainly spirited. He *ought* to get on if he wants to. Does he do nothing but his researches?"

"He lectures in the Spring Term," said Marjorie.

"Ah!" said Aunt Plessington with a triumphant note: "you must alter all that. You must interest him in wider things. You must bring him out of his shell, and let him

see what it is to deal with Affairs. Then he wouldn't talk
such nonsense about our Work."

Marjorie was at a momentary loss for a reply, and in the
instant's respite Aunt Plessington turned to the jam and
pickle lady and asked in a bright, encouraging note :
" Well ! And how's the Village Club getting on ? " . . .

She had another lunge at Trafford as he took his leave.
" You must come again soon," she said. " I *love* a good
wrangle, and Hubert and I never want to talk about our
Movement to any one but unbelievers. You don't know
the beginnings of it yet. Only I warn you they have a
way of getting converted. I warn you." . . .

On this occasion there was no kissing in the cab.
Trafford was exasperated.

" Of all the intolerable women ! " he said, and was
silent for a time.

" The astounding part of it is," he burst out, " that
this sort of thing, this Movement and all the rest of it,
does really give the quality of English public affairs. It's
like a sample—dredged. The—the *cheapness* of it !
Raised voices, rash assertions, sham investigations, meetings and committees and meetings, that's the stuff of it,
and politicians really have to attend to it, and silly,
ineffective, irritating bills really get drafted and messsed
about with and passed on the strength of it. Public affairs
are still in the Dark Ages. Nobody now would think of
getting together a scratch committee of rich old women
and miscellaneous conspicuous people to design an electric
tram, and jabbering and jabbering and jabbering, and if
any one objects "—a note of personal bitterness came
into his voice—" jabbering faster ; but nobody thinks
it ridiculous to attempt the organisation of poor people's
affairs in that sort of way. This project of the supersession
of Wages by Payment in Kind—oh ! it's childish. If it
wasn't it would be outrageous and indecent. Your uncle
and aunt haven't thought for a moment of any single one
of the necessary consequences of these things they say
their confounded Movement aims at, effects upon the race,
upon public spirit, upon people's habits and motives.
They've just a queer craving to feel powerful and influential,
which they think they can best satisfy by upsetting the
lives of no end of harmless poor people—the only people
they dare upset—and that's about as far as they go. . . .
Your aunt's detestable, Marjorie."

Marjorie had never seen him so deeply affected by

anything but herself. It seemed to her he was needlessly disturbed by a trivial matter. He sulked for a space, and then broke out again.

"That confounded woman talks of my physical science," he said, "as if research were an amiable weakness, like collecting postage stamps. And it's changed human conditions more in the last ten years than all the parliamentary wire-pullers and legislators and administrative experts have done in two centuries. And for all that, there's more clerks in Whitehall than professors of physics in the whole of England. . . ."

"I suppose it's the way that sort of thing gets done," said Marjorie, after an interval.

"That sort of thing doesn't get done," snapped Trafford. "All these people burble about with their movements and jobs and lectures and stuff—and *things happen*. Like some one getting squashed to death in a crowd. Nobody did it, but anybody in the muddle can claim to have done it—if only they've got the cheek of your Aunt Plessington."

He seemed to have finished.

"*Done !*" he suddenly broke out again. "Why ! people like your Aunt Plessington don't even know where the handle is. If they ventured to look for it, they'd give the whole show away ! Done, indeed ! "

"Here we are ! " said Marjorie, a little relieved to find the hansom turning out of King's Road into their own side street. . . .

And then Marjorie wore the blue dress with great success at the Carmels'. The girls came and looked at it and admired it—it was no mere politeness. They admitted there was style about it, a quality—there was no explaining. "You're *wonderful*, Madge ! " cried the younger Carmel girl.

The Carmel boy, seizing the opportunity of a momentary seclusion in a corner, ended a short but rather portentous silence with, "I say, you *do* look ripping," in a voice that implied the keenest regret for the slacknesses of a summer that was now infinitely remote to Marjorie. It was ridiculous that the Carmel boy should have such emotions—he was six years younger than Trafford and only a year older than Marjorie, and yet she was pleased by his manifest wound. . . .

There was only one little thing at the back of her mind that alloyed her sense of happy and complete living that night, and that was the ghost of an addition sum. At home, in her pretty bureau, a little gathering pile of bills, as yet unpaid, and an empty cheque-book with appealing counterfoils, awaited her attention.

Marjorie had still to master the fact that all the fine braveries and interests and delights of life that offer themselves so amply to the favoured children of civilisation, trail, and, since the fall of man at any rate, have trailed after them something—something, the justification of morality, the despair of all easy, happy souls, the unavoidable drop of bitterness in the cup of pleasure—the Reckoning.

CHAPTER THE SECOND

THE CHILD OF THE AGES

§ 1

WHEN the intellectual history of this time comes to be written, nothing I think will stand out more strikingly than the empty gulf in quality between the superb and richly fruitful scientific investigations that are going on and the general thought of other educated sections of the community. I do not mean that the scientific men are, as a whole, a class of supermen, dealing with and thinking about everything in a way altogether better than the common run of humanity, but that in their own field, they think and work with an intensity, an integrity, a breadth, boldness, patience, thoroughness and faithfulness that (excepting only a few artists) puts their work out of all comparison with any other human activity. Often the field in which the work is done is very narrow, and almost universally the underlying philosophy is felt rather than apprehended. A scientific man may be large and deep-minded, deliberate and personally detached in his work, and hasty, commonplace, and superficial in every other relation of life. Nevertheless it is true that in these particular directions the human mind has achieved a new and higher quality of attitude and gesture, a veracity, self-detachment, and self-abnegating vigour of criticism that tend to spread out and must ultimately spread out to every other human affair. In these uncontroversial issues at least mankind has learnt the rich rewards that ensue from patience and infinite pains.

The peculiar circumstances of Trafford's birth and upbringing had accentuated his natural disposition toward this new thoroughness of intellectual treatment which has always distinguished the great artist, and which to-day is also the essential quality of the scientific method. He had lived apart from any urgency to produce and compete in the common business of the world ; his natural curiosities, fed and encouraged by his natural gifts, had grown into a steady passion for clarity and knowledge. But with him there was no specialisation. He brought out from his laboratory into the everyday affairs of the world the same sceptical restraint of judgment which is the touchstone of scientific truth. This made him a tepid and indeed rather a scornful spectator of political and social life. Party formulæ, international rivalries, social customs, and very much of the ordinary law of our state impressed him as a kind of fungoid growth out of a fundamental intellectual muddle. It all maintained itself hazardously, changing and adapting itself unintelligently to unseen conditions. He saw no ultimate truth in this seething welter of human efforts, no tragedy as yet in its defeats, no value in its victories. It had to go on, he believed, until the spreading certitudes of the scientific method pierced its unsubstantial thickets, burst its delusive films, drained away its folly. Aunt Plessington's talk of order and progress and the influence of her Movement impressed his mind very much as the cackle of some larger kind of hen—which cackles because it must. Only Aunt Plessington being human simply imagined the egg. She laid— on the plane of the ideal. When the great nonsensical issues between liberal and conservative, between socialist and individualist, between " Anglo-Saxon " and " Teuton," between the " white race " and the " yellow race " arose in Trafford's company, he would if he felt cheerful take one side or the other as chance or his amusement with his inter- locutors determined, and jest and give at the opponent's inconsistencies, and if on the other hand he chanced to be irritable he would lose his temper at this " chewing of mesembryanthemum " and sulk into silence. " Chewing mesembryanthemum " was one of Trafford's favourite images—no doubt the reader knows that abundant fleshy Mediterranean weed and the weakly unpleasant wateriness of its substance. He went back to his laboratory and his proper work after such discussions with a feeling of escape, as if he shut a door upon a dirty and undisciplined market- place crowded with mental defectives. Yet even before he met and married Marjorie, there was a queer little undertow of thought in his mind which insisted that this business could not end with door-slamming, that he didn't altogether leave the social confusion outside his panels when he stood alone before his apparatus, and that sooner or later that babble of voices would force his defences and overcome his disdain.

His particular work upon the intimate constitution of matter had broadened very rapidly in his hands. The drift of his work had been to identify all colloids as liquid solutions of variable degrees of viscosity, and to treat crystalline bodies as the only solids. He had dealt with oscillating processes in colloid bodies with especial reference to living matter. He had passed from a study of the melting and toughening of glass to the molecular structure of a number of elastic bodies, and, so, by a characteristic leap into botanical physiology, to the states of resinous and gummy substances at the moment of secretion. He worked at first upon a false start, and then resumed to discover a growing illumination. He found himself in the presence of phenomena that seemed to him to lie near the still un-discovered threshold to the secret processes of living proto-plasm. He was, as it were, breaking into biology by way of molecular physics. He spent many long nights of deep excitement, calculating and arranging the development of these seductive intimations. It was this work which his marriage had interrupted, and to which he was now returning.

He was surprised to find how difficult it was to take it up again. He had been only two months away from it, and yet already it had not a little of the feeling of a relic taken from a drawer. Something had faded. It was at first as if a film had come over his eyes, so that he could no longer see these things clearly and subtly and closely. His senses, his emotions, had been living in a stirring and vivid illumination. Now in this cool quietude bright clouds of coloured memory-stuff swam distractingly before his eyes. Phantom kisses on his lips, the memory of touches and the echoing vibrations of an adorable voice, the thought of a gay delightful fireside and the fresh recollection of a companion intensely felt beside him, effaced the delicate profundities of this dim place. Durgan hovered about him, helpful and a mute reproach. Trafford had to force his attention daily for the better part of two weeks before he had fully recovered the fine enchanting interest of that suspended work.

§ 2

At last one day he had the happiness of possession again. He had exactly the sensation one gets when some hitherto intractable piece of a machine one is putting together, clicks neatly and beyond all hoping, into its place. He found himself working in the old style, with the hours slipping by disregarded. He sent out Durgan to get him tobacco and tea and smoked-salmon sandwiches, and he stayed in the laboratory all night. He went home about half-past five, and found a white-faced, red-eyed Marjorie still dressed, wrapped in a travelling-rug, and crumpled and asleep in his study arm-chair beside the gray ashes of an extinct fire.

In the instant before she awoke he could see what a fragile and pitiful being a healthy and happy young wife can appear. Her pose revealed an unsuspected slender weakness of body, her face something infantile and wistful he had still to reckon with. She awoke with a start and stared at him for a moment, and at the room about her. " Oh, where have you been ? " she asked almost querulously. " Where *have* you been ? "

" But, my dear ! " he said, as one might speak to a child, " why aren't you in bed ? It's just dawn."

" Oh," she said, " I waited and I waited. It seemed you *must* come. I read a book. And then I fell asleep." And then with a sob of feeble self-pity, " And here I am ! " She rubbed the back of her hand into one eye and shivered. " I'm cold," she said, " and I want some tea."

" Let's make some," said Trafford.

" It's been horrible waiting," said Marjorie, without moving ; " horrible ! Where have you been ? "

" I've been working. I got excited by my work. I've been at the laboratory. I've had the best spell of work I've ever had since our marriage."

"But I have been up all night !" she cried, with her face and voice softening to tears. "How *could* you ? How *could* you ?"

He was surprised by her weeping. He was still more surprised by the self-abandonment that allowed her to continue. " I've been working," he repeated, and then looked about him with a man's helplessness for the tea apparatus. One must have hot water and a teapot and a kettle ; he would find those in the kitchen. He strolled thoughtfully out of the room, thinking out the further details of tea-making all mixed up with amazement at Marjorie, while she sat wiping her eyes with a crumpled

pocket-handkerchief. Presently she followed him down
with the rug about her like a shawl, and stood watching
him as he lit a fire of wood and paper among the ashes in
the kitchen fireplace. " It's been dreadful," she said, not
offering to help.

" You see," he said, on his knees, " I'd really got hold
of my work at last."

" But you should have sent——"

" I was thinking of my work. I clean forgot."

" Forgot ? "

" Absolutely."

" Forgot—*me* ! "

" Of course," said Trafford, with a slightly puzzled air ;
" you don't see it as I do."

The kettle engaged him for a time. Then he threw out
a suggestion. " We'll have to have a telephone."

" I couldn't imagine where you were. I thought of all
sorts of things. I almost came round—but I was so
horribly afraid I mightn't find you."

He renewed his suggestion of a telephone.

" So that if I really want you——" said Marjorie. " Or
if I just want to feel you're there."

" Yes," said Trafford slowly, jabbing a piece of firewood
into the glow ; but it was chiefly present in his mind that much
of that elaborate experimenting of his wasn't at all
a thing to be cut athwart by the exasperating gusts of a
telephone bell clamouring for attention. Hitherto the
laboratory telephone had been in the habit of disconnecting
itself early in the afternoon.

And yet after all it was this instrument, the same
twisted wire and little quivering tympanum, that had
brought back Marjorie into his life.

§ 3

And now Trafford fell into a great perplexity of mind.
His banker had called his attention to the fact that his
account was overdrawn to the extent of three hundred and
thirteen pounds, and he had been under that vague sort of
impression one always has about one's current account
that he was a hundred and fifty or so to the good. His
first impression was that those hitherto infallible beings,
those unseen gnomes of the pass-book whose lucid figures
neat tickings, and unrelenting additions constituted banks
to his imagination, must have made a mistake ; his second

that some one had tampered with a cheque. His third thought pointed to Marjorie and the easy circumstances of his home. For a fortnight now she had been obviously ailing, oddly irritable ; he did not understand the change in her, but it sufficed to prevent his taking the thing to her at once and going into it with her as he would have done earlier. Instead he had sent for his pass-book, and in the presence of its neat columns realised for the first time the meaning of Marjorie's " three hundred pounds." Including half a dozen cheques to Oxbridge tradesmen for her old debts, she had spent, he discovered, nearly seven hundred and fifty.

He sat before the little bundle of crumpled strips of pink and white, perforated, purple stamped, and effaced, in a state of extreme astonishment. It was no small factor in his amazement to note how very carelessly some of those cheques of Marjorie's had been written. Several she had not even crossed. The effect of it all was that she'd just spent his money—freely—with an utter disregard of the consequences.

Up to that moment it had never occurred to Trafford that anybody one really cared for could be anything but punctilious about money. Now here, with an arithmetical exactitude of demonstration, he perceived that Marjorie wasn't.

It was so tremendous a discovery for him, so disconcerting and startling, that he didn't for two days say a word to her about it. He couldn't think of a word to say. He felt that even to put these facts before her amounted to an accusation of disloyalty and selfishness that he hadn't the courage to make. His work stopped altogether. He struggled hourly with that accusation. Did she realise——? There seemed no escape from his dilemma ; either she didn't care or she didn't understand !

His thoughts went back to the lake of Orta, when he had put all his money at her disposal. She had been surprised, and now he perceived she had also been a little frightened. The chief excuse he could find for her was that she was inexperienced—absolutely inexperienced.

Even now, of course, she was drawing fresh cheques. . . .

He would have to pull himself together, and go into the whole thing—for all its infinite disagreeableness—with her. . . .

But it was Marjorie who broached the subject.

He had found work at the laboratory unsatisfactory, and after lunching at his club he had come home and gone to his study in order to think out the discussion he contemplated with her. She came in to him as he sat at his

desk. " Busy ? " she said. " Not very," he answered ;
and she came up to him, kissed his head, and stood beside
him with her hand on his shoulder.

" Pass-book ? " she asked.

He nodded.

" I've been overrunning."

" No end."

The matter was opened. What would she say ?

She bent to his ear and whispered, " I'm going to over-
run some more."

His voice was resentful. " You *can't*," he said compactly without looking at her. " You've spent—enough."

" There's—things."

" What things ? "

Her answer took some time in coming. " We'll have to
give a wedding present to Daffy. . . I shall want—some
more furniture."

Well, he had to go into it now. " I don't think you can
have it," he said, and then as she remained silent,
" Marjorie, do you know how much money I've got ? ',

" Six thousand."

" I *had*. But we've spent nearly a thousand pounds.
Yes—one thousand pounds—over and above income. We
meant to spend four hundred. And now, we've got—
hardly anything over five."

" Five thousand," said Marjorie.

" Five thousand."

" And there's your salary."

" Yes, but at this pace——"

" Dear," said Marjorie, and her hands came about his
neck, " dear—there's something——"

She broke off. An unfamiliar quality in her voice struck
into him. He turned his head to see her face, rose to his
feet, staring at her.

This remarkable young woman had become soft and
wonderful as April hills across which clouds are sweeping.
Her face was as if he had never seen it before ; her eyes
bright with tears.

" Oh ! don't let's spoil things by thinking of money,"
she said. " I've got something——" Her voice fell to
a whisper. Don't let's spoil things by thinking of
money. . . . It's too good, dear, to be true. It's too
good to be true. It makes everything perfect. . . .
We'll have to furnish that little room. I didn't dare to
hope it—somehow. I've been so excited and afraid. But

we've got to furnish that little room there—that empty little
room upstairs, dear, that we left over. . . . Oh, my *dear* !
my *dear* ! "

§ 4

The world of Trafford and Marjorie was filled and transfigured by the advent of their child.

For two days of abundant silences he had been preparing
a statement of his case for her, he had been full of the
danger to his research and all the waste of his life that her
extravagance threatened. He wanted to tell her just all
that his science meant to him, explain how his income and
life had all been arranged to leave him, mind and time
and energy, free for these commanding investigations. His
life was to him the service of knowledge—or futility. He
had perceived that she did not understand this in him ;
that for her, life was a blaze of eagerly sought experiences
and gratifications. So far he had thought out things and
had them ready for her. But now all this impending discussion vanished out of his world. Their love was to be
crowned by the miracle of parentage. This fact flooded
his outlook and submerged every other consideration.

This manifest probability came to him as if it were an
unforeseen marvel. It was as if he had never thought of
such a thing before, as though a fact entirely novel in the
order of the universe had come into existence. Marjorie
became again magical and wonderful for him, but in a
manner new and strange, she was grave, solemn, significant. He was filled with a passionate solicitude for her
welfare, and a passionate desire to serve her. It seemed
impossible to him that only a day or so ago he should have
been accusing her in his heart of disloyalty, and searching
for excuses and mitigations. . . .

All the freshness of his first love for Marjorie returned,
his keen sense of the sweet gallantry of her voice and bearing, his admiration for the swift, falcon-like swoop of her
decisions, for the grace and poise of her body, and the
steady frankness of her eyes ; but now it was all charged
with his sense of this new joint life germinating at the heart
of her slender vigour, spreading throughout her being to
change it altogether into womanhood for ever. In this
new light his passion for research and all the scheme of his
life appeared faded and unworthy, as much egotism as if
he had been devoted to hunting or golf or any such aimless
preoccupation. Fatherhood gripped him and faced him

about. It was manifestly a monstrous thing that he should ever have expected Marjorie to become a mere undisturbing accessory to the selfish intellectualism of his career, to shave and limit herself to a mere bachelor income, and play no part of her own in the movement of the world. He knew better now. Research must fall into its proper place, and for his immediate business he must set to work to supplement his manifestly inadequate resources.

At first he could form no plan at all for doing that. He determined that research must still have his morning hours until lunch-time, and, he privately resolved, some part of the night. The rest of his day, he thought, he would set aside for a time to money-making. But he was altogether inexperienced in the methods of money-making ; it was a new problem, and a new sort of problem to him altogether. He discovered himself helpless and rather silly in the matter. The more obvious possibilities seemed to be that he might lecture upon his science or write. He communicated with a couple of lecture agencies, and was amazed at their scepticism : no doubt he knew his science, on that point they were complimentary in a profuse, unconvincing manner, but could he interest like X—and here they named a notorious quack—could he *draw* ? He offered Science Notes to a weekly periodical ; the editor answered that for the purposes of his publication he preferred, as between professors and journalists, journalists. " You real scientific men," he said, " are no doubt a thousand times more accurate and novel and all that, but as no one seems able to understand you——" He went to his old fellow-student, Gwenn, who was editing *The Scientific Review*, and through him he secured some semi-popular lectures, which involved, he found, travelling about twenty-nine miles weekly at the rate of four-and-sixpence a mile—counting nothing for the lectures. Afterwards Gwenn arranged for some regular notes on physics and micro-chemistry. Trafford made out a weekly time-table, on whose white of dignity, leisure, and the honourable pursuit of knowledge, a diaper of red marked the claims of domestic necessity.

§ 5

It was astonishing how completely this coming child dominated the whole atmosphere and all the circumstances of the Traffords. It became their central fact, to which everything else turned and pointed. Its effect on Marjorie's circle of school and college friends was prodigious. She was the first of their company to cross the mysterious boundaries of a woman's life. She became to them a heroine mingled with something of the priestess. They called upon her more abundantly and sat with her, noted the change in her eyes and voice and bearing, talking with a kind of awe and a faint diffidence of the promised new life.

Many of them had been deeply tinged by the woman's suffrage movement, the feminist note was strong among them, and when one afternoon Ottiline Winchelsea brought round Agatha Alimony, the novelist, and Agatha said in that deep-ringing voice of hers : " I hope it will be a girl, so that presently she may fight the battle of her sex," there was the profoundest emotion. But when Marjorie conveyed that to Trafford he was lacking in response.

" I want a boy," he said, and, being pressed for a reason, explained : " Oh, one likes to have a boy. I want him with just your quick eyes and ears, my dear, and just my own safe and certain hands."

Mrs. Pope received the news with that depth and aimless complexity of emotion which had now become her habitual method with Marjorie. She kissed and clasped her daughter, and thought confusedly over her shoulder, and said : " Of course, dear—— Oh, I *do* so hope it won't annoy your father." Daffy was " nice," but vague, and sufficiently feminist to wish it a daughter, and the pseudo-twins said " *Hoo*-ray ! " and changed the subject at the earliest possible opportunity. But Theodore was deeply moved at the prospect of becoming an uncle, and went apart and mused deeply and darkly thereon for some time. It was difficult to tell just what Trafford's mother thought ; she was complex and subtle, and evidently did not show Marjorie all that was in her mind ; but at any rate it was clear the prospect of a grandchild pleased and interested her. And about Aunt Plessington's views there was no manner of doubt at all. She thought, and remarked judicially, as one might criticise a game of billiards, that on the whole it was just a little bit too soon.

§ 6

Marjorie kept well throughout March and April, and then suddenly she grew unutterably weary and uncomfortable in London. The end of April came hot and close and dry—it might have been July for the heat—the scrap of garden wilted, and the streets were irritating with fine dust and blown scraps of paper and drifting straws, she could think of nothing but the shade of trees, and corn-fields under sunlight and the shadows of passing clouds. So Trafford took out an old bicycle and wandered over the home counties for three days, and at last hit upon a little country cottage near Great Missenden, a cottage a couple of girl artists had furnished and now wanted to let. It had a long, untidy vegetable garden and a small orchard and drying-ground, with an old, superannuated humbug of a pear-tree near the centre surrounded by a green seat, and high hedges with the promise of honeysuckle and dog-roses, and gaps that opened into hospitable beech-woods—woods not so thick but that there were glades of bluebells, bracken, and, to be exact, in places embattled stinging-nettles. He took it and engaged a minute, active, interested, philoprogenitive servant girl for it, and took Marjorie thither in a taxi-cab. She went out, wrapped in a shawl, and sat under the pear-tree and cried quietly with weakness and sentiment and the tenderness of afternoon sunshine, and forthwith began to pick up wonderfully, and was presently writing to Trafford to buy her a dog to go for walks with, while he was away in London.

Trafford was still struggling along with his research in spite of a constant gravitation to the cottage and Marjorie's side, but he was also doing his best to grapple with the difficulties of his financial situation. His science notes, which were very uncongenial and difficult to do, and his lecturing, still left his income far behind his expenditure, and the problem of minimising the inevitable fresh inroads on his capital was insistent and distracting. He discovered that he could manage his notes more easily and write a more popular article if he dictated to a typist instead of writing out the stuff in his own manuscript. Dictating made his sentences more copious and open, and the effect of the young lady's by no means acquiescent back was to make him far more explicit than he tended to be pen in hand. With a pen and alone he felt the boredom of the job unendurably, and, to be through with it, became more and more terse, allusive, and compactly technical, after the style of his original papers. One or two articles by him were accepted and published by the monthly magazines, but as he took what the editors sent him, he did not find this led to any excessive opulence. . . .

But his heart was very much with Marjorie through all

this time. Hitherto he had taken her health and vigour
and companionship for granted, and it changed his attitudes
profoundly to find her now an ailing thing, making an
invincible appeal for restraint and consideration and help.
She changed marvellously, she gained a new dignity, and
her complexion took upon itself a fresh, soft beauty. He
would spend three or four days out of a week at the cottage,
and long hours of that would be at her side, paper and notes
of some forthcoming lecture at hand neglected, talking to
her consolingly and dreamingly. His thoughts were full
of ideas about education ; he was obsessed, as are most
intelligent young parents of the modern type, by the
enormous possibilities of human improvement that might
be achieved—if only one could begin with a baby from the
outset, on the best lines, with the best methods, training
and preparing it—presumably for a cleaned and chastened
world. Indeed, he made all the usual discoveries of intelligent modern young parents very rapidly, fully and
completely, and overlooked most of those practical difficulties that finally reduce them to human dimensions again
in quite the normal fashion.

"I sit and muse sometimes when I ought to be com-
puting," he said. "Old Durgan watches me and grunts.
But think, if we take reasonable care, watch its phases,
stand ready with a kindergarten toy directly it stretches
out its hand—think what we can make of it ! " . .

"We will make it the most wonderful child in the world,"
said Marjorie. "Indeed what else can it be ? "

"Your eyes," said Trafford, "and my hands."

" A girl."

" A boy."

He kissed her white and passive wrist.

§ 7

The child was born a little before expectation at the
cottage throughout a long summer's night and day in early
September. Its coming into the world was a long and
painful struggle ; the general practitioner who had seemed
two days before a competent and worthy person enough,
revealed himself as hesitating, old-fashioned, and ill-
equipped. He had a lingering theological objection to the
use of chloroform, and the nurse from London sulked under
his directions and came and discussed his methods scorn-
fully with Trafford. From sundown until daylight Trafford

chafed in the little sitting-room and tried to sleep, and hovered listening at the foot of the narrow staircase to the room above. He lived through interminable hours of moaning and suspense. . . .

The dawn and sunrise came with a quality of beautiful horror. For years afterwards that memory stood out among other memories as something peculiarly strange and dreadful. Day followed an interminable night and broke slowly. Things crept out of darkness, awoke, as it were, out of mysteries and reclothed themselves in unsubstantial shadows and faint-hued forms. All through that slow infiltration of the world with light and then with colour, the universe it seemed was moaning and endeavouring; and a weak and terrible struggle went on and kept on in that forbidden room whose windows opened upon the lightening world, dying to a sobbing silence, rising again to agonising cries, fluctuating, a perpetual obstinate failure to achieve a tormenting end. He went out, and behold the sky was a wonder of pink-flushed level clouds and golden hope, and nearly ever star except the morning star had gone, the supine moon was pale and half-dissolved in blue, and the grass which had been gray and wet, was green again, and the bushes and trees were green. He returned and hovered in the passage, washed his face, listened outside the door for age-long moments, and then went out again to listen under the window. . . .

He went to his room and shaved, sat for a long time thinking, and then suddenly knelt by his bed and prayed. He had never prayed before in all his life. . . .

He returned to the garden, and there neglected and wet with dew was the camp-chair Marjorie had sat on the evening before, the shawl she had been wearing, the novel she had been reading. He brought these things in as if they were precious treasures. . . .

Light was pouring into the world again now. He noticed with an extreme particularity the detailed dewy delicacy of grass and twig, the silver edges to the leaves of briar and nettle, the soft clearness of the moss on bank and wall. He noted the woods with the first warmth of autumn tinting their green, the clear, calm sky, with just a wisp or so of purple cloud waning to a luminous pink on the brightening east, the exquisite freshness of the air. And still through the open window, incessant, unbearable, came this sound of Marjorie moaning, now dying away, now reviving, now weakening again. . . .

Was she dying ?   Were they murdering her ?   It was
incredible this torture could go on.   Somehow it must end.
Chiefly he wanted to go in and kill the doctor.   But it
would do no good to kill the doctor !

At last the nurse came out, looking a little scared, to
ask him to cycle three miles away and borrow some special
sort of needle that the fool of a doctor had forgotten.   He
went, outwardly meek, and returning was met by the little
interested servant, very alert and excited and rather
superior—for here was something no man can do—with
the news that he had a beautiful little daughter, and that
all was well with Marjorie.

He said, " Thank God, thank God ! " several times, and
then went out into the kitchen and began to eat some
flabby toast and drink some lukewarm tea he found there.
He was horribly fatigued.   " Is she all right ? " he asked
over his shoulder, hearing the doctor's footsteps on the
stairs. . . .

They were very pontifical and official with him.

Presently they brought out a strange, wizened little
animal, wailing very stoutly, with a face like a very, very
old woman, and reddish skin and hair—it had quite a lot
of wet blackish hair of an incredible delicacy of texture.
It kicked with a stumpy monkey's legs and inturned feet.
He held it ;   his heart went out to it.   He pitied it beyond
measure, it was so weak and ugly.   He was astonished and
distressed by the fact of its extreme endearing ugliness.
He had expected something strikingly pretty.   It clenched
a fist, and he perceived it had all its complement of fingers,
and ridiculous, pretentious little finger-nails.   Inside that
fist it squeezed his heart. . . . He did not want to give it
back to them.   He wanted to protect it.   He felt they
could not understand it or forgive, as he could forgive, its
unjustifiable feebleness. . . .

Later, for just a little while, he was permitted to see
Marjorie—Marjorie so spent, so unspeakably weary, and
yet so reasssuringly vital and living, so full of gentle pride
and gentler courage amidst the litter of surgical precaution,
that the tears came streaming down his face and he sobbed
shamelessly as he kissed her.   " Little daughter," she
whispered and smiled—just as she had always smiled—
that sweet, dear smile of hers !—and closed her eyes and
said no more. . . .

Afterwards as he walked up and down the garden he
remembered their former dispute, and thought how

characteristic of Marjorie it was to have a daughter in spite of all his wishes.

§ 8

For weeks and weeks this astonishing and unprecedented being filled the Trafford's earth and sky. Very speedily its minute quaintness passed, and it became a vigorous delightful baby that was, as the nurse explained repeatedly and very explicitly, not only quite exceptional and distinguished, but exactly everything that a baby should be. Its weight became of supreme importance ; there was a splendid week when it put on nine ounces, and an indifferent one when it added only one. And then came a terrible crisis. It was ill ; some sort of infection had reached it, an infantile cholera. Its temperature mounted to a hundred and three and a half. It became a flushed misery, wailing with a pathetic feeble voice. Then it ceased to wail. Marjorie became white-lipped and heavy-eyed from want of sleep, and it seemed to Trafford that perhaps his child might die. It seemed to him that the spirit of the universe must be a monstrous Caliban, since children had to die. He went for a long walk through the October beech-woods, under a windy sky and in a drift of falling leaves, wondering with a renewed freshness at the haunting futilities of life. Life was not futile—anything but that, but futility seemed to be stalking it, waiting for it. . . . When he returned the child was already better, and in a few days it was well again—but very light and thin.

When they were sure of its safety, Marjorie and he confessed the extremity of their fears to one another. They had not dared to speak before, and even now they spoke in undertones of the shadow that had hovered and passed over the dearest thing in their lives.

CHAPTER THE THIRD

THE NEW PHASE

§ 1

IN the course of the next six months the child of the ages became an almost ordinary healthy baby, and Trafford began to think consecutively about his scientific work again—in the intervals of effort of a more immediately practical sort.

The recall of molecular physics and particularly of the internal condition of colloids to something like their old importance in his life was greatly accelerated by the fact that a young Oxford don named Behrens was showing extraordinary energy in what had been for a time Trafford's distinctive and undisputed field. Behrens was one of those vividly clever energetic people who are the despair of originative men. He had begun as Trafford's pupil and sedulous ape; he had gone on to work that imitated Trafford's in everything except its continual freshness, and now he was ransacking every scrap of suggestion to be found in Trafford's work, and developing it with an intensity of uninspired intelligence that most marvellously simulated originality. He was already being noted as an authority; sometimes in an article his name would be quoted and Trafford's omitted in relation to Trafford's ideas, and in every way his emergence and the manner of his emergence threatened and stimulated his model and master. A great effort had to be made. Trafford revived the drooping spirits of Durgan by a renewed punctuality in the laboratory. He began to stay away from home at night and work late again, now, however, under no imperative inspiration, but simply because it was only by such an invasion of the evening and night that it would be possible to make headway against Behrens's unremitting industry. And this new demand upon Trafford's already strained mental and nervous equipment began very speedily to have its effect upon his domestic life.

It is only in romantic fiction that a man can work strenuously to the limit of his power and come home to be sweet, sunny, and entertaining. Trafford's preoccupation involved a certain negligence of Marjorie, a certain indisposition to be amused or interested by trifling things, a certain irritability. . . .

§ 2

And now, indeed, the Traffords were coming to the most difficult and fatal phase in marriage. They had had that taste of defiant adventure which is the crown of a spirited love affair, they had known the sweetness of a maiden passion for a maid, and they had felt all those rich and solemn emotions, those splendid fears and terrible hopes that weave themselves about the great partnership in parentage. And now, so far as sex was concerned, there might be much joy and delight still, but no more wonder, no fresh discoveries of incredible new worlds and unsuspected stars. Love, which had been a new garden, an unknown land, a sunlit sea to launch upon, was now a rich treasure-house of memories. And memories, although they afford a perpetually increasing enrichment to emotion, are not sufficient in themselves for the daily needs of life.

For this, indeed, is the truth of passionate love, that it works out its purpose and comes to an end. A day arrives in every marriage when the lovers must face each other, disillusioned, stripped of the last shred of excitement—undisguisedly themselves. And our two were married; they had bound themselves together under a penalty of scandalous disgrace, to take the life-long consequences of their passionate association.

It was upon Trafford that this exhaustion of the sustaining magic of love pressed most severely, because it was he who had made the greatest adaptations to the exigencies of their union. He had crippled, he perceived more and more clearly, the research work upon which his whole being had once been set, and his hours were full of tiresome and trivial duties and his mind engaged and worried by growing financial anxieties. He had made these abandonments in a phase of exalted passion for the one woman in the world and her unprecedented child, and now he saw, in spite of all his desire not to see, that she was just a weak human being among human beings, and neither she nor little Margharita so very marvellous.

But while Marjorie shrank to the dimensions of reality, research remained still a luminous and commanding dream. In love one fails or one wins home, but the lure of research is for ever beyond the hills, every victory is a new desire. Science has inexhaustibly fresh worlds to conquer. . . .

He was beginning now to realise the dilemma of his life, the reality of the opposition between Marjorie and child and home on the one hand and on the other this big wider thing, this remoter, severer demand upon his being. He had long perceived these were distinct and different things, but now it appeared more and more inevitable that they should be antagonistic and mutually disregardful things. Each claimed him altogether, it seemed, and suffered compromise impatiently. And this is where the particular stress of his situation came in. Hitherto he had believed that nothing of any importance was secret or inexplicable between himself and Marjorie. His ideal of his relationship had assumed a complete sympathy of feeling, an almost instinctive identity of outlook. And now it was manifest they were living in a state of inadequate understanding, that she knew only in the most general and opaque forms the things that interested him so profoundly, and had but the most superficial interest in his impassioned curiosities. And missing as she did the strength of his intellectual purpose she missed too, she had no inkling of, the way in which her careless expansiveness pressed upon him. She was unaware that she was destroying an essential thing in his life.

He could not tell how far this antagonism was due to inalterable discords of character, how far it might not be an ineradicable sex difference, a necessary aspect of marriage. The talk of old Sir Roderick Dover at the Winton Club germinated in his mind, a branching and permeating suggestion. And then would come a phase of keen sympathy with Marjorie ; she would say brilliant and penetrating things, display a swift cleverness that drove all these intimations of incurable divergence clean out of his head again. Then he would find explanations in the differences in his and Marjorie's training and early associations. He perceived his own upbringing had had a steadfastness and consistency that had been altogether lacking in hers. He had had the rare advantage of perfect honesty in the teaching and tradition of his home. There had never been any shams or sentimentalities for him to find out and abandon. From boyhood his mother's hand had pointed steadily to the search for truth as the supreme ennobling fact in life. She had never preached this to him, never delivered discourses upon his father's virtues, but all her conversation and life was saturated with this idea. Compared with this atmosphere of high and sustained direction, the intellectual and moral quality of the Popes, he saw, was the quality of an agitated rag-bag. They had thought nothing out, joined nothing together, they seemed to believe everything and nothing, they were neither religious nor irreligious, neither moral nor adventurous. In the place of a religion, and tainting their entire atmosphere, they had the decaying remains of a dead Anglicanism ; it was clear they did not believe in its creed, and as clear that they did not want to get rid of it ; it afforded them no guidance, but only vague pretensions, and the dismal exercises of Silas Root flourished in its shadows, a fungus, a post-mortem activity of the soul. None of them had any idea of what they were for or what their lives as a whole might mean ; they had no standards, but only instincts and an instinctive fear of instincts ; Pope wanted to be tremendously respected and complimented by everybody and get six per cent. for his money ; Mrs. Pope wanted things to go smoothly ; the young people had a general indisposition to do anything that might " look bad," and otherwise " have a good time." But neither Marjorie nor any of them had any test for a good time, and so they fluctuated in their conceptions of what they wanted from day to day. Now it was Plessingtonian standards, now Carmel standards, now the standards of Agatha Alimony ; now it was a stimulating novel, now a gleam of æsthetic imaginativeness come, Heaven knows whence, that dominated her mood. He was beginning to understand all this at last, and to see the need of coherence in Marjorie's mood.

He realised the unfairness of keeping his thoughts to himself, the need of putting his case before her, and making her realise their fatal and widening divergence. He wanted to infect her with his scientific passion, to give her his sense of the gravity of their practical difficulties. He would sit amidst his neglected work in his laboratory framing explanatory phrases. He would prepare the most lucid and complete statements, and go about with these in his mind for days waiting for an opportunity of saying what he felt so urgently had to be said.

But the things that seemed so luminous and effective in the laboratory had a curious way of fading and shrinking beside the bright colours of Marjorie's Bokhara hangings, in the presence of little Margharita pink and warm and entertaining in her bath, or amidst the fluttering rustle of the afternoon tea-parties that were now becoming frequent in his house. And when he was alone with her he discovered they didn't talk now any more—except in terms of a constrained and formal affection.

What had happened to them ? What was the matter between himself and Marjorie that he couldn't even intimate his sense of their divergence ? He would have liked to discuss the whole thing with his mother, but somehow that seemed disloyal to Marjorie. . . .

One day they quarrelled.

He came in about six in the afternoon, jaded from the delivery of a suburban lecture, and the consequent tedium of suburban travel, and discovered Marjorie examining the effect of a new picture which had replaced the German

print of sunlit waves over the dining-room mantelpiece.
It was a painting in the post-impressionist manner, and it
had arrived after the close of the exhibition in Weldon
Street, at which Marjorie had bought it. She had bought
it in obedience to a sudden impulse, and its imminence had
long weighed upon her conscience. She had gone to the
show with Sydney Flor and old Mrs. Flor, Sydney's
mother, and a kind of excitement had come upon them
at the idea of possessing this particular picture. Mrs. Flor
had already bought three Herbins, and her daughter wanted
to dissuade her from more. " But they're so delightful,"
said Mrs. Flor. " You're overrunning your allowance,"
said Sydney. Disputing the point, they made inquiries for
the price, and learnt that this bright epigram in colour was
going begging—was even offered at a reduction from the
catalogue price. A reduced price always had a strong
appeal nowadays to Marjorie's mind. " If you don't get
it," she said abruptly, " I shall."

The transition from that attitude to ownership was
amazingly rapid. Then nothing remained but to wait
for the picture. She had dreaded a mistake, a blundering
discord, but now with the thing hung she could see her
quick eye had not betrayed her. It was a mass of reds,
browns, purples, and vivid greens and grays ; an effect of
roof and brick house facing upon a Dutch canal, and it lit
up the room and was echoed and reflected by all the rest
of her courageous colour scheme, like a coal-fire amidst
mahogany and metal. It justified itself to her completely,
and she faced her husband with a certain confidence.

" Hallo ! " he cried.

" A new picture," she said.   " What do you think of it ? "

" What is it ? "

" A town or something—never mind. Look at the
colour. It heartens everything."

Trafford looked at the painting with a reluctant admiration.

" It's brilliant—and impudent. He's an artist—who-
ever he is. He hits the thing. But—I say—how did
you get it ? "

" I bought it."

" Bought it ! Good Lord ! How much ? "

" Oh ! ten guineas," said Marjorie, with an affectation
of ease ; " it will be worth thirty in ten years' time."

Trafford's reply was to repeat : " Ten guineas ! "

Their eyes met, and there was singularly little tenderness in their eyes.

" It was priced at thirteen," said Marjorie, ending a pause, and with a sinking heart.

Trafford had left her side. He walked to the window and sat down in a chair.

" I think this is too much," he said, and his voice had disagreeable notes in it she had never heard before. " I have just been earning two guineas at Croydon, of all places, administering comminuted science to fools—and here I find—this exploit ! Ten guineas' worth of picture. To say we can't afford it is just to waste a mild expression. It's—mad extravagance. It's waste of money—it's—oh ! —monstrous disloyalty. Disloyalty ! " He stared resentful at the cheerful, unhesitating daubs of the picture for a moment. Its affected carelessness goaded him to fresh words. He spoke in a tone of absolute hostility. " I think this winds me up to something," he said. " You'll have to give up your cheque-book, Marjorie."

" Give up my cheque-book ! "

He looked up at her and nodded. There was a warm flush in her cheeks, her lips panted apart, and tears of disappointment and vexation were shining beautifully in her eyes. She mingled the quality of an indignant woman with the distress and unreasonable resentment of a child.

" Because I've bought this picture ? "

" Can we go on like this ? " he asked, and felt how miserably he had bungled in opening this question that had been in his mind so long.

" But it's *beautiful* ! " she said.

He disregarded that. He felt now that he had to go on with these long-premeditated expostulations. He was tired and dusty from his third-class carriage, his spirit was tired and dusty, and he said what he had to say without either breadth or power, an undignified statement of personal grievances, a mere complaint of the burthen of work that falls upon a man. That she missed the high aim in him, and all sense of the greatness they were losing had vanished from his thoughts. He had too heavy a share of the common burthen, and she pressed upon him unthinkingly ; that was all he could say. He girded at her with a bitter and loveless truth ; it was none the less cruel that in her heart she knew these things he said were true. But he went beyond justice—as every quarrelling human being does ; he called the things she had bought and the harmonies she had created, " this litter and rubbish for which I am wasting my life." That stabbed into her

pride acutely and deeply. She knew anyhow that it
wasn't so simple and crude as that. It was not mere
witlessness she contributed to their trouble. She tried to
indicate her sense of that. But she had no power of
ordered reasoning, she made futile interruptions, she was
inexpressive of anything but emotion, she felt gagged against
his flow of indignant, hostile words. They blistered her.

Suddenly she went to her little desk in the corner, unlocked it with trembling hands, snatched her cheque-book
out of a heap of still unsettled bills, and having locked
that anti-climax safe away again, turned upon him. " Here
it is," she said, and stood poised for a moment. Then she
flung down the little narrow gray cover—nearly empty,
it was, of cheques—on the floor before him.

" Take it," she cried, " take it. I never asked you to
give it me."

A memory of Orta and its reeds and sunshine and love
rose like a luminous mist between them. . . .

She ran weeping from the room.

He leapt to his feet as the door closed. " Marjorie ! "
he cried.

But she did not hear him.

§ 3

The disillusionment about marriage which had discovered Trafford a thwarted, overworked, and worried
man, had revealed Marjorie with time on her hands,
superabundant imaginative energy, and no clear intimation of any occupation. With them, as with thousands of
young couples in London to-day, the bread-winner was
overworked, and the spending partner's duty was chiefly
the negative one of not spending. You cannot consume
your energies merely in not spending money. Do what
she could, Marjorie would not contrive to make house and
child fill the waking hours. She was far too active and
irritable a being to be beneficial company all day for genial,
bubble-blowing little Margharita ; she could play with
that young lady and lead her into ecstasies of excitement
and delight, and she could see with an almost instinctive
certainty when anything was going wrong ; but for the
rest that little life reposed far more beneficially upon the
passive acquiescence of May, her pink and wholesome
nurse. And the household generally was in the hands of
a trustworthy cook-general, who maintained a tolerable

routine. Marjorie did not dare to have an idea about food
or domestic arrangements ; if she touched that routine
so much as with her little finger it sent up the bills. She
could knock off butcher and greengrocer and do every
scrap of household work that she could touch, in a couple
of hours a day. She tried to find some work to fill her
leisure ; she suggested to Trafford that she might help
him by writing up his Science Notes from rough pencil
memoranda, but when it became clear that the first step
to her doing this would be the purchase of a Remington
typewriter and a special low table to carry it, he became
bluntly discouraging. She thought of literary work, and
sat down one day to write a short story and earn guineas,
and was surprised to find that she knew nothing of any
sort of human being about whom she could invent a story.
She tried a cheap subscription at Mudie's and novels, and
they filled her with a thirst for events ; she tried needlework, and found her best efforts æsthetically feeble and
despicable, and that her mind prowled above the silks and
colours like a hungry wolf.

The early afternoons were the worst time, from two to
four, before calling began. The devil was given great
power over Marjorie's early afternoon. She could even
envy her former home life then, and reflect that there,
at any rate, one had a chance of a game or a quarrel with
Daffy or Syd or Rom or Theodore. She would pull herself
together and go out for a walk, and whichever way she
went there were shops and shops and shops, a glittering
array of tempting opportunities for spending money.
Sometimes she would give way to spending exactly as a
struggling drunkard decides to tipple. She would fix on
some object, some object trivial and a little rare and not
too costly, as being needed—when she knew perfectly well
it wasn't needed—and choose the remotest shops and
display the exactest insistence upon her requirements.
Sometimes she would get home from these raids without
buying at all. After four the worst of the day was over ;
one could call on people or people might telephone and
follow up with a call ; and there was a chance of Trafford
coming home. . . .

One day at the Carmels' she found herself engaged in
a vigorous flirtation with young Carmel. She hadn't
noticed it coming on, but there she was in a window-seat
talking quite closely to him. He said he was writing a
play, a wonderful passionate play about St. Francis, and

only she could inspire and advise him. Wasn't there some afternoon in the week when she sat and sewed, so that he might come and sit by her and read to her and talk to her ? He made his request with a certain confidence, but it filled her with a righteous panic ; she pulled him up with an abruptness that was almost inartistic. On her way home she was acutely ashamed of herself ; this was the first time she had let any man but Trafford think he might be interesting to her, but once or twice on former occasions she had been on the verge of such provocative intimations. This sort of thing anyhow mustn't happen.

But if she didn't dress with any distinction—because of the cost—and didn't flirt and trail men in her wake, what was she to do at the afternoon gatherings which were now her chief form of social contact ? What was going to bring people to her house ? She knew that she was more than ordinarily beautiful and that she could talk well, but that does not count for much if you are rather dowdy, and quite uneventfully virtuous.

It became the refrain of all her thoughts that she must find something to do.

There remained " Movements."

She might take up a movement. She was a rather exceptionally good public speaker. Only her elopement and marriage had prevented her being president of her college Debating Society. If she devoted herself to some movement she would be free to devise an ostentatiously simple dress for herself and stick to it, and she would be able to give her little house a significance of its own, and present herself publicly against what is perhaps quite the best of all backgrounds for a good-looking, clear-voiced, self-possessed woman, a platform. Yes ; she had to go in for a Movement.

She reviewed the chief contemporary Movements much as she might have turned over dress fabrics in a draper's shop, weighing the advantages and disadvantages of each. . . .

London, of course, is always full of Movements. Essentially they are absorbents of superfluous feminine energy. They have a common flavour of progress and revolutionary purpose, and common features in abundant meetings, officials, and organisation generally. Few are expensive, and still fewer produce any tangible results in the world. They direct themselves at the most various ends ; the Poor, that favourite butt, either as a whole or in such typical sections as the indigent invalid or the indigent aged, the young, public health, the woman's cause, the prevention of animal food, anti-vivisection, the gratuitous advertisement of Shakespeare (that neglected poet), novel but genteel modifications of medical or religious practice, dress reform, the politer aspects of socialism, the encouragement of aeronautics, universal military service, garden suburbs, domestic arts, proportional representation, duodecimal arithmetic, and the liberation of the drama. They range in size and importance from campaigns on a Plessingtonian scale to sober little intellectual Beckingham things that arrange to meet half-yearly, and die quietly before the second assembly. If Heaven by some miracle suddenly gave every Movement in London all it professed to want, our world would be standing on its head and everything would be extremely unfamiliar and disconcerting. But, as Mr. Roosevelt once remarked, the justifying thing about life is the effort and not the goal, and few Movements involve any real and impassioned struggle to get to the ostensible object. They exist as an occupation ; they exercise the intellectual and moral activities without undue disturbance of the normal routines of life. In the days when everybody was bicycling an ingenious mechanism called Hacker's Home Bicycle used to be advertised. Hacker's Home Bicycle was a stand bearing small rubber wheels upon which one placed one's bicycle (properly equipped with a cyclometer) in such a way that it could be mounted and ridden without any sensible forward movement whatever. In bad weather, or when the state of the roads made cycling abroad disagreeable, Hacker's Home Bicycle could be placed in front of an open window and ridden furiously for any length of time. Whenever the rider tired, he could descend—comfortably at home again—and examine the cyclometer to see how far he had been. In exactly the same way the ordinary London Movement gives scope for the restless and progressive impulse in human nature without the risk of personal entanglements or any inconvenient disturbance of the milieu.

Marjorie considered the Movements about her. She surveyed the accessible aspects of socialism, but that old treasure-house of constructive suggestion had an effect like a rich château which had been stormed and looted by a mob. For a time the proposition that " we are all Socialists nowadays " had prevailed. The blackened and discredited frame remained, the contents were scattered ; Aunt Plessington had a few pieces, the Tory Democrats had taken freely, the Liberals were in possession of a hastily compiled collection. There wasn't, she perceived, and there never had been a Socialist Movement; the socialist idea which had now become part of the general consciousness, had always been too big for polite domestication. She weighed Aunt Plessington, too, in the balance, and found her not so much wanting indeed as excessive. She felt that a Movement with Aunt Plessington in it couldn't possibly offer even elbow-room for anybody else. Philanthropy generally she shunned. The movements that aim at getting poor people into rooms and shouting at them in an improving, authoritative way, aroused an instinctive dislike in her. Her sense of humour, again, would not let her patronise Shakespeare or the stage, or raise the artistic level of the country by means of green-dyed deal, and the influence of Trafford on her mind debarred her from attempting the physical and moral regeneration of humanity by means of beans and nut butter. It was indeed rather by the elimination of competing movements than by any positive preference that she found herself declining at last towards Agatha Alimony's section of the suffrage movement. . . . It was one of the less militant sections, but it held more meetings and passed more resolutions than any two others.

One day Trafford, returning from an afternoon of forced and disappointing work in his laboratory—his mind had been steadfastly sluggish and inelastic—discovered Marjorie's dining-room crowded with hats and all the rustle and colour which plays so large a part in constituting contemporary feminine personality. Buzard, the feminist writer, and a young man just down from Cambridge who had written a decadent poem, were the only men present. The chairs were arranged meeting-fashion, but a little irregularly to suggest informality; the post-impressionist picture was a rosy benediction on the gathering, and at a table in the window sat Mrs. Pope in the chair, looking quietly tactful in an unusually becoming bonnet, supported by her daughter and Agatha Alimony. Marjorie was in a simple gown of bluish-gray, hatless amidst a froth of foolish bows and feathers, and she looked not only beautiful and dignified but deliberately and conscientiously patient until she perceived the new arrival. Then he noted she was a little concerned for him, and made some futile sign he did not comprehend. The meeting was debating the behaviour of women at the approaching census, and a

small, earnest, pale-faced lady with glasses was standing
against the fireplace with a crumpled envelope covered
with pencil notes in her hand, and making a speech.
Trafford wanted his tea badly, but he had not the wit to
realise that his study had been converted into a refresh-
ment room for the occasion ; he hesitated, and seated
himself near the doorway, and so he was caught ; he
couldn't, he felt, get away and seem to slight a woman
who was giving herself the pains of addressing him.

The small lady in glasses was giving a fancy picture of
the mind of Mr. Asquith and its attitude to the suffrage
movement, and telling with a sort of inspired intimacy
just how Mr. Asquith had hoped to " bully women down,"
and just how their various attempts to bring home to him
the eminent reasonableness of their sex by breaking his
windows, interrupting his meetings, booing at him in the
streets, and threatening his life, had time after time baffled
this arrogant hope. There had been many signs lately
that Mr. Asquith's heart was failing him. Now here was
a new thing to fill him with despair. When Mr. Asquith
learnt that women refused to be counted in the census,
then at least she was convinced he must give in. When
he gave in it would not be long—she had her information
upon good authority—before they got the Vote. So what
they had to do was not to be counted in the census. That
was their paramount duty at the present time. The
women of England had to say quietly but firmly to the
census man when he came round : " No, we don't count
in an election, and we won't count now. Thank you." No
one could force a woman to fill in a census paper she didn't
want to, and for her own part, said the little woman with
the glasses, she'd starve first. (Applause.) For her own
part she was a householder with a census paper of her own,
and across that she was going to write quite plainly and
simply what she thought of Mr. Asquith. Some of those
present wouldn't have census papers to fill up ; they would
be sent to the man, the so-called Head of the House. But
the W.S.P.U. had foreseen that. Each householder had
to write down the particulars of the people who slept in
his house on Sunday night, or who arrived home before
midday on Monday ; the reply of the women of England
must be not to sleep in a house that night where census
papers were properly filled, and not to go home until the
following afternoon. All through that night the women
of England must be abroad. She herself was prepared,

and her house would be ready. There would be coffee and refreshments enough for an unlimited number of refugees, there would be twenty or thirty sofas and mattresses and piles of blankets for those who chose to sleep safe from all counting. In every quarter of London there would be houses of refuge like hers. And so they would make Mr. Asquith's census fail, as it deserved to fail, as every census would fail until women managed these affairs in a sensible way. For she supposed they were all agreed that only women could manage these things in a sensible way. That was *her* contribution to this great and important question. (Applause, amidst which the small lady with the glasses resumed her seat.)

Trafford glanced doorward, but before he could move another speaker was in possession of the room. This was a very young, tall, fair, round-shouldered girl who held herself with an unnatural rigidity, fixed her eyes on the floor just in front of the chairwoman, and spoke with knitted brows and an effect of extreme strain. She remarked that some people did not approve of this proposed boycott of the census. She hung silent for a moment, as if ransacking her mind for something mislaid, and then proceeded to remark that she proposed to occupy a few moments in answering that objection—if it could be called an objection. They said that spoiling the census was an illegitimate extension of the woman movement. Well, she objected— she objected fiercely—to every word of that phrase. Nothing was an illegitimate extension of the woman movement. Nothing could be. (Applause.) That was the very principle they had been fighting for all along. So that, examined in this way, this so-called objection resolved itself into a mere question-begging phrase. Nothing more. And her reply therefore to those who made it was that they were begging the question, and however well that might do for men, it would certainly not do, they would find, for women. (Applause.) For the freshly awakened consciousness of women. (Further applause.) This was a war in which quarter was neither asked nor given ; if it were not so things might be different. She remained silent after that for a space of twenty seconds perhaps, and then remarked that that seemed to be all she had to say, and sat down amidst loud encouragement.

Then with a certain dismay Trafford saw his wife upon her feet. He was afraid of the effect upon himself of what she was going to say, but he need have had no reason for his fear. Marjorie was a seasoned debater, self-possessed, with a voice very well controlled and a complete mastery of that elaborate appearance of reasonableness which is so essential to good public speaking. She could speak far better than she could talk. And she startled the meeting in her opening sentence by declaring that she meant to stay at home on the census night, and supply her husband with every scrap of information he hadn't got already that might be needed to make the return an entirely perfect return. (Marked absence of applause.)

She proceeded to avow her passionate interest in the feminist movement of which this agitation for the vote was merely the symbol. (A voice: " No ! ") No one could be more aware of the falsity of woman's position at the present time than she was—she seemed to be speaking right across the room to Trafford—they were neither pets nor partners, but something between the two ; now indulged like spoilt children, now blamed like defaulting partners ; constantly provoked to use the arts of their sex, constantly mischievous because of that provocation. She caught her breath and stopped for a moment, as if she had suddenly remembered the meeting intervening between herself and Trafford. No, she said, there was no more ardent feminist and suffragist than herself in the room. She wanted the vote and everything it implied with all her heart. With all her heart. But every way to get a thing wasn't the right way, and she felt with every fibre of her being that this petulant hostility to the census was a wrong way and an inconsistent way, and likely to be an unsuccessful way— one that would lose them the sympathy and help of just that class of men they should look to for support, the cultivated and scientific men. (A voice: " *Do* we want them ? ") What was the commonest charge made by the man in the street against women ?—that they were un- reasonable and unmanageable, that it was their way to get things by crying and making an irrelevant fuss. And here they were, as a body, doing that very thing ! Let them think what the census and all that modern organisa- tion of vital statistics of which it was the central feature stood for. It stood for order, for the replacement of guesses and emotional generalisation by a clear knowledge of facts, for the replacement of instinctive and violent methods, by which women had everything to lose (a voice: " No ! ") by reason and knowledge and self-restraint, by which women had everything to gain. To her the advancement of science, the progress of civilisation, and the emancipation of womanhood were nearly synonymous terms. At any rate, they were different phases of one thing. They were different aspects of one wider purpose. When they struck at the census, she felt, they struck at themselves. She glanced at Trafford as if she would convince him that this was the real voice of the suffrage movement, and sat down amidst a brief, polite applause, that warmed to rapture as Agatha Alimony, the deep-voiced, stirring Agatha, rose to reply.

Miss Alimony, who was wearing an enormous hat with three nodding ostrich feathers, a purple bow, a gold buckle and numerous minor ornaments of various origin and substance, said they had all of them listened with the greatest appreciation and sympathy to the speech of their hostess. Their hostess was a new-comer to the movement, she knew she might say this without offence, and was passing through a phase, an early phase, through which many of them had passed. This was the phase of trying to take a reasonable view of an unreasonable situation. (Applause.) Their hostess had spoken of science, and no doubt science was a great thing; but there was something greater than science, and that was the ideal. It was woman's place to idealise. Sooner or later their hostess would discover, as they had all discovered, that it was not to science but the ideal that women must look for freedom. Consider, she said, the scientific men of to-day. Consider, for example, Sir James Crichton-Browne, the physiologist. Was he on their side ? On the contrary, he said the most unpleasant things about them on every occasion. He went out of his way to say them. Or consider Sir Almroth Wright, did he speak well of women ? Or Sir Ray Lankester, the biologist, who was the chief ornament of the Anti-Suffrage Society. Or Sir Roderick Dover, the physicist, who—forgetting Madame Curie, a far more celebrated physicist than himself, she ventured to say—had recently gone outside his province altogether to abuse feminine research. There were your scientific men. Mrs. Trafford had said their anti-census campaign would annoy scientific men ; well, under the circumstances, she wanted to annoy scientific men. (Applause.) She wanted to annoy everybody. Until women got the vote (loud applause) the more annoying they were the better. When the whole world was impressed by the idea that voteless women were an intolerable nuisance, then there would cease to be voteless women. (Enthusiasm.) Mr. Asquith had said——

And so on for quite a long time. . . .

Buzard rose out of waves of subsiding emotion. Buzard
was a slender, long-necked, stalk-shaped man with gilt
glasses, uneasy movements, and a hypersensitive manner.
He didn't so much speak as thrill with thought vibrations ;
he spoke like an entranced but still quite gentlemanly sibyl.
After Agatha's deep trumpet calls, he sounded like a solo
on the piccolo. He picked out all his more important
words with a little stress as though he gave them capitals.
He said their hostess's remarks had set him thinking. He
thought it was possible to stew the Scientific Argument in
its own Juice. There was something he might call the
Factuarial Estimate of Values. Well, it was a High
Factuarial Value on their side, in his opinion at any rate,
when Anthropologists came and told him that the Primitive Human Society was a Matriarchate. (" But it wasn't !"
said Trafford to himself.) It had a High Factuarial Value
when they assured him that Every One of the Great
Primitive Inventions was made by a Woman, and that it
was to Women they owed Fire and the early Epics and Sagas.
(" Good Lord ! " said Trafford.) It had a High Factuarial
Value when they not only asserted but proved that for Thousands of Years, and perhaps for Hundreds of Thousands of
Years, Women had been in possession of Articulate Speech
before men rose to that Level of Intelligence. . . .

It occurred suddenly to Trafford that he could go now ;
that it would be better to go ; that indeed he *must* go ;
it was no doubt necessary that his mind should have to
work in the same world as Buzard's mental processes, but
at any rate those two sets of unsympathetic functions need
not go on in the same room. Something might give way.
He got up, and with those elaborate efforts to be silent
that lead to the violent upsetting of chairs, got himself out
of the room and into the passage, and was at once rescued
by the sympathetic cook-general, in her most generalised
form, and given fresh tea in his study—which impressed
him as being catastrophically disarranged. . . .

§ 4

When Marjorie was at last alone with him she found
him in a state of extreme mental stimulation. " Your
speech," he said, " was all right. I didn't know you
could speak like that, Marjorie. But it soared like the
dove above the waters. Waters ! I never heard such a

flood of rubbish. . . . You know, it's a mistake to *mass* women. It brings out something silly. . . . It affected Buzard as badly as any one. The extraordinary thing is they have a case, if only they'd be quiet. Why did you get them together ? "

" It's our local branch."

" Yes, but *why* ? "

" Well, if they talk about things—Discussions like this clear up their minds."

" Discussion ! It wasn't discussion."

" Oh ! it was a beginning."

" Chatter of that sort isn't the beginning of discussion, it's the end. It's the death-rattle. Nobody was meeting the thoughts of any one. I admit Buzard, who's a man, talked the worst rubbish of all. That Primitive Matri-archate of his ! So it isn't sex. I've noticed before that the men in this movement of yours are worse than the women. It isn't sex. It's something else. It's a foolish-ness. It's a sort of irresponsible looseness." He turned on her gravely. " You ought not to get all these people here. It's contagious. Before you know it you'll find your own mind liquefy and become enthusiastic and slop about. You'll begin to talk monomania about Mr. Asquith."

" But it's a great movement, Rag, even if incidentally they say and do silly things ! "

" My dear ! aren't I feminist ? Don't I want women fine and sane and responsible ? Don't I want them to have education, to handle things, to vote like men and bear themselves with the gravity of men ? And these meetings—all hat and flutter ! These displays of weak, untrained, hysterical vehemence ! These gatherings of open-mouthed impressionable young girls to be trained in incoherence ! You can't go on with it ! "

Marjorie regarded him quietly for a moment. " I must go on with something," she said.

" Well, not this."

" Then *what* ? "

" Something sane."

" Tell me what."

" It must come out of yourself."

Marjorie thought sullenly for a moment. " Nothing comes out of myself," she said.

" I don't think you realise a bit what my life has become," she went on ; " how much I'm like some one who's been put in a pleasant, high-class prison."

" This house ! It's your own ! "

" It doesn't give me an hour's mental occupation in the day. It's all very well to say I might do more in it. I can't—without absurdity. Or expenditure. I can't send the girl away and start scrubbing. I can't make jam or do ornamental needlework. The shops do it better and cheaper, and I haven't been trained to it. I've been trained *not* to do it. I've been brought up on games and school-books, and fed on mixed ideas. I can't sit down and pacify myself with a needle as women used to do. Besides, I not only detest doing needlework, but I hate it —the sort of thing a woman of my kind does anyhow— when it's done. I'm no artist. I'm not sufficiently interested in outside things to spend my time in serious systematic reading, and after four or five novels—oh, these meetings are better than that ! You see, you've got a life—too much of it—*I* haven't got enough. I wish almost I could sleep away half the day. Oh ! I want something *real*, Rag ; something more than I've got." A sudden inspiration came to her. " Will you let me come to your laboratory and work with you ? "

She stopped abruptly. She caught up her own chance question and pointed it at him, a vitally important challenge. " Will you let me come to your laboratory and work ? " she repeated.

Trafford thought. " No," he said.

" Why not ? "

" Because I'm in love with you. I can't think of my work when you're about. . . . And you're too much behind. Oh, my dear ! don't you see how you're behind ? " He paused. " I've been soaking in this stuff of mine for ten long years."

" Yes," assented Marjorie flatly.

He watched her downcast face, and then it lifted to him with a helpless appeal in her eyes and lift in her voice. " But look here, Rag ! " she cried—" what on earth am I to *DO* ? "

§ 5

At least there came out of these discussions one thing, a phrase, a purpose, which was to rule the lives of the Traffords for some years. It expressed their realisation that instinct and impulse had so far played them false, that life for all its rich gifts of mutual happiness wasn't adjusted between them. " We've got," they said, " to

talk all this out between us. We've got to work this out."
They didn't mean to leave things at a misfit, and that was
certainly their present relation. They were already at the
problem of their joint lives, like a tailor with his pins and
chalk. Marjorie hadn't rejected a humorist and all his
works in order to decline at last to the humorous view of
life, that rather stupid, rather pathetic, grin-and-bear-it
attitude compounded in incalculable proportions of goodwill, evasion, indolence, slovenliness, and (nevertheless)
spite (masquerading indeed as jesting comment), which
supplies the fabric of everyday life for untold thousands
of educated middle-class people. She hated the misfit.
She didn't for a moment propose to pretend that the ungainly twisted sleeve, the puckered back, was extremely
jolly and funny. She had married with a passionate
anticipation of things fitting and fine, and it was her nature
in great matters as in small, to get what she wanted
strenuously before she counted the cost. About both
their minds there was something sharp and unrelenting,
and if Marjorie had been disposed to take refuge from
facts in swathings of æsthetic romanticism, whatever
covering she contrived would have been torn to rags very
speedily by that fierce and steely veracity which swung
down out of the laboratory into her home.

One may want to talk things out long before one hits
upon the phrases that will open up the matter.

There were two chief facts in the case between them,
and so far they had looked only one in the face—the fact
that Marjorie was unemployed to a troublesome and
distressing extent, and that there was nothing in her
nature or training to supply, and something in their circumstances and relations to prevent, any adequate use of
her energies. With the second fact neither of them cared
to come to close quarters as yet, and neither as yet saw
very distinctly how it was linked to the first, and that was
the steady excess of her expenditure over their restricted
means. She was secretly surprised at her own weakness.
Week by week and month by month, they were spending all
his income and eating into that little accumulation of capital
that had once seemed so sufficient against the world. . . .

And here it has to be told that although Trafford knew
that Marjorie had been spending too much money, he
still had no idea of just how much money she had spent.
She was doing her utmost to come to an understanding
with him, and at the same time—I don't explain it, I don't

excuse it—she was keeping back her bills from him,
keeping back urgent second and third and fourth demands,
that she had no cheque-book now to stave off even by
the most partial satisfaction. It kept her awake at nights,
that catastrophic explanation, that all unsuspected by
Trafford hung over their attempts at mutual elucidation ;
it kept her awake but she could not bring it to the speaking
point, and she clung, in spite of her own intelligence, to a
persuasion that *after* they had got something really settled
and defined then it would be time enough to broach the
particulars of this second divergence. . . .

Talking one's relations over isn't particularly easy
between husband and wife at any time ; we are none of
us so sure of one another as to risk loose phrases or make
experiments in expression in matters so vital ; there is
inevitably an excessive caution on the one hand and an
abnormal sensitiveness to hints and implications on the
other. Marjorie's bills were only an extreme instance of
these unavoidable suppressions that always occur. Moreover, when two people are continuously together, it is
amazingly hard to know when and where to begin ; where
intercourse is unbroken it is as a matter of routine being
constantly interrupted. You cannot broach these broad
personalities while you are getting up in the morning, or
over the breakfast-table while you make the coffee, or when
you meet again after a multitude of small events at tea,
or in the evening when one is rather tired and trivial after
the work of the day. Then Miss Margharita Trafford
permitted no sustained analysis of life in her presence.
She synthesised things fallaciously, but for the time con-
vincingly ; she insisted that life wasn't a thing you discussed, but pink and soft and jolly, which you crowed at
and laughed at and addressed as " Goo." Even without
Margharita there were occasions when the Traffords were
a forgetfulness to one another. After an ear has been
pinched or a hand has been run through a man's hair, or a
pretty bare shoulder kissed, all sorts of broader interests
lapse into a temporary oblivion. They found discussion
much more possible when they walked together. A walk
seemed to take them out of the everyday sequence, isolate
them from their household, abstract them a little from one
another. They set out one extravagant spring Sunday to
Great Missenden, and once in spring also they discovered
the Waterlow Park. On each occasion they seemed to get
through an enormous amount of talking. But the Great

Missenden walk was all mixed up with a sweet keen wind, and beech-woods just shot with spring green and bursting hedges and the extreme earliness of honeysuckle, which Trafford noted for the first time, and a clamorous rejoicing of birds. And in the Waterlow Park there was a great discussion of why the yellow crocus comes before white and purple, and the closest examination of the manner in which daffodils and narcissi thrust their green noses out of the garden beds. Also they found the ugly, ill-served, aggressively propagandist non-alcoholic refreshment-room in that gracious old house a scandal and disappointment, and Trafford scolded at the stupidity of officialdom that can control so fine a thing so ill.

Though they talked on these walks they were still curiously evasive. Indeed, they were afraid of each other. They kept falling away from their private thoughts and intentions. They generalised, they discussed Marriage and George Gissing and Bernard Shaw and the suffrage movement and the agitation for the reform of the divorce laws. They pursued imaginary cases into distant thickets of contingency remotely far from the personal issues between them.

§ 6

One day came an incident that Marjorie found wonderfully illuminating. Trafford had a fit of rage. Stung by an unexpected irritation, he forgot himself, as people say, and swore, and was almost physically violent, and the curious thing was that so he lit up things for her as no premeditated attempt of his had ever done.

A copy of the *Scientific Bulletin* fired the explosion. He sat down at the breakfast-table with the heaviness of a rather overworked and worried man, tasted his coffee, tore open a letter and crumpled it with his hand, turned to the *Bulletin*, regarded its list of contents with a start, opened it, read for a minute, and expressed himself with an extraordinary heat of manner in these amazing and unprecedented words :—

" Oh ! Damnation and damnation ! "

Then he shied the paper into the corner of the room and pushed his plate from him.

" Damn the whole scheme of things ! " he said, and met the blank amazement of Marjorie's eye.

" Behrens ! " he said, with an air of explanation.

" Behrens ? " she echoed, with a note of inquiry.

" He's doing my stuff ! "

He sat darkling for a time, and then hit the table with his fist so hard that the breakfast things seemed to jump together—to Marjorie's infinite amazement. " I can't *stand* it ! " he said.

She waited some moments. " I don't understand," she began. " What has he done ? "

" Oh ! " was Trafford's answer. He got up, recovered the crumpled paper and stood reading. "Fool and thief," he said.

Marjorie was amazed beyond measure. She felt as though she had been effaced from Trafford's life. " Ugh ! " he cried, and slapped back the *Bulletin* into the corner with quite needless violence. He became aware of Marjorie again.

" He's doing my work," he said.

And then as if he completed the explanation : " And I've got to be in Croydon by half-past ten to lecture to a pack of spinsters and duffers, because they're too stupid to get the stuff from books. It's all in books—every bit of it."

He paused and went on in tones of unendurable wrong.

" It isn't as though he was doing it right. He isn't. He can't. He's a fool. He's a clever, greedy, dishonest fool with a twist. Oh ! the pile, the big Pile of silly muddled technicalities he's invented already ! The solemn mess he's making of it ! And there he is, I can't get ahead of him, I can't get at him. I've got no time. I've got no room or leisure to swing my mind in ! Oh, curse these engagements, curse all these silly fretting entanglements of lecture and article ! I never get the time, I can't get the time, I can't get my mind clear ! I'm worried ! I'm badgered ! And meanwhile Behrens—— ! "

" Is he discovering what you want to discover ? "

" Behrens ! *No !* He's going through the breaches I made. He's guessing out what I meant to do. And he's getting it set out all wrong—misleading terminology— distinctions made in the wrong place. Oh, the fool he is ! '

" But afterwards—— "

" Afterwards I may spend my life—removing the obstacles he's made. He'll be established and I shan't. You don't know anything of these things. You don't understand."

She didn't. Her next question showed as much. " Will it affect your F.R.S. ? " she asked.

" Oh ! *that's* safe enough, and it doesn't matter anyhow. The F.R.S. ! Confound the silly little F.R.S. ! As if that mattered. It's seeing all my great openings—misused.

It's seeing all I might be doing. This brings it all home to me. Don't you understand, Marjorie? Will you never understand? I'm getting away from all *that*! I'm being hustled away by all this work, this silly everyday work to get money. Don't you see that unless I can have time for thought and research, life is just darkness to me? I've made myself master of that stuff. I had, at any rate. No one can do what I can do there. And when I find myself—oh, shut out, shut out! I come near raving. As I think of it I want to rave again." He paused. Then with a swift transition : " I suppose I'd better eat some breakfast. Is that egg boiled ? "

She gave him an egg, brought him coffee, put things before him, seated herself at the table. For a little while he ate in silence. Then he cursed Behrens.

" Look here ! " she said. " Bad as I am, you've got to reason with me, Rag. I didn't know all this. I didn't understand. . . . I don't know what to do."

" What *is* there to do ? "

" I've got to do something. I'm beginning to see things. It's just as though everything had become clear suddenly." She was weeping. "Oh, my dear ! I want to help you. I have so wanted to help you. Always. And it's come to this ! "

" But it's not *your* fault. I didn't mean that. It's—it's in the nature of things."

" It's my fault."

" It's not your fault."

" It is."

" Confound it, Marjorie. When I swear at Behrens I'm not swearing at you."

" It's my fault. All this is my fault. I'm eating you up. What's the good of your pretending, Rag ? You know it is. Oh ! When I married you I meant to make you happy, I had no thought but to make you happy, to give myself to you, my body, my brains, everything, to make life beautiful for you——"

" Well, *haven't* you ? " He thrust out a hand she did not take.

" I've broken your back," she said.

An unwonted resolution came into her face. Her lips whitened. " Don't you know, Rag," she said, forcing herself to speak—" don't you guess ? You don't know half ! In that bureau there——. In there ! It's stuffed with bills. Unpaid bills."

She was weeping, with no attempt to wipe the streaming

tears away ; terror made the expression of her wet face
almost fierce. " Bills," she repeated. " More than a
hundred pounds still. Yes ! Now. *Now !* "

He drew back, stared at her, and with no trace of
personal animus, like one who hears of a common disaster,
remarked with a quiet emphasis : " Oh, *damn* ! "

" I know," she said, " Damn ! " and met his eyes. There
was a long silence between them. She produced a handkerchief
and wiped her eyes. " That's what I amount to," she said.

" It's your silly upbringing," he said, after a long pause.

" And my silly self."

She stood up, unlocked and opened her littered desk,
turned and held out the key to him.

" Why ? " he asked.

" Take it. You gave me a cheque-book of my own and
a corner of my own, and they—they are just ambushes—
against you."

He shook his head.

" Take it," said Marjorie with quiet insistence.

He obeyed. She stood with her eyes on the crumpled
heap of bills. They were not even tidily arranged. That
seemed to her now an extreme aggravation of her offence.

" I ought to be sent to the chemist's," she remarked,
" as one sends a worthless cat."

Trafford weighed this proposition soberly for some
moments. " You're a bother, Marjorie," he said, with
his eyes on the desk ; " no end of a bother. I'd better
have those bills."

He looked at her, stood up, put his hands on her
shoulders, drew her to him and kissed her forehead. He
did it without passion, without tenderness, with something
like resignation in his manner. She clung to him tightly,
as though by clinging she could warm and soften him.

" Rag," she whispered, " all my heart is yours. . . . I
want to help you. . . . And this is what I have done."

" I know," he said—almost grimly.

He repeated his kiss.

Then he seemed to explode again. " Gods ! " he cried,
" look at the clock. I shall miss that Croydon lecture ! "
He pushed her from him. " Where are my boots ? . . ."

§ 7

Marjorie spent the forenoon and the earlier part of the
afternoon repeating and reviewing this momentous

conversation.   Her mind was full of the long disregarded
problem of her husband's state of mind.   She thought
with a sympathetic astonishment of his swearing, of his
startling blow upon the table.   She hadn't so far known
he could swear.   But this was the real thing, the relief
of vehement and destructive words.   His voice, saying
" damnation and damnation," echoed and re-echoed in her
ears.   Somehow she understood that as she had never
understood any sober statement of his case.   Such women as
Marjorie, I think, have an altogether keener understanding
of people who have lost control of themselves than they have
of reasoned cases.   Perhaps that is because they themselves
always reserve something when they state a reasoned case.

She went on to the apprehension of a change in him that
hitherto she had not permitted herself to see—a change in
his attitude to her.   There had been a time when she had
seemed able without an effort to nestle inside his heart.
Now she felt distinctly for the first time that that hadn't
happened.   She had instead a sense of her embrace sliding
over a rather deliberately contracted exterior. . . . Of
course he had been in a hurry. . . .

She tried to follow him on his long journey to Croydon
Now he'd have just passed out of London Bridge.   What
was he thinking and feeling about her in the train ?   Now
he would be going into the place, wherever it was, where
he gave his lecture.   Did he think of Behrens and curse
her under his breath as he entered that tiresome room ? . . .

It seemed part of the prevailing inconvenience of life
that Daffy should see fit to pay an afternoon call.

Marjorie heard the sobs and uproar of an arrested motor,
and glanced discreetly from the window to discover the
dark green car with its green-clad chauffeur which now
adorned her sister's life, and which might, under different
circumstances, have adorned her own.   Wilkins—his name
was Wilkins, his hair was sandy and his expression discreet,
and he afforded material for much quiet humorous observation—descended smartly and opened the door.   Daffy
appeared in black velvet, with a huge black fur muff, and
an air of being unaware that there were such things as
windows in the world.

It was just four, and the cook-general, who ought to
have been now in her housemaid's phase, was still upstairs
divesting herself of her more culinary characteristics.
Marjorie opened the door.

" Hallo, old Daffy ! " she said.

" Hallo, old Madge ! " and there was an exchange of
sisterly kisses and a mutual inspection.

" Nothing wrong ? " asked Daffy, surveying her.

" *Wrong ?* "

" You look pale and—tired about the eyes," said Daffy,
leading the way into the drawing-room. " Thought you
might be a bit off it, that's all. No offence, Madge."

" I'm all right," said Marjorie, getting her back to the
light. " Want a holiday, perhaps. How's every one ? "

" All right. *We're* off to Lake Garda next week. This
new play has taken it out of Will tremendously. He
wants a rest and fresh surroundings. It's to be the biggest
piece of work he's done—so far, and it's straining him. And
people worry him here ; receptions, first nights, dinners,
speeches. He's so neat, you know, in his speeches. . . .
But it wastes him. He wants to get away. How's Rag ? "

" Busy."

" Lecturing ? "

" And his Research, of course."

" Oh ! of course. How's the Babe ? "

" Just in. Come up and see the little beast, Daffy !
It is getting so pretty, and it talks——"

Margharita dominated intercourse for a time. She
was one of those tactful infants who exactly resemble
their fathers and exactly resemble their mothers, and have
a charm and individuality quite distinctly their own, and
she was now beginning to converse with startling enterprise
and intelligence.

" Big, big, bog," she said, at the sight of Daffy.

" Remembers you," said Marjorie.

" Bog ! Go ta-ta ! " said Margharita.

" There ! " said Marjorie, and May, the nurse in the
background, smiled unlimited appreciation.

" Bably," said Margharita.

" That's herself ! " said Marjorie, falling on her knees.
"She talks like this all day. Oh, de sweetums, den ! *Was* it ?"

Daffy made amiable gestures and canary-like noises
with her lips, and Margharita responded jovially.

" You darling ! " cried Marjorie, " you delight of life,"
kneeling by the cot and giving the crowing, healthy little
mite a passionate hug.

" It's really the nicest of babies," Daffy conceded, and
reflected. . . .

" I don't know what I should do with a kiddy," said
Daffy, as the infant worship came to an end ; " I'm really

glad we haven't one—yet. He'd love it, I know. But it would be a burthen in some ways. They *are* a tie. As he says, the next few years means so much for him. Of course, here his reputation is immense, and he's known in Germany, and there are translations into Russian; but he's still got to conquer America, and he isn't really well known yet in France. They read him, of course, and buy him in America, but they're—*restive*. Oh! I do so wish they'd give him the Nobel prize, Madge, and have done with it! It would settle everything. Still, as he says, we mustn't think of that—yet, anyhow. He isn't—venerable enough. It's doubtful, he thinks, that they would give the Nobel prize to any humorist now that Mark Twain is dead. Mark Twain was different, you see, because of the German Emperor and all that white hair and everything."

At this point Margharita discovered that the conversation had drifted away from herself, and it was only when they got downstairs again that Daffy could resume the thread of Magnet's career, which had evidently become the predominant interest in her life. She brought out all the worst elements of Marjorie's nature and their sisterly relationship. There were moments when it became nakedly apparent that she was magnifying Magnet to belittle Trafford. Marjorie did her best to counter-brag. She played her chief card in the F.R.S.

"They always ask Will to the Royal Society Dinner," threw out Daffy; "but of course he can't always go. He's asked to so many things."

Five years earlier Marjorie would have kicked her shins for that.

Instead she asked pointedly, offensively, if Magnet was any balder.

"He's not really bald," said Daffy unruffled, and went on to discuss the advisability of a second motor car—purely for town use. "I tell him I don't want it," said Daffy, "but he's frightfully keen upon getting one."

§ 8

When Daffy had at last gone Marjorie went back into Trafford's study and stood on the hearthrug regarding its appointments, with something of the air of one who awakens from a dream. She had developed a new, appalling thought. Was Daffy really a better wife than herself? It was dawning upon Marjorie that she hadn't been doing the

right thing by her husband, and she was as surprised as
if it had been suddenly brought home to her that she was
neglecting Margharita. This was her husband's study—
and it showed just a little dusty in the afternoon sunshine,
and everything about it denied the pretensions of serene
sustained work that she had always made to herself. Here
were the crumpled galley proofs of his science notes ; here
were unanswered letters. There—she dare not touch
them—were computations, under a glass paper-weight.
What did they amount to now ? On the table under the
window were back numbers of the *Scientific Bulletin* in a
rather untidy pile, and on the footstool by the arm-chair
she had been accustomed to sit at his feet when he stayed
at home to work, and look into the fire, and watch him
furtively, and sometimes give way to an overmastering
tenderness and make love to him. The thought of Magnet,
pampered, fenced around, revered in his industrious tiresome repetitions, variations, dramatisations, and so forth
of the half-dozen dry little old jokes which the British
public accepted as his characteristic offering and rewarded
him for so highly, contrasted vividly with her new realisation of Trafford's thankless work and worried face.

And she loved him, she loved him—*so*. She told herself
in the presence of all these facts, and without a shadow of
doubt in her mind that all she wanted in the world was
to make him happy.

It occurred to her as a rather drastic means to this end
that she might commit suicide.

She had already gone some way in the composition of a
touching letter of farewell to him, containing a luminous
analysis of her own defects, before her common sense
swept away this imaginative exercise.

Meanwhile, as if it had been working at her problem all
the time that this exciting farewell epistle had occupied
the foreground of her thoughts, her natural lucidity emerged
with the manifest conclusion that she had to alter her way
of living. She had been extraordinarily regardless of him,
she only began to see that, and now she had to take up
the problem of his necessities. Her self-examination, now
that it had begun, was thorough. She had always told
herself before that she had made a most wonderful and
beautiful little home for him. But had she made it for
him ? Had he, as a matter of fact, ever wanted it, except
that he was glad to have it through her ? No doubt it had
given him delight and happiness, it had been a marvellous

little casket of love for them, but how far did that out-
weigh the burthen and limitation it had imposed upon
him ?   She had always assumed he was beyond measure
grateful to her for his home, in spite of all her bills, but
was he ?   It was like sticking a knife into herself to ask
that, but she was now in a phase heroic enough for the
task—was he ?   She had always seen herself as the giver
of bounties ; greatest bounty of all was Margharita.   She
had faced pains and terrors and the shadow of death to
give him Margharita.   Now with Daffy's illuminating conversation in her mind, she could turn the light upon a
haunting doubt that had been lurking in the darkness for
a long time.   Had he really so greatly wanted Margharita ?
Had she ever troubled to get to the bottom of that before ?
Hadn't she, as a matter of fact, wanted Margharita ten
thousand times more than he had done ?   Hadn't she, in
effect, imposed Margharita upon him, as she had imposed
her distinctive and delightful home upon him, regardlessly,
because these things were the natural and legitimate
developments of herself ?

These things were not his end.

Had she hitherto ever really cared what his ends might be ?

A phrase she had heard abundantly enough in current
feminist discussion recurred to her mind, " the economic
dependence of women," and now for the first time it was
charged with meaning.   She had imposed these things
upon him not because she loved him, but because these
things that were the expansions and consequences of her
love for him were only obtainable through him.   A woman
gives herself to a man out of love, and remains clinging
parasitically to him out of necessity.   Was there no way
of evading that necessity ?

For a time she entertained dreams of marvellous social
reconstructions.   Suppose the community kept all its
women, suppose all property in homes and furnishings
and children vested in them !   That was Marjorie's version
of that idea of the Endowment of Womanhood which has
been creeping into contemporary thought during the last
two decades.   Then every woman would be a Princess
to the man she loved. . . . She became more definitely
personal.   Suppose she herself was rich, then she could
play the Princess to Trafford ; she could have him free,
unencumbered, happy, and her lover !   Then, indeed, her
gifts would be gifts, and all her instincts and motives would
but crown his unhampered life !   She could not go on from

that idea, she lapsed into a golden reverie, from which she was roused by the clock striking five.

In half an hour perhaps Trafford would be home again. She could at least be so much of a princess as to make his home sweet for his home-coming. There should be tea in here, where callers did not trouble. She glanced at an empty copper case. It ached. There was no light in the room. There would be just time to dash out into the High Street and buy some flowers for it before he came. . . .

§ 9

Spring and a renewed and deepened love for her husband were in Marjorie's blood. Her mind worked rapidly during the next few days, and presently she found herself clearly decided upon her course of action. She had to pull herself together and help him, and if that meant a Spartan and strenuous way of living, then manifestly she must be Spartan and strenuous. She must put an end once for all to her recurrent domestic deficits, and since this could only be done by getting rid of May, she must get rid of May and mind the child herself. (Every day, thank Heaven! Margharita became more intelligent, more manageable, and more interesting.) Then she must also make a far more systematic and thorough study of domestic economy than she had hitherto done, and run the shopping and housekeeping on severer lines ; she bought fruit carelessly, they had far too many joints ; she never seemed able to restrain herself when it came to flowers. And in the evenings, which would necessarily be very frequently lonely evenings if Trafford's researches were to go on, she would typewrite, and either acquire great speed at that or learn shorthand, and so save Trafford his present expenditure on a typist. That unfortunately would mean buying a typewriter. . . .

She found one afternoon in a twopenny book-box, with which she was trying to allay her craving for purchases, a tattered little pamphlet entitled : " Proposals for the Establishment of an Order of Samurai," which fell in very exactly with her mood. The title " dated " ; it carried her mind back to her middle girlhood and the defeats of Kuropatkin and the futile earnest phase in English thought which followed the Boer War. The order was to be a sort of self-appointed nobility serving the world. It shone with the light of a generous dawn, but cast, I fear, the shadow

of the prig. Its end was the Agenda Club. . . . She read
and ceased to read—and dreamt.

The project unfolded the picture of a new method of
conduct to her, austere, yet picturesque and richly noble.
These Samurai, it was intimated, were to lead lives of
hard discipline and high effort, under self-imposed rule
and restraint. They were to stand a little apart from
the excitements and temptations of everyday life, to eat
sparingly, drink water, resort greatly to self-criticism and
self-examination, and harden their spirits by severe and
dangerous exercises. They were to dress simply, work
hard, and be the conscious and deliberate salt of the world.
They were to walk among mountains. Incidentally, great
power was to be given them. Such systematic effort and
self-control as this seemed to Marjorie to give just all she
wasn't and needed to be, to save her life and Trafford's
from a common disaster. . . .

It particularly appealed to her that they were to walk
among mountains. . . .

But it is hard to make a change in the colour of one's
life amidst the routine one has already established about
oneself, in the house that is grooved by one's weaknesses,
amidst hangings and ornaments living and breathing with
the life of an antagonistic and yet insidiously congenial
ideal. A great desire came upon Marjorie to go away with
Trafford for a time, out of their everyday life into strange
and cool and spacious surroundings. She wanted to leave
London and its shops, and the home and the movements
and the callers and rivalries, and even dimpled little
Margharita's insistent claims, and get free, and think. It
was the first invasion of their lives by this conception, a
conception that was never afterwards to leave them
altogether, of retreat and reconstruction. She knelt upon
the white sheepskin hearthrug at Trafford's feet one night,
and told him of her desire. He, too, was tired of his work
and his vexations, and ripe for this suggestion of an altered
life. The Easter holiday was approaching, and nearly
twenty unencumbered days. Mrs. Trafford, they knew,
would come into the house, meanwhile, and care for
Margharita. They would go away somewhere together
and walk, no luggage but a couple of knapsacks, no hotel
but some homely village inn. They would be in the air
all day, until they were saturated with sweet air and the
spirit of clean restraints. They would plan out their new
rule, concentrate their aims. "And I could think," said

Trafford, " of this new work I can't begin here. I might make some notes." Presently came the question of where the great walk should be. Manifestly, it must be among mountains, manifestly, and Marjorie's eye saw those mountains with snow upon their summits and cold glaciers on their flanks. Could they get to Switzerland ? If they travelled second class throughout, and took the cheaper way, as Samurai should ? . . .

§ 10

That holiday seemed to Marjorie as if they had found a lost and forgotten piece of honeymoon. She had that same sense of fresh beginnings that had made their first walk in Italian Switzerland so unforgettable. She was filled with the happiness of recovering Trafford when he had seemed to be slipping from her. All day they talked of their outlook, and how they might economise away the need of his extra work, and so release him for his research again. For the first time he talked of his work to her, and gave her some intimation of its scope and quality. He became enthusiastic with the sudden invention of experimental devices, so that it seemed to her almost worth while if instead of going on they bolted back, he to his laboratory and she to her nursery, and so at once inaugurate the new régime. But they went on, to finish the holiday out. And the delight of being together again, with unfettered hours of association ! They rediscovered each other, the same— and a little changed. If their emotions were less bright and intense, their interest was far wider and deeper.

The season was too early for high passes, and the weather was changeable. They started from Fribourg and walked to Thun and then back to Bulle, and so to Bultigen, Saanen, Montbovon, and the Lake of Geneva. They had rain several days, the sweet, soft, windless mountain rain that seems so tolerable to those who are accustomed to the hard and driven downpours of England, and in places they found mud and receding snow ; the inns were at their homeliest, and none the worse for that, and there were days of spring sunshine when a multitude of minute and delightful flowers came out, as it seemed, to meet them—it was impossible to suppose so great a concourse universal—and spread in a scented carpet before their straying feet. The fruit trees in the valleys were powdered with blossom, and the new grass seemed rather green-tinted sunlight than merely green. And they walked with a sort of stout leisureliness, knapsacks well hung and cloaks about them, with their faces fresh and bright under the bracing weather, and their lungs deep charged with mountain air, talking of the new austerer life that was now beginning. With great snow-capped mountains in the background, streaming precipices overhead, and a sward of flowers to go upon, that strenuous prospect was altogether delightful. They went as it pleased them, making detours into valleys, coming back upon their steps. The interludes of hot, bright April sunshine made them indolent, and they would loiter and halt where some rock or wall invited, and sit basking like happy animals, talking very little, for long hours together. Trafford seemed to have forgotten all the strain and dis-appointment of the past two years, to be amazed but in no-wise incredulous at this enormous change in her and in their outlook ; it filled her with a passion of pride and high resolve to think that so she could recover and uplift him.

He was now very deeply in love with her again. He talked, indeed, of his research, but so that it might interest her, and when he thought alone, he thought, not of it, but of her, making again the old discoveries, his intense delight in the quality of her voice, his joy in a certain indescribable gallantry in her bearing. He pitied all men whose wives could not carry themselves, and whose voices failed and broke under the things they had to say. And then again there was the way she moved her arms, the way her hands took hold of things, the alert lucidity of her eyes, and then that faint, soft shadow of a smile upon her lips when she walked thinking or observant, all unaware that he was watching her.

It rained in the morning of their eleventh day, and then gave way to warmth and sunshine, so that they arrived at Les Avants in the afternoon a little muddy and rather hot. At one of the tables under the trees outside the Grand Hotel was a small group of people dressed in the remarkable and imposing costume which still in those days distinguished the motorist. They turned from their tea to a more or less frank inspection of the Traffords, and suddenly broke out into cries of recognition and welcome. Solomonson—for the most part brown leather—emerged with extended hands, and behind him, nestling in the midst of immense and costly furs, appeared the kindly salience and brightness of his Lady's face. " Good luck ! " cried Solomonson. " Good luck ! Come and have tea with us ! But this is a happy encounter ! "

THE NEW PHASE

" We're dirty—but so healthy ! " cried Marjorie, saluting
Lady Solomonson.

" You look, oh !—splendidly well," that lady responded.

" We've been walking."

" With just that knapsack ! "

" It's been glorious."

" But the courage ! " said Lady Solomonson, and did not
add, " the tragic hardship ! " though her tone conveyed
it. She had all the unquestioning belief of her race in the
sanity of comfort. She had ingrained in her the most
definite ideas of man's position and woman's, and that
any one, man or woman, should walk in mud except under
dire necessity, was outside the range of her philosophy.
She thought Marjorie's thick boots and short skirts quite
the most appalling feminine costume she had ever seen.
She saw only a ruined complexion and damaged womanhood in Marjorie's rain-washed, sun-bit cheek. Her
benevolent heart rebelled at the spectacle. It was dreadful, she thought, that nice young people like the Traffords
should have come to this.

The rest of the party were now informally introduced.
They were all very splendid and disconcertingly free from
mud. One was Christabel Morrison, the actress, a graceful
figure in a green baize coat and brown fur, who looked ever
so much more charming than her innumerable post cards
and illustrated-paper portraits would have led one to
expect ; her neighbour was Solomonson's cousin Lee, the
organiser of the Theatre Syndicate, a brown-eyed, attenuated, quick-minded little man with an accent that struck
Trafford as being, on the whole, rather Dutch, and the
third lady was Lady Solomonson's sister, Mrs. Lee. It
appeared they were all staying at Lee's villa above Vevey,
part of an amusing assembly of people who were either
vividly rich or even more vividly clever, an accumulation
which the Traffords in the course of the next twenty
minutes were three times invited, with an increasing
appreciation and earnestness, to join.

From the first our two young people were not indisposed
to do so. For eleven days they had maintained their
duologue at the very highest level, seven days remained
to them before they must go back to begin the hard new
life in England, and there was something very attractive—
they did not for a moment seek to discover the elements
of that attractiveness—in this proposal of five or six days
of luxurious indolence above the lake, a sort of farewell

to the worldly side of worldly things, before they set forth
upon the high and narrow path they had resolved to tread.

" But we've got no clothes," cried Marjorie, " no clothes
at all ! We've these hobnail boots and a pair each of
heelless slippers.

" My dear ! " cried Lady Solomonson in real distress,
and as much aside as circumstances permitted, " my dear !
My sister can manage all that ! " Her voice fell to earnest
undertones. " We can really manage all that. The house
is packed with things. We'll come to dinner in fancy
dress. And Scott, my maid, is so clever."

" But really ! " said Marjorie.

" My dear ! " said Lady Solomonson. " Everything."
And she changed places with Lee in order to be perfectly
confidential and explicit. " Rachel ! " she cried, and
summoned her sister for confirmatory assurances. . . .

" But my husband ! " Marjorie became audible.

" We've long Persian robes," said Mrs. Lee, with a
glance of undisguised appraisement. " He'll be splendid.
He'll look like a Soldan. . . ."

The rest of the company forced a hectic conversation
in order not to seem to listen, and presently Lady Solomonson and her sister were triumphant. They packed Marjorie
into the motor car, and Trafford and Solomonson returned
to Vevey by the train and thence up to the villa by a hired
automobile.

§ 11

They didn't go outside the magic confines of the Lees'
villa for three days, and when they did they were still
surrounded by their host's service and possessions ; they
made an excursion to Chillon in his motor cars, and went
in his motor boat to lunch with the Maynards in their lake-
side villa close to Geneva. During all that time they
seemed lifted off the common earth into a world of fine
fabrics, agreeable sounds, noiseless unlimited service, and
ample untroubled living. It had an effect of enchantment,
and the long healthy arduous journey thither seemed a
tale of incredible effort amidst these sunny excesses. The
weather had the whim to be serenely fine, sunshine like
summer and the bluest of skies shone above the white wall
and the ilex thickets and cypresses that bounded them in
from the great world of crowded homes and sous and small
necessities. And through the texture of it all for Trafford
ran a thread of curious new suggestion. An intermittent

discussion of economics and socialism was going on between himself and Solomonson, and an agreeable little stammering man in brown named Minter, who walked up in the afternoon from Vevey—he professed to be writing a novel during the earlier half of the day. Minter displayed the keenest appreciation of everything in his entertainment, and blinked cheerfully and expressed opinions of the extremist socialistic and anarchistic flavour to an accompaniment of grateful self-indulgence. " Your port-wine is wonderful, Lee,' he would say, sipping it. " A terrible retribution will fall upon you some day for all this."

The villa had been designed by Lee to please his wife, and if it was neither very beautiful nor very dignified, it was, at any rate, very pretty and amusing. It might have been built by a Parisian dressmaker—in the châteauesque style. It was of grayish-white stone, with a roof of tiles. It had little balconies and acutely roofed turrets, and almost burlesque buttresses, pierced by doors and gates ; and sun-trap loggias, as pleasantly casual as the bows and embroideries of a woman's dress ; and its central hall, with an impluvium that had nothing to do with rain-water, and its dining-room, to which one ascended from this hall between pillars up five broad steps, were entirely irrelevant to all its exterior features. Unobtrusive men-servants in gray with scarlet facings hovered serviceably.

From the little terrace, all set with orange-trees in tubs. one could see, through the branches and stems of evergreens and over a foreground of budding, starting vineyard, the clustering roofs of Vevey below, an agglomeration veiled ever so thinly in the mornings by a cobweb of wood smoke, against the blue background of lake with its winged sailing-boats and sombre Alpine distances. Minter made it all significant by a wave of the hand. " All this," he said, and of the crowded work-a-day life below, " all that."

" All this," with its rich litter of stuffs and ornaments, its fine profusion, its delicacies of flower and food and furniture, its frequent inconsecutive pleasures, its noiseless, ready service, was remarkably novel and yet remarkably familiar to Trafford. For a time he could not understand this undertone of familiarity, and then a sunlit group of hangings in one of the small rooms that looked out upon the lake took his mind back to his own dining-room, and the little, inadequate, but decidedly good, Bokhara embroidery that dominated it like a flag, that lit it, and now lit his understanding, like a confessed desire. Of course,

Mrs. Lee—happy woman !—was doing just everything that Marjorie would have loved to do. Marjorie had never confessed as much, perhaps she had never understood as much, but now in the presence of Mrs. Lee's æsthetic exuberances, Trafford at least understood. He surveyed the little room, whose harmonies he had at first simply taken for granted, noted the lustre-ware that answered to the gleaming Persian tiles, the inspiration of a metallic thread in the hangings, and the exquisite choice of the deadened paint upon the woodwork, and realised for the first time how little aimless extravagance can be, and all the timid, obstinately insurgent artistry that troubled his wife. He stepped through the open window into a little loggia, and stared unseeingly over glittering, dark-green leaves to the mysteries of distance in the great masses above St. Gingolph, and it seemed for the first time that perhaps in his thoughts he had done his wife a wrong. He had judged her fickle, impulsive, erratic, perhaps merely because her mind followed a different process from his, because while he went upon the lines of constructive truth, her guide was a more immediate and instinctive sense of beauty.

He was very much alive to her now, and deeply in love with her. He had reached Les Avants with all his sense of their discordance clean washed and walked out of his mind, by rain and sun and a flow of high resolutions, and the brotherly swing of their strides together. They had come to the Lees' villa, mud-splashed, air-sweet comrades, all unaware of the subtle differences of atmosphere they had to encounter. They had no suspicion that it was only about half of each other that had fraternised. Now here they were in a company that was not only altogether alien to their former mood, but extremely interesting and exciting and closely akin to the latent factors in Marjorie's composition. Their hostess and her sister had the keen, quick æsthetic sensibilities of their race, with all that freedom of reading and enfranchisement of mind which is the lot of Western women. Lee had an immense indulgent affection for his wife ; he regarded her arrangements and exploits with an admiration that was almost American. And Mrs. Lee's imagination had run loose in pursuit of beautiful and remarkable people and splendours rather than harmonies of line and colour. Lee, like Solomonson, had that inexplicable alchemy of mind which distils gold from the commerce of the world (" All this," said Minter to Trafford, " is an exhalation from all that ") ; he accumulated wealth as one grows a beard, and found his interest in his uxorious satisfactions, and so Mrs. Lee, with her bright watchful eyes, quick impulsive movements and instinctive command, had the utmost freedom to realise her ideals.

In the world at large Lee and Solomonson seemed both a little short and a little stout, and a little too black and bright for their entirely conventional clothing, but for the dinner and evening of the villa they were now, out of consideration for Trafford, at their ease, and far more dignified in Oriental robes. Trafford was accommodated with a long, black, delicately embroidered garment that reached to his feet, and suited something upstanding and fine in his bearing ; Minter, who had stayed on from an afternoon call, was gorgeous in Chinese embroidery. The rest of the men clung boldly or bashfully to evening dress. . . .

On the evening of his arrival Trafford, bathed and robed, found the rest of the men assembling about an open wood fire in the smaller hall at the foot of the main staircase. Lee was still upstairs, and Solomonson, with a new grace of gesture begotten by his costume, made the necessary introductions ; a little man with fine-cut features and a Galway accent was Rex the playwright ; a tall, gray-haired, clean-shaven man was Bright from the New York Central Museum ; and a bearded giant with a roof of red hair and a remote eye was Radlett Barns, the great portrait-painter, who consents to paint your portrait for posterity as the King confers a knighthood. These were presently joined by Lee and Pacey, the blond-haired musician, and Mottersham, whose patents and inventions control electric lighting and heating all over the world. And then, with the men duly gathered and expectant, the women came down the wide staircase.

The staircase had been planned and lit for these effects, and Mrs. Lee meant to make the most of her new discovery. Her voice could be heard in the unseen corridor above arranging the descent : " You go first, dear. Will you go with Christabel ? " The conversation about the fire checked and ceased with the sound of voices above and the faint rustle of skirts. Then came Christabel Morrison, her slender grace beautifully contrasted with the fuller beauties of that great lady of the stage, Marion Rufus. Lady Solomonson descended confidentially in a group of three, with Lady Mottersham and sharp-tongued little Mrs. Rex, all very rich and splendid. After a brief interval their hostess preceded Marjorie, and was so much of an artist

that she had dressed herself merely as a foil to this new
creation. She wore black and scarlet, that made the white
face and bright eyes under her sombre hair seem the face
of an inspiring spirit. A step behind her and to the right
of her came Marjorie, tall and wonderful, as if she were
the queen of earth and sunshine, swathed barbarically in
gold and ruddy brown, and with her abundant hair bound
back by a fillet of bloodstones and gold. Radlett Barns
exclaimed at the sight of her. She was full of the manifest
consciousness of dignity as she descended, quite conscious
and quite unembarrassed ; two borrowed golden circlets
glittered on her shining arm, and a thin chain of gold and
garnets broke the contrast of the warm, sun-touched neck
above, with the unsullied skin below.

She sought and met her husband's astonishment with
the faintest, remotest of smiles. It seemed to him that
never before had he appreciated her beauty. His daily
companion had become this splendour in the sky. She
came close by him with hand extended to greet Sir Philip
Mottersham. He was sensible of the glow of her, as it
were of a scented aura about her. He had a first full
intimation of the cult and worship of women and the
magnificence of women, old as the Mediterranean and its
goddesses, and altogether novel to his mind. . . .

Christabel Morrison found him a pleasant but not very
entertaining or exciting neighbour at the dinner-table, and
was relieved when the time came for her to turn an ear to
the artistic compliments of Radlett Barns. But Trafford
was too interested and amused by the general effect of the
dinner to devote himself to the rather heavy business of
really exhilarating Christabel. He didn't give his mind to
her. He found the transformation of Sir Rupert into a
turbaned Oriental who might have come out of a picture
by Carpaccio, gently stimulating and altogether delightful.
His attention returned again and again to that genial
swarthiness. Mrs. Lee, on his left, lived in her eyes, and
didn't so much talk to him as rattle her mind at him almost
absent-mindedly, as one might dangle keys at a baby while
one talked to its mother. Yet it was evident she liked the
look of him. Her glance went from his face to his robe,
and up and down the table, at the bright dresses, the
shining arms, the glass and light and silver. She asked him
to tell her just where he had tramped and just what he
had seen, and he had scarcely begun answering her question
before her thoughts flew off to three trophies of china and

silver, struggling groups of china boys bearing up great
silver shells of fruit and flowers that stood down the centre
of the table. "What do you think of my chubby boys ?"
she asked. " They're German work. They came from a
show at Düsseldorf last week. Ben saw I liked them, and
sent back for them secretly, and here they are ! I thought
they might be too colourless. But are they ? "

" No," said Trafford ; " they're just cool. Under that
glow of fruit. Is this salt-cellar English cut glass ? "

" Old Dutch," said Mrs. Lee. " Isn't it jolly ? " She
embarked with a roving eye upon the story of her Dutch
glass, which was abundant and admirable, and broke off
abruptly to say, " Your wife is wonderful.

" Her hair goes back," she said, " like music. You
know what I mean—a sort of easy rhythm. You don't
mind my praising your wife ? "

Trafford said he didn't.

" And there's a sort of dignity about her. All my life,
Mr. Trafford, I've wanted to be tall. It stopped my growth."

She glanced off at a tangent. " Tell me, Mr. Trafford,"
she asked, " was your wife beautiful like this when you
married her ? I mean—of course she was a beautiful girl and
adorable and all that ; but wasn't she just a slender thing ? "

She paused, but if she had a habit of asking disconcerting
questions she did not at any rate insist upon answers, and
she went on to confess that she believed she would be a
happier woman poor than rich—" not that Ben isn't all
he should be "—but that then she would have been a
fashionable dressmaker. " People want help," she said, " so
much more help than they get. They go about with
themselves—what was it Mr. Radlett Barns said the other
night ?—oh ! like people leading horses they daren't ride.
I think he says such good things at times, don't you ? So
wonderful to be clever in two ways like that. Just look
now at your wife—now, I mean, that they've drawn that
peacock-coloured curtain behind her. My brother-in-law
has been telling me you keep the most wonderful and
precious secrets locked up in your breast ; that you know
how to make gold and diamonds and all sorts of things.
If I did—I should make them."

She pounced suddenly upon Rex at her left with questions about the Keltic Renascence, was it still going on—
or what ? and Trafford was at liberty for a time to enjoy
the bright effects about him, the shadowed profile and black
hair of Christabel to the right of him, and the coruscating

refractions and reflections of Lady Solomonson across the
white and silver and ivory and blossom of the table. Then
Mrs. Lee dragged him into a sudden conflict with Rex, by
saying abruptly,—

" Of course, Mr. Trafford wouldn't believe that."

He looked perhaps a little lost.

" I was telling Mrs. Lee," said Rex, " that I don't
believe there's any economy of human toil in machinery
whatever. I mean that the machine itself really embodies
all the toil it seems to save, toil that went to the making
of it and preparing of it and getting coal for it. . . ."

§ 12

Next morning they found their hostess at breakfast in
the dining-room, and now the sun was streaming through
a high triple window that had been curtained overnight,
and they looked out through clean, bright plate-glass upon
mountains half-dissolved in a luminous mist, and a mist-
veiled lake below. Great stone jars upon the terrace bore
a blaze of urged and early blossom, and beyond were
cypresses. Their hostess presided at one of two round
tables; at a side-table various breakfast dishes kept warm
over spirit lamps, and two men-servants dispensed tea and
coffee. In the bay of the window was a fruit table, with
piled fruit-plates and finger-bowls.

Mrs. Lee waved a welcoming hand, and drew Marjorie
to a seat beside her. Rex was consuming trout and
Christabel peaches, and Solomonson, all his overnight
Orientalism abandoned, was in outspoken tweeds and quite
under the impression that he was interested in gold.
Trafford got frizzled bacon for Marjorie and himself, and
dropped into a desultory conversation, chiefly sustained by
Christabel, about the peculiarly exalting effect of beautiful
scenery on Christabel's mind. Mrs. Lee was as usual distraught, and kept glancing towards the steps that led up
from the hall. Lady Solomonson appeared with a rustle
in a wrapper of pink Chinese silk. " I came down after
all," she said. " I lay in bed weighing rolls and coffee
and relaxed muscles against your English breakfast downstairs. And suddenly I remembered your little sausages ! "

She sat down with a distribution of handkerchief, bag,
letters, a gold fountain pen, and such-like equipments, and
Trafford got her some of the coveted delicacies. Mrs. Lee
suddenly cried out, " *Here* they come ! *Here* they come ! "

and simultaneously the hall resonated with children's voices and the yapping of a Skye terrier.

Then a gay little procession appeared ascending the steps. First came a small but princely little boy of three, with a ruddy face and curly black hair, behind him was a slender, rather awkward girl of perhaps eleven, and a sturdier daughter of Israel of nine. A nurse in artistic purple followed, listening inattentively to some private whisperings of a knickerbockered young man of five, and then came another purple-robed nurse against contingencies, and then a nurse of a different, white-clad, and more elaborately costumed sort, carrying a sumptuous baby of eight or nine months. " Ah ! the *darlings* ! ' cried Christabel, springing up quite beautifully, and Lady Solomonson echoed the cry. The procession broke against the tables and split about the breakfast party. The small boy in petticoats made a confident rush for Marjorie, Christabel set herself to fascinate his elder brother, the young woman of eleven scrutinised Trafford with speculative interest and edged towards him coyly, and Mrs. Lee interviewed her youngest born. The amiable inanities suitable to the occasion had scarcely begun before a violent clapping of hands announced the appearance of Lee.

It was Lee's custom, Mrs. Lee told Marjorie over her massively robed baby, to get up very early and work on rolls and coffee ; he never breakfasted nor joined them until the children came. All of them rushed to him for their morning kiss, and it seemed to Trafford that Lee at least was an altogether happy creature as he accepted the demonstrative salutation of this struggling, elbowing armful of offspring, and emerged at last like a man from a dive, flushed and ruffled and smiling, to wish his adult guests good-morning.

" Come upstairs with us, Daddy," cried the children, tugging at him. " Come upstairs ! "

Mrs. Lee ran her eye about her table and rose. " It's the children's hour," she said to Marjorie. " You don't I hope, mind children ? "

" But," said Trafford incredulous, and with a friendly arm about his admirer, " is this tall young woman yours ? "

The child shot him a glance of passionate appreciation for this scrap of flattery.

" We began young," said Mrs. Lee, with eyes of uncritical pride for the ungainly one, and smiled at her husband.

" Upstairs," cried the boy of five and the girl of nine.
" Upstairs ! "

" May we come ? " asked Marjorie.

" May we all come ? " asked Christabel, determined to
be in the movement.

Rex strolled towards the cigars, with disentanglement
obviously in his mind.

" Do you really care ? " asked Mrs. Lee. " You know,
I'm so proud of their nursery. Would you care—— ?
Always I go up at this time."

" I've my little nursery too," said Marjorie.

" Of course ! " cried Mrs. Lee, " I forgot. Of course ; "
and overwhelmed Marjorie with inquiries as she followed
her husband. Every one joined the nurseryward procession except Rex, who left himself behind with an air of
inadvertency, and escaped to the terrace and a cigar. . . .

It was a wonderful nursery, a suite of three bedrooms,
a green and white, well-lit schoolroom, and a vast playroom,
and hovering about the passage Trafford remarked a third
purple nurse and a very efficient and serious-looking Swiss
governess. The schoolroom and the nursery displayed a
triumph of judicious shopping and arrangement, the best
of German and French and English things had been blended
into a harmony at once hygienic and pedagogic and humanly
charming. For once Marjorie had to admire the spending
of another woman, and admit to herself that even she
could not have done better with the money.

There were clever little desks for the elder children to
work at, adjustable desks scientifically lit so that they
benefited hands and shoulders and eyes ; there were
artistically coloured and artistically arranged pictures,
and a little library held all the best of Lang and Lucas,
rare good things like *Uncle Lubin*, Maurice Baring's story
of *Forget-me-Not*, *Johnny Crow's Garden*, *The Bad Child's
Book of Beasts*, animals books and bird books, costume
books and story books, colour books and rhyme books,
abundant, yet every one intelligently chosen, no costly
meretricious printed rubbish such as silly Gentile mothers
buy. Then in the great nursery, with its cork carpet on
which any toy would stand or run, was an abundance of
admirable possessions and shelving for everything, and
great fat cloth elephants to ride, and go-carts, and hooks
for a swing. Marjorie's quick eye saw, and she admired
effusively and envied secretly, and Mrs. Lee appreciated
her appreciation. A skirmishing romp of the middle children

and Lee went on about the two of them, and Trafford was led off by his admirer into a cubby-house in one corner (with real glass windows made to open) and the muslin curtains were drawn while he was shown a secret under vows. Lady Solomonson discovered some soldiers, and was presently on her knees in a corner with the five-year-old boy.

"These are like my Teddy's," she was saying. "My Billy has some of these."

Trafford emerged from the cubby-house, which was perhaps a little cramped for him, and surveyed the room, with his admirer lugging at his arm unheeded, and whispering: "Come back with me."

Of course this was the clue to Lee and Solomonson. How extremely happy Lee appeared to be! Enormous vistas of dark philoprogenitive parents and healthy little Jews and Jewesses seemed to open out to Trafford hygienically reared, exquisitely trained and educated. And he and Marjorie had just one little daughter—with a much poorer educational outlook. She had no cloth elephant to ride, no elaborate cubby-house to get into, only a half-dozen picture-books or so, and later she wouldn't when she needed it get that linguistic Swiss.

He wasn't above the normal human vanity of esteeming his own race and type the best, and certain vulgar aspects of what nowadays one calls Eugenics crossed his mind.

§ 13

During those few crowded days of unfamiliar living Trafford accumulated a vast confused mass of thoughts and impressions. He realised acutely the enormous gulf between his attitudes towards women and those of his host and Solomonson—and indeed of all the other men. It had never occurred to him before that there was any other relationship possible between a modern woman and a modern man but a frank comradeship and perfect knowledge, helpfulness, and honesty. That had been the continual implication of his mother's life and of all that he had respected in the thought and writing of his time. But not one of these men in their place—with the possible exception of Minter, who remained brilliant but ambiguous —believed anything of the sort. It necessarily involved in practice a share of hardship for women, and it seemed fundamental to them that women should have no hardship. He sought for a word, and hung between chivalry and orientalism. He inclined towards chivalry. Their women were lifted a little off the cold ground of responsibility. Charm was their obligation. " A beautiful woman should be beautifully dressed," said Radlett Barns in the course of the discussion of a contemporary portrait painter. Lee nodded to endorse an obvious truth. " But she ought to dress herself," said Barns. " It ought to be herself to the points of the old lace—chosen and assimilated. It's just through not being that, that so many rich women are —detestable. Heaps of acquisition. Caddis-women. . . ."

Trafford ceased to listen, he helped himself to a cigar and pinched its end and lit it, while his mind went off to gnaw at: " A beautiful woman should be beautifully dressed," as a dog retires with a bone. He couldn't escape from its shining truth, and withal it was devastating to all the purposes of his life.

He rejected the word " orientalism "; what he was dealing with here was chivalry. " All this," was indeed, under the thinnest of disguises, the castle and the pavilion, and Lee and Solomonson were valiant knights, who entered the lists not indeed with spear and shield but with prospectus and ingenious enterprise, who drew cheques instead of swords for their ladies' honour, who held " all that " in fee and subjection that these exquisite and wonderful beings should flower in rich perfection. All these women lived in a magic security and abundance, far above the mire and adventure of the world ; their knights went upon quests for them and returned with villas and pictures and diamonds and historical pearls. And not one of them all was so beautiful a being as his Marjorie, whom he made his squaw, whom he expected to aid and follow him, and suffer uncomplainingly the rough services of the common life. Not one was half so beautiful as Marjorie, nor half so sweet and wonderful. . . .

If such thoughts came in Lee's villa, they returned with redoubled force when Trafford found himself packed painfully with Marjorie in the night train to Paris. His head ached with the rattle and suffocation of the train, and he knew hers must ache more. The windows of the compartment and the door were all closed, the litigious little commercial traveller in shiny gray had insisted upon that, there was no corner seat either for Marjorie or himself, the dim big package over her head swayed threateningly. The green shade over the light kept opening with the vibration of the train, the pallid old gentleman with the beard had twisted himself into a ghastly resemblance to a broken-necked corpse, and pressed his knees hard and stiffly against Trafford, and the small, sniffing, bow-legged little boy beside the rusty widow woman in the corner smelt mysteriously and penetratingly of Roquefort cheese. For the seventeenth time the little commercial traveller jumped up with an unbecoming expletive, and pulled the shade over the light, and the silent young man in the fourth corner stirred and readjusted his legs.

For a time until the crack of light overhead had widened again every one became a dark head-dangling outline. . . .

He watched the dim shape before him and noted the weary droop of her pose. He wished he had brought water. He was intolerably thirsty, and his thirst gave him the measure of hers. This jolting fetid compartment was a horrible place for her, an intolerably horrible place. And she was standing it, for all her manifest suffering, with infinite gallantry and patience. What a gallant soul indeed she was ! Whatever else she did she never failed to rise to a challenge. Her very extravagance that had tried their lives so sorely was perhaps just one aspect of that same quality. It is so easy to be saving if one is timid ; so hard if one is unaccustomed to fear. How beautiful she had shone at times in the lights and glitter of that house behind there ! and now she was back in her weather-stained tweeds again, like a shining sword thrust back into a rusty old sheath.

Was it fair that she should come back into the sheath because of this passion of his for a vast inexhaustible research ?

He had never asked himself before if it was fair to assume she would follow his purpose and his fortunes. He had taken that for granted. And she, too, had taken that for granted, which was so generously splendid of her. All her disloyalties had been unintentional, indeed almost instinctive, breaches of her subordination to this aim which was his alone. These breaches he realised had been the reality of her nature fighting against her profoundest resolutions.

He wondered what Lee must think of this sort of married life. How ugly and selfish it must seem from that point of view !

He perceived for the first time the fundamental incongruity of Marjorie's position ; she was made to shine, elaborately prepared and trained to shine, desiring keenly to shine, and then imprisoned and hidden in the faded obscurity of a small poor home. How conspicuously, how extremely he must be wanting in just that sort of chivalry in which Lee excelled ! Those business men lived for their women to an extent he had hitherto scarcely dreamt of doing. . . .

His want of chivalry was beyond dispute. And was there not also an extraordinary egotism in this concentration upon his own purposes, a self-esteem, a vanity ? Had her life no rights ? Suppose now he were to give her—two years, three years perhaps of his life—altogether. Or even four. Was it too much to grudge her four ? Solomonson had been at his old theme with him, a theme the little man had never relinquished since their friendship first began years ago, possibilities of a business alliance and the application of a mind of exceptional freshness and penetration to industrial development. Why shouldn't that be tried ? Why not ' make money ' for a brief strenuous time, and then come back, when Marjorie's pride and comfort were secured ? . . .

(Poor dear, how weary she looked !)

He wondered how much more remained of this appalling night. It would have made so little difference if they had taken the day train and travelled first-class. Wasn't she indeed entitled to travel first-class ? Pictures of the immense spaciousness, the softness, cleanliness, and dignity of first-class compartments appeared in his mind. . . .

He would have looked at his watch, but to get at it would mean disturbing the silent young man on his left.

Outside in the corridor there broke out a noisy dispute about a missing coupon, a dispute in that wonderful language that is known to the facetious as *entente cordiale*, between an Englishman and the conductor of the train. . . .

§ 14

In Paris there was a dispute with an extortionate cabman, and the crossing from Dieppe to Newhaven was rough and bitterly cold. They were both ill. They reached home very dirty and weary, and among the pile of letters and papers on Trafford's desk was a big bundle of Science Note proofs, and two letters from Croydon and Pinner to alter the hours of his lectures for various plausible and irritating reasons.

The little passage looked very small and rather bare as the door shut behind them, and the worn places that had begun to be conspicuous during the last six months, and which they had forgotten during the Swiss holiday, re-asserted themselves. The dining-room, after spacious rooms flooded with sunshine, betrayed how dark it was, and how small. Those Bokhara embroideries that had once shone so splendid now, after Mrs. Lee's rich and unlimited harmonies, seemed skimpy and insufficient, mere loin-cloths for the artistic nakedness of the home. They felt, too, they were beginning to find out their post-impressionist picture. They had not remembered it as nearly so crude as it now appeared. The hole a flying coal had burnt in the unevenly faded dark-blue carpet looked larger than it had ever done before, and was indeed the only thing that didn't appear faded and shrunken.

§ 15

The atmosphere of the Lees' villa had disturbed Marjorie's feelings and ideas even more than it had Trafford's. She came back struggling to recover those high resolves that had seemed so secure when they had walked down to Les Avants. There was a curiously tor-menting memory of that vast, admirable nursery, and the princely procession of children that would not leave her mind. No effort of her reason could reconcile her to the inferiority of Margharita's equipment. She had a detestable craving for a uniform for May. But May was going. . . .

But indeed she was not so sure that May was going.

She was no longer buoyantly well, she was full of indefinable apprehensions of weakness and failure. She struggled to control an insurgence of emotions that rose out of the deeps of her being. She had now, she knew, to take on her share of the burden, to become one of the Samurai, to show her love no longer as a demand but as a service. Yet from day to day she procrastinated under the shadow of apprehended things ; she forbore to dismiss May, to buy that second-hand typewriter she needed, to take any irrevocable step towards the realisation of the new way of living. She tried to think away her fears, but they would not leave her. She felt that Trafford watched her pale face with a furtive solicitude and wondered at her hesitations ; she tried in vain to seem cheerful and careless in his presence, with an anxiety, with premonitions that grew daily.

There was no need to worry him unduly. . . .

But soon the matter was beyond all doubting. One night she gathered her courage together suddenly, and came down into his study in her dressing-gown with her hair about her shoulders. She opened the door, and her heart failed her.

" Rag," she whispered.

"Yes," he said busily from his desk, without looking round.

" I want to speak to you," she answered, and came slowly, and stood beside him silently.

" Well, old Marjorie ? " he said presently, drawing a little intricate pattern in the corner of his blotting paper, and wondering whether this was a matter of five pounds or ten.

" I meant so well," she said, and caught herself back into silence again.

He started at a thought, at a depth and meaning in her voice, turned his chair about to look at her, and discovered she was weeping and choking noiselessly. He stood up close to her, moving very slowly and silently, his eyes full of this new surmise, and now without word or gesture from her he knew his thought was right. " My dear," he whispered.

She turned her face from him. " I meant so well," she sobbed. " My dear ! I meant so well." Still with an averted face her arms came out to him in a desperate, un- reasoning appeal for love. He took her and held her close to him. " Never mind, dear," he said. " Don't mind." Her passion now was unconstrained. " I thought——" he began, and left the thing unsaid.

" But your work," she said ; " your research ? "

" I must give up research," he said.

" Oh, my dearest ! "

" I must give up research," he repeated. " I've been seeing it for days. Clearer and clearer. *This*, dear, just settles things. Even—as we were coming home in that train—I was making up my mind. At Vevey I was talking to Solomonson."

" My dear," she whispered, clinging to him.

" I talked to Solomonson. He has ideas—a proposal."

" No," she said.

" Yes," he said. " I've left the thing too long."

He repeated. " I must give up research—for years. I ought to have done it long before."

" I had meant so well," she said. " I meant to work. I meant to deny myself. . . ."

" I'm glad," he whispered. " Glad ! Why should you weep ? " It seemed nothing to him then, that so he should take a long farewell to the rare, sweet air of that wonderland his mind had loved so dearly. All he remembered was that Marjorie was very dear to him, very dear to him, and that all her being was now calling out for him and his strength. " I had thought anyhow of giving up research," he repeated. " This merely decides. It happens to decide. I love you, dear. I put my research at your feet. Gladly. This is the end, and I do not care, my dear, at all. I do not care at all—seeing I have you. . . ."

He stood beside her for a moment, and then sat down again, sideways, upon his chair.

" It isn't you, my dear, or me," he said, " but life that beats us—that beautiful, irrational mother. . . . Life does not care for research or knowledge, but only for life. Oh ! the world has to go on yet for tens of thousands of years before—before we are free for that. I've got to fight—as other men fight. . . ."

He thought in silence for a time, oddly regardless of her. " But if it was not you," he said, staring at the fireplace with knitted brows, " if I did not love you. . . . Thank God, I love you, dear ! Thank God, our children are love children ! I want to live—to my finger-tips, but if I didn't love you—oh ! love you ! then I think now—I'd be glad —I'd be glad, I think, to cheat life of her victory."

" Oh, my dear ! " she cried, and clung weeping to him, and caught at him and sat herself upon his knees, and put her arms about his head, and kissed him passionately with tear-salt lips, with her hair falling about his face.

" My dear," she whispered. . . .

§ 16

So soon as Trafford could spare an afternoon amidst his crowded engagements he went to talk to Solomonson, who was now back in London. " Solomonson," he said, " you were talking about rubber at Vevey."

" I remember," said Solomonson, with a note of welcome.

" I've thought it over."

" I *thought* you would."

" I've thought things over. I'm going to give up my professorship—and science generally, and come into business—if that is what you are meaning."

Solomonson turned his paper-weight round very carefully

before replying. Then he said : " You mustn't give up your professorship yet, Trafford. For the rest—I'm glad."

He reflected, and then his bright eyes glanced up at Trafford. " I knew," he said, " you would."

" I didn't," said Trafford. " Things have happened since."

" Something was bound to happen. You're too good—for what it gave you. I didn't talk to you out there for nothing. I saw things. . . . Let's go into the other room, and smoke and talk it over." He stood up as he spoke.

" I thought you would," he repeated, leading the way. " I knew you would. You see—one *has* to. You can't get out of it.

" It was all very well before you were married," said Solomonson, stopping short to say it, " but when a man's married he's got to think. He can't go on devoting himself to his art and his science and all that—not if he's married anything worth having. No. Oh, I understand. He's got to look about him, and forget the distant prospect for a bit. I saw you'd come to it. *I* came to it. Had to. I had ambitions—just as you have. I've always had an inclination to do a bit of research on my own. I *like* it you know. Oh! I could have done things. I'm sure I could have done things. I'm not a born money-maker. But——" He became very close and confidential. " It's —*them*. You said good-bye to science for a bit when you flopped me down on that old croquet-lawn, Trafford." He went off to reminiscences. " Lord, how we went over ! No more aviation for me, Trafford ! "

He arranged chairs, and produced cigars. " After all—this, of course—it's interesting. Once you get into the movement of it, it takes hold of you. It's a game."

" I've thought over all you said," Trafford began, using premeditated phrases. " Bluntly—I want three thousand a year, and I don't make eight hundred. It's come home to me. I'm going to have another child."

Solomonson gesticulated a congratulation.

" All the same, I hate dropping research. It's stuff I'm made to do. About that, Solomonson, I'm almost super-stitious. I could say I had a call. . . . It's the maddest state of affairs ! Now that I'm doing absolutely my best work for mankind, work I firmly believe no one else can do, I just manage to get six hundred—nearly two hundred of my eight hundred is my own. What does the world think I could do better—that would be worth four times as much."

"The world doesn't think anything at all about it," said Solomonson.

"Suppose it did!"

The thought struck Sir Rupert. He knitted his brows and looked hard obliquely at the smoke of his cigar. "Oh, it won't," he said, rejecting a disagreeable idea. "There isn't any world—not in that sense. That's the mistake you make, Trafford."

"It's not what your work is worth," he explained. "It's what your advantages can get for you. People are always going about supposing—just what you suppose—that people ought to get paid in proportion to the good they do. It's forgetting what the world is, to do that. Very likely some day civilisation will get to that, but it hasn't got to it yet. It isn't going to get to it for hundreds and hundreds of years."

His manner became confidential. "Civilisation's just a fight, Trafford—just as savagery is a fight, and being a wild beast is a fight—only you have paddeder gloves on and there's more rules. We aren't out for everybody, we're out for ourselves—and a few friends perhaps—within limits. It's no good hurrying ahead and pretending civilisation's something else when it isn't. That's where all these Socialists and people come a howler. Oh, I know the Socialists. I see 'em at my wife's At Homes. They come along with the literary people and the artists' wives and the actors and actresses, and none of them take much account of me because I'm just a business man and rather dark and short, and so I get a chance of looking at them from the side that isn't on show while the other's turned to the women, and they're just as fighting as the rest of us, only they humbug more and they don't seem to me to have a decent respect for any of the common rules. And that's about what it all comes to, Trafford."

Sir Rupert paused, and Trafford was about to speak when the former resumed again, his voice very earnest, his eyes shining with purpose. He liked Trafford, and he was doing his utmost to make a convincing confession of the faith that was in him. "It's when it comes to the women," said Sir Rupert, "that one finds it out. That's where *you've* found it out. You say, I'm going to devote my life to the service of Humanity in general. You'll find Humanity in particular, in the shape of all the fine, beautiful, delightful, and desirable women you come across, preferring a narrower turn of devotion. See? That's all.

Caeteris paribus, of course. That's what I found out, and that's what you've found out, and that's what everybody with any sense in his head finds out, and there you are ! "

" You put it—graphically," said Trafford.

" I feel it graphically. I may be all sorts of things, but I do know a fact when I see it. I'm here with a few things I want and a woman or so I have and want to keep, and the kids upstairs, bless 'em ! and I'm in league with all the others who want the same sort of things. Against any one or anything that upsets us. We stand by the law and each other, and that's what it all amounts to. That's as far as my patch of Humanity goes. Humanity at large ! Humanity be blowed ! *Look* at it ! It isn't that I'm hostile to Humanity, mind you, but that I'm not disposed to go under as I should do if I didn't say that. So I say it. And that's about all it is, and there you are ! "

He regarded Trafford over his cigar, drawing fiercely at it for some moments. Then seeing Trafford on the point of speaking, he snatched it from his lips, demanded silence by waving it at his hearer, and went on.

" I say all this in order to dispose of any idea that you can keep up the open-minded tell-everybody-everything scientific attitude if you come into business. You can't. Put business in two words and what is it ? Keeping something from somebody else, and making him pay for it——"

" Oh, look here ! " protested Trafford. " That's not the whole of business."

" There's making him want it, of course, advertisement and all that, but that falls under making him pay for it, really."

" But a business man organises public services, consolidates, economises."

Sir Rupert made his mouth look very wide by sucking in the corners. " Incidentally," he said, and added after a judicious pause : " Sometimes. . . . I thought we were talking of making money."

" Go on," said Trafford."

" You set me thinking," said Solomonson. " It's the thing I always like about you. I tell you, Trafford, I don't believe that the majority of people who make money help civilisation forward any more than the smoke that comes out of the engine helps the train forward. If you put it to me, I don't. I've got no illusions of that sort. They're

about as much help as—fat. They accumulate because
things happen to be arranged so."

"Things will be arranged better some day,"

"They aren't arranged better now. Grip that! *Now*,
it's a sort of paradox. If you've got big gifts and you
choose to help forward the world, if you choose to tell all
you know and give away everything you can do in the
way of work, you've got to give up the ideas of wealth and
security, and that means fine women and children. You've
got to be a *deprived* sort of man. ' All right,' you say,
' That's me ! ' But how about your wife being a deprived
sort of woman ? Eh ? That's where it gets you ! And
meanwhile, you know, while *you* make your sacrifices and
do your researches, there'll be little mean sharp active
beasts making money all over you like maggots on a
cheese. And if everybody who'd got gifts and altruistic
ideas gave themselves up to it, then evidently only the
mean and greedy lot would breed and have the glory.
They'd get everything. Every blessed thing. There
wouldn't be an option they didn't hold. And the other
chaps would produce the art and the science and the literature, as far as the men who'd got hold of things would let
'em, and perish out of the earth altogether. . . . There you
are ! Still, that's how things are made. . . .

"But it isn't worth it. It isn't worth extinguishing
oneself in order to make a world for those others, anyhow.
Them and their children. Is it ? Eh ? It's like building
a temple for flies to buzz in. . . . There is such a thing as
a personal side to Eugenics, you know."

Solomonson reflected over the end of his cigar. "It
isn't good enough," he concluded.

"You're infernally right," said Trafford.

"Very well," said Solomonson, "and now we can get
to business."

§ 17

The immediate business was the systematic exploitation
of the fact that Trafford had worked out the problem of
synthesising india-rubber. He had done so with an entire
indifference to the commercial possibilities of the case,
because he had been irritated by the enormous publicity
given to Behrens's assertion that he had achieved this long-
sought end. Of course the production of artificial rubbers
and rubber-like substances had been one of the activities

of the synthetic chemist for many years, from the appearance of Tilden's isoprene rubber onward, and there was already a formidable list of collaterals, dimethybutadiene, and so forth, by which the coveted goal could be approached. Behrens had boldly added to this list as his own a number of variations upon a theme of Trafford's, originally designed to settle certain curiosities about elasticity. Behrens's products were not only more massively rubber-like than anything that had gone before them, but also extremely cheap to produce, and his bold announcement of success had produced a check in rubber sales and widespread depression in the quiveringly sensitive market of plantation shares. Solomonson had consulted Trafford about this matter at Vevey, and had heard with infinite astonishment that Trafford had already roughly prepared and was proposing to complete and publish, unpatented and absolutely unprotected, first a smashing demonstration of the unsoundness of Behrens's claim, and then a lucid exposition of just what had to be done and what could be done to make an indiarubber absolutely indistinguishable from the natural product. The business man could not believe his ears.

" My dear chap, positively—you mustn't," Solomonson had screamed, and he had opened his fingers and humped his shoulders and for all his public school and university training lapsed undisguisedly into the Oriental. " Don't you *see* all you are throwing away ? " he squealed.

" I suppose it's our quality to throw such things away," said Trafford, when at last Solomonson's point of view became clear to him. They had embarked upon a long rambling discussion of that issue of publication, a discussion they were now taking up again. "When men dropped that idea of concealing knowledge, alchemist gave place to chemist," said Trafford, " and all that is worth having in modern life, all that makes it better and safer and more hopeful than the ancient life, began."

" My dear fellow," said Solomonson, " I know, I know. But to give away the synthesis of rubber ! To just shove it out of the window into the street ! *Gare l'eau !* Oh ! And when you could do with so much too ! " . . .

Now they resumed the divergent threads of that Vevey talk.

Solomonson had always entertained the warmest friendship and admiration for Trafford, and it was no new thing that he should desire a business co-operation. He had been working for that in the old days at Riplings ; he had never altogether let the possibility drop out of sight between them in spite of Trafford's repudiations. He believed himself to be a scientific man turned to business, but indeed his whole passion was for organisation and finance. He knew he could do everything but originate, and in Trafford he recognised just that rare combination of an obstinate and penetrating simplicity with constructive power which is the essential blend in the making of great intellectual initiatives. To Trafford belonged the secret of novel and unsuspected solutions ; what were fixed barriers and unsurmountable conditions to trained investigators and commonplace minds, would yield to his gift of magic inquiry. He could startle the accepted error into self-betrayal. Other men might play the game of business infinitely better than he—Solomonson knew, indeed, quite well that he himself could play the game infinitely better than Trafford—but it rested with Trafford by right divine of genius to alter the rules. If only he could be induced to alter the rules secretly, unostentatiously, on a business footing, instead of making catastrophic plunges into publicity ! And everything that had made Trafford up to the day of his marriage was antagonistic to such strategic reservations. The servant of science has as such no concern with personal consequences ; his business is the steady, relentless clarification of knowledge. The human affairs he changes, the wealth he makes or destroys, are no concern of his ; once these things weigh with him, become primary, he has lost his honour as a scientific man.

" But you *must* think of consequences," Solomonson had cried during those intermittent talks at Vevey. " Here you are, shying this cheap synthetic rubber of yours into the world—for it's bound to be cheap ! any one can see that—like a bomb into a market-place. What's the good of saying you don't care about the market-place, that *your* business is just to make bombs and drop them out of the window ? You smash up things just the same. Why ! you'll ruin hundreds and thousands of people, people living on rubber shares, people working in plantations, old, inadaptable workers in rubber works. . . ."

Sir Rupert was now still a little incredulous of Trafford's change of purpose, and for a time argued conceded points. Then slowly he came to the conditions and methods of the new relationship. He sketched out a scheme of co-operation and understandings between his firm and Trafford, between them both and his associated group in the city.

Behrens was to have rope and produce his slump in plantation shares, then Trafford was to publish his criticism of Behrens, reserving only that catalytic process which was his own originality, the process that was to convert the inert, theoretically correct synthetic rubber, with a mysterious difference in the quality of its phases, into the real right thing. With Behrens exploded, plantation shares would recover, and while their friends in the city manipulated that, Trafford would resign his professorship and engage himself to an ostentatious promotion syndicate for the investigation of synthetic rubber. His discovery would follow immediately the group had cleared itself of plantation shares; indeed he could begin planning the necessary works forthwith; the large scale operations in the process were to be protected as far as possible by patents, but its essential feature, the addition of a specific catalytic agent, could be safely dealt with as a secret process.

" I hate secrecy," said Trafford.

" Business," interjected Solomonson, and went on with his exposition of the relative advantages of secrecy and patent rights. It was all a matter of just how many people you had to trust. As that number increased, the more and more advisable did it become to put your cards on the table and risk the complex uncertain protection of the patent law. They went into elaborate calculations, clerks were called upon to hunt up facts and prices, and the table was presently littered with waste arithmetic.

" I believe we can do the stuff at tenpence a pound," said Solomonson, leaning back in his chair at last and rattling his fountain pen between his teeth, " so soon, that is, as we deal in quantity. Tenpence ! We can lower the price and spread the market, sixpence by sixpence. In the end—there won't be any more plantations. Have to grow tea. . . . I say, let's have an invalid dinner of chicken and champagne, and go on with this. It's fascinating. You can telephone."

They dined together, and Solomonson on champagne rather than chicken. His mind, which had never shown an instant's fatigue, began to glow and sparkle. This enterprise, he declared, was to be only the first of a series of vigorous exploitations. The whole thing warmed him. He would rather make ten thousand by such developments, than a hundred thousand by mere speculation. Trafford had but scratched the surface of his mine of knowledge. " Let's think of other thing," said Sir Rupert Solomonson. " Diamonds ! No ! They've got too many tons stowed away already. A diamond now—it's an absolutely artificial value. At any time a new discovery and one wild proprietor might bust that show. Lord !—diamonds ! Metals ? Of course you've worked the colloids chiefly. I suppose there's been more done in metals and alloys than anywhere. There's a lot of other substances. Business has hardly begun to touch substances yet, you know, Trafford— flexible glass, for example, and things like that. So far we've always taken substances for granted. On our side, I mean. It's extraordinary how narrow the outlook of business and finance is—still. It never seems to lead to things, never thinks ahead. In this case of rubber, for example——"

" When men fight for their own hands and for profit and position in the next ten years or so, I suppose they tend to become narrow."

" I suppose they must." Sir Rupert's face glowed with a new idea, and his voice dropped a little lower. " But what a pull they get, Trafford, if perhaps—they don't, eh ? "

" No," said Trafford, with a smile and a sigh, " the other sort gets the pull. "

" Not *this* time," said Solomonson ; " not with you to spot processes and me to figure out the cost "—he waved his hands to the litter that had been removed to a side table—" and generally see how the business end of things is going. . . ."

BOOK THE THIRD

MARJORIE AT LONELY HUT

CHAPTER THE FIRST

SUCCESSES

§ 1

I FIND it hard to trace the accumulation of moods and feelings that led Trafford and Marjorie at last to make their extraordinary raid upon Labrador. In a week more things happen in the thoughts of such a man as Trafford, changes, revocations, deflections, than one can chronicle in the longest of novels. I have already in an earlier passage of this story sought to give an image of the confused content of a modern human mind, but that pool was to represent a girl of twenty, and Trafford now was a man of nearly thirty-five, and touching life at a hundred points for one of the undergraduate Marjorie's. Perhaps that made him less confused, but it certainly made him fuller. Let me attempt, therefore, only the broad outline of his changes of purpose and activity until I come to the crucial mood that made these two lives a little worth telling about, amidst the many thousands of such lives that people are living to-day. . . .

It took him seven years from his conclusive agreement with Solomonson to become a rich and influential man. It took him only seven years, because already by the mere accidents of intellectual interest he was in possession of knowledge of the very greatest economic importance, and because Solomonson was full of that practical loyalty and honesty that distinguishes his race. I think that in any case Trafford's vigour and subtlety of mind would have achieved the prosperity he had found necessary to himself, but it might have been, under less favourable auspices, a much longer and more tortuous struggle. Success and security were never so abundant nor so easily attained by men with capacity and a sense of proportion as they are in the varied and flexible world of to-day. We live in an affluent age with a nearly incredible continuous fresh

increment of power pouring in from mechanical invention,
and compared with our own most other periods have been
meagre and anxious and hard-up times. Our problems
are constantly less the problems of submission and consola-
tion and continually more problems of opportunity. . . .
Trafford found the opening campaign, the operation
with the plantation shares and his explosion of Behrens's
pretensions extremely uncongenial. It left upon his mind
a confused series of memories of interviews and talks in
offices for the most part dingy and slovenly, of bales of
press-cuttings and blue-pencilled financial publications,
of unpleasing encounters with a number of bright-eyed,
flushed, excitable, and extremely cunning men, of having
to be reserved and limited in his talk upon all occasions,
and of all the worst aspects of Solomonson. All that
part of the new treatment of life that was to make him
rich gave him sensations as though he had ceased to wash
himself mentally, until he regretted his old life in his laboratory as a traveller in a crowded night train among filthy
people might regret the bathroom he had left behind him. . . .
But the development of his manufacture of rubber was
an entirely different business, and for a time profoundly
interesting. It took him into a new astonishing world,
the world of large-scale manufacture and industrial organisation. The actual planning of the works was not in itself
anything essentially new to him. So far as all that went
it was scarcely more than the problem of arranging an
experiment upon a huge and permanent scale, and all that
quick ingenuity, that freshness and directness of mind that
had made his purely scientific work so admirable had
ample and agreeable scope. Even the importance of cost
and economy at every point in the process involved no
system of considerations that was altogether novel to him.
The British investigator knows only too well the necessity
for husbanded material and inexpensive substitutes. But
strange factors came in, a new region of interest was opened
with the fact that instead of one experimenter working
with the alert responsive assistance of Durgan, a multitude
of human beings—even in the first drafts of his project
they numbered already two hundred, before the handling
and packing could be considered—had to watch, control,
assist or perform every stage in a long elaborate synthesis.
For the first time in his life Trafford encountered the reality
of Labour, as it is known to the modern producer.
It will be difficult in the future, when things now subtly

or widely separated have been brought together by the receding perspectives of time, for the historian to realise just how completely out of the thoughts of such a young man as Trafford the millions of people who live and die in organised productive industry had been. That vast world of toil and weekly anxiety, ill-trained and stupidly directed effort and mental and moral feebleness, had been as much beyond the living circle of his experience as the hosts of Genghis Khan or the social life of the Forbidden City. Consider the limitations of this world. In all his life hitherto he had never been beyond a certain prescribed area of London's immensities, except by the most casual and uninstructive straying. He knew Chelsea and Kensington and the north bank and (as a boy) Battersea Park, and all the strip between Kensington and Charing Cross, with some scraps of the Strand as far as the Law Courts, a shop or so in Tottenham Court Road and fragments about the British Museum and Holborn and Regent's Park, a range up Edgware Road to Maida Vale, the routes west and south-west through Uxbridge and Putney to the country, and Wimbledon Common and Putney Heath. He had never been on Hampstead Heath nor visited the Botanical Gardens nor gone down the Thames below London Bridge, nor seen Sydenham nor Epping Forest nor the Victoria Park. Take a map and blot all he knew and see how vast is the area left untouched. All industrial London, all wholesale London, great oceans of human beings fall into that excluded area. The homes he knew were comfortable homes, the poor he knew were the parasitic and dependent poor of the West, the shops, good retail shops, the factories for the most part engaged in dressmaking.

Of course he had been informed about this vast rest of London. He knew that as a matter of fact it existed, was populous, portentous, puzzling. He had heard of "slums," read *Tales of Mean Streets*, and marvelled in a shallow, transitory way at such wide wildernesses of life, apparently supported by nothing at all in a state of gray, darkling but prolific discomfort. Like the princess who wondered why the people having no bread did not eat cake, he could never clearly understand why the population remained there, did not migrate to more attractive surroundings. He had discussed the problems of those wildernesses as young men do, rather confidently, very ignorantly, had dismissed them, recurred to them, and forgotten them amidst a press of other interests, but now it all suddenly became real to him with the intensity of a startling and intimate contact. He discovered this limitless unknown greater London, this London of the majority, as if he had never thought of it before. He went out to inspect favourable sites in regions whose very names were unfamiliar to him, travelled on dirty little intra-urban railway lines to hitherto unimagined railway stations, found parks, churches, workhouses, institutions, public-houses, canals, factories, gas-works, warehouses, foundries and sidings, amidst a multitudinous dinginess of mean houses, shabby backyards, and ill-kept streets. There seemed to be no limits to this threadbare side of London, it went on northward, eastward, and over the Thames southward, for mile after mile—endlessly. The factories and so forth clustered in lines and banks upon the means of communication, the homes stretched between, an infinitude of parallelograms of grimy boxes with public-houses at the corners and churches and chapels in odd places, towering over which rose the council schools, big, blunt, truncated-looking masses, the means to an education as blunt and truncated, born of tradition and confused purposes, achieving by accident what they achieve at all.

And about this sordid-looking wilderness went a population that seemed at first as sordid. It was in no sense a tragic population. But it saw little of the sun, felt the wind but rarely, and so had a white, dull skin that looked degenerate and ominous to a West End eye. It was not naked or barefooted, but it wore cheap clothes that were tawdry when new, and speedily became faded, discoloured, dusty, and draggled. It was slovenly and almost wilfully ugly in its speech and gestures. And the food it ate was rough and coarse if abundant, the eggs it consumed " tasted "—everything " tasted " ; its milk, its beer, its bread was degraded by base adulterations, its meat was hacked red stuff that hung in the dusty air until it was sold ; east of the city Trafford could find no place where by his standards he could get a tolerable meal tolerably served. The entertainment of this eastern London was jingle, its religion clap-trap, its reading feeble and sensational rubbish without kindliness or breadth. And if this great industrial multitude was neither tortured nor driven nor cruelly treated—as the slaves and common people of other days have been—yet it was universally anxious, perpetually anxious about urgent small necessities and petty dissatisfying things. . . .

That was the general effect of this new region in which he had sought out and found the fortunate site for his manufacture of rubber, and against this background it was that he had now to encounter a crowd of selected individuals, and weld them into a harmonious and successful "process." They came out from their millions to him, dingy, clumsy, and at first it seemed without any individuality. Insensibly they took on character, rounded off by unaccustomed methods into persons as marked and distinctive as any he had known.

There was Dowd, for instance, the technical assistant, whom he came to call in his private thoughts Dowd the Disinherited. Dowd had seemed a rather awkward, potentially insubordinate young man of unaccountably extensive and curiously limited attainments. He had begun his career in a crowded home behind and above a baker's shop in Hoxton; he had gone as a boy into the works of a Clerkenwell electric engineer, and there he had developed that craving for knowledge which is so common in poor men of the energetic type. He had gone to classes, read with a sort of fury, feeding his mind on the cheap and adulterated instruction of grant-earning crammers and on stale, meretricious and ill-chosen books; his mental food indeed was the exact parallel of the rough, abundant, cheap, and nasty groceries and meat that gave the East-ender his spots and dyspeptic complexion, the cheap text-books were like canned meat and dangerous with intellectual ptomaines, the rascally encyclopædias like weak and whitened bread, and Dowd's mental complexion, too, was leaden and spotted. Yet essentially he wasn't, Trafford found, by any means bad stuff; where his knowledge had had a chance of touching reality it became admirable, and he was full of energy in his work and a sort of honest zeal about the things of the mind. The two men grew from an acute mutual criticism into a mutual respect.

At first it seemed to Trafford that when he met Dowd he was only meeting Dowd, but a time came when it seemed to him that in meeting Dowd he was meeting all that cast new England outside the range of ruling-class dreams, that multitudinous greater England, cheaply treated, rather out of health, angry, energetic, and now becoming intelligent and critical, that England which organised industrialism has created. There were nights when he thought for hours about Dowd. Other figures grouped themselves round him—Markham, the head clerk, the quintessence of East

End respectability, with a house almost on the Victoria Park ; Casement, who saw to the packing ; Miss Peckover, an ex-telegraph operator, a woman so entirely reliable and unobservant that the most betraying phase of the secret process could be confidently entrusted to her hands. Behind them were clerks, workmen, motor-van men, work-girls, a crowd of wage-earners, from amidst which some individual would assume temporary importance and interest by doing something wrong, getting into trouble, becoming insubordinate, and having contributed a little vivid story to Trafford's gathering impressions of life, drop back again into undistinguished subordination.

Down became at last entirely representative.

When first Trafford looked Dowd in the eye, he met something of the hostile interest one might encounter in a swordsman ready to begin a duel. There was a watchful-ness, an immense reserve. They discussed the work and the terms of their relationship, and all the while Trafford felt there was something almost threateningly not mentioned.

Presently he learnt from a Silvertown employer what that concealed aspect was. Dowd was " the sort of man who makes trouble," disposed to strike rather than not upon a grievance, with a taste for open-air meetings, a member, obstinately adherent in spite of friendly remon-strance, of the Social Democratic Party. This in spite of his clear duty to a wife and two small white knobby children. For a time he would not talk to Trafford of anything but business—Trafford was so manifestly the enemy, not to be trusted, the adventurous plutocrat, the exploiter—when at last Dowd did open out he did so defiantly, throwing opinions at Trafford as a mob might hurl bricks at windows. At last they achieved a sort of friendship and understanding, an amiability as it were in hostility, but never from first to last would he talk to Trafford as one gentleman to another ; between them, and crossed only by flimsy temporary bridges, was his sense of incurable grievances and fundamental injustice. He seemed incapable of forgetting the disadvantages of his birth and upbringing, the inferiority and disorder of the house that sheltered him, the poor food that nourished him, the dead-ened air he breathed, the limited leisure, the inadequate books. Implicit in his every word and act was the assur-ance that but for this handicap he could have filled Trafford's place, while Trafford would certainly have failed in his.

For all these things Dowd made Trafford responsible;
he held him to that inexorably.

" *You* sweat us," he said, speaking between his teeth ;
" *you* limit us, *you* stifle us, and away there in the West
End, *you* and the women you keep waste the plunder."

Trafford attempted palliation. " After all," he said,
" it's not me so particularly——"

" But it is," said Dowd.

" It's the system things go upon."

" You're the responsible part of it. *You* have freedom,
you have power and endless opportunity——"

Trafford shrugged his shoulders.

" It's because your sort wants too much," said Dowd,
" that my sort hasn't enough."

" Tell me how to organise things better."

" Much you'd care. They'll organise themselves. Everything is drifting to class separation, the growing discontent,
the growing hardship of the masses. . . . Then you'll see."

" Then what's going to happen ? "

" Overthrow. And social democracy."

" How is that going to work ? "

Dowd had been cornered by that before. " I don't care
if it *doesn't* work," he snarled, " so long as we smash up
this. We're getting too sick to care what comes after."

" Dowd," said Trafford abruptly, " *I'm* not so satisfied
with things."

Dowd looked at him askance. " You'll get reconciled
to it," he said. " It's ugly here—but it's all right there—
at the spending end. . . . Your sort has got to grab, your
sort has got to spend—until the thing works out and the
social revolution makes an end of you."

" And then ? "

Dowd became busy with his work.

Trafford stuck his hands in his pockets and stared out
of the dingy factory window.

" I don't object so much to your diagnosis," he said,
" as to your remedy. It doesn't strike me as a remedy."

" It's an end," said Dowd, " anyhow. My God ! When
I think of all the women and shirkers flaunting and fritter-
ing away there in the West, while here men and women
toil and worry and starve. . . ." He stopped short like
one who feels too full for controlled speech.

" Dowd," said Trafford, after a fair pause, " what would
you do if you were me ? "

" Do ! " said Dowd.

" Yes," said Trafford, as one who reconsiders it, " what would you do ? "

" Now that's a curious question, Mr. Trafford," said Dowd, turning to regard him. " Meaning—if I were in your place ? "

" Yes," said Trafford. " What would you do in my place ? "

" I should sell out of this place jolly quick," he said.

" *Sell !* " said Trafford softly.

" Yes—sell. And start a socialist daily right off. An absolutely independent, unbiased socialist daily."

" And what would that do ? "

" It would stir people up. Every day it would stir people up."

" But you see I can't edit. I haven't the money for half a year of a socialist daily. . . . And meanwhile people want rubber."

Dowd shook his head. " You mean that you and your wife want to have the spending of six or eight thousand a year," he said.

" I don't make half of that," said Trafford.

" Well—half of that," pressed Dowd. " It's all the same to me."

Trafford reflected. " The point where I don't agree with you," he said, " is in supposing that my scale of living— over there, is directly connected with the scale of living —about here."

" Well, isn't it ? "

" ' Directly,' I said. No. If we just stopped it—over there—there'd be no improvement here. In fact, for a time it would mean dislocations. It might mean per-manent, hopeless, catastrophic dislocation. You know that as well as I do. Suppose the West End became— Tolstoyan ; the East would become chaos."

" Not much likelihood," sneered Dowd.

" That's another question. That we earn together here and that I spend alone over there, it's unjust and bad, but it isn't a thing that admits of any simple remedy. Where we differ, Dowd, is about that remedy. I admit the disease as fully as you do. I, as much as you, want to see the dawn of a great change in the ways of human living. But I don't think the diagnosis is complete and satisfactory ; our problem is an intricate muddle of disorders, not one simple disorder, and I don't see what treatment is indicated."

" Socialism," said Dowd, " is indicated."

" You might as well say that health is indicated," said Trafford, with a note of impatience in his voice. " Does any one question that if we could have this socialist state in which every one is devoted and every one is free, in which there is no waste and no want, and beauty and brother-hood prevail universally, we wouldn't ? But——. You socialists have no scheme of government, no scheme of economic organisation, no intelligible guarantees of personal liberty, no method of progress, no ideas about marriage, no plan—except those little pickpocket plans of the Fabians that you despise as much as I do—for making this order into that other order you've never yet taken the trouble to work out even in principle. Really, you know, Dowd, what is the good of pointing at my wife's dresses and waving the red flag at me, and talking of human miseries——"

" It seems to wake you up a bit," said Dowd, with characteristic irrelevance.

§ 2

The accusing finger of Dowd followed Trafford into his dreams.

Behind it was his gray-toned, intelligent, resentful face, his smouldering eyes, his slightly frayed collar and vivid, ill-chosen tie. At times Trafford could almost hear his flat, insistent voice, his measured h-less speech. Dowd was so penetratingly right—and so ignorant of certain essentials, so wrong in his forecasts and ultimates. It was true beyond disputing that Trafford as compared with Dowd, had oppor-tunity, power of a sort, the prospect and possibility of leisure. He admitted the liability that followed on that advantage. It expressed so entirely the spirit of his training that with Trafford the noble maxim of the older socialists : " from each according to his ability, to each according to his need," received an intuitive acquiescence. He had no more doubt than Dowd that Dowd was the victim of a subtle, evasive injustice, innocently and help-lessly underbred, underfed, cramped, and crippled, and that all his own surplus made him, in a sense, Dowd's debtor.

But Dowd's remedies !

Trafford made himself familiar with the socialist and labour newspapers, and he was as much impressed by their

honest resentments and their enthusiastic hopefulness as
he was repelled by their haste and ignorance, their cocksure
confidence in untried reforms and impudent teachers, their
indiscriminating progressiveness, their impulsive lapses
into hatred, misrepresentation and vehement personal
abuse. He was in no mood for the humours of human
character, and he found the ill-masked feuds and jealousies
of the leaders, the sham statecraft of G. B. Magdeberg,
M.P., the sham Machiavellism of Dorvil, the sham persistent
good-heartedness of Will Pipes, discouraging and irritating.
Altogether it seemed to him the conscious popular movement in politics, both in and out of Parliament, was a mere
formless and indeterminate aspiration. It was a confused
part of the general confusion, symptomatic perhaps, but
exercising no controls and no direction.

His attention passed from the consideration of this
completely revolutionary party to the general field of
social reform. With the naïve directness of a scientific
man, he got together the published literature of half a
dozen flourishing agitations and philanthropies, interviewed prominent and rather embarrassed personages,
attended meetings, and when he found the speeches too
tiresome to follow watched the audience about him. He
even looked up Aunt Plessington's Movement, and filled
her with wild hopes and premature boastings about a
promising convert "Marjorie's brought him round at
last!" said Aunt Plessington. " I knew I could trust my
little Madge!" His impression was not the cynic's impression of these wide shallows of activity. Progress and
social reform are not, he saw, mere cloaks of hypocrisy ; a
wealth of good intention lies behind them in spite of their
manifest futility. There is much dishonesty due to the
blundering desire for consistency in people of hasty intention, much artless and a little calculated self-seeking, but
far more vanity and amiable feebleness of mind in their
general attainment of failure. The Plessingtons struck
him as being after all very typical of the publicist at large,
quite devoted, very industrious, extremely presumptuous
and essentially thin-witted. They would cheat like ill-
bred children, for example, on some petty point of reputation, but they could be trusted to expend, ineffectually
indeed, but with the extremest technical integrity, whatever sums of money their adherents could get together. . . .

He emerged from this inquiry into the proposed remedies
and palliatives for Dowd's wrongs with a better opinion of

people's hearts and a worse one of their heads than he had
hitherto entertained.

Pursuing this line of thought, he passed from the
politicians and practical workers to the economists and
sociologists. He spent the entire leisure of the second
summer after the establishment of the factory upon sociological and economic literature. At the end of that bout
of reading he attained a vivid realisation of the garrulous
badness that rules in this field of work, and the prevailing
slovenliness and negligence in regard to it. He chanced
one day to look up the article on Socialism in the new
Encyclopædia Britannica, and found in its entire failure
to state the case for or against modern Socialism, to trace
its origins, or to indicate any rational development in the
movement, a symptom of the universal laxity of interest
in these matters. Indeed, the writer did not appear to
have heard of modern Socialism at all ; he discussed
collective and individualist methods very much as a rather
ill-read schoolgirl in a hurry for her college debating
society might have done. Compared with the treatment of
engineering or biological science in the same compilation,
this article became almost symbolical of the prevailing
habitual incompetence with which all this system of
questions is still handled. The sciences were done scantily
and carelessly enough, but they admitted at any rate the
possibility of completeness ; this did not even pretend to
thoroughness.

One might think such things had no practical significance.
And at the back of it all was Dowd, remarkably more
impatient each year, confessing the failure of parliamentary
methods, of trades unionism, hinting more and more plainly
at the advent of a permanent guerilla war against capital,
at the general strike and sabotage.

" It's coming to that," said Dowd ; " it's coming to
that."

" *What's the good of it ?* " he said, echoing Trafford's
words. " It's a sort of relief to the feelings. Why
shouldn't we ? "

§ 3

But you must not suppose that at any time these huge
gray problems of our social foundations and the riddle of
intellectual confusion one reaches through them, and the
yet broader riddles of human purpose that open beyond,

constituted the whole of Trafford's life during this time.
When he came back to Marjorie and his home, a curtain
of unreality fell between him and all these things. It was
as if he stepped through such boundaries as Alice passed
to reach her Wonderland ; the other world became a
dream again ; as if he closed the pages of a vivid book
and turned to things about him. Or again it was as if he
drew down the blind of a window that gave upon a landscape, grave, darkling, ominous, and faced the warm realities
of a brightly illuminated room. . . .

In a year or so he had the works so smoothly organised
and Dowd so reconciled, trained and encouraged that his
own daily presence was unnecessary, and he would go
three and then only two mornings a week to conduct those
secret phases in the preparation of his catalytic that even
Dowd could not be trusted to know. He reverted more
and more completely to his own proper world.

And the first shock of discovering that greater London
which " isn't in it " passed away by imperceptible degrees.
Things that had been as vivid and startling as new wounds
became unstimulating and ineffective with repetition. He
got used to the change from Belgravia to East Ham from
East Ham to Belgravia. He fell in with the unusual persuasion in Belgravia, that, given a firm and prompt Home
Secretary, East Ham could be trusted to go on—for quite
a long time anyhow. One cannot sit down for all one's life
in the face of insoluble problems. He had a motor-car now
that far outshone Magnet's, and he made the transit from
west to east in the minimum of time and with the minimum
of friction. It ceased to be more disconcerting that he
should have workers whom he could dismiss at a week's
notice to want or prostitution than that he should have a
servant waiting behind his chair. Things were so. The
main current of his life—and the main current of his life
flowed through Marjorie and his home—carried him on.
Rubber was his, but there were still limitless worlds to
conquer. He began to take up, working under circumstances of considerable secrecy at Solomonson's laboratories
at Riplings, (to which he would now go by motor-car for
two or three days at a time) the possibility of a cheap,
resilient, and very tough substance, rubber glass, that was
to be, Solomonson was assured, the road surface of the
future. . . .

§ 4

The confidence of Solomonson had made it possible for Trafford to alter his style of living almost directly upon the conclusion of their agreement. He went back to Marjorie to broach a financially emancipated phase. They took a furnished house at Shackleford, near Godalming in Surrey, and there they lived for nearly a year—using their Chelsea home only as a town apartment for Trafford when business held him in London. And there it was, in the pretty Surrey country, with the sweet air of pine and heather in Marjorie's blood, that their second child was born. It was a sturdy little boy, whose only danger in life seemed to be the superfluous energy with which he resented its slightest disrespect of his small but important requirements.

When it was time for Marjorie to return to London, spring had come round again, and Trafford's conceptions of life were adapting themselves to the new scale upon which they were now to do things. While he was busy creating his factory in the East End, Marjorie was displaying an equal if a less original constructive energy in Sussex Square, near Lancaster Gate, for there it was the new home was to be established. She set herself to furnish and arrange it so as to produce the maximum of surprise and chagrin in Daphne, and she succeeded admirably. The Magnets now occupied a flat in Whitehall Court; the furniture Magnet had insisted upon buying himself with all the occult cunning of the humorist in these matters, and not even Daphne could blind herself to the superiority both in arrangement and detail of Marjorie's home. That was very satisfactory, and so too was the inevitable exaggeration of Trafford's financial importance. " He can do what he likes in the rubber world," said Marjorie. " In Mincing Lane, where they deal in rubber shares, they used to call him and Sir Rupert the Invaders ; now they call them the Conquering Heroes. . . . Of course, it's mere child's play to Godwin, but, as he said, ' We want money.' It won't really interfere with his more important interests. . . ."

I do not know why both those sisters were more vulgarly competitive with each other than with any one else ; I have merely to record the fact that they were so.

The effect upon the rest of Marjorie's family was equally gratifying. Mr. Pope came to the house-warming as though he had never had the slightest objection to Trafford's antecedents, and told him casually after dinner that

Marjorie had always been his favourite daughter, and that from the first he had expected great things of her. He told Magnet, who was the third man of the party, that he only hoped Syd and Rom would do as well as their elder sisters. Afterwards, in the drawing-room, he whacked Marjorie suddenly and very startlingly on the shoulder-blade—it was the first bruise he had given her since Buryhamstreet days. " You've made a man of him, Maggots," he said.

The quiet smile of the Christian Scientist was becoming now the fixed expression of Mrs. Pope's face, and it scarcely relaxed for a moment as she surveyed her daughter's splendours. She had triumphantly refused to worry over a rather serious speculative disappointment, but her faith in her prophet's spiritual power had been strengthened rather than weakened by the manifest insufficiency of his financial prestidigitations, and she was getting through life quite radiantly now, smiling at (but not, of course, giving way to) beggars, smiling at toothaches and head-aches, both her own and other people's, smiling away doubts, smiling away everything that bows the spirit of those who are still in the bonds of the flesh. . . .

Afterwards the children came round, Syd and Rom now with skirts down and hair up, and rather stiff in the fine big rooms, and Theodore in a high collar and very anxious to get Trafford on his side in his ambition to chuck a proposed bank clerkship and go in for professional aviation. . . .

It was pleasant to be respected by her family again, but the mind of Marjorie was soon reaching out to the more novel possibilities of her changed position. She need no longer confine herself to teas and afternoons. She could now, delightful thought ! give dinners. Dinners are mere vulgarities for the vulgar, but in the measure of your brains does a dinner become a work of art. There is the happy blending of a modern and distinguished sim-plicity with a choice of items essentially good and delightful and just a little bit not what was expected. There is the still more interesting and difficult blending and arrange-ment of the diners. From the first Marjorie resolved on a round table, and the achievement of that rare and wonder-ful thing, general conversation. She had a clear centre, with a circle of silver bowls filled with short cut flowers and low, shaded, old silver candlesticks adapted to the electric light. The first dinner was a nervous experience for her, but happily Trafford seemed unconscious of the

importance of the occasion and talked very easily and
well ; at last she attained her old ambition to see Sir
Roderick Dover in her house ; and there was Remington,
the editor of the *Blue Weekly*, and his silent, gracious wife ;
Edward Crampton, the historian, full of surprising new
facts about Kosciusko ; the Solomonsons and Mrs. Millingham, and Mary Gasthorne the novelist. It was a good
talking lot. Remington sparred agreeably with the old
Toryism of Dover, flank attacks upon them both were
delivered by Mrs. Millingham and Trafford, Crampton
instanced Hungarian parallels, and was happily averted
by Mary Gasthorne with travel experiences in the Car-
pathians ; the diamonds of Lady Solomonson and Mrs.
Remington flashed and winked across the shining table, as
their wearers listened with unmistakable intelligence, and
when the ladies had gone upstairs Sir Rupert Solomonson
told all the men exactly what he thought of the policy of
the *Blue Weekly*, a balanced, common-sense judgment.
Upstairs Lady Solomonson betrayed a passion of admiration for Mrs. Remington, and Mrs. Millingham mumbled
depreciation of the same lady's intelligence in Mary
Gasthorne's unwilling ear. " She's *passive*," said Mrs.
Millingham. " She bores him. . . ."

For a time Marjorie found dinner-giving delightful—it
is like picking and arranging posies of human flowers—and
fruits—and perhaps a little dried grass, and it was not long
before she learnt that she was esteemed a success as a
hostess. She gathered her earlier bunches in the Carmel
and Solomonson circle, with a stiffening from among the
literary and scientific friends of Trafford and his mother,
and one or two casual and undervalued blossoms from
Aunt Plessington's active promiscuities. She had soon a
gaily flowering garden of her own to pick from. Its
strength and finest display lay in its increasing proportion
of political intellectuals, men in and about the House who
relaxed their minds from the tense detailed alertness needed
in political intrigues by conversation that rose at times
to the level of the smarter sort of article in the half-crown
reviews. The women were more difficult than the men,
and Marjorie found herself wishing at times that girl
novelists and playwrights were more abundant, or women
writers, on the average, younger. These talked generally
well, and one or two capable women of her own type talked
and listened with an effect of talking ; so many other
women either chattered disturbingly, or else did not listen,

with an effect of not talking at all, and so made gaps about the table. Many of these latter had to be asked because they belonged to the class of inevitable wives, *sine qua nons*, and through them she learnt the value of that priceless variety of kindly unselfish men who can create the illusion of attentive conversation in the most uncomfortable and suspicious natures without producing backwater and eddy in the general flow of talk.

Indisputably Marjorie's dinners were successful. Of course, the abundance and æsthetic achievements of Mrs. Lee still seemed to her immeasurably out of reach, but it was already possible to show Aunt Plessington how the thing ought really to be done, Aunt Plessington with her narrow, lank, austerely served table, with a sort of quarter-deck at her own end and a subjugated forecastle round Hubert. And accordingly the Plessingtons were invited and shown, and to a party, too, that restrained Aunt Plessington from her usual conversational prominence. . . .

These opening years of Trafford's commercial phase were full of an engaging activity for Marjorie as for him, and for her far more completely than for him were the profounder solicitudes of life lost sight of in the bright succession of immediate events.

Marjorie did not let her social development interfere with her duty to society in the larger sense. Two years after the vigorous and resentful Godwin came a second son, and a year and a half later a third. " That's enough," said Marjorie, " now we've got to rear them." The nursery at Sussex Square had always been a show part of the house, but it became her crowning achievement. She had never forgotten the Lee display at Vevey, the shining splendours of modern maternity, the books, the apparatus, the space and light and air. The whole second floor was altered to accommodate these four triumphant beings, who absorbed the service of two nurses, a Swiss nursery governess, and two housemaids—not to mention those several hundred obscure individuals who were yielding a sustaining profit in the East End. At any rate, they were very handsome and promising children, and little Margharita could talk three languages with a childish fluency, and invent and write a short fable in either French or German—with only as much misspelling as any child of eight may be permitted. . . .

Then there sprang up a competition between Marjorie and the able, pretty wife of Halford Wallace, most promising of under-secretaries. They gave dinners against each other, they discovered young artists against each other, they went to first-nights and dressed against each other. Marjorie was ruddy and tall, Mrs. Halford Wallace dark and animated ; Halford Wallace admired Marjorie, Trafford was insensible to Mrs. Halford Wallace. They played for points so vague that it was impossible for any one to say which was winning, but none the less they played like artists, for all they were worth. . . .

Trafford's rapid prosperity and his implicit promise of still wider activities and successes brought him innumerable acquaintances and many friends. He joined two or three distinguished clubs, he derived an uncertain interest from a series of week-end visits to ample, good-mannered households, and for a time he found a distraction in little flashes of travel to countries that caught at his imagination, Morocco, Montenegro, Southern Russia.

I do not know whether Marjorie might not have been altogether happy during this early Sussex Square period, if it had not been for an unconquerable uncertainty about Trafford. But ever and again she became vaguely apprehensive of some perplexing unreality in her position. She had never had any such profundity of discontent as he experienced. It was nothing clear, nothing that actually penetrated, distressing her. It was at most an uneasiness. For him the whole fabric of life was, as it were, torn and pierced by a provocative sense of depths unplumbed that robbed it of all its satisfactions. For her these glimpses were as yet rare, mere moments of doubt that passed again and left her active and assured.

§ 5

It was only after they had been married six or seven years that Trafford began to realise how widely his attitudes to Marjorie varied. He emerged slowly from a naïve unconsciousness of his fluctuations—a naïve unconsciousness of inconsistency that for most men and women remains throughout life. His ruling idea that she and he were friends, equals, confederates, knowing everything about each other, co-operating in everything, was very fixed and firm. But indeed that had become the remotest rendering of their relationship. Their lives were lives of intimate disengagement. They came nearest to fellowship in relation to their children ; there they shared an immense

common pride. Beyond that was a less confident appreciation of their common house and their joint effect. And
then they liked and loved each other tremendously. They
could play upon each other and please each other in a
hundred different ways, and they did so, quite consciously,
observing each other with the completest externality. She
was still in many ways for him the bright girl he had
admired in the examination, still the mysterious dignified
transfiguration of that delightful creature on the tragically
tender verge of motherhood ; these memories were of more
power with him than the present realities of her full-grown
strength and capacity. He petted and played with the
girl still ; he was still tender and solicitous for that early
woman. He admired and co-operated also with the
capable, narrowly ambitious, beautiful lady into which
Marjorie had developed, but those remoter experiences it
was that gave the deeper emotions to their relationship.

The conflict of aims that had at last brought Trafford
from scientific investigation into business, had left behind
it a little scar of hostility. He felt his sacrifice. He felt
that he had given something for her that she had had no
right to exact, that he had gone beyond the free mutualities
of honest love and paid a price for her ; he had deflected
the whole course of his life for her and he was entitled
to repayments. Unconsciously he had become a slightly
jealous husband. He resented inattentions and absences.
He felt she ought to be with him and orient all her proceedings towards him. He did not like other people to
show too marked an appreciation of her. She had a healthy
love of admiration, and in addition her social ambitions
made it almost inevitable that at times she should use her
great personal charm to secure and retain adherents. He
was ashamed to betray the resentments thus occasioned,
and his silence widened the separation more than any
protest could have done. . . .

For his own part he gave her no cause for a reciprocal
jealousy. Other women did not excite his imagination
very greatly, and he had none of the ready disposition to
lapse to other comforters which is so frequent a characteristic of the husband out of touch with his life's companion.
He was perhaps an exceptional man in his steadfast loyalty
to his wife. He had come to her as new to love as she
had been. He had never in his life taken that one decisive
illicit step which changes all the aspects of sexual life for
a man even more than for a woman. Love for him was a

thing solemn, simple, and unspoilt. He perceived that it
was not so for most other men, but that did little to modify
his own private attitude. In his curious scrutiny of the
people about him, he did not fail to note the drift of
adventures and infidelities that glimmers along beneath
the even surface of our social life. One or two of his
intimate friends, Solomonson was one of them, passed
through "affairs." Once or twice those dim proceedings
splashed upward to the surface in an open scandal. There
came Remington's startling elopement with Isabel Rivers,
the writer, which took two brilliant and inspiring con-
temporaries suddenly and distressingly out of Trafford's
world. Trafford felt none of that rage and forced and
jealous contempt for the delinquents in these matters
which is common in the ill-regulated, virtuous mind. Indeed, he was far more sympathetic with than hostile to
the offenders. He had brains and imagination to appreciate
the grim pathos of a process that begins as a hopeful quest,
full of the suggestion of noble possibilities, full of the
craving for missed intensities of fellowship and realisation,
that loiters involuntarily towards beauties and delights,
and ends at last too often, after the gratification of an
appetite, in artificially hideous exposures, and the pelting
misrepresentations of the timidly well-behaved vile. But
the general effect of pitiful evasions, of unavoidable mean-
nesses, of draggled heroics and tortuously insincere
explanations confirmed him in his aversion from this
labyrinthine trouble of extraneous love. . . .

But if Trafford was a faithful husband, he ceased to be
a happy and confident one. There grew up in him a vast
hinterland of thoughts and feelings, an accumulation of
unspoken and largely of unformulated things in which
his wife had no share. And it was in that hinterland that
his essential self had its abiding-place. . . .

It came as a discovery, it remained for ever after a
profoundly disturbing perplexity, that he had talked to
Marjorie most carelessly, easily and seriously, during their
courtship and their honeymoon. He remembered their
early intercourse now as an immense happy freedom in
love. Then afterwards a curtain had fallen. That almost
delirious sense of escaping from oneself, of having at last
found some one from whom there need be no concealment,
some one before whom one could stand naked-souled and
assured of love as one stands before one's God, faded so
that he scarce observed its passing, but only discovered

at last that it had· gone.   He misunderstood and met
misunderstanding.   He found he could hurt her by the
things he said, and be exquisitely hurt by her failure to
apprehend the spirit of some ill-expressed intention.   And
it was so vitally important not to hurt, not to be hurt.
At first he only perceived that he reserved himself ; then
there came the intimation of the question, was she also
perhaps in such another hinterland as his, keeping herself
from him ?

He had perceived the cessation of that first bright
outbreak of self-revelation, this relapse into the secrecies
of individuality, quite early in their married life.   I have
already told of his first efforts to bridge their widening
separation by walks and talks in the country, and by the
long pilgrimage among the Alps that had ended so un-
expectedly at Vevey.   In the retrospect the years seemed
punctuated with phases when " we must talk " dominated
their intercourse, and each time the impulse of that recognised need passed away by insensible degrees again—with
nothing said.

§ 6

Marjorie cherished an obstinate hope that Trafford
would take up political questions and go into Parliament.
It seemed to her that there was something about him
altogether graver and wider than most of the active politicians she knew.   She liked to think of those gravities
assuming a practicable form, of Trafford very rapidly and
easily coming forward into a position of cardinal significance.   It gave her general expenditure a quality of
concentration without involving any uncongenial limitation
to suppose it aimed at the preparation of a statesman's
circle whenever Trafford chose to need that.   Little men
in great positions came to her house and talked with opaque
self-confidence at her table ; she measured them against
her husband while she played the admiring female disciple
to their half-confidential talk.   She felt that he could take
up these questions and measures that they reduced to trite
twaddle, open the wide relevances behind them, and make
them magically significant, sweep away the encrusting
pettiness, the personalities and arbitrary prejudices.   But
why didn't he begin to do it ?   She threw out hints he
seemed blind towards, she exercised miracles of patience
while he ignored her baits.   She came near intrigue in her
endeavour to entangle him in political affairs.   For a time

it seemed to her that she was succeeding—I have already told of his phase of inquiry and interest in socio-political work—and then he relapsed into a scornful restlessness, and her hopes weakened again.

But he could not concentrate his mind, he could not think where to begin. Day followed day, each with its attack upon his attention, its petty just claims, its attractive novelties of aspect. The telephone bell rang, the letters flopped into the hall, Malcolm the butler seemed always at hand with some distracting oblong on his salver. Dowd was developing ideas for a reconstructed organisation of the factory, Solomonson growing enthusiastic about rubber-glass, his house seemed full of women, Marjorie had an engagement for him to keep or the children were coming in to say good-night. To his irritated brain the whole scheme of his life presented itself at last as a tissue of interruptions which prevented his looking clearly at reality. More and more definitely he realised he wanted to get away and think. His former life of research became invested with an effect of immense dignity and of a steadfast singleness of purpose. . . .

But Trafford was following his own lights, upon his own lines. He was returning to that faith in the supreme importance of thought and knowledge, upon which he had turned his back when he left pure research behind him. To that familiar end he came by an unfamiliar route, after his long, unsatisfying examination of social reform movements and social and political theories. Immaturity, haste, and presumption vitiated all that region, and it seemed to him less and less disputable that the only escape for mankind from a continuing extravagant futility lay through the attainment of a quite unprecedented starkness and thoroughness of thinking about all these questions. This conception of a needed Renascence obsessed him more and more, and the persuasion, deeply felt if indistinctly apprehended, that somewhere in such an effort there was a part for him to play. . . .

Life is too great for us or too petty. It gives us no tolerable middle way between baseness and greatness. We must die daily on the levels of ignoble compromise or perish tragically among the precipices. On the one hand is a life—unsatisfying and secure, a plane of dulled gratifications, mean advantages, petty triumphs, adaptations, acquiescences and submissions, and on the other a steep and terrible climb, set with sharp stones and bramble thickets and the possibilities of grotesque dislocations, and the snares of such temptation as comes only to those whose minds have been quickened by high desire, and the challenge of insoluble problems and the intimations of issues so complex and great, demanding such a nobility of purpose, such a steadfastness, alertness, and openness of mind, that they fill the heart of man with despair. . . .

There were moods when Trafford would, as people say, pull himself together, and struggle with his gnawing discontent. He would compare his lot with that of other men, reproach himself for a monstrous greed and ingratitude. He remonstrated with himself as one might remonstrate with a pampered child refusing to be entertained by a whole handsome nursery full of toys. Other men did their work in the world methodically and decently, did their duty by their friends and belongings, were manifestly patient through dullness, steadfastly cheerful, ready to meet vexations with a humorous smile, and grateful for orderly pleasures. Was he abnormal ? Or was he in some unsuspected way unhealthy ? Trafford neglected no possible explanations. Did he want this great Renascence of the human mind because he was suffering from some subtle form of indigestion ? He invoked, independently of each other, the aid of two distinguished specialists. They both told him in exactly the same voice and with exactly the same air of guineas well earned : " What you want, Mr. Trafford, is a change."

Trafford brought his mind to bear upon the instances of contentment about him. He developed an opinion that all men and many women were potentially at least as restless as himself. A huge proportion of the usage and education in modern life struck upon him now as being a training in contentment. Or rather in keeping quiet and not upsetting things. The serious and responsible life of an ordinary prosperous man fulfilling the requirements of our social organisation fatigues and neither completely satisfies nor completely occupies. Still less does the responsible part of the life of a woman of the prosperous classes engage all her energies or hold her imagination. And there has grown up a great informal organisation of employments, games, ceremonies, social routines, travel, to consume these surplus powers and excessive cravings, which might otherwise change or shatter the whole order of human living. He began to understand the forced preoccupation with cricket and golf, the shooting, visiting,

and so forth, to which the young people of the economically
free classes in the community are trained. He discovered
a theory for hobbies and specialised interests. He began
to see why people go to Scotland to get away from
London, and come to London to get away from Scotland,
why they crowd to and fro along the Riviera, swarm over
Switzerland, shoot, yacht, hunt, and maintain an immense
apparatus of racing and motoring. Because so they are
able to remain reasonably contented with the world as it
is. He perceived, too, that a man who has missed or
broken through the training of this kind of life, does not
again very readily subdue himself to the security of these
systematised distractions. His own upbringing had been
antipathetic to any such adaptations ; his years of research
had given him the habit of naked intimacy with truth,
filled him with a craving for reality, and the destructive
acids of a relentless critical method.

He began to understand something of the psychology
of vice, to comprehend how small a part mere sensuality,
how large a part the spirit of adventure and the craving
for illegality, may play in the lives of those who are called
evil livers. Mere animal impulses and curiosities it had
always seemed possible to him to control, but now he was
beginning to apprehend the power of that passion for
escape, at any cost, in any way, from the petty, weakly
stimulating, competitive motives of low-grade and law-
abiding prosperity. . . .

For a time Trafford made an earnest effort to adjust
himself to the position in which he found himself, and make
a working compromise with his disturbing forces. He
tried to pick up the scientific preoccupation of his earlier
years. He made extensive schemes, to Solomonson's great
concern, whereby he might, to a large extent, disentangle
himself from business. He began to hunt out forgotten
note-books and yellowing sheets of memoranda. He found
the resumption of research much more difficult than he
had ever supposed possible. He went so far as to plan a
laboratory, and to make some inquiries as to site and the
cost of building, to the great satisfaction, not only of
Marjorie, but of his mother. Old Mrs. Trafford had never
expressed her concern at his abandonment of molecular
physics for money-making, but now in her appreciation of
his return to pure investigation she betrayed her sense of
his departure.

But in his heart he felt that this methodical establishment

of virtue by limitation would not suffice for him. He said no word of this scepticism as it grew in his mind. Marjorie was still under the impression that he was returning to research, and that she was free to contrive the steady preparation for that happier day when he should assume his political inheritance. And then presently a queer little dispute sprang up between them. Suddenly, for the first time since he took to business, Trafford found himself limiting her again. She was disposed, partly through the natural growth of her circle and her setting, and partly through a movement on the part of Mrs. Halford Wallace, to move from Sussex Square into a larger, more picturesquely built house in a more central position. She particularly desired a good staircase. He met her intimations of this development with a curious and unusual irritation. The idea of moving bothered him. He felt that exaggerated annoyance which is often a concomitant of overwrought nerves. They had a dispute that was almost a quarrel, and though Marjorie dropped the matter for a time, he could feel she was still at work upon it.

CHAPTER THE SECOND

TRAFFORD DECIDES TO GO

§ 1

A HAUNTING desire to go away into solitude grew upon Trafford very steadily. He wanted intensely to think, and London and Marjorie would not let him think. He wanted, therefore, to go away out of London and Marjorie's world. He wanted, he felt, to go away alone and face God, and clear things up in his mind. By imperceptible degrees this desire anticipated its realisation. His activities were affected more and more by intimations of a determined crisis. One eventful day it seemed to him that his mind passed quite suddenly from desire to resolve. He found himself with a project, already broadly definite. Hitherto he hadn't been at all clear where he could go. From the first almost he had felt that this change he needed, the change by which he was to get out of the thickets of work and perplexity and distraction that held him captive, must be a physical as well as a mental removal; he must go somewhere, still and isolated, where sustained, detached thinking was possible. . . . His preference, if he had one, inclined him to some solitude among the Himalaya Mountains. That came perhaps from Kim and the precedent of the Hindoo's religious retreat from the world. But this retreat he contemplated was a retreat that aimed at a return, a clarified and strengthened resumption of the world. And then suddenly, as if he had always intended it, Labrador flashed through his thoughts, like a familiar name that had been for a time quite unaccountably forgotten.

The word " Labrador " drifted to him one day from an adjacent table as he sat alone at lunch in the Liberal Union Club. Some bore was reciting the substance of a lecture to a fellow-member. " Seems to be a remarkable country," said the speaker. " Mineral wealth hardly glanced at, you know. Furs and a few score Indians. And at our doors. Practically—at our doors."

Trafford ceased to listen. His mind was taking up this idea of Labrador. He wondered why he had not thought of Labrador before.

He had two or three streams of thought flowing in his mind, as a man who muses alone is apt to do. Marjorie's desire to move had reappeared ; a particular group of houses between Berkeley Square and Park Lane had taken hold of her fancy, she had urged the acquisition of one upon him that morning, and this kept coming up into consciousness like a wrong thread in a tapestry. Moreover, he was watching his fellow-members with a critical rather than a friendly eye. A half-speculating, half-hostile contemplation of his habitual associates was one of the queer aspects of this period of unsettlement. They exasperated him by their massive contentment with the surface of things. They came in one after another patting their ties, or pulling at the lapels of their coats, and looked about them for vacant places with a conscious ease of manner that irritated his nerves. No doubt they were all more or less successful and distinguished men, matter for conversation and food for anecdotes, but why did they trouble to give themselves the air of it ? They halted or sat down by friends, enunciated vapid remarks in sonorous voices, and opened conversations in trite phrases, about London architecture, about the political situation or the morning's newspaper, conversations that ought, he felt, to have been thrown away unopened, so stale and needless they seemed to him. They were judges, lawyers of all sorts, bankers, company promoters, railway managers, stockbrokers, pressmen, politicians, men of leisure. He wondered if indeed they were as opaque as they seemed, wondered with the helpless wonder of a man of exceptional mental gifts whether any of them at any stage had had such thoughts as his, had wanted as acutely as he did now to get right out of the world. Did old Booch over there, for example, guzzling oysters, cry at times upon the unknown God in the vast silences of the night ? But Booch, of course, was a member or something of the House of Laymen, and very sound on the Thirty-nine Articles—a man who ate oysters like that could swallow anything—and in the vast silences of the night he was probably heavily and noisily asleep. . . .

Blenkins, the gentlemanly colleague of Denton in the control of the *Old Country Gazette*, appeared on his way to the pay-desk, gesticulating amiably *en route* to any possible friend. Trafford returned his salutation, and pulled himself together immediately after in fear that he had scowled, for he hated to be churlish to any human being. Blenkins, too, it might be, had sorrow and remorse and periods of passionate self-distrust and self-examination; maybe Blenkins could weep salt tears, as Blenkins no doubt under suitable sword-play would reveal heart and viscera as quivering and oozy as any man's.

But to Trafford's jaundiced eye just then, it seemed that if you slashed Blenkins across, he would probably cut like a cheese. . . .

Now, in Labrador . . .

So soon as Blenkins had cleared, Trafford followed him to the pay-desk, and went on upstairs to the smoking-room, thinking of Labrador. Long ago he had read the story of Wallace and Hubbard in that wilderness.

There was much to be said for a winter in Labrador. It was cold, it was clear, infinitely lonely, with a keen edge of danger and hardship and never a letter or a paper.

One could provision a hut and sit wrapped in furs, watching the Northern Lights. . . .

" I'm off to Labrador," said Trafford, and entered the smoking-room.

It was, after all, perfectly easy to go to Labrador. One had just to go. . . .

As he pinched the end of his cigar, he became aware of Blenkins, with a gleam of golden glasses and a flapping white cuff, beckoning across the room to him. With that probable scowl on his conscience, Trafford was moved to

respond with an unreal warmth, and strolled across to
Blenkins and a group of three or four other people, including that vigorous young politician, Weston Massinghay,
and Hart, K.C., about the farther fireplace. "We were
talking of you," said Blenkins. "Come and sit down with
us. Why don't you come into Parliament ? "

" I've just arranged to go for some months to Labrador."

" Industrial development ? " asked Blenkins, all alive.

" No.   Holiday."

No Blenkins believes that sort of thing, but of course,
if Trafford chose to keep his own counsel——

" Well, come into Parliament as soon as you get back."

Trafford had had that old conversation before. He
pretended insensibility when Blenkins gestured to a vacant
chair. " No," he said, still standing, " we settled all that.
And now I'm up to my neck in—detail about Labrador.
I shall be starting—before the month is out."

Blenkins and Hart simulated interest. " It's immoral,"
said Blenkins, " for a man of your standing to keep out
of politics."

" It's more than immoral," said Hart ; " it's American."

" Solomonson comes in to represent the firm," smiled
Trafford, signalled the waiter for coffee, and presently
disentangled himself from their company.

For Blenkins Trafford concealed an exquisite dislike
and contempt ; and Blenkins had a considerable admiration for Trafford, based on extensive misunderstandings.
Blenkins admired Trafford because he was good-looking
and well-dressed, with a beautiful and successful wife,
because he had become reasonably rich very quickly and
easily, was young and a Fellow of the Royal Society with
a reputation that echoed in Berlin, and very perceptibly
did not return Blenkins's admiration. All these things
filled Blenkins with a desire for Trafford's intimacy, and
to become the associate of the very promising political
career that it seemed to him, in spite of Trafford's repudiations, was the natural next step in a deliberately and
honourably planned life. He mistook Trafford's silences
and detachment for the marks of a strong, silent man, who
was scheming the immense, vulgar, distinguished-looking
achievements that appeal to the Blenkins mind. Blenkins
was a sentimentally loyal party Liberal, and as he said at
times to Hart and Weston Massinghay : " If those other
fellows get hold of him—— ! "

Blenkins was the fine flower of Oxford Liberalism and

the Tennysonian days. He wanted to be like King Arthur and Sir Galahad, with the merest touch of Launcelot, and to be perfectly upright and splendid and very, very successful. He was a fair, tenoring sort of person, with an Arthurian moustache and a disposition to long frock-coats. It had been said of him that he didn't dress like a gentleman, but that he dressed more like a gentleman than a gentleman ought to dress. It might have been added that he didn't behave like a gentleman, but that he behaved more like a gentleman than a gentleman ought to behave. He didn't think, but he talked and he wrote more thoughtfully in his leaders, and in the little dialogues he wrote in imitation of Sir Arthur Helps, than any other person who didn't think could possibly do. He was an orthodox Churchman, but very, very broad ; he held all the doctrines, a distinguished sort of thing to do in an age of doubt, but there was a quality about them as he held them—as though they had been run over by something rather heavy. It was a flattened and slightly obliterated breadth—nothing was assertive, but nothing, under exam-ination, proved to be altogether gone. His profuse thought-fulness was not confined to his journalistic and literary work, it overflowed into Talks. He was a man for Great Talks, interminable rambling floods of boyish observation, emotional appreciation, and silly, sapient comment. He loved to discuss " Who are the Best Talkers now Alive ? " He had written an essay, *Talk in the Past*. He boasted of week-ends when the Talk had gone on from the moment of meeting in the train to the moment of parting at Euston or Paddington or Waterloo ; and one or two hostesses with embittered memories could verify his boasting. He did his best to make a club the Talking Club, and loved to summon men to a growing circle of chairs. . . .

Trafford had been involved in Talks on one or two occasions, and now, as he sat alone in the corridor and smoked and drank his coffee, he could imagine the Talk he had escaped, the Talk that was going on in the smoking-room—the platitudes, the sagacities, the digressions, the sudden revelation of deep, irrational convictions. He reflected upon the various Talks at which he had assisted. His chief impression of them all was of an intolerable fluidity. Never once had he known a Talk thicken to adequate discussion ; never had a new idea or a new view come to him in a Talk. He wondered why Blenkins and his like talked at all. Essentially they lived for pose, not for expression ; they did not greatly desire to discover, make, or be ; they wanted to seem and succeed. Talking perhaps was part of their pose of great intellectual activity, and Blenkins was fortunate to have an easy, unforced running of the mind. . . .

Over his cigar Trafford became profoundly philosophical about Talk. And after the manner of those who become profoundly philosophical he spread out the word beyond its original and proper intentions to all sorts of kindred and parallel things. Blenkins and his miscellany of friends in their circle of chairs were, after all, only a crude rendering of very much of the intellectual activity of mankind. Men talked so often as dogs bark. Those Talkers never came to grips, fell away from topic to topic, pretended depth and evaded the devastating horrors of sincerity. Listening was a politeness amongst them that was presently rewarded with utterance. Tremendously like dogs they were, in a dog-fancying neighbourhood on a summer week-day afternoon. Fluidity, excessive abundance, inconsecutiveness ; these were the things that made Talk hateful to Trafford. . . .

Wasn't most literature in the same case ? Wasn't nearly all present philosophical and sociological discussion in the world merely a Blenkins circle on a colossal scale, with every one looming forward to get in a deeply thoughtful word edgeways at the first opportunity ? Imagine any one in distress about his soul or about mankind, going to a professor of economics or sociology or philosophy ! He thought of the endless, big, expensive, fruitless books, the windy expansions of industrious pedantry that mocked the spirit of inquiry. The fields of physical and biological science alone had been partially rescued from the floods of human inconsecutiveness. There, at least, a man must, on the whole, join on to the work of other men, stand a searching criticism, justify himself. Philosophically this was an age of relaxed schoolmen. He thought of Doctor Codger at Cambridge, bubbling away with his iridescent Hegelianism like a salted snail ; of Doctor Quiller at Oxford, ignoring Bergson and fulminating a preposterous insular Pragmatism. Each contradicted the other fundamentally upon matters of universal concern ; neither ever joined issue with the other. Why in the name of humanity didn't some one take hold of those two excellent gentlemen, and bang their busy heads together hard and frequently until they either compromised or cracked ?

§ 2

He forgot these rambling speculations as he came out
into the spring sunshine of Pall Mall, and halting for a
moment on the topmost step, regarded the tidy pavements,
the rare, dignified shops, the waiting taxi-cabs, the pleasant,
prosperous passers-by. His mind lapsed back to the
thought that he meant to leave all this and go to Labrador.
His mind went a step further, and reflected that he would
not only go to Labrador, but—it was highly probable—
come back again.

And then ?

Why, after all, should he go to Labrador at all ? Why
shouldn't he make a supreme effort here ?

Something entirely irrational within him told him with
conclusive emphasis that he had to go to Labrador. . . .

He remembered there was this confounded business of
the proposed house in Mayfair to consider. . . .

§ 3

It occurred to him that he would go a little out of his
way, and look at the new great laboratories at the Romeike
College, of which his old bottle-washer Durgan was, he
knew, extravagantly proud. Romeike's widow was dead
now and her will executed, and her substance half turned
already to bricks and stone and glazed tiles and all those
excesses of space and appliance which the rich and authoritative imagine must needs give us Science, however ill-
selected and underpaid and slighted the users of those
opportunities may be. The architects had had great fun
with the bequest ; a quarter of the site was devoted to a
huge square surrounded by dignified, if functionless, colonnades, and adorned with those stone seats of honour which
are always so chill and unsatisfactory as resting-places in
our island climate. The laboratories, except that they
were a little shaded by the colonnades, were everything a
laboratory should be ; the benches were miracles of convenience, there wasn't anything the industrious investigator
might want, steam, high pressures, electric power, that
he couldn't get by pressing a button or turning a switch,
unless, perhaps, it was inspiring ideas. And the new
library at the end, with its grays and greens, its logarithmic
computators at every table, was a miracle of mental
convenience.

Durgan showed his old professor the marvels.

" If he *chooses* to do something here," said Durgan, not too hopefully, " a man can." . . .

" What's become of the little old room where we two used to work ? " asked Trafford.

" They'll turn 'em all out presently," said Durgan, " when this part is ready, but just at present it's very much as you left it. There's been precious little research done there since you went away—not what *I* call research. Females chiefly—and boys. Playing at it. Making themselves into D.Sc.'s by a baby research instead of a man's examination. It's like broaching a thirty-two gallon cask full of Pap to think of it. Lord, sir, the swill ! Research ! Counting and weighing things ! Professor Lake's all right, I suppose, but his work was mostly mathematical ; he didn't do much of it here. No, the old days ended, sir, when you——"

He arrested himself, and obviously changed his words. " Got busy with other things."

Trafford surveyed the place ; it seemed to him to have shrunken a little in the course of the three years that had intervened since he resigned his position. On the wall at the back there still hung, fly-blown and a little crumpled, an old table of constants he had made for his elasticity researches. Lake had kept it there, for Lake was a man of generous appreciations, and rather proud to follow in the footsteps of an investigator of Trafford's subtlety and vigour. The old sink in the corner where Trafford had once swilled his watch glasses and filled his beakers had been replaced by one of a more modern construction, and the combustion cupboard was unfamiliar, until Durgan pointed out that it had been enlarged. The ground-glass window at the east end showed still the marks of an explosion that had banished a clumsy student from this sanctuary at the very beginning of Trafford's career.

" By Jove ! " he said, after a silence, " but I did some good work here."

" You did, sir," said Durgan.

" I wonder—— I may take it up again presently."

" I doubt it, sir," said Durgan.

" Oh ! But suppose I come back ? "

" I don't think you would find yourself coming back, sir," said Durgan, after judicious consideration.

He adduced no shadow of a reason for his doubt, but some mysterious quality in his words carried conviction

to Trafford's mind. He knew that he would never do
anything worth doing in molecular physics again. He
knew it now conclusively for the first time.

§ 4

He found himself presently in Bond Street. The bright
May day had brought out great quantities of people, so
that he had to come down from altitudes of abstraction to
pick his way among them.

He was struck by the prevailing interest and contentment in the faces he passed. There was no sense of
insecurity betrayed, no sense of the deeps and mysteries
upon which our being floats like a film. They looked solid,
they looked satisfied ; surely never before in the history
of the world has there been so great a multitude of secure-
feeling, satisfied-looking, uninquiring people as there is
to-day. All the tragic great things of life seem stupendously
remote from them ; pain is rare, death is out of sight,
religion has shrunken to an inconsiderable comfortable
reassuring appendage of the daily life. And with the bright
small things of immediacy they are so active and alert.
Never before has the world seen such multitudes, and a
day must come when it will cease to see them for evermore.

As he shouldered his way through the throng before the
Oxford Street shop windows he appreciated a queer effect,
almost, as it were, of insanity, about all this rich and
abundant and ultimately aimless life, this tremendous
spawning and proliferation of uneventful humanity. These
individual lives signified, no doubt, enormously to the
individuals, but did all the shining, reflecting, changing
existence that went by like bubbles in a stream, signify
collectively anything more than the leaping, glittering
confusion of shoaling mackerel on a sunlit afternoon ?
The pretty girl looking into the window schemed picturesque
achievements with lace and ribbon, the beggar at the curb
was alert for any sympathetic eye, the chauffeur on the
waiting taxi-cab watched the twopences ticking on with a
quiet satisfaction ; each followed a keenly sought immediate
end, but altogether ? Where were they going together ?
Until he knew that, where was the sanity of statecraft, the
excuse of any impersonal effort, the significance of anything
beyond a life of appetites and self-seeking instincts ?

He found that perplexing suspicion of priggishness
affecting him again. Why couldn't he take the gift of life

as it seemed these people took it ? Why was he continually
lapsing into these sombre, dimly religious questionings and
doubts ? Why, after all, should he concern himself with
these riddles of some collective and ultimate meaning in
things ? Was he, for all his ability and security, so afraid
of the accidents of life that on that account he clung to
this conception of a larger impersonal issue which the
world in general seemed to have abandoned so cheerfully ?
At any rate he did cling to it—and his sense of it made the
abounding active life of this stirring, bristling thoroughfare
an almost unendurable perplexity. . . .

By the Marble Arch a little crowd had gathered at the
pavement edge. He remarked other little knots towards
Paddington, and then still others, and inquiring, found the
King was presently to pass. They promised themselves
the gratification of seeing the King go by. They would
see a carriage, they would see horses and coachmen,
perhaps even they might catch sight of a raised hat and
a bowing figure. And this would be a gratification to them,
it would irradiate the day with a sense of experiences,
exceptional and precious. For that some of them had
already been standing about for two or three hours.

He thought of these waiting people for a time, and then
he fell into a speculation about the King. He wondered
if the King ever lay awake at three o'clock in the morning
and faced the riddle of the eternities, or whether he did
really take himself seriously and contentedly as being in
himself the vital function of the State, performed his
ceremonies, went hither and thither through a wilderness
of gaping watchers, slept well on it. Was the man
satisfied ? Was he satisfied with his empire as it was and
himself as he was, or did some vision, some high, ironical
intimation of the latent and lost possibilities of his empire
and of the world of Things Conceivable that lies beyond
the poor tawdry splendours of our present loyalties, ever
dawn upon him ?

Trafford's imagination conjured up a sleepless King
Emperor agonising for humanity. . . .

He turned to his right out of Lancaster Gate into Sussex
Square, and came to a stop at the pavement edge.

From across the road he surveyed the wide white front
and portals of the house that wasn't big enough for Marjorie.

§ 5

He let himself in with his latchkey.

Malcolm, his man, hovered at the foot of the staircase, and came forward for his hat and gloves and stick.

" Mrs. Trafford in ? " asked Trafford.

" She said she would be in by four, sir."

Trafford glanced at his watch and went slowly upstairs. On the landing there had been a rearrangement of the furniture, and he paused to survey it. The alterations had been made to accommodate a big cloisonné jar, that now glowed a wonder of white and tinted whites and luminous blues upon a dark, deep-shining stand. He noted now the curtain of the window had been changed from something—surely it had been a reddish curtain !—to a sharp clear blue with a black border, that reflected upon and sustained and encouraged the jar tremendously. And the wall behind——? Yes. Its deep brown was darkened to an absolute black behind the jar, and shaded up between the lacquer cabinets on either hand by insensible degrees to the general hue. It was wonderful, perfectly harmonious, and so subtly planned that it seemed it all might have grown, as flowers grow. . . .

He entered the drawing-room and surveyed its long and handsome spaces. Post-impressionism was over and gone ; three long pictures by young Rogerson and one of Redwood's gallant bronzes faced the tall windows between the white marble fireplaces at either end. There were two lean jars from India, a young boy's head from Florence, and in a great bowl in the remotest corner a radiant mass of azaleas. . . .

His mood of wondering at familiar things was still upon him. It came to him as a thing absurd and incongruous that this should be his home. It was all wonderfully arranged into one dignified harmony, but he felt now that at a touch of social earthquake, with a mere momentary lapse towards disorder, it would degenerate altogether into litter, lie heaped together confessed the loot it was. He came to a stop opposite one of the Rogersons, a stiffly self-conscious shop girl in her Sunday clothes, a not unsuccessful emulation of Nicholson's wonderful Mrs. Stafford of Paradise Row. Regarded as so much brown and gray and amber-gold, it was coherent in Marjorie's design, but regarded as a work of art, as a piece of expression, how madly irrelevant was its humour and implications to that

room and the purposes of that room ! Rogerson wasn't
perhaps trying to say much, but at any rate he was trying
to say something, and Redwood too was asserting freedom
and adventure, and the thought of that Florentine of the
bust, and the patient, careful Indian potter, and every
maker of all the little casual articles about him, produced
an effect of muffled, stifled assertions. Against this subdued
and disciplined background of muted, inarticulate cries—
cries for beauty, for delight, for freedom, Marjorie and her
world moved and rustled and chattered and competed—
wearing the skins of beasts, the love-plumage of birds, the
woven cocoon cases of little silkworms. . . .

" Preposterous," he whispered.

He went to the window and stared out ; turned about
and regarded the gracious variety of that long, well-lit room
again, then strolled thoughtfully upstairs. He reached the
door of his study, and a sound of voices from the schoolroom—it had recently been promoted from the rank of day
nursery to this level—caught his mood. He changed his
mind, crossed the landing, and was welcomed with shouts.

The rogues had been dressing up. Margharita, that child
of the dreadful dawn, was now a sturdy and domineering
girl of eight, and she was attired in a gilt paper mitre and
her governess's white muslin blouse so tied at the wrists
as to suggest lawn sleeves, a broad crimson band doing
duty as a stole. She was Becket prepared for martyrdom
at the foot of the altar. Godwin, his eldest son, was a
hot-tempered, pretty-featured, pleasantly self-conscious
boy of nearly seven, and very happy now in a white
dragoon's helmet and rude but effective brown paper
breastplate and greaves, as the party of assassin knights.
A small acolyte in what was in all human probability one
of the governess's more intimate linen garments assisted
Becket, while the general congregation of Canterbury was
represented by Edward, aged two, and the governess,
disguised with a Union Jack tied over her head after the
well-known fashion of the Middle Ages. After the children
had welcomed their father and explained the bloody work
in hand, they returned to it with solemn earnestness, while
Trafford surveyed the tragedy. Godwin slew with admirable gusto, and I doubt if the actual Thomas of Canterbury
showed half the stately dignity of Margharita.

The scene finished, they went on to the penance of Henry
the Second ; and there was a tremendous readjustment
of costumes, with much consultation and secrecy.

Trafford's eyes went from his offspring to the long, white-painted room, with its gay frieze of ships and gulls and its rug-variegated cork carpet of plain brick-red. Everywhere it showed his wife's quick cleverness, the clean, serviceable decorativeness of it all, the pretty patterned window-curtains, the writing-desks, the little library, the flowers and bulbs in glasses, the counting blocks and bricks and jolly toys, the blackboard on which the children learnt to draw in bold wide strokes, the big, well-chosen German colour prints upon the walls. And the children did credit to their casket ; they were not only full of vitality but full of ideas, even Edward was already a person of conversation. They were good stuff anyhow. . . .

It was fine in a sense, Trafford thought, to have given up his own motives and curiosities to afford this airy pleasantness of upbringing for them, and then came a qualifying thought. Would they in their turn for the sake of another generation have to give up fine occupations for mean occupations, deep thoughts for shallow ? Would the world get them in turn ? Would the girls be hustled and flattered into advantageous marriages, that dinners and drawing-rooms might still prevail ? Would the boys, after this gracious beginning, presently have to swim submerged in another generation of Blenkinses and their Talk, toil in arduous self-seeking, observe, respect and manipulate shams, succeed or fail, and succeeding, beget amidst hope and beautiful emotions yet another generation doomed to insincerities and accommodations, and so die at last—as he must die ? . . .

He heard his wife's clear voice in the hall below, and went down to meet her. She had gone into the drawing-room, and he followed her in and through the folding doors to the hinder part of the room, where she stood ready to open a small bureau. She turned at his approach, and smiled a pleasant, habitual smile. . . .

She was no longer the slim, quick-moving girl who had come out of the world to him when he crawled from beneath the wreckage of Solomonson's plane, no longer the half-barbaric young beauty who had been revealed to him on the staircase of the Vevey villa. She was now a dignified, self-possessed woman, controlling her house and her life with a skilful, subtle appreciation of her every point and possibility. She was wearing now a simple walking dress of brownish-fawn colour, and her hat was touched with a steely blue that made her blue eyes seem handsome and hard, and toned her hair to a merely warm brown. She had, as it were, subdued her fine colours into a sheath in order that she might presently draw them again with more effect.

" Hallo, old man ! " she said, " you home ? "

He nodded. " The club bored me—and I couldn't work."

Her voice had something of a challenge and defiance in it. " I've been looking at a house," she said. " Alice Carmel told me of it. It isn't in Berkeley Square, but it's near it. It's rather good."

He met her eye. " That's—premature," he said.

" We can't go on living in this one."

" I won't go to another."

" But why ? "

" I just won't."

" It isn't the money ? "

" No," said Trafford, with sudden fierce resentment. " I've overtaken you and beaten you there, Marjorie."

She stared at the harsh bitterness of his voice. She was about to speak when the door opened, and Malcolm ushered in Aunt Plessington and Uncle Hubert. Husband and wife hung for a moment, and then realised their talk was at an end. . . .

Marjorie went forward to greet her aunt, careless now of all that once stupendous Influence might think of her. She had long ceased to feel even the triumph of victory in her big house, her costly, dignified clothes, her assured and growing social importance. For five years Aunt Plessington had not even ventured to advise ; had once or twice admired. All that business of Magnet was—even elaborately—forgotten. . . .

Seven years of feverish self-assertion had left their mark upon both the Plessingtons. She was leaner, more gauntly untidy, more aggressively ill-dressed. She no longer dressed carelessly, she defied the world with her clothes, waved her tattered and dingy banners in its face. Uncle Hubert was no fatter, but in some queer way he had ceased to be thin. Like so many people whose peripheries defy the manifest quaint purpose of Providence, he was in a state of thwarted adiposity, and with all the disconnected-ness and weak irritability characteristic of this condition. He had developed a number of nervous movements, chin-strokings, cheek-scratchings, and incredulous pawings at his more salient features.

" Isn't it a lark ? " began Aunt Plessington, with some-thing like a note of apprehension in her high-pitched voice, and speaking almost from the doorway, " we're making a call together. I and Hubert ! It's an attack in force."

Uncle Hubert goggled in the rear and stroked his chin, and tried to get together a sort of facial expression.

The Traffords made welcoming noises, and Marjorie advanced to meet her aunt.

" We want you to do something for us," said Aunt Plessington, taking two hands with two hands. . . .

In the intervening years the Movement had had ups and downs ; it had had a boom, which had ended abruptly in a complete loss of voice for Aunt Plessington—she had tried to run it on a patent non-stimulating food, and then it had entangled itself with a new cult of philanthropic theosophy from which it had been extracted with difficulty and in a damaged condition. It had never completely recovered from that unhappy association. Latterly Aunt Plessington had lost her nerve, and she had taken to making calls upon people with considerable and sometimes embarrassing demands for support, urging them to join committees, take chairs, stake reputations, speak and act as foils for her. If they refused she lost her temper very openly and frankly, and became industriously vindictive. She circulated scandals or created them. Her old assurance had deserted her ; the strangulated contralto was losing its magic power, she felt, in this degenerating England it had ruled so long. In the last year or so she had become extremely snappy with Uncle Hubert. She ascribed much of the Movement's futility to the decline of his administrative powers and the increasing awkwardness of his gestures, and she did her utmost to keep him up to the mark. Her only method of keeping him up to the mark was to jerk the bit. She had now come to compel Marjorie to address a meeting that was to inaugurate a new phase in the Movement's history, and she wanted Marjorie because she particularly wanted a daring, liberal, and spiritually amorous bishop, who had once told her with a note of profound conviction that Marjorie was a very beautiful woman. She was so intent upon her purpose that she scarcely noticed Trafford. He slipped from the room unobserved under cover of her playful preliminaries, and went to the untidy little apartment overhead which served in that house as his study. He sat down at the big desk, pushed his methodically arranged papers back, and drummed on the edge with his fingers.

" I'm damned if we have that bigger house," said Trafford.

§ 6

He felt he wanted to confirm and establish this new
resolution, to go right away to Labrador for a year. He
wanted to tell some one the thing definitely. He would
have gone downstairs again to Marjorie, but she was
submerged and swimming desperately against the voluble
rapids of Aunt Plessington's purpose. It might be an hour
before that attack withdrew. Presently there would be
other callers. He decided to have tea with his mother and
talk to her about this new break in the course of his life.

Except that her hair was now gray and her brown eyes
by so much contrast brighter, Mrs. Trafford's appearance
had altered very little in the ten years of her only son's
marriage. Whatever fresh realisations of the inevitably
widening separation between parent and child these years
had brought her, she had kept to herself. She had watched
her daughter-in-law sometimes with sympathy, sometimes
with perplexity, always with a jealous resolve to let no
shadow of jealousy fall between them. Marjorie had been
sweet and friendly to her, but after the first outburst of
enthusiastic affection, she had neither offered nor invited
confidences. Old Mrs. Trafford had talked of Marjorie to
her son guardedly, and had marked and respected a growing
indisposition on his part to discuss his wife. For a year
or so after his marriage she had ached at times with a
sense of nearly intolerable loneliness, and then the new
interests she had found for herself had won their way against
this depression. The new insurrectionary movement of
women that had distinguished those years had attracted
her by its emotion and repelled her by its crudity, and she
had resolved, quite in the spirit of the man who had shaped
her life, to make a systematic study of all the contributory
strands that met in this difficult tangle. She tried to write,
but she found that the poetic gift, the gift of the creative
and illuminating phrase which alone justifies writing, was
denied to her, and so she sought to make herself wise, to
read and hear, and discuss and think over these things,
and perhaps at last inspire and encourage writing in others.

Her circle of intimates grew, and she presently remarked
with a curious interest that while she had lost the confidences of her own son and his wife, she was becoming the
confidante of an increasing number of other people. They
came to her, she perceived, because she was receptive and
sympathetic and without a claim upon them or any

interest to complicate the freedoms of their speech with her. They came to her, because she did not belong to them nor they to her. It is, indeed, the defect of all formal and established relationship, that it embarrasses speech, and taints each phase in intercourse with the flavour of diplomacy. One can be far more easily outspoken to a casual stranger one may never see again than to that inseparable other, who may misinterpret, who may disapprove or misunderstand, and who will certainly in the measure of that discord remember. . . .

It became at last a matter of rejoicing to Mrs. Trafford that the ties of the old instinctive tenderness between herself and her son, the memories of pain and tears and the passionate conflict of childhood, were growing so thin and lax and inconsiderable, that she could even hope some day to talk to him again—almost as she talked to the young men and young women who drifted out of the unknown to her and sat in her little room and sought to express their perplexities and listened to her advice. . . .

It seemed to her that afternoon the wished-for day had come.

Trafford found her just returned from a walk in Kensington Gardens and writing a note at her desk under the narrow sunlit window that looked upon the High Street. " Finish your letter, little mother," he said, and took possession of the hearthrug.

When she had sealed and addressed her letter, she turned her head and found him looking at his father's portrait.

" Done ? " he asked, becoming aware of her eyes.

She took her letter into the hall and returned to him, closing the door behind her.

" I'm going away, little mother," he said, with an unconvincing off-handedness. " I'm going to take a holiday."

" Alone ? "

" Yes. I want a change. I'm going off somewhere—untrodden ground as near as one can get it nowadays—Labrador."

Their eyes met for a moment.

" Is it for long ? "

" The best part of a year."

" I thought you were going on with your research work again."

" No." He paused. " I'm going to Labrador."

" Why ? " she asked.

" I'm going to think."

She found nothing to say for a moment. " It's good,"
she remarked, " to think." Then, lest she herself should
seem to be thinking too enormously, she rang the bell
to order the tea that was already on its way.

" It surprises a mother," she said, when the maid had
come and gone, " when her son surprises her."

" You see," he repeated, as though it explained everything, " I want to think."

Then after a pause she asked some questions about
Labrador ; wasn't it very cold, very desert, very dangerous
and bitter, and he answered informingly. How was he
going to stay there ? He would go up the country with an
expedition, build a hut and remain behind. Alone ? Yes
—thinking. Her eyes rested on his face for a time. " It
will be—lonely," she said, after a pause.

She saw him as a little still speck against immense
backgrounds of snowy wilderness.

The tea-things came before mother and son were back
at essentials again. Then she asked abruptly : " Why
are you going away like this ? "

" I'm tired of all this business and finance," he said,
after a pause.

" I thought you would be," she answered as deliberately.

" Yes. I've had enough of things. I want to get clear.
And begin again somehow."

She felt they both hung away from the essential aspect.
Either he or she must approach it. She decided that she
would, that it was a less difficult thing for her than for him.

" And Marjorie ? " she asked.

He looked into his mother's eyes very quietly. " You
see," he went on, deliberately disregarding her question,
" I'm beached. I'm aground. I'm spoilt now for the old
researches—spoilt altogether. And I don't like this life
I'm leading. I detest it. While I was struggling it had a
kind of interest. There was an excitement in piling up
the first twenty thousand. But *now*—— ! It's empty,
it's aimless, it's incessant." . . .

He paused. She turned to the tea-things, and lit the
spirit lamp under the kettle. It seemed a little difficult
to do, and her hand trembled. When she turned on him
again it was with an effort.

" Does Marjorie like the life you are leading ? " she
asked, and pressed her lips together tightly.

He spoke with a bitterness in his voice that astonished
her. " Oh, *she* likes it."

" Are you sure ? "

He nodded.

" She won't like it without you."

" Oh, that's too much ! It's her world. It's what she's done—what she's made. She can have it ; she can keep it. I've played my part and got it for her. But now— now I'm free to go. I will go. She's got everything else. I've done my half of the bargain. But my soul's my own. If I want to go away and think, I will. Not even Marjorie shall stand in the way of that."

She made no answer to this outburst for a couple of seconds. Then she threw out, " Why shouldn't Marjorie think, too ? "

He considered that for some moments. " She doesn't." he said, as though the words came from the roots of his being.

" But you two——"

" We don't talk. It's astonishing—how we don't. We don't. We can't. We try to, and we can't. And she goes her way, and now—I will go mine."

" And leave her ? "

He nodded.

" In London ? "

" With all the things she cares for."

" Except yourself."

" I'm only a means——"

She turned her quiet face to him. " You know," she said, " that isn't true." . . .

" No," she repeated to his silent contradiction.

" I've watched her," she went on. " You're *not* a means. I'd have spoken long ago if I had thought that. Haven't I watched ? Haven't I lain awake through long nights thinking about her and you, thinking over every casual mood, every little sign—longing to help—helpless." . . . She struggled with herself, for she was weeping. " *It has come to this*," she said in a whisper, and choked back a flood of tears.

Trafford stood motionless, watching her. She became active. She moved round the table. She looked at the kettle, moved the cups needlessly, made tea, and stood waiting for a moment before she poured it out. " It's so hard to talk to you," she said, " and about all this. . . . I care so much. For her. And for you. . . . Words don't come, dear. . . . One says stupid things."

She poured out the tea, and left the cups steaming, and came and stood before him.

" You see," she said, " you're ill. You aren't just.
You've come to an end. You don't know where you are
and what you want to do. Neither does she, my dear.
She's as aimless as you—and less able to help it. Ever so
much less able."

" But she doesn't show it. She goes on. She wants
things and wants things——"

" And you want to go away. It's the same thing. It's
exactly the same thing. It's dissatisfaction. Life leaves
you empty and craving—leaves you with nothing to do
but little immediate things that turn to dust as you do
them. It's her trouble, just as it's your trouble."

" But she doesn't show it."

" Women don't. Not so much. Perhaps even she
doesn't know it. Half the women in our world don't
know—and for a woman it's so much easier to go on—
so many little things." . . .

Trafford tried to grasp the intention of this. " Mother,"
he said, " I mean to go away."

" But think of her ! "

" I've thought. Now I've got to think of myself."

" You can't—without her."

" I will. It's what I'm resolved to do."

" Go right away ? "

" Right away."

" And think ? "

He nodded.

" Find out—what it all means, my boy ? "

" Yes. So far as I'm concerned."

" And then——? "

" Come back, I suppose. I haven't thought."

" To her ? "

He didn't answer. She went and stood beside him,
leaning upon the mantel. " Godwin," she said, " she'd only
be farther behind. . . . You've got to take her with you."

He stood still and silent.

" You've got to think things out with her. If you
don't——"

" I can't."

" Then you ought to go away from her——" She
stopped.

" For good ? " he asked.

" Yes."

They were both silent for a space. Then Mrs. Trafford
gave her mind to the tea that was cooling in the cups, and

added milk and sugar. She spoke again with the table between them.

" I've thought so much of these things," she said, with the milk-jug in her hand. " It's not only you two, but others. And all the movement about us. . . . Marriage isn't what it was. It's become a different thing because women have become human beings. Only—— You know, Godwin, all these things are so difficult to express. Woman's come out of being a slave, and yet she isn't an equal. . . . We've had a sort of sham emancipation, and we haven't yet come to the real one."

She put down the milk-jug on the tray with an air of grave deliberation. " If you go away from her and make the most wonderful discoveries about life and yourself, it's no good—unless she makes them too. It's no good at all. . . . You can't live without her in the end, any more than she can live without you. You may think you can, but I've watched you. You don't want to go away from her ; you want to go away from the world that's got hold of her, from the dresses and parties and the competition, and all this complicated flatness we have to live in. . . . It wouldn't worry you a bit, if it hadn't got hold of her. You don't want to get out of it for your own sake. You *are* out of it. You are as much out of it as any one can be. Only she holds you in it, because she isn't out of it. Your going away will do nothing. She'll still be in it— and still have her hold on you. . . . You've got to take her away. Or else—if you go away—in the end it will be just like a ship, Godwin, coming back to its moorings."

She watched his thoughtful face for some moments, then arrested herself just in time in the act of putting a second portion of sugar into each of the cups. She handed her son his tea, and he took it mechanically. " You're a wise little mother," he said. " I didn't see things in that light. . . . I wonder if you're right ? "

" I know I am," she said.

" I've thought more and more—it was Marjorie."

" It's the world."

" Women made the world. All the dress and display and competition."

Mrs. Trafford thought. " Sex made the world. Neither men nor women. But the world has got hold of the women tighter than it has the men. They're deeper in." She looked up into his face. " Take her with you," she said simply.

" She won't come," said Trafford, after considering it.

Mrs. Trafford reflected. " She'll come—if you make her," she said.

" She'll want to bring two housemaids."

" I don't think you know Marjorie as well as I do."

" But she can't——"

" She can. It's you—you'll want to take two house-maids for her. Even you. . . . Men are not fair to women."

Trafford put his untasted tea upon the mantelshelf, and confronted his mother with a question point blank. " Does Marjorie care for me ? " he asked.

" You're the sun of her world."

" But she goes her way."

" She's clever, she's full of life, full of activities, eager to make and arrange and order ; but there's nothing she is, nothing she makes, that doesn't centre on you."

" But if she cared, she'd understand ! "

" My dear, do *you* understand ? "

He stood musing. " I had everything clear," he said. " I saw my way to Labrador. . . ."

Her little clock pinged the hour. " Good God ! " he said, " I'm to be at dinner somewhere at seven. We're going to a first night. With the Bernards, I think. Then I suppose we'll have a supper. Always life is being slashed to tatters by these things. Always. One thinks in snatches of fifty minutes. It's dementia. . . ."

§ 7

They dined at the Loretto Restaurant with the Bernards and Richard Hampden and Mrs. Godwin Capes, the dark-eyed, quiet-mannered wife of the dramatist, a woman of impulsive speech and long silences, who had subsided from an early romance (Capes had been divorced for her while she was still a mere girl) into a markedly correct and exclusive mother of daughters. Through the dinner Marjorie was watching Trafford and noting the deep preoccupation of his manner. He talked a little to Mrs. Bernard until it was time for Hampden to entertain her, then finding Mrs. Capes was interested in Bernard, he lapsed into thought. Presently Marjorie discovered his eye scrutinising herself.

She hoped the play would catch his mind, but the play seemed devised to intensify his sense of the tawdry unreality of contemporary life. Bernard filled the intervals with a conventional enthusiasm. Capes didn't appear.

" He doesn't seem to care to see his things," his wife explained.

" It's so brilliant," said Bernard.

" He has to do it," said Mrs. Capes slowly, her sombre eyes estimating the crowded stalls below. " It isn't what he cares to do."

The play was, in fact, an admirable piece of English stagecraft, and it dealt exclusively with that unreal other world of beings the English theatre has for its own purposes developed. Just as Greece through the ages evolved and polished and perfected the idealised life of its Homeric poems, so the British mind has evolved their Stage Land to embody its more honourable dreams, full of heroic virtues, incredible honour, genial worldliness, childish villainies, profound but amiable waiters and domestics, pathetic shepherds and preposterous crimes. Capes, needing an income, had mastered the habits and customs of this imagined world as one learns a language ; success endorsed his mastery ; he knew exactly how deeply to underline an irony and just when it is fit and proper for a good man to call upon " God ! " or cry out " Damn ! " In this play he had invented a situation in which a charming and sympathetic lady had killed a gross and drunken husband in self-defence, almost but not quite accidentally, and had then appealed to the prodigious hero for assistance in the resulting complications. At a great cost of mental suffering to himself he had told his First and Only Lie to shield her. Then years after he had returned to England —the first act happened, of course, in India—to find her on the eve of marrying, without any of the preliminary confidences common among human beings, an old school friend of his. (In plays all Gentlemen have been at school together, and one has been the other's fag.) The audience had to be interested in the problem of what the prodigious hero was to do in this prodigious situation. Should he maintain a colossal silence, continue his shielding, and let his friend marry the murderess saved by his perjury, or——? . . . The dreadful quandary ! Indeed, the absolute—inconvenience !

Marjorie watched Trafford in the corner of the box, as he listened rather contemptuously to the statement of the evening's Problem and then lapsed again into a brooding quiet. She wished she understood his moods better. She felt there was more in this than a mere resentment at her persistence about the new house. . . .

Why didn't he go on with things ? . . .

This darkling mood of his had only become manifest to her during the last three or four years of their life. Previously, of course, he had been irritable at times.

Were they less happy now than they had been in the little house in Chelsea ? It had really been a horrible little house. And yet there had been a brightness then—a nearness. . . .

She found her mind wandering away upon a sort of stock-taking expedition. How much of real happiness had she and Trafford had together ? They ought by every standard to be so happy. . . .

She declined the Bernard's invitation to a chafing-dish supper, and began to talk so soon as she and Trafford had settled into the car.

" Rag," she said, " something's the matter ? "

" Well—yes."

" The house ? "

" Yes—the house."

Marjorie considered through a little interval.

" Old man, why are you so prejudiced against a bigger house ? "

" Oh, because the one we have bores me, and the next one will bore me more."

" But try it."

" I don't want to."

" Well," she said, and lapsed into silence.

" And then," he asked, " what are we going to do ? "

" Going to do—when ? "

" After the new house——"

" I'm going to open out," she said.

He made no answer.

" I want to open out. I want you to take your place in the world, the place you deserve."

" A four-footman place ? "

" Oh ! the house is only a means."

He thought upon that. " A means," he asked, " to what ? Look here, Marjorie, what do you think you are up to with me and yourself ? What do you see me doing —in the years ahead ? "

She gave him a silent and thoughtful profile for a second or so.

" At first, I suppose, you are going on with your researches."

" Well ? "

" Then—— I must tell you what I think of you, Rag. Politics——"

" Good Lord ! "

" You've a sort of power.   You could make things noble."

" And then ?   Office ? "

" Why not ?   Look at the little men they are."

" And then perhaps a still bigger house ? "

" You're not fair to me."

He pulled up the bearskin over his knees.

" Marjorie ! " he said.   " You see—— We aren't going to do any of those things at all. . . . *No !* . . .

" I can't go on with my researches," he explained. " That's what you don't understand. I'm not able to get back to work. I shall never do any good research again. That's the real trouble, Marjorie, and it makes all the difference. As for politics—— I can't touch politics. I despise politics. I think this empire and the monarchy and Lords and Commons and patriotism and social reform and all the rest of it, silly, *silly* beyond words ; temporary, accidental, foolish, a mere stop-gap—like a gipsy's round-about in a place where one will presently build a house. . . . You don't help make the house by riding on the roundabout. . . . There's no clear knowledge—no clear purpose. . . . Only research matters—and expression per-haps—I suppose expression is a sort of research—until we get that—that sufficient knowledge. And you see, I can't take up my work again. I've lost something. . . ."

She waited.

" I've got into this stupid struggle for winning money," he went on, " and I feel like a woman must feel who's made a success of prostitution. I've been prostituted. I feel like some one fallen and diseased. . . . Business and prostitution ; they're the same thing. All business is a sort of prostitution, all prostitution is a sort of business. Why should one sell one's brains any more than one sells one's body ? . . . It's so easy to succeed if one has good brains and cares to do it, and doesn't let one's attention or imagination wander—and it's so degrading. Hopelessly degrading. . . . I'm sick of this life, Marjorie. I don't want to buy things. I'm sick of buying. I'm at an end. I'm clean at an end. It's exactly as though suddenly in walking through a great house one came on a passage that ended abruptly in a door, which opened—on nothing ! Nothing ! "

" This is a mood," she whispered to his pause.

" It isn't a mood, it's fact. . . . I've got nothing ahead, and I don't know how to get back. My life's no good to me any more. I've spent myself."

She looked at him with dismayed eyes. " But," she said, " this *is* a mood."

" No," he said, " no mood, but conviction. I *know*. . . ."

He started. The car had stopped at their house, and Malcolm was opening the door of the car. They descended silently, and went upstairs in silence.

He came into her room presently and sat down by her fireside. She had gone to her dressing-table and unfastened a necklace ; now with this winking and glittering in her hand she came and stood beside him.

" Rag," she said, " I don't know what to say. This isn't so much of a surprise. . . . I *felt* that somehow life was disappointing you, that I was disappointing you. I've felt it endless times, but more so lately. I haven't, perhaps, dared to let myself know just how much. . . . But isn't it what life is ? Doesn't every wife disappoint her husband ? We're none of us inexhaustible. After all, we've had a good time ; isn't it a little ungrateful to forget ? . . .

" Look here, Rag," she said. " I don't know what to do. If I did know, I would do it. . . . What are we to do ? "

" Think," he suggested.

" We've got to live as well as think."

" It's the immense troublesome futility of—everything," he said.

" Well, let us cease to be futile. Let us *do*. You say there is no grip for you in research, that you despise politics . . . There's no end of trouble and suffering. Cannot we do social work, social reform, change the lives of others less fortunate than ourselves ? . . ."

" Who are we that we should tamper with the lives of others ? "

" But one must do something."

He thought that over.

" No," he said, " that's the universal blunder nowadays. One must do the right thing. And we don't know the right thing, Marjorie. That's the very heart of the trouble. . . . Does this life satisfy *you* ? If it did would you always be so restless ? . . ."

" But," she said, " think of the good things in life."

" It's just the good, the exquisite things in life, that make me rebel against this life we are leading. It's because I've seen the streaks of gold that I know the rest for dirt. When I go cheating and scheming to my office, and come back to find you squandering yourself upon a horde of chattering, overdressed women, when I think that that is our substance and everyday and what we are, then it is I remember most the deep and beautiful things. . . . It is impossible, dear, it is intolerable that life was made beautiful for us—just for these vulgarities."

" Isn't there——" She hesitated. " Love—still ? "

" But—— Has it been love ? Love is a thing that grows. But we took it—as people take flowers out of a garden, cut them off, put them in water. . . . How much of our daily life has been love ? How much of it mere consequences of the love we've left behind us ? . . . We've just cohabited and ' made love '—you and I—and thought of a thousand other things. . . ."

He looked up at her. " Oh, I love a thousand things about you," he said. " But do I love *you*, Marjorie ? Have I got you ? Haven't I lost you—haven't we both lost something, the very heart of it all ? Do you think that we were just cheated by instinct, that there wasn't something in it we felt and thought was there ? And where is it now ? Where is that brightness and wonder, Marjorie, and the pride and the immense unlimited hope ? "

She was still for a moment ; then knelt very swiftly before him and held out her arms.

" Oh, Rag ! " she said, with a face of tender beauty. He took her finger-tips in his, dropped them and stood up above her.

" My dear," he cried, " my dear ! why do you always want to turn love into—touches ? . . . Stand up again. Stand up, there, my dear ; don't think I've ceased to love you, but stand up there and let me talk to you as one man to another. If we let this occasion slide to embraces. . . ."

He stopped short.

She crouched before the fire at his feet. " Go on," she said, " go on."

" I feel now that all our lives now, Marjorie—— We have come to a crisis. I feel that now—*now* is the time. Either we shall save ourselves now or we shall never save ourselves. It is as if something had gathered and accumulated and could wait no longer. If we do not seize this opportunity—— Then our lives will go on as they have gone on, will become more and more a matter of small excitements and elaborate comforts and distractions. . . ."

He stopped this halting speech and then broke out again.

"Oh! why *should* the life of every day conquer us? Why should generation after generation of men have these fine beginnings, these splendid dreams of youth, attempt so much, achieve so much, and then, then become—*this*! Look at this room, this litter of little satisfactions! Look at your pretty books there, a hundred minds you have pecked at, bright things of the spirit that attracted you as jewels attract a jackdaw. Look at the glass and silver, and that silk from China! And we are in the full tide of our years, Marjorie. Now is the very crown and best of our lives. And this is what we do, we sample, we accumulate. For this we loved, for this we hoped. Do you remember when we were young—that life seemed so splendid—it was intolerable we should ever die? . . . The splendid dream! The intimations of greatness! . . . The miserable failure!"

He raised clenched fists. "I won't stand it, Marjorie. I won't endure it. Somehow, in some way, I will get out of this life—and you with me. I have been brooding upon this and brooding, but now I know. . . ."

"But how?" asked Marjorie, with her bare arms about her knees, staring into the fire. "*How?*"

"We must get out of its constant interruptions, its incessant vivid, petty appeals. . . ."

"We might go away—to Switzerland."

"We *went* to Switzerland. Didn't we agree?—it was our second honeymoon. It isn't a honeymoon we need. No, we'll have to go farther than that."

A sudden light broke upon Marjorie's mind. She realised he had a plan. She lifted a fire-lit face to him and looked at him with steady eyes, and asked,—

"Where?"

"Ever so much farther."

"Where?"

"I don't know."

"You do. You've planned something."

"I don't know, Marjorie. At least—I haven't made up my mind. Where it is very lonely. Cold and remote. Away from all this——" His mind stopped short, and he ended with a cry: "Oh! God! how I want to get out of all this!"

He sat down in her arm-chair, and bowed his face on his hands.

Then abruptly he stood up and went out of the room.

§ 8

When in five minutes' time he came back into her room she was still upon her hearthrug before the fire, with her necklace in her hand, the red reflections of the flames glowing and winking in her jewels and in her eyes. He came and sat again in her chair.

" I have been ranting," he said. " I feel I've been—eloquent. You make me feel like an actor-manager, in a play by Capes. . . . You are the most difficult person for me to talk to in all the world—because you mean so much to me."

She moved impulsively and checked herself and crouched away from him. " I mustn't touch your hand," she whispered.

" I want to explain."

" You've got to explain."

" I've got quite a definite plan. . . . But a sort of terror seized me. It was like—shyness."

" I know. I knew you had a plan."

" You see. . . . I mean to go to Labrador."

He leant forward with his elbows on his knees and his hands extended, explanatory. He wanted intensely that she should understand and agree, and his desire made him clumsy, now slow and awkward, now glibly and unsatisfyingly eloquent. But she comprehended his quality better than he knew. They were to go away to Labrador, this snowy desert of which she had scarcely heard, to camp in the very heart of the wilderness, two hundred miles or more from any human habitation——

" But how long ? " she asked abruptly.

" The better part of a year."

" And we are to talk ? "

" Yes," he said, " talk and think ourselves together—oh !—the old phrases carry it all—find God. . . ."

" It is what I dreamt of, Rag, years ago."

" Will you come," he cried, " out of all this ? "

She leant across the hearthrug, and seized and kissed his hand. . . .

Then, with one of those swift changes of hers, she was in revolt. " But, Rag," she exclaimed, " this is dreaming. We are not free. There are the children, Rag ! We cannot leave the children ! "

" We can," he said. " We must."

" But, my dear !—our duty ! "

" *Is* it a mother's duty always to keep with her children ?
They will be looked after, their lives are organised, there
is my mother close at hand. . . . What is the good of
having children at all—unless their world is to be better
than our world ? . . . What are we doing to save them
from the same bathos as this—to which we have come ?
We give them food and health and pictures and lessons,
that's all very well while they are just little children ; but
we've got no religion to give them, no aim, no sense of a
general purpose. What is the good of bread and health—
and no worship ? . . . What can we say to them when
they ask us why we brought them into the world ?—*We*
happened—*you* happened. What are we to tell them
when they demand the purpose of all this training, all
these lessons ? When they ask what we are preparing them
for ? Just that *you*, too, may have children ! Is that any
answer ? Marjorie, it's common sense to try this over—to
make this last supreme effort—just as it will be common sense
to separate if we can't get the puzzle solved together."

" Separate ! "

" Separate. Why not ? We can afford it. Of course
we shall separate."

" But, Rag !—separate ! "

He faced her protest squarely. " Life is not worth
living," he said, " unless it has more to hold it together
than ours has now. If we cannot escape together, then—
I will go alone." . . .

§ 9

They parted that night resolved to go to Labrador
together, with the broad outline of their subsequent journey
already drawn. Each lay awake far into the small hours
thinking of this purpose and of one another, with a strange
sense of renewed association. Each woke to a morning
of sunshine heavy-eyed. Each found that overnight
decision remote and incredible. It was like something in
a book or a play that had moved them very deeply. They
came down to breakfast, and helped themselves after the
wonted fashion of several years, Marjorie with a skilful
eye to the large order of her household ; *The Times* had
one or two characteristic letters which interested them
both ; there was the usual picturesque irruption of the
children and a distribution of early strawberries among
them. Trafford had two notes in his correspondence which

threw a new light upon the reconstruction of the Norton-Batsford company in which he was interested ; he formed a definite conclusion upon the situation, and went quite normally to his study and the telephone to act upon that.

It was only as the morning wore on that it became real to him that he and Marjorie had decided to leave the world. Then, with the Norton-Batsford business settled, he sat at his desk and mused. His apathy passed. His imagination began to present first one picture and then another of his retreat. He walked along Oxford Street to his club thinking—" soon we shall be out of all this." By the time he was at lunch in his club, Labrador had become again the magic refuge it had seemed the day before. After lunch he went to work in the library, finding out books about Labrador, and looking up the details of the journey.

But his sense of futility and hopeless oppression had vanished. He walked along the corridor and down the great staircase, and without a trace of the despairful hostility of the previous day, passed Blenkins, talking gray bosh with infinite thoughtfulness. He nodded easily to Blenkins. He was going out of it all, as a man might do who discovers after years of weary incarceration that the walls of his cell are made of thin paper. The time when Blenkins seemed part of a prison-house of routine and invincible stupidity seemed ten ages ago.

In Pall Mall Trafford remarked Lady Grampians and the Countess of Claridge, two women of great influence, in a big green car, on the way, no doubt, to create or sustain or destroy ; and it seemed to him that it was limitless ages since these poor old dears with their ridiculous hats and their ridiculous airs, their luncheons and dinners and dirty aggressive old minds, had sent tidal waves of competitive anxiety into his home. . . .

He found himself jostling through the shopping crowd on the sunny side of Regent Street. He felt now that he looked over these swarming, preoccupied heads at distant things. He and Marjorie were going out of it all, going clean out of it all. They were going to escape from society and shopping, and petty engagements and incessant triviality—as a bird flies up out of weeds.

§ 10

But Marjorie fluctuated more than he did.

There were times when the expedition for which he was

now preparing rapidly and methodically seemed to her the most adventurously-beautiful thing that had ever come to her, and times when it seemed the maddest and most hopeless of eccentricities. There were times when she had devastating premonitions of filth, hunger, strain, and fatigue, damp and cold, when her whole being recoiled from the project, when she could even think of staying secure in London and letting him go alone. She developed complicated anxieties for the children ; she found reasons for further inquiries, for delay. " Why not," she suggested, " wait a year ? "

" No," he said, " I won't. I mean we are to do this, and do it now, and nothing but sheer physical inability to do it will prevent my carrying it out. . . . And you ? Of course, you are to come. I can't drag you shrieking all the way to Labrador ; short of that I'm going to *make* you come with me." . . . .

She sat and looked up at him with dark lights in her upturned eyes, and a little added warmth in her cheek. " You've never forced my will like this before," she said in a low voice. " Never."

He was too intent upon his own resolves to heed her tones.

" It hasn't seemed necessary somehow," he said, considering her statement. " Now it does."

" This is something final," she said.

" It is final."

She found an old familiar phrasing running through her head, as she sat crouched together, looking up at his rather gaunt, very intent face, the speech of another woman echoing to her across a vast space of years : " Whither thou goest I will go——"

" In Labrador," he began. . . .

CHAPTER THE THIRD

THE PILGRIMAGE TO LONELY HUT

§ 1

MARJORIE was surprised to find how easy it was at last to part from her children and go with Trafford.

" I am not sorry," she said, " not a bit sorry—but I am fearfully afraid. I shall dream they are ill. . . . Apart from that, it's strange how you grip me—and they don't. . . ."

In the train to Liverpool she watched Trafford with the

queer feeling which comes to all husbands and wives at
times that that other partner is indeed an undiscovered
stranger, just beginning to show perplexing traits—full of
inconceivable possibilities.

For some reason his tearing her up by the roots in this
fashion had fascinated her imagination. She felt a strange
new wonder at him that had in it just a pleasant faint
flavour of fear. Always before she had felt a curious
aversion and contempt for those servile women who are
said to seek a master, to want to be mastered, to be eager
even for the physical subjugations of brute force. Now
she could at least understand, sympathise even with them.
Not only Trafford surprised her but herself. She found
she was in an unwonted perplexing series of moods. All
her feelings struck her now as being incorrect as well as
unexpected ; not only had life become suddenly full of
novelty, but she was making novel responses. She felt
that she ought to be resentful and tragically sorry for her
home and children. She felt this departure ought to have
the quality of an immense sacrifice, a desperate and heroic
undertaking for Trafford's sake. Instead she could detect
little beyond an adventurous exhilaration when presently
she walked the deck of the steamer that was to take her to
St. John's. She had visited her cabin, seen her luggage
stowed away, and now she surveyed the Mersey and its
shipping with a renewed freshness of mind. She was
reminded of the day, now nearly nino years ago, when she
had crossed the sea for the first time—to Italy. Then,
too, Trafford had seemed a being of infinitely wonderful
possibilities. . . . What were the children doing ?—that
ought to have been her preoccupation. She didn't know ;
she didn't care ! Trafford came and stood beside her,
pointed out this and that upon the landing stage, no longer
heavily sullen, but alert, interested, almost gay. . . .

Neither of them could find any way to the great discussion they had set out upon, in this voyage to St. John's.
But there was plenty of time before them. Plenty of
time ! They were both the prey of that uneasy distraction
which seems the inevitable quality of a passenger steamship.
They surveyed and criticised their fellow-travellers, and
prowled up and down through the long swaying days and
the cold dark nights. They slept uneasily amidst fog-horn
hootings and the startling sounds of waves swirling against
the ports. Marjorie had never had a long sea voyage
before ; for the first time in her life she saw all the world,

through a succession of days, as a circle of endless blue
waters, with the stars and planets and sun and moon rising
sharply from its rim. Until one has had a voyage no one
really understands that old Earth is a watery globe. . . .
They ran into thirty hours of storm, which subsided, and
then came a slow time among icebergs, and a hooting,
dreary passage through fog. The first three icebergs were
marvels, the rest bores ; a passing collier out of her course
and pitching heavily, a lonely black and dirty ship with a
manner almost derelict, filled their thoughts for half a day.
Their minds were in a state of tedious inactivity, eager for
such small interests and only capable of such small interests.
There was no hurry to talk, they agreed, no hurry at all,
until they were settled away ahead there among the snows.
" There we shall have plenty of time for everything. . . ."

Came the landfall and then St. John's, and they found
themselves side by side watching the town draw near,
The thought of landing and transference to another ship
refreshed them both. . . .

They were going, Trafford said, in search of God, but it
was far more like two children starting out upon a holiday.

§ 2

There was trouble and procrastination about the half-
breed guides that Trafford had arranged should meet them
at St. John's, and it was three weeks from their reaching
Newfoundland before they got themselves and their guides
and equipment and general stores aboard the boat for Port
Dupré. Thence he had planned they should go in the
Gibson schooner to Manivikovik, the Marconi station at
the mouth of the Green River, and thence past the new
pulp-mills up river to the wilderness. There were delays
and a few trivial, troublesome complications in carrying
out this scheme, but at last a day came when Trafford
could wave good-bye to the seven people and eleven dogs
which constituted the population of Peter Hammond's,
that last rude outpost of civilisation twenty miles above
the pulp-mill, and turn his face in good earnest towards
the wilderness.

Neither he nor Marjorie looked back at the headland for
a last glimpse of the little settlement they were leaving.
Each stared ahead over the broad, smooth sweep of water,
broken by one transverse bar of foaming shallows, and
scanned the low-tree-clad hills beyond that drew together

at last in the distant gorge out of which the river came.
The morning was warm and full of the promise of a hot
noon, so that the veils they wore against the assaults of
sand-flies and mosquitoes were already a little inconvenient.
It seemed incredible in this morning glow that the wooded
slopes along the shore of the lake were the border of a land
in which nearly half the inhabitants die of starvation.
The deep-laden canoes swept almost noiselessly through
the water with a rhythmic alternation of rush and pause
as the dripping paddles drove and returned. Altogether
there were four long canoes and five Indian breeds in their
party, and when they came to pass through shallows both
Marjorie and Trafford took a paddle.

They came to the throat of the gorge towards noon,
and found strong flowing deep water between its high
purple cliffs. All hands had to paddle again, and it was
only when they came to rest in a pool to eat a midday
meal and afterwards to land upon a mossy corner for a
stretch and a smoke, that Marjorie discovered the peculiar
beauty of the rock about them. On the dull, purplish-gray
surfaces played the most extraordinary mist of luminous
iridescence. It fascinated her. Here was a land whose
common substance had this gemlike opalescence. But
her attention was very soon withdrawn from these glancing
splendours.

She had had to put aside her veil to eat, and presently
she felt the vividly painful stabs of the black-fly and
discovered blood upon her face. A bigger fly, the size and
something of the appearance of a small wasp, with an evil
buzz, also assailed her and Trafford. It was a bad corner
for flies ; the breeds even were slapping their wrists and
swearing under the torment, and every one was glad to
embark and push on up the winding gorge. It opened out
for a time, and then the wooded shores crept in again, and
in another half-hour they saw ahead of them a long rush
of foaming waters among tumbled rocks that poured down
from a brimming, splashing line of light against the sky.
They crossed the river, ran the canoes into an eddy under
the shelter of a big stone and began to unload. They had
reached their first portage.

The rest of the first day was spent in packing and lugging
first the cargoes and then the canoes up through thickets
and over boulders and across stretches of reindeer moss
for the better part of two miles to a camping ground about
halfway up the rapids. Marjorie and Trafford tried to

help with the carrying, but this evidently shocked and
distressed the men too much, so they desisted and set to
work cutting wood and gathering moss for the fires and
bedding of the camp. When the iron stove was brought
up the man who had carried it showed them how to put
it up on stakes and start a fire in it, and then Trafford
went to the river to get water, and Marjorie made a kind
of flour-cake in the frying pan, in the manner an American
woman from the wilderness had once shown her, and boiled
water for tea. The twilight had deepened to night while
the men were still stumbling up the trail with the last two
canoes.

It gave Marjorie a curiously homeless feeling to stand
there in the open with the sunset dying away below the
black scrubby outlines of the treetops uphill to the north-
west, and to realise the nearest roof was already a day's
toilsome journey away. The cool night breeze blew upon
her bare face and arms—for now the insects had ceased
from troubling and she had cast aside gloves and veil and
turned up her sleeves to cook—and the air was full of the
tumult of the rapids tearing seaward over the rocks below.
Struggling through the bushes towards her was an immense,
headless quadruped with unsteady legs and hesitating
paces, two of the men carrying the last canoe. Two others
were now assisting Trafford to put up the little tent that
was to shelter her, and the fifth was kneeling beside her
very solemnly and respectfully cutting slices of bacon for
her to fry. The air was very sweet, and she wished she
could sleep not in the tent but under the open sky.

It was queer, she thought, how much of the wrappings
of civilisation had slipped from them already. Every day
of the journey from London had released them or deprived
them—she hardly knew which—of a multitude of petty
comforts and easy accessibilities. The afternoon toil uphill intensified the effect of having clambered up out of
things—to this loneliness, this twilight openness, this
simplicity.

The men ate apart at a fire they made for themselves,
and after Trafford and Marjorie had supped on damper,
bacon, and tea, he smoked. They were both too healthily
tired to talk very much. There was no moon, but a frosty
brilliance of stars, the air which had been hot and sultry
at midday grew keen and penetrating, and after she had
made him tell her the names of constellations she had
forgotten, she suddenly perceived the wisdom of the tent,

went into it—it was sweet and wonderful with sprigs of the Labrador tea-shrub—undressed, and had hardly rolled herself up into a cocoon of blankets before she was fast asleep.

She was awakened by a blaze of sunshine pouring into the tent, a smell of fried bacon, and Trafford's voice telling her to get up. "They've gone on with the first loads," he said. "Get up, wrap yourself in a blanket, and come and bathe in the river. It's as cold as ice."

She blinked at him. "Aren't you stiff ? " she asked.

"I was stiffer before I bathed," he said.

She took the tin he offered her. (They weren't to see china cups again for a year.) "It's woman's work getting tea," she said, as she drank.

"You can't be a squaw all at once," said Trafford.

§ 3

After Marjorie had taken her dip, dried roughly behind a bush, twisted her hair into a pigtail and coiled it under her hat, she amused herself and Trafford as they clambered up through rocks and willows to the tent again by cataloguing her apparatus of bath and toilette at Sussex Square and tracing just when and how she had parted from each item on the way to this place.

"But I say ! " she cried, with a sudden, sharp note of dismay, "we haven't soap ! This is our last cake almost. I never thought of soap."

"Nor I," said Trafford.

He spoke again presently. "We don't turn back for soap," he said.

"We don't turn back for anything," said Marjorie. "Still—I didn't count on a soaplesss winter."

"I'll manage something," said Trafford, a little doubtfully. "Trust a chemist. . . ."

That day they finished the portage and came out upon a wide lake with sloping shores and a distant view of snow-topped mountains, a lake so shallow that at times their loaded canoes scraped on the glaciated rock below and they had to alter their course. They camped in a lurid sunset ; the night was warm and mosquitoes were troublesome, and towards morning came a thunderstorm and wind and rain.

The dawn broke upon a tearing race of waves and a wild drift of slanting rain sweeping across the lake before a gale. Marjorie peered out at this as one peers out under

the edge of an umbrella. It was manifestly impossible to
go on, and they did nothing that day but run up a canvas
shelter for the men and shift the tent behind a thicket of
trees out of the full force of the wind. The men squatted
stoically, and smoked and yarned. Everything got coldly
wet, and for the most part the Traffords sat under the tent
and stared blankly at this summer day in Labrador.

"Now," said Trafford, "we ought to begin talking."

"There's nothing much to do else," said Marjorie.

"Only one can't begin," said Trafford.

He was silent for a time. "We're getting out of things,"
he said. . . .

The next day began with a fine drizzle, through which
the sun broke suddenly about ten o'clock. They made a
start at once, and got a good dozen miles up the lake before
it was necessary to camp again. Both Marjorie and
Trafford felt stiff and weary and uncomfortable all day,
and secretly a little doubtful now of their own endurance.
They camped on an island on turf amidst slippery rocks,
and the next day were in a foaming, difficult river again,
with glittering shallows that obliged every one to get out
at times to wade and push. All through the afternoon
they were greatly beset by flies. And so they worked
their way on through a third day's journey towards the
silent inland of Labrador.

Day followed day of toilsome and often tedious travel ;
they fought rapids, they waited while the men stumbled
up long portages under vast loads, going and returning,
they camped and discussed difficulties and alternatives.
The flies sustained an unrelenting persecution, until faces
were scarred in spite of veils and smoke fires, until wrists
and necks were swollen and the blood in a fever. As they
got higher and higher towards the central plateau, the
midday heat increased and the nights grew colder, until
they would find themselves toiling, wet with perspiration,
over rocks that sheltered a fringe of ice beneath their
shadows. The first fatigues and lassitudes, the shrinking
from cold water, the ache of muscular effort, gave place to
a tougher and tougher endurance ; skin seemed to have
lost half its capacity for pain without losing a tithe of its
discrimination, muscles attained a steely resilience ; they
were getting seasoned. "I don't feel philosophical," said
Trafford, "but I feel well."

"We're getting out of things."

"Suppose we are getting out of our problems !" . . .

One day as they paddled across a mile-long pool, they saw three bears prowling in single file high up on the hillside. "Look," said the man, and pointed with his paddle at the big, soft, furry black shapes, magnified and startling in the clear air. All the canoes rippled to a stop, the men, at first still, whispered softly. One passed a gun to Trafford, who hesitated and looked at Marjorie.

The air of tranquil assurance about these three huge loafing monsters had a queer effect on Marjorie's mind. They made her feel that they were at home and that she was an intruder. She had never in her life seen any big wild animals except in a menagerie. She had developed a sort of unconscious belief that all big wild animals were in menageries nowadays, and this spectacle of beasts entirely at large startled her. There was never a bar between these creatures, she felt, and her sleeping self. They might, she thought, do any desperate thing to feeble men and women who came their way.

"Shall I take a shot?" asked Trafford.

"No," said Marjorie, pervaded by the desire for mutual toleration. "Let them be."

The big brutes disappeared in a gully, reappeared, came out against the skyline one by one and vanished.

"Too long a shot," said Trafford, handing back the gun. . . .

Their journey lasted altogether a month. Never once did they come upon any human being save themselves, though in one place they passed the poles—for the most part overthrown—of an old Indian encampment. But this desolation was by no means lifeless. They saw great quantities of water-birds, geese, divers, Arctic partridge, and the like, they became familiar with the banshee cry of the loon. They lived very largely on geese and partridge. Then for a time about a string of lakes, the country was alive with migrating deer going south, and the men found traces of a wolf. They killed six caribou, and stayed to skin and cut them up and dry the meat to replace the bacon they had consumed, caught, fried, and ate great quantities of trout, and became accustomed to the mysterious dance of the northern lights as the sunset afterglow faded.

Everywhere, except in the river gorges, the country displayed the low hummocky lines and tarn-like pools of intensely glaciated land ; everywhere it was carpeted with reindeer moss growing upon peat and variegated by bushes

of flowering, sweet-smelling Labrador tea. In places this
was starred with little harebells and diversified by tussocks
of heather and rough grass, and over the rocks trailed
delicate dwarf shrubs and a very pretty and fragrant
pink-flowered plant of which neither she nor Trafford
knew the name.   There was an astonishing amount of
wild fruit, raspberries, cranberries, and a white kind of
strawberry that was very delightful.   The weather, after
its first outbreak, remained brightly serene. . . .

And at last it seemed fit to Trafford to halt and choose
his winter quarters.   He chose a place on the side of a
low, razor-backed rocky mountain ridge, about fifty feet
above the river—which had now dwindled to a thirty-foot
stream.   His site was near a tributary rivulet that gave
convenient water, in a kind of lap that sheltered between
two rocky knees, each bearing thickets of willow and
balsam.   Not a dozen miles away from them now they
reckoned was the Height of Land, the low watershed between the waters that go to the Atlantic and those that go
to Hudson's Bay.   Close beside the site he had chosen a
shelf of rock ran out and gave a glimpse up the narrow
rocky valley of the Green River's upper waters and a broad
prospect of hill and tarn towards the south-east.   North
and north-east of them the country rose to a line of low
crests, with here and there a yellowing patch of last year's
snow, and across the valley were slopes covered in places
by woods of stunted pine.   It had an empty spaciousness
of effect ; the one continually living thing seemed to be
the Green River, hurrying headlong, noisily, perpetually,
in an eternal flight from this high desolation.   Birds were
rare here, and the insects that buzzed and shrilled and
tormented among the rocks and willows in the gorge came
but sparingly up the slopes to them.

" Here, presently," said Trafford, " we shall be in
peace."

" It is very lonely," said Marjorie.

" The nearer to God."

" Think ! Not one of these hills has ever had a name."

" Well ? "

" It might be in some other planet."

" Oh !—we'll christen them.   That shall be Marjorie
Ridge, and that Rag Valley.   This space shall be—oh !
Bayswater ! Before we've done with it, this place and
every feature of it will be as familiar as Sussex Square.
More so—for half the houses there would be stranger to

us, if we could see inside them, than anything in this
wilderness. . . . As familiar, say—as your drawing-room.
That's better."

Marjorie made no answer, but her eyes went from the
reindeer moss and scrub and thickets of the foreground
to the low rocky ridges that bounded the view north and
east of them. The scattered boulders, the tangles of wood,
the barren upper slopes, the dust-soiled survivals of the
winter's snowfall, all contributed to an effect at once
carelessly desert and hopelessly untidy. She looked westward, and her memory was full of interminable streaming
rapids, wastes of ice-striated rocks, tiresome struggles
through woods and wild, wide stretches of tundra and tarn,
trackless and treeless, infinitely desolate. It seemed to her
that the sea-coast was but a step from London and ten
thousand miles away from her.

§ 4

The men had engaged to build the framework of hut
and store-shed before returning, and to this under Trafford's
direction they now set themselves. They were all half-
breeds, mingling Indian with Scottish or French blood,
sober and experienced men. Three were named Mackenzie,
two brothers and a cousin, and another, Raymond Noyes,
was a relation and acquaintance of that George Elson who
was with Wallace and Leonidas Hubbard, and afterwards
guided Mrs. Hubbard in her crossing of Labrador. The
fifth was a boy of eighteen named Lean. They were all
familiar with the idea of summer travel in this country ;
quite a number, a score or so, that is to say, of adventurous
people, including three or four women, had ventured far
in the wake of the Hubbards into these great wildernesses
during the decade that followed that first tragic experiment
in which Hubbard died. But that any one not of Indian
or Esquimaux blood should propose to face out the
Labrador winter was a new thing to them. They were
really very sceptical at the outset whether these two
highly civilised-looking people would ever get up to the
Height of Land at all, and it was still with manifest in-
credulity that they set about the building of the hut and
the construction of the sleeping-bunks for which they had
brought up planking. A stream of speculative talk had
flowed along beside Marjorie and Trafford ever since they
had entered the Green River ; and it didn't so much come

to an end as get cut off at last by the necessity of their
departure.

Noyes would stand, holding a hammer and staring at
the narrow little berth he was fixing together.

" You'll not sleep, in this," he said.

" I will," replied Marjorie.

" You'll come back with us."

" Not me."

" There'll be wolves come and howl."

" Let 'em."

" They'll come right up to the door here. Winter
makes 'em hidjus bold."

Marjorie shrugged her shoulders.

" It's that cold I've known a man have his nose froze
while he lay in bed," said Noyes.

" Up here ? "

" Down the coast. But they say it's 'most as cold up
here. Many's the man it's starved and froze." . . .

He and his companions told stories—very circumstantial and pitiful stories, of Indian disasters. They were
all tales of weariness and starvation, of the cessation of
food, because the fishing gave out, because the caribou did
not migrate by the customary route, because the man of
a family group broke his wrist, and then of the start of
all or some of the party to the coast to get help and provisions, of the straining, starving fugitives caught by
blizzards, losing the track, devouring small vermin raw,
gnawing their own skin garments until they toiled half
naked in the snow,—becoming cannibals, becoming delirious,
lying down to die. Once there was an epidemic of influenza,
and three families of seven and twenty people just gave up
and starved and died in their lodges, and were found, still
partly frozen, a patient, pitiful company, by trappers in
the spring. . . .

Such, they said, were the common things that happened
in a Labrador winter. Did the Traffords wish to run such
risks ?

A sort of propagandist enthusiasm grew up in the men.
They felt it incumbent upon them to persuade the Traffords
to return. They reasoned with them rather as one does
with wilful children. They tried to remind them of the
delights and securities of the world they were deserting.
Noyes drew fancy pictures of the pleasures of London by
way of contrast to the bitter days before them. " You've
got everything there, everything. Suppose you feel a bit

ill, you go out, and every block there's a drug store got everything—all the new rem'dies—p'raps twenty, thirty sorts of rem'dy. Lit up, nice. And chaps in collars—like gentlemen. Or you feel a bit dull, and you go into the streets and there's people. Why! when I was in New York I used to spend hours looking at the people. Hours! And everything lit up, too. Sky signs! Readin' everywhere. You can spend hours and hours in New York——"

" London," said Marjorie.

" Well, London—just going about and reading the things they stick up. Every blamed sort of thing. Or you say, let's go somewhere. Let's go out and be a bit lively. See? Up you get on a car and there you are! Great big restaurants, blazing with lights, and you can't think of a thing to eat they haven't got. Waiters all round you, dressed tremendous, fair asking you to have more. Or you say, let's go to a theatre. Very likely," said Noyes, letting his imagination soar, " you order up one of these automobillies."

" By telephone," helped Trafford.

" By telephone," confirmed Noyes. " When I was in New York there was a telephone in each room in the hotel. Each room. I didn't use it ever, except once when they didn't answer—but there it was. I know about telephones all right." . . .

Why had they come here? None of the men were clear about that. Marjorie and Trafford would overhear them discussing this question at their fire night after night; they seemed to talk of nothing else. They indulged in the boldest hypotheses, even in the theory that Trafford knew of deposits of diamonds and gold, and would trust no one but his wife with the secret. They seemed also attracted by the idea that our two young people had " done something." Lean, with memories of some tattered sixpenny novel that had drifted into his hands from England, had even some notion of an elopement, of a pursuing husband or a vindictive wife. He was young and romantic, but it seemed incredible he should suggest that Marjorie was a royal princess. Yet there were moments when his manner betrayed a more than personal respect . . .

One night after a hard day's portage Mackenzie was inspired by a brilliant idea. " They got no children," he said, in a hoarse, exceptionally audible whisper. " It worries them. Them as is Catholics goes pilgrimages, but these ain't Catholics. See? "

" I can't stand that," said Marjorie. " It touches my pride. I've stood a good deal. Mr. Mackenzie ! . . . Mr. . . . Mackenzie."

The voice at the men's fire stopped and a black head turned round. " What is it, Mrs. Trafford ? " asked Mackenzie.

She held up four fingers. " Four ! " she said.

" Eh ? "

" Three sons and a daughter," said Marjorie.

Mackenzie did not take it in until his younger brother had repeated her words.

" And you've come from them to *this* ! . . . Sir, what *have* you come for ? "

" We want to be here," shouted Trafford to their listening pause. Their silence was incredulous.

" We wanted to be alone together. There was too much—over there—too much everything."

Mackenzie, in silhouette against the fire, shook his head, entirely dissatisfied. He could not understand how there could be too much of anything. It was beyond a trapper's philosophy.

" Come back with us, sir," said Noyes. " You'll weary of it." . . .

Noyes clung to the idea of dissuasion to the end. " I don't care to leave ye," he said, and made a sort of by-word of it that served when there was nothing else to say.

He made it almost his last words. He turned back for another handclasp as the others under their light returning packs went filing down the hill.

" I don't care to leave ye," he said.

" Good luck ! " said Trafford.

" You'll need it," said Noyes, and looked at Marjorie very gravely and intently before he turned about and marched off after his fellows. . . .

Both Marjorie and Trafford felt a queer emotion, a sense of loss and desertion, a swelling in the throat, as that file of men receded over the rocky slopes, went down into a dip, reappeared presently small and remote cresting another spur, going on towards the little wood that hid the head of the rapids. They halted for a moment on the edge of the wood and looked back, then turned again one by one and melted stride by stride into the trees. Noyes was the last to go. He stood, in an attitude that spoke as plainly as words, " I don't care to leave ye." Something white waved and flickered ; he had whipped out the

letters they had given him for England, and he was waving
them. Then, as if by an effort, he set himself to follow
the others, and the two still watchers on the height above
saw him no more.

CHAPTER THE FOURTH

LONELY HUT

§ 1

MARJORIE and Trafford walked slowly back to the hut.
"There is much to do before the weather breaks," he
said, ending a thoughtful silence. "Then we can sit inside
there and talk about the things we need to talk about."

He added awkwardly: "Since we started, there has
been so much to hold the attention. I remember a mood
—an immense despair. I feel it's still somewhere at the back
of things, waiting to be dealt with. It's our essential fact.
But meanwhile we've been busy, looking at fresh things."

He paused. "Now it will be different perhaps. . . ."

For nearly four weeks indeed they were occupied very
closely, and crept into their bunks at night as tired as
wholesome animals who drop to sleep. At any time the
weather might break; already there had been two overcast days and a frowning conference of clouds in the north.
When at last storms began they knew there would be
nothing for it but to keep in the hut until the world froze up.

There was much to do to the hut. The absence of
anything but stunted and impoverished timber and the
limitation of time had forbidden a log hut, and their home
was really only a double framework, rammed tight between
inner and outer frame with a mixture of earth and boughs
and twigs of willow, pine, and balsam. The floor was
hammered earth carpeted with balsam twigs and a caribou-
skin. Outside and within wall and roof were faced with
coarse canvas—that was Trafford's idea—and their bunks
occupied two sides of the hut. Heating was done by the
sheet-iron stove they had brought with them, and the
smoke was carried out to the roof by a thin sheet-iron pipe
which had come up outside a roll of canvas. They had
made the roof with about the pitch of a Swiss chalet, and
it was covered with nailed waterproof canvas, held down
by a large number of big lumps of stone. Much of the
canvasing still remained to do when the men went down,

and then the Traffords used every scrap of packing-paper
and newspaper that had come up with them and was not
needed for lining the bunks in covering any crack or join
in the canvas wall.

Two decadent luxuries, a rubber bath and two rubber
hot-water bottles, hung behind the door. They were
almost the only luxuries. Kettles and pans and some
provisions stood on a shelf over the stove ; there was also
a sort of recess cupboard in the opposite corner, reserve
clothes were in canvas trunks under the bunks, they kept
their immediate supply of wood under the eaves just outside the door, and there was a big can of water between
stove and door. When the winter came they would have
to bring in ice from the stream.

This was their home. The tent that had sheltered
Marjorie on the way up was erected close to this hut to
serve as a rude scullery and outhouse, and they also made
a long, roughly thatched roof with a canvas cover, supported on stakes, to shelter the rest of the stores. The stuff
in tins and cases and jars they left on the ground under
this ; the rest—the flour, candles, bacon, dried caribou
beef, and so forth, they hung, as they hoped, out of the
reach of any prowling beast. And finally and most important was the wood pile. This they accumulated to the
north and east of the hut, and all day long with a sort of
ant-like perseverance Trafford added to it from the thickets
below. Once or twice, however, tempted by the appearance of birds, he went shooting, and one day he got five
geese that they spent a day upon, plucking, cleaning,
boiling, and putting up in all their store of empty cans,
letting the fat float and solidify on the top to preserve
this addition to their provision until the advent of the
frost rendered all other preservatives unnecessary. They
also tried to catch trout in the river below, but though they
saw many fish the catch was less than a dozen.

It was a discovery to both of them to find how com-
panionable these occupations were, how much more side
by side they could be amateurishly cleaning out a goose
and disputing about its cooking, than they had ever
contrived to be in Sussex Square.

"These things are so infernally interesting," said
Trafford, surveying the row of miscellaneous cans upon
the stove he had packed with disarticulated goose. "But
we didn't come here to picnic. All this is eating us up.
I have a memory of some immense tragic purpose——"

"That tin's *boiling*!" screamed Marjorie sharply.

He resumed his thread after an active interlude.

"We'll keep the wolf from the door," he said.

"Don't talk of wolves!" said Marjorie.

"Is it only when men have driven away the wolf from the door—oh! altogether away, that they find despair in the sky? I wonder——"

"What?" asked Marjorie, in his pause.

"I wonder if there is nothing really in life but this, the food hunt and the love hunt? Is life just all hunger and need, and are we left with nothing—nothing at all—when these things are done? . . . We're infernally uncomfortable here."

"Oh, nonsense!" cried Marjorie.

"Think of your carpets at home! Think of the great, warm, beautiful house that wasn't big enough!—And yet here, we're happy."

"We *are* happy," said Marjorie, struck by the thought. "Only——"

"Yes."

"I'm afraid. And I long for the children. And the wind *nips*."

"It may be those are good things for us. No! This is just a lark as yet, Marjorie. It's still fresh and full of distractions. The discomforts are amusing. Presently we'll get used to it. Then we'll talk out—what we have to talk out. . . . I say, wouldn't it keep and improve this goose of ours if we put in a little brandy?" . . .

§ 2

The weather broke at last. One might say it smashed itself over their heads. There came an afternoon darkness swift and sudden, a wild gale and an icy sleet that gave place in the night to snow, so that Trafford looked out next morning to see a maddening chaos of small white flakes, incredibly swift, against something that was neither darkness nor light. Even with the door but partly ajar a cruelty of cold put its claw within, set everything that was movable swaying and clattering, and made Marjorie hasten shuddering to heap fresh logs upon the fire. Once or twice Trafford went out to inspect tent and roof and store-shed, several times wrapped to the nose he battled his way for fresh wood, and for the rest of the blizzard they kept to the hut. It was slumberously stuffy, but comfortingly full of flavours of tobacco and food. There were two days of

intermission and a day of gusts and icy sleet again, turning
with one extraordinary clap of thunder to a wild down-
pour of dancing lumps of ice, and then a night when it
seemed all Labrador, earth and sky together, was in
hysterical protest against inconceivable wrongs.

And then the break was over; the annual freezing-up
was accomplished, winter had established itself, the snowfall moderated and ceased, and an icebound world shone
white and sunlit under a cloudless sky.

§ 3

Through all that time they got no further with the
great discussion for which they had faced that solitude.
They attempted beginnings.

"Where had we got to when we left England ? " tried
Marjorie. " You couldn't work, you couldn't rest—you
hated our life."

"Yes, I know. I had a violent hatred of the lives
we were leading. I thought—we had to get away. To
think. . . . But things don't leave us alone here."

He covered his face with his hands.

" Why did we come here ? " he asked.

" You wanted—to get out of things."

" Yes. But with you. . . . Have we, after all, got out
of things at all ? I said coming up, perhaps we were
leaving our own problem behind. In exchange for other
problems—old problems men have had before. We've
got nearer necessity ; that's all. Things press on us just
as much. There's nothing more fundamental in wild
nature, nothing profounder—only something earlier. One
doesn't get out of life by going here or there. . . . But I
wanted to get you away—from all the things that had
such a hold on you. . . .

" When one lies awake at nights, then one seems to get
down into things. . . ."

He went to the door, opened it, and stood looking out.
Against a wan daylight the snow was falling noiselessly
and steadily.

" Everything goes on," he said. . . . " Relentlessly." . . .

§ 4

That was as far as they had got when the storms ceased
and they came out again into an air inexpressibly fresh

and sharp and sweet, and into a world blindingly clean and golden white under the rays of the morning sun.

" We will build a fire out here," said Marjorie ; " make a great pile. There is no reason at all why we shouldn't live outside all through the day in such weather as this."

§ 5

One morning Trafford found the footmarks of some catlike creature in the snow near the bushes where he was accustomed to get firewood ; they led away very plainly up the hill, and after breakfast he took his knife and rifle and snowshoes and went after the lynx—for that, he decided, the animal must be. There was no urgent reason why he should want to kill a lynx, unless, perhaps, that killing it made the store-shed a trifle safer, but it was the first trail of any living thing for many days ; it promised excitement ; some primordial instinct perhaps urged him.

The morning was a little overcast, and very cold between the gleams of wintry sunshine. " Good-bye, dear wife ! " he said, and then as she remembered afterwards, came back a dozen yards to kiss her. " I'll not be long," he said. " The beast's prowling, and if it doesn't get wind of me I ought to find it in an hour." He hesitated for a moment. " I'll not be long," he repeated, and she had an instant's wonder whether he hid from her the same dread of loneliness that she concealed. Or perhaps he only knew her secret. Up among the tumbled rocks he turned, and she was still watching him. " Good-bye ! " he cried and waved, and the willow thickets closed about him.

She forced herself to the petty duties of the day, made up the fire from the pile he had left for her, set water to boil, put the hut in order, brought out sheets and blankets to air, and set herself to wash up. She wished she had been able to go with him. The sky cleared presently, and the low December sun lit all the world about her, but it left her spirit desolate.

She did not expect him to return until midday, and she sat herself down on a log before the fire to darn a pair of socks as well as she could. For a time this unusual occupation held her attention, and then her hands became slow and at last inactive, and she fell into a reverie. She thought at first of her children and what they might be doing ; in England across there to the east it would be about five hours later, four o'clock in the afternoon, and

the children would be coming home through the warm
muggy London sunshine with Fraulein Otto to tea. She
wondered if they had the proper clothes, if they were well ;
were they perhaps quarrelling or being naughty or skylark-
ing gaily across the Park. Of course, Fraulein Otto was
all right, quite to be trusted, absolutely trustworthy, and
their grandmother would watch for a flushed face or an
irrational petulance, or any of the little signs that herald
trouble, with more than a mother's instinctive alertness.
No need to worry about the children, no need whatever.
. . . The world of London opened out behind these
thoughts ; it was so queer to think that she was in almost
the same latitude as the busy, bright traffic of the autumn
season in Kensington Gore ; that away there in ten
thousand cleverly furnished drawing-rooms the ringing
tea-things were being set out for the rustling advent of
smart callers and the quick leaping gossip. And there
would be all sorts of cakes and little things ; for a while
her mind ran on cakes and little things, and she thought in
particular whether it wasn't time to begin cooking. . . .
Not yet. What was it she had been thinking about ?
Ah ! the Solomonsons and the Capeses and the Bernards
and the Carmels and the Lees. Would they talk of her
and Trafford ? It would be strange to go back to it all.
Would they go back to it all ? She found herself thinking
intently of Trafford.

What a fine human being he was ! And how touchingly
human ! The thought of his moments of irritation, his
baffled silences, filled her with a wild passion of tenderness.
She had disappointed him ; all that life failed to satisfy
him. Dear master of her life ! what was it he needed ?
She, too, wasn't satisfied with life, but while she had been
able to assuage herself with a perpetual series of petty
excitements, theatres, new books, and new people, meetings,
movements, dinners, shows, he had grown to an immense
discontent. He had most of the things men sought,
wealth, respect, love, children. . . . So many men might
have blunted their heartache with—adventures. There
were pretty women, clever women, unoccupied women.
She felt she wouldn't have minded—*much*—if it made him
happy. . . . It was so wonderful he loved her still. . . .
It wasn't that he lacked occupation ; on the whole he
overworked. His business interests were big and wide.
Ought he to go into politics ? Why was it that the researches that had held him once, could hold him now no

more ? That was the real pity of it. Was she to blame
for that ? She couldn't state a case against herself, and
yet she felt she was to blame. She had taken him away
from those things, forced him to make money. . . .

She sat chin on hand staring into the fire, the sock
forgotten on her knee.

She could not weigh justice between herself and him.
If he was unhappy it was her fault. She knew that with
a woman's irrational simplicity of conviction ; if he was
unhappy it was no excuse that she had not known, had
been misled, had a right to her own instincts and purposes.
She had got to make him happy. But what was she to
do, what was there for her to do ? . . .

Only he could work out his own salvation, and until
he had light, all she could do was to stand by him, help
him, cease to irritate him, watch, wait. Anyhow she
could at least mend his socks as well as possible, so that
the threads would not chafe him. . . .

She flashed to her feet. What was that ?

It seemed to her she had heard the sound of a shot,
and a quick brief wake of echoes. She looked across the
icy waste of the river, and then up the tangled slopes of
the mountain. Her heart was beating very fast. It must
have been up there, and no doubt he had killed his beast.
Some shadow of doubt she would not admit crossed that
obvious suggestion.

This wilderness was making her as nervously responsive
as a creature of the wild.

Came a second shot ; this time there was no doubt of
it. Then the desolate silence closed about her again.

She stood for a long time staring at the shrubby slopes
that rose to the barren rock wilderness of the purple
mountain crest. She sighed deeply at last, and set herself
to make up the fire and prepare for the midday meal. Once
far away across the river she heard the howl of a wolf.

Time seemed to pass very slowly that day. She found
herself going repeatedly to the space between the day tent
and the sleeping-hut from which she could see the stunted
wood that had swallowed him up, and after what seemed
a long hour her watch told her it was still only half-past
twelve. And the fourth or fifth time that she went to
look out she was set atremble again by the sound of a
third shot. And then at regular intervals out of that
distant brown purple jumble of thickets against the snow
came two more shots. " Something has happened," she

said, " something has happened," and stood rigid. Then she became active, seized the rifle that was always at hand when she was alone, fired into the sky and stood listening.

Prompt came an answering shot.

" He wants me," said Marjorie. " Something—— Perhaps he has killed something too big to bring ! "

She was for starting at once, and then remembered this was not the way of the wilderness.

She thought and moved very rapidly. Her mind catalogued possible requirements, rifle, hunting-knife, the oilskin bag with matches, and some chunks of dry paper, the rucksack—and he would be hungry. She took a saucepan and a huge chunk of cheese and biscuit. Then a brandy flask is sometimes handy—one never knows. Though nothing was wrong, of course. Needles and stout thread, and some cord. Snowshoes. A waterproof cloak could be easily carried. Her light hatchet for wood. She cast about to see if there was anything else. She had almost forgotten cartridges—and a revolver. Nothing more. She kicked a stray brand or so into the fire, put on some more wood, damped the fire with an armful of snow to make it last longer, and set out towards the willows into which he had vanished·

There was a rustling and snapping of branches as she pushed her way through the bushes, a little stir that died insensibly into quiet again ; and then the camping-place became very still. . . .

Scarcely a sound occurred, except for the little shuddering and stirring of the fire, and the reluctant infrequent drip from the icicles along the sunny edge of the log hut roof. About one o'clock the amber sunshine faded out altogether, a veil of clouds thickened and became grayly ominous, and a little after two the first flakes of a snowstorm fell hissing into the fire. A wind rose and drove the multiplying snowflakes in whirls and eddies before it. The icicles ceased to drip, but one or two broke and fell with a weak tinkling. A deep soughing, a shuddering groaning of trees and shrubs, came ever and again out of the ravine, and the powdery snow blew like puffs of smoke from the branches.

By four the fire was out, and the snow was piling high in the darkling twilight against tent and hut. . . .

§ 6

Trafford's trail led Marjorie through the thicket of dwarf willows and down to the gully of the rivulet which they had called Marjorie Trickle ; it had long since become a trough of snow-covered ice ; the trail crossed this, and, turning sharply uphill, went on until it was clear of shrubs and trees, and in the windy open of the upper slopes it crossed a ridge and came over the lip of a large desolate valley with slopes of ice and icy snow. Here she spent some time in following his loops back on the homeward trail before she saw what was manifestly the final trail running far away out across the snow, with the spoor of the lynx, a lightly-dotted line, to the right of it. She followed this suggestion of the trail, put on her snowshoes, and shuffled her way across this valley, which opened as she proceeded. She hoped that over the ridge she would find Trafford, and scanned the sky for the faintest discoloration of a fire, but there was none. That seemed odd to her, but the wind was in her face, and perhaps it beat the smoke down. Then as her eyes scanned the hummocky ridge ahead, she saw something, something very intent and still, that brought her heart into her mouth. It was a big, gray wolf, standing with back hunched and head down, watching and winding something beyond there, out of sight.

Marjorie had an instinctive fear of wild animals, and it still seemed dreadful to her that they should go at large uncaged. She suddenly wanted Trafford violently, wanted him by her side. Also she thought of leaving the trail, going back to the bushes. She had to take herself in hand. In the wastes one did not fear wild beasts. One had no fear of them. But why not fire a shot to let him know she was near ?

The beast flashed round with an animal's instantaneous change of pose, and looked at her. For a couple of seconds, perhaps, woman and brute regarded one another across a quarter of a mile of snowy desolation.

Suppose it came towards her !

She would fire—and she would fire at it. She made a guess at the range, and aimed very carefully. She saw the snow fly two yards ahead of the grisly shape, and then in an instant it had vanished over the crest.

She reloaded, and stood for a moment waiting for Trafford's answer. No answer came. " Queer ! " she

whispered, "queer!"—and suddenly such a horror of
anticipation assailed her that she started running and
floundering through the snow to escape it. Twice she
called his name, and once she just stopped herself from
firing a shot.

Over the ridge she would find him. Surely she would
find him over the ridge.

She found herself among rocks, and there was a beaten
and trampled place where Trafford must have waited and
crouched. Then on and down a slope of tumbled boulders.
There came a patch where he had either thrown himself
down or fallen.

It seemed to her he must have been running. . . .

Suddenly, a hundred feet or so away, she saw a patch
of violently disturbed snow—snow stained a dreadful
colour, a snow of scarlet crystals! Three strides, and
Trafford was in sight.

She had a swift conviction he was dead. He was lying
in a crumpled attitude on a patch of snow between convergent rocks, and the lynx, a mass of blood-smeared
silvery fur, was in some way mixed up with him. She
saw as she came nearer that the snow was disturbed round
about them, and discoloured copiously, yellow widely,
and in places bright red, with congealed and frozen blood.
She felt no fear now, and no emotion ; all her mind was
engaged with the clear, bleak perception of the fact before
her. She did not care to call to him again. The lynx
hid his head, it was as if he was burrowing underneath the
creature ; his legs were twisted about each other in a
queer, unnatural attitude.

Then, as she dropped off a boulder and came nearer,
Trafford moved. A hand came out and gripped the rifle
beside him ; he suddenly lifted a dreadful face, horribly
scarred and torn, and crimson with frozen blood ; he
pushed the gray beast aside, rose on an elbow, wiped his
sleeve across his eyes, stared at her, grunted, and flopped
forward. He had fainted.

She was now as clear-minded and as self-possessed as a
woman in a shop. In another moment she was kneeling
by his side. She saw, by the position of his knife and the
huge rip in the beast's body, that he had stabbed the lynx
to death as it clawed his head ; he must have shot and
wounded it and then fallen upon it. His knitted cap was
torn to ribbons, and hung upon his neck. Also his leg
was manifestly injured ; how, she could not tell. It was

chiefly evident he must freeze if he lay here. It seemed to her that perhaps he had pulled the dead brute over him to protect his torn skin from the extremity of cold. The lynx was already rigid, its clumsy paws asprawl—the torn skin and clot upon Trafford's face were stiff as she put her hands about his head to raise him. She turned him over on his back—how heavy he seemed !—and forced brandy between his teeth. Then, after a moment's hesitation, she poured a little brandy on his wounds.

She glanced at his leg, which was surely broken, and back at his face. Then she gave him more brandy, and his eyelids flickered. He moved his hand weakly. " The blood," he said, " kept getting in my eyes."

She gave him brandy once again, wiped his face and glanced at his leg. Something ought to be done to that, she thought. But things must be done in order.

She stared up at the darkling sky with its gray promise of snow, and down the slopes of the mountain. Clearly they must stay the night here. They were too high for wood among these rocks, but three or four hundred yards below there were a number of dwarfed fir-trees. She had brought her axe, so that a fire was possible. Should she go back to the camp and get the tent ?

Trafford was trying to speak again. " I got——" he said.

" Yes ? "

" Got my leg in that crack. Damn—damned nuisance."

Was he able to advise her ? She looked at him, and then perceived she must bind up his head and face. She knelt behind him and raised his head on her knee. She had a thick silk neck muffler, and this she supplemented by a band she cut and tore from her inner vest. She bound this, still warm from her body, about him, wrapped her cloak round him. The next thing was a fire. Five yards away, perhaps, a great mass of purple gabbro hung over a patch of nearly snowless moss. A hummock to the westward offered shelter from the weakly bitter wind, the icy draught, that was soughing down the valley. Always in Labrador, if you can, you camp against a rock surface ; it shelters you from the wind, reflects your fire, guards your back.

" Rag ! " she said.

" Rotten hole," said Trafford.

" What ? " she cried sharply.

" Got you in a rotten hole," he said. " Eh ? "

"Listen," she said, and shook his shoulder. "Look!
I want to get you up against that rock."

"Won't make much difference," said Trafford, and
opened his eyes. "Where?" he asked.

"There."

He remained quite quiet for a second perhaps. "Listen
to me," he said. "Go back to camp."

"Yes," she said.

"Go back to camp. Make a pack of all the strongest
food—strenthin'—strengthnin' food—you know?" He
seemed troubled to express himself.

"Yes," she said.

"Down the river. Down—down. Till you meet help."

"Leave you?"

He nodded his head and winced.

"You're always plucky," he said. "Look facts in the
face. Kiddies. Thought it over while you were coming."
A tear oozed from his eye. "Not be a fool, Madge. Kiss
me good-bye. Not be a fool. I'm done. Kids."

She stared at him, and her spirit was a luminous mist
of tears. "You old *coward*," she said in his ear, and
kissed the little patch of rough and bloody cheek beneath
his eye. Then she knelt up beside him. "*I'm* boss now,
old man," she said. "I want to get you to that place
there under the rock. If I drag, can you help?"

He answered obstinately: "You'd better go."

"I'll make you comfortable first," she answered,
"anyhow."

He made an enormous effort, and then with her quick
help and with his back to her knee, had raised himself on
his elbows.

"And afterwards?" he asked.

"Build a fire."

"Wood?"

"Down there."

"Two bits of wood tied on my leg—splints. Then I
can drag myself. See? Like a blessed old walrus."

He smiled, and she kissed his bandaged face again.

"Else it hurts," he apologised, "more than I can stand."

She stood up again, thought, put his rifle and knife to
his hand for fear of that lurking wolf, abandoning her own
rifle with an effort, and went striding and leaping from
rock to rock towards the trees below. She made the chips
fly, and was presently towing three venerable pine dwarfs,
bumping over rock and crevice, back to Trafford. She

flung them down, stood for a moment bright and breathless, then set herself to hack off the splints he needed from
the biggest stem. " Now," she said, coming to him.

" A fool," he remarked, " would have made the splints
down there. You're—*good*, Marjorie."

She lugged his leg out straight, put it into the natural
and least painful pose, padded it with moss and her torn
handkerchief, and bound it up. As she did so a handful
of snowflakes came whirling about them. She was now
braced up to every possibility. " It never rains," she
said grimly, " but it pours," and went on with her bone-
setting. He was badly weakened by pain and shock, and
once he swore at her sharply. " Sorry," he said.

She rolled him over on his chest, and left him to struggle
to the shelter of the rock while she went for more wood.

The sky alarmed her. The mountains up the valley
were already hidden by driven rags of slaty snowstorm.
This time she found a longer but easier path for dragging
her boughs and trees ; she determined she would not
start the fire until nightfall, nor waste any time in preparing
food until then. There were dead boughs for kindling—
more than enough. It was snowing quite fast by the time
she got up to him with her second load, and a premature
twilight already obscured and exaggerated the rocks and
mounds about her. She gave some of her cheese to
Trafford, and gnawed some herself on her way down to the
wood again. She regretted that she had brought neither
candles nor lantern, because then she might have kept
on until the cold of night stopped her, and she reproached
herself bitterly because she had brought no tea. She
could forgive herself the lantern, she had never expected
to be out after dark, but the tea was inexcusable. She
muttered self-reproaches while she worked like two men
among the trees, panting puffs of mist that froze upon
her lips and iced the knitted wool that covered her chin.
Why don't they teach a girl to handle an axe ? . . .

When at last the wolfish cold of the Labrador night
had come, it found Trafford and Marjorie seated almost
warmly on a bed of pine boughs between the sheltering
dark rock behind and a big but well husbanded fire in
front, drinking a queer-tasting but not unsavoury soup of
lynx-flesh, that she had fortified with the remainder of the
brandy. Then they tried roast lynx and ate a little, and
finished with some scraps of cheese and deep draughts of
hot water. Then—oh, Tyburnia and Chelsea and all that

is becoming !—they smoked Trafford's pipe for alternate
minutes, and Marjorie found great comfort in it.

The snowstorm poured incessantly out of the darkness
to become flakes of burning fire in the light of the flames
and then vanish magically, but it only reached them and
wetted them in occasional gusts. What did it matter for
the moment if the dim snow-heaps rose and rose about
them ? A glorious fatigue, an immense self-satisfaction
possessed Marjorie ; she felt that they had both done
well.

" I am not afraid of to-morrow now," she said at last—
a thought matured. " *No !* "

Trafford had the pipe and did not speak for a moment.
" Nor I," he said at last. " Very likely we'll get through
with it." He added after a pause : " I thought I was
done for. A man—loses heart. After a loss of blood."

" The leg's better ? "

" Hot as fire." His humour hadn't left him. " It's a
treat," he said. " The hottest thing in Labrador."

" I've been a good squaw this time, old man ? " she
asked suddenly.

He seemed not to hear her ; then his lips twitched and
he made a feeble movement for her hand. " I cursed
you," he said. . . .

She slept, but on a spring as it were, lest the fire should
fall. She replenished it with boughs, tucked in the half-
burnt logs, and went to sleep again. Then it seemed to her
that some invisible hand was pouring a thin spirit on the
flames that made them leap and crackle and spread north
and south until they filled the heavens. Her eyes were
open and the snowstorm overpast, leaving the sky clear,
and all the westward heaven alight with the trailing,
crackling, leaping curtains of the Aurora, brighter than
she had ever seen them before. Quite clearly visible
beyond the smoulder of the fire, a wintry waste of rock
and snow, boulder beyond boulder, passed into a dun
obscurity. The mountain to the right of them lay long
and white and stiff, a shrouded death. All earth was dead
and waste and nothing, and the sky alive and coldly
marvellous, signalling and astir. She watched the changing,
shifting colours, and they made her think of the gathering
banners of inhuman hosts, the stir and marshalling of icy
giants for ends stupendous and indifferent to all the trivial
impertinence of man's existence. . . .

That night the whole world of man seemed small and

shallow and insecure to her, beyond comparison. One came, she thought, but just a little way out of its warm and sociable cities hither, and found this homeless wilderness ; one pricked the thin appearances of life with microscope or telescope and came to an equal strangeness. All the pride and hope of human life goes to and fro in a little shell of air between this ancient globe of rusty nickel-steel and the void of space ; faint specks we are within a film ; we quiver between the atom and the infinite, beings hardly more substantial than the glow within an oily skin that drifts upon the water. The wonder and the riddle of it ! Here she and Trafford were ! Phantasmal shapes of unsubstantial fluid thinly skinned against evaporation and wrapped about with woven wool and the skins of beasts, that yet reflected and perceived, suffered and sought to understand ; that held a million memories, framed thoughts that plumbed the deeps of space and time—and another day of snow or icy wind might leave them just scattered bones and torn rags gnawed by a famishing wolf ! . . .

She felt a passionate desire to pray. . . .

She glanced at Trafford beside her, and found him awake and staring. His face was very pale and strange in that livid, flickering light. She would have spoken, and then she saw his lips were moving, and something, something she did not understand, held her back from doing so.

§ 7

The bleak, slow dawn found Marjorie intently busy. She had made up the fire, boiled water, and washed and dressed Trafford's wounds, and made another soup of lynx. But Trafford had weakened in the night, the stuff nauseated him, he refused it and tried to smoke and was sick, and then sat back rather despairfully after a second attempt to persuade her to leave him there to die. This failure of his spirit distressed her and a little astonished her, but it only made her more resolute to go through with her work. She had awakened cold, stiff, and weary, but her fatigue vanished with movement ; she toiled for an hour replenishing her pile of fuel, made up the fire, put his gun ready to his hand, kissed him, abused him lovingly for the trouble he gave her until his poor torn face lit in response, and then parting on a note of cheerful confidence set out to return to the hut. She found the way not altogether easy to make out, wind and snow had left scarcely a trace of

their tracks, and her mind was full of the stores she must
bring and the possibility of moving him nearer to the hut.
She was startled to see by the fresh, deep spoor along the
ridge how near the wolf had dared approach them in the
darkness. . . .

Ever and again Marjorie had to halt and look back to
get her direction right. As it was, she came through the
willow scrub nearly half a mile above the hut, and had to
follow the steep bank of the frozen river down. At one
place she nearly slipped upon an icy slope of rock.

One possibility she did not dare to think of during that
time : a blizzard now would cut her off absolutely from
any return to Trafford. Short of that she believed she
could get through.

Her quick mind was full of all she had to do. At first
she had thought chiefly of his immediate necessities, of
food and some sort of shelter. She had got a list of things
in her head—meat extract, bandages, corrosive sublimate
by way of antiseptic, brandy, a tin of beef, some bread and
so forth ; she went over that several times to be sure of it,
and then for a time she puzzled about a tent. She thought
she could manage a bale of blankets on her back, and that
she could rig a sleeping-tent for herself and Trafford with
one and some bent sticks. The big tent would be too
much to strike and shift. And then her mind went on to
a bolder enterprise, which was to get him home. The
nearer she could bring him to the log hut, the nearer they
would be to supplies. She cast about for some sort of
sledge. The snow was too soft and broken for runners,
especially among the trees, but if she could get a flat of
smooth wood she thought she might be able to drag him.
She decided to try the side of her bunk. She could easily
get that off. She would have, of course, to run it edgewise
through the thickets and across the ravine, but after that
she would have almost clear going until she reached the
steep place of broken rocks within two hundred yards of
him. The idea of a sledge grew upon her, and she planned
to nail a rope along the edge and make a kind of harness
for herself.

She found the camping-place piled high with drifted
snow, which had invaded tent and hut, and that some
beast, a wolverine she guessed, had been into the hut,
devoured every candle-end and the uppers of Trafford's
well-greased second boots, and had then gone to the corner
of the store shed and clambered up to the stores. She

made no account of its depredations there, but set herself
to make a sledge and get her supplies together. There
was a gleam of sunshine, but she did not like the look of
the sky, and she was horribly afraid of what might be
happening to Trafford. She carried her stuff through the
wood and across the ravine, and returned for her improvised
sledge. She was still struggling with that among the trees
when it began to snow again.

It was hard then not to be frantic in her efforts. As
it was, she packed her stuff so loosely on the planking that
she had to repack it, and she started without putting on
her snowshoes, and floundered fifty yards before she discovered that omission. The snow was now falling fast,
darkling the sky and hiding everything but objects close
at hand, and she had to use all her wits to determine
her direction ; she knew she must go down a long slope
and then up to the ridge, and it came to her as a happy
inspiration that if she bore to the left she might strike
some recognisable vestige of her morning's trail. She had
read of people walking in circles when they have no light
or guidance, and that troubled her until she bethought
herself of the little compass on her watch-chain. By that
she kept her direction. She wished very much she had
timed herself across the waste, so that she could tell when
she approached the ridge.

Soon her back and shoulders were aching violently,
and the rope across her chest was tugging like some evil-
tempered thing. But she did not dare to rest. The snow
was now falling thick and fast, the flakes traced white
spirals and made her head spin, so that she was constantly
falling away to the south-westward and then correcting
herself by the compass. She tried to think how this
zig-zagging might affect her course, but the snow-whirls
confused her mind and a growing anxiety would not let her
pause to think. She felt blinded ; it seemed to be snowing
inside her eyes so that she wanted to rub them. Soon
the ground must rise to the ridge, she told herself ; it
must surely rise. Then the sledge came bumping at her
heels and she perceived she was going downhill. She
consulted the compass, and she found she was facing south.
She turned sharply to the right again. The snowfall
became a noiseless, pitiless torture to sight and mind.

The sledge behind her struggled to hold her back, and
the snow balled under her snowshoes. She wanted to stop
and rest, take thought, sit for a moment. She struggled

with herself and kept on. She tried walking with shut
eyes, and tripped and came near sprawling. " O God ! "
she cried, " O God ! " too stupefied for more articulate
prayers.

Would the rise of the ground to the ribs of rock never
come ?

A figure, black and erect, stood in front of her suddenly,
and beyond appeared a group of black, straight antagonists.
She staggered on towards them, gripping her rifle with
some muddled idea of defence, and in another moment
she was brushing against the branches of a stunted fir,
which shed thick lumps of snow upon her feet. What
trees were these ? Had she ever passed any trees ? No !
There were no trees on her way to Trafford. . . .

She began whimpering like a tormented child. But
even as she wept she turned her sledge about to follow
the edge of the wood. She was too much downhill, she
thought, and she must bear up again.

She left the trees behind, made an angle uphill to the
right, and was presently among trees again. Again she
left them and again came back to them. She screamed
with anger at them and twitched her sledge away. She
wiped at the snowstorm with her arm as though she would
wipe it away. She wanted to stamp on the universe. . . .

And she ached, she ached. . . .

Something caught her eye ahead, something that
gleamed ; it was exactly like a long, bare, rather pinkish
bone standing erect on the ground. Just because it was
strange and queer she ran forward to it. Then as she
came nearer she perceived it was a streak of barked
trunk ; a branch had been torn off a pine tree and the
bark stripped down to the root. And then her foot hit
against a freshly hewn stump, and then came another,
poking its pinkish wounds above the snow. And there
were chips ! This filled her with wonder. Some one had
been cutting wood ! There must be Indians or trappers
near, she thought, and then realised the wood-cutter could
be none other than herself.

She turned to the right and saw the rocks rising steeply
close at hand. " Oh, Rag ! " she cried, and fired her rifle
in the air.

Ten seconds, twenty seconds, and then so loud and near
it amazed her, came his answering shot. It sounded like
the hillside bursting.

In another moment she had discovered the trail she

had made overnight and that morning by dragging fire-wood. It was now a shallow soft white trench. Instantly her despair and fatigue had gone from her. Should she take a load of wood with her ? she asked herself, in addition to the weight behind her, and had a better idea. She would unload and pile her stuff here, and bring him down on the sledge closer to the wood. She looked about and saw two rocks that diverged with a space between. She flashed schemes. She would trample the snow hard and flat, put her sledge on it, pile boughs and make a canopy of blanket overhead and behind. Then a fire in front.

She saw her camp admirable. She tossed her provisions down and ran up the broad windings of her pine-tree trail to Trafford, with the unloaded sledge bumping behind her. She ran as lightly as though she had done nothing that day.

She found him markedly recovered, weak, and quiet, with snow drifting over his feet, his rifle across his knees, and his pipe alight. " Back already," he said, " but——'
He hesitated. " No grub ? "

She knelt over him, gave his rough, unshaven cheek a swift kiss, and very rapidly explained her plan.

§ 8

In three days' time they were back at the hut, and the last two days they wore blue spectacles because of the midday glare of the sunlit snow.

It amazed Marjorie to discover as she lay awake in the camp on the edge of the ravine close to the hut to which she had lugged Trafford during the second day, that she was deeply happy. It was preposterous that she should be so, but those days of almost despairful stress were irradiated now by a new courage. She was doing this thing, against all Labrador and the snow-driving wind that blew from the polar wilderness, she was winning. It was a great discovery to her that hardship and effort almost to the breaking-point could ensue in so deep a satisfaction. She lay and thought how deep and rich life had become for her, as though in all this effort and struggle some unsuspected veil had been torn away. She perceived again, but now with no sense of desolation, that same infinite fragility of life which she had first perceived when she had watched the Aurora Borealis flickering up the sky. Beneath that realisation and carrying it, as a river flood may carry scum, was a sense of herself as something deeper, greater, more enduring than mountain or wilderness or sky, or any of those monstrous forms of nature that had dwarfed her physical self to nothingness.

She had a persuasion of self-detachment and illumination, and withal of self-discovery. She saw her life of time and space for what it was. Away in London the children, with the coldest of noses and the gayest of spirits, would be scampering about their bedrooms in the mild morning sunlight of a London winter ; Elsie, the parlourmaid, would be whisking dexterous about the dining-room, the bacon would be cooking and the coffee-mill at work, the letters of the morning delivery perhaps just pattering into the letter-box, and all the bright little household she had made, with all the furniture she had arranged, all the characteristic decoration she had given it, all the clever convenient arrangements, would be getting itself into action for another day—and *it wasn't herself* ! It was the extremest of her superficiality.

She had come out of all that, and even so it seemed she had come out of herself ; this weary woman lying awake on the balsam boughs with a brain cleared by underfeeding and this continuous, arduous bath of toil in snow-washed, frost-cleansed, starry air, this, too, was no more than a momentarily clarified window for her unknown and indefinable reality. What was that reality ? what was she herself ? She became interested in framing an answer to that, and slipped down from the peace of soul she had attained. Her serenity gave way to a reiteration of this question, reiterations increasing and at last oppressing like the snowflakes of a storm, perpetual whirling repetitions that at last confused her and hid the sky. . . .

She fell asleep. . . .

§ 9

With their return to the hut, Marjorie had found herself encountering a new set of urgencies. In their absence that wretched little wolverine had found great plenty and happiness in the tent and store-shed ; its traces were manifest nearly everywhere, and it had particularly assailed the candles, after a destructive time among the frozen caribou beef. It had clambered up on the packages of sardines and jumped thence on to a sloping pole that it could claw along into the frame of the roof. She rearranged the packages, but that was no good. She could not leave Trafford in order to track the brute down, and for a night or so she could not think of any way of checking its depredations. It came each night. . . . Trafford kept her close at home. She had expected that when he was back in his bunk, secure and warm, he would heal rapidly, but instead he suddenly developed all the symptoms of a severe feverish cold, and his scars, which had seemed healing, became flushed and ugly-looking. Moreover, there was something wrong with his leg, an ominous ache that troubled her mind. Every woman, she decided, ought to know how to set a bone. He was unable to sleep by reason of these miseries, though very desirous of doing so. He became distressingly weak and inert, he ceased to care for food, and presently he began to talk to himself with a complete disregard of her presence. Hourly she regretted her ignorance of medicine that left her with no conceivable remedy for all the aching and gnawing that worried and weakened him, except bathing with antiseptics and a liberal use of quinine.

And his face became strange to her, for over his flushed and sunken cheeks, under the raw spaces of the scar a blond beard bristled and grew. Presently, Trafford was a bearded man.

Incidentally, however, she killed the wolverine by means of a trap of her own contrivance, a loaded rifle with a bait of what was nearly her last candles, rigged to the trigger.

But this loss of the candles brought home to them the steady lengthening of the nights. Scarcely seven hours of day remained now in the black, cold grip of the darkness. And through those seventeen hours of chill aggression they had no light but the red glow of the stove. She had to close the door of the hut and bar every chink and cranny against the icy air, that became at last a murderous, freezing wind. Not only did she line the hut with every scrap of skin and paper she could obtain, but she went out with the spade toiling for three laborious afternoons in piling and beating snow against the outer frame. And now it was that Trafford talked at last, talked with something of the persistence of delirium, and she sat and listened hour by hour, silently, for he gave no heed to her or to anything she might say. He talked, it seemed, to God. . . .

§ 10

Darkness about a sullen glow of red, and a voice speaking.

The voice of a man, fevered and in pain, wounded and amidst hardship and danger, struggling with the unrelenting riddle of his being. Ever and again when a flame leapt she would see his face, haggard, bearded, changed, and yet infinitely familiar.

His voice varied, now high and clear, now mumbling, now vexed and expostulating, now rich with deep feeling, now fagged and slow ; his matter varied too ; now he talked like one who is inspired, and now like one lost and confused, stupidly repeating phrases, going back upon a misleading argument, painfully, laboriously beginning over and over again. Marjorie sat before the stove watching it burn and sink, replenishing it, preparing food, and outside the bitter wind moaned and blew the powdery snow before it, and the shortening interludes of pallid, diffused daylight which pass for days in such weather, came and went. Intense cold had come now with leaden snowy days and starless nights.

Sometimes his speech filled her mind, seemed to fill all her world ; sometimes she ceased to listen, following thoughts of her own. Sometimes she dozed ; sometimes she awakened from sleep to find him talking. But slowly she realised a thread in his discourse, a progress and development.

Sometimes he talked of his early researches, and then he would trace computations with his hands as if he were using a blackboard, and became distressed to remember what he had written. Sometimes he would be under the claws of the lynx again, and fighting for his eyes. " Ugh ! " he said, " keep those hind legs still. Keep your hind legs still ! Knife ? Knife ? Ah ! got it. Gu—u—u, you *Beast* ! "

But the gist of his speech was determined by the purpose of his journey to Labrador. At last he was reviewing his life and hers, and all that their life might signify, even as he determined to do. She began to perceive that whatever else drifted into his mind and talk, this recurred and grew, that he returned to the conclusion he had reached, and not to the beginning of the matter, and went on from that. . . .

" You see," he said, " our lives are nothing—nothing in themselves. I know that ; I've never had any doubts of that. We individuals just pick up a mixed lot of things out of the powers that begat us, and lay them down again presently a little altered, that's all—heredities, traditions, the finger-nails of my grandfather, a great-aunt's lips, the faith of a sect, the ideas of one's time. We live and then we die, and the threads run, dispersing this way and that. To make other people again. Whatever's immortal isn't that, our looks or our habits, our thoughts or our memories —just the shapes, these are, of one immortal stuff. . . . One immortal stuff." . . .

The. voice died away as if he was baffled. Then it resumed.

" But we ought to *partake* of immortality ; that's my point. We ought to partake of immortality.

" I mean we're like the little elements in a magnet ; ought not to lie higgledy-piggledy, ought to point the same way, be polarised—— Something microcosmic, you know, ought to be found in a man.

" Analogies run away with one. Suppose the bar isn't magnetised yet ! Suppose purpose has to come ; suppose the immortal stuff isn't yet, isn't being but struggling to be. Struggling to be. . . . Gods ! that morning ! When the child was born ! And afterwards she was there—with a smile on her lips, and a little flushed and proud—as if nothing had happened so very much out of the way. Nothing so wonderful. And we had another life besides our own ! " . . .

Afterwards he came back to that. " That was a good image," he said, " something trying to exist, which isn't substance, doesn't belong to space or time, something stifled and enclosed, struggling to get through. Just confused birth cries, eyes that hardly see, deaf ears, poor little thrusting hands. A thing altogether blind at first, a twitching and thrusting of protoplasm under the waters, and then the plants creeping up the beaches, the insects and reptiles on the margins of the rivers, beasts with a flicker of light in their eyes answering the sun. And at last, out of the long interplay of desire and fear, an ape, an ape that stared and wondered, and scratched queer pictures on a bone." . . .

He lapsed into silent thought for a time, and Marjorie glanced at his dim face in the shadows.

" I say nothing of ultimates," he said at last.

He repeated that twice before his thoughts would flow again.

" This is as much as I see, in time as I know it and space as I know it—*something struggling to exist*. It's true to the end of my limits. What can I say beyond

that ? It struggles to exist, becomes conscious, becomes
now conscious of itself. That is where I come in, as a
part of it. Above the beast in me is that—the desire to
know better, to know—beautifully, and to transmit my
knowledge. That's all there is in life for me beyond food
and shelter and tidying up. This Being—opening its eyes,
listening, trying to comprehend. Every good thing in
man is that ; —looking and making pictures, listening and
making songs, making philosophies and sciences, trying
new powers, bridge and engine, spark and gun. At the
bottom of my soul, *that*. We began with bone-scratching.
We're still—near it. I am just a part of this beginning—
mixed with other things. Every book, every art, every
religion is that, the attempt to understand and express—
mixed with other things. Nothing else matters, nothing
whatever. I tell you—— Nothing whatever !

"I've always believed that. All my life I've believed
that.

"Only I've forgotten.

"Every man with any brains believes that at the
bottom of his heart. Only he gets busy and forgets. He
goes shooting lynxes and breaks his leg. Odd, instinctive,
brutal thing to do—to go tracking down a lynx to kill it !
I grant you that, Marjorie. I grant you that."

"Grant me what ? " she cried, startled beyond measure
to hear herself addressed.

"Grant you that it is rather absurd to go hunting a
lynx. And what big paws it has—disproportionately big !
I wonder if that's an adaptation to snow ? Tremendous
paws they are. . . . But the real thing, I was saying, the
real thing is to get knowledge, and express it. All things
lead up to that. Civilisation, social order, just for that.
Except for that, all the life of man, all his affairs, his laws
and police, his morals and manners—nonsense, nonsense,
nonsense. Lynx hunts ! Just ways of getting themselves
mauled and clawed perhaps—into a state of understanding.
Who knows ? " . . .

His voice became low and clear.

"Understanding spreading like a dawn. . . .

"Logic and language, clumsy implements, but rising
to our needs, rising to our needs, thought clarified, enriched,
reaching out to every man alive—some day—presently—
touching every man alive, harmonising acts and plans,
drawing men into gigantic co-operations, tremendous
co-operations. . . .

" Until man shall stand upon this earth as upon a footstool and reach out his hand among the stars. . . .

" And then I went into the rubber market, and spent seven years of my life driving shares up and down and into a net ! . . . Queer game indeed ! Stupid ass, Behrens was—at bottom. . . .

" There's a flaw in it somewhere." . . .

He came back to that several times before he seemed able to go on from it.

" There *is* a collective mind," he said, " a growing general consciousness—growing clearer. Something put me away from that, but I know it. My work, my thinking, was a part of that. That's why I was so mad about Behrens."

" Behrens ? "

" Of course. He'd got a twist, a wrong twist. It makes me angry now. It will take years, it will eat up some brilliant man to clean up after Behrens——

" Yes, but the point is "—his voice became acute— " why did I go making money and let Behrens in ? Why generally and in all sorts of things does Behrens come in ? " . . .

He was silent for a long time, and then he began to answer himself. " Of course," he said, " I said it—or somebody said it—about this collective mind being mixed with other things. It's something arising out of life—not the common stuff of life. An exhalation. . . . It's like the little tongues of fire that came at Pentecost. . . . Queer how one comes drifting back to these images. Perhaps I shall die a Christian yet. . . . The other Christians won't like me if I do. What was I saying ? . . . It's what I reach up to, what I desire shall pervade me, not what I am. Just as far as I give myself purely to knowledge, to making feeling and thought clear in my mind and words, to the understanding and expression of the realities and relations of life, just so far do I achieve Salvation. . . . Salvation ! . . .

" I wonder, is Salvation the same for every one ? Perhaps for one man Salvation is research and thought, and for another expression in art, and for another nursing lepers. Provided he does it in the spirit. He has to do it in the spirit." . . .

There came a silence as though some difficulty baffled him, and he was feeling back to get his argument again.

" This flame that arises out of life, that redeems life

from purposeless triviality, *isn't* life. Let me get hold of
that. That's a point. That's a very important point."

Something had come to him.

" I've never talked of this to Marjorie. I've lived with
her nine years and more, and never talked of religion.
Not once. That's so queer of us. Any other couple in
any other time would have talked religion no end. . . .
People ought to."

Then he stuck out an argumentative hand. " You see,
Marjorie *is* life," he said.

" She took me."

He spoke slowly, as though he traced things carefully.
" Before I met her I suppose I wasn't half alive. No!
Yet I don't remember. I felt particularly incomplete.
Women were interesting, of course ; they excited me at
times, that girl at Yonkers !—H'm. I stuck to my work.
It was fine work ; I forget half of it now, the half-concealed
intimations, I mean—queer how one forgets !—but I know
I felt my way to wide, deep things. It was like exploring
caves—monstrous, limitless caves. Such caves ! . . .
Very still—underground. Wonderful and beautiful. . . .
They're lying there now for other men to seek. Other
men will find them. . . . Then *she* came, as though she
was taking possession. The beauty of her, oh ! the life
and bright eagerness, and the incompatibility ! That's
the riddle ! I've loved her always. When she came to my
arms it seemed to me the crown of life. Caves indeed !
Old caves ! Nothing else seemed to matter. But something did. All sorts of things did. I found that out soon
enough. And when that first child was born. That for a
time was supreme. . . . Yes—she's the quintessence of
life, the dear greed of her, the appetite, the clever appetite
for things. She grabs. She's so damned clever ! The
light in her eyes ! Her quick, sure hands ! . . . Only my
work was crowded out of my life and ended, and she didn't
seem to feel it, she didn't seem to mind it. There was a
sort of disregard. Disregard. As though all that didn't
really matter." . . .

" *My dear !* " whispered Marjorie, unheeded. She wanted
to tell him it mattered now, mattered supremely, but she
knew he had no ears for her.

His voice flattened. " It's perplexing," he said. " The
two different things."

Then suddenly he cried out harshly : " I ought never
to have married her—never, never ! I had my task. I

gave myself to her. Oh! the high immensities, the great and terrible things open to the mind of man! And we breed children and live in littered houses and play with our food and chatter, chatter, chatter. Oh, the chatter of my life! The folly! The women with their clothes. I can hear them rustle now, whiff the scent of it! The scandals—as though the things they did with themselves and each other mattered a rap; the little sham impromptu clever things, the trying to keep young—and underneath it all that continual cheating, cheating, cheating, damning struggle for money! . . .

"Marjorie, Marjorie, Marjorie! Why is she so good and no better! Why wasn't she worth it altogether? . . .

"No! I don't want to go on with it any more—ever. I want to go back.

"I want my life over again, and to go back.

"I want research, and the spirit of research that has died in me, and that still, silent room of mine again, that room, as quiet as a cell, and the toil that led to light. Oh! the coming of that light, the uprush of discovery, the solemn joy as the generalisation rises like a sun upon the facts—floods them with a common meaning. That is what I want. That is what I have always wanted. . . .

"Give me my time, O God! again; I am sick of this life I have chosen. I am sick of it! This—busy death! Give me my time again. . . . Why did You make me, and then waste me like this? Why are we made for folly upon folly? Folly! and brains made to scale high heaven, smeared into the dust! Into the dust, into the dust. Dust!" . . .

He passed into weak, wandering repetitions of disconnected sentences, that died into whispers and silence, and Marjorie watched him and listened to him, and waited with a noiseless dexterity upon his every need.

§ 11

One day, she did not know what day, for she had lost count of the days, Marjorie set the kettle to boil and opened the door of the hut to look out, and the snow was ablaze with diamonds, and the air was sweet and still. It occurred to her that it would be well to take Trafford out into that brief brightness. She looked at him and found his eyes upon the sunlight, quiet and rather wondering eyes.

"Would you like to get out into that!" she asked abruptly

" Yes," he said, and seemed disposed to get up.

" You've got a broken leg," she cried, to arrest his movement, and he looked at her and answered : " Of course—I forgot."

She was all atremble that he should recognise her and speak to her. She pulled her rude old sledge alongside his bunk, and kissed him, and showed him how to shift and drop himself upon the plank. She took him in her arms and lowered him. He helped weakly but understandingly, and she wrapped him up warmly on the planks and lugged him out and built up a big fire at his feet, wondering, but as yet too fearful to rejoice, at the change that had come to him.

He said no more, but his eyes watched her move about with a kind of tired curiosity. He smiled for a time at the sun, and shut his eyes, and still faintly smiling, lay still. She had a curious fear that if she tried to talk to him this new lucidity would vanish again. She went about the business of the morning, glancing at him ever and again, until suddenly the calm of his upturned face smote her, and she ran to him and crouched down to him between hope and a terrible fear, and found that he was sleeping, and beathing very lightly, sleeping with the deep unconsciousness of a child. . . .

When he awakened the sun was red in the west. His eyes met hers, and he seemed a little puzzled.

" I've been sleeping, Madge ? " he said.

She nodded.

" And dreaming ? I've a vague sort of memory of preaching and preaching in a kind of black, empty place, where there wasn't anything. . . . A fury of exposition . . . a kind of argument. . . . I say !—Is there such a thing in the world as a new-laid egg—and some bread-and-butter ? "

He seemed to reflect. " Of course," he said, " I broke my leg. Golly ! I thought that beast was going to claw my eyes out. Lucky, Madge, it didn't get my eyes. It was just a chance it didn't."

He stared at her.

" I say," he said, " you've had a pretty rough time ! How long has this been going on ? "

He amazed her by raising himself on his elbow and sitting up.

" Your leg ! " she cried.

He put his hand down and felt it. " Pretty stiff," he

said. " You get me some food—there *were* some eggs,
Madge, frozen new-laid, anyhow—and then we'll take these
splints off and feel it about a bit. Eh! why not? How
did you get me out of that scrape, Madge? I thought
I'd got to be frozen as safe as eggs. (Those eggs ought to
be all right, you know. If you put them on in a saucepan
and wait until they boil.) I've a sort of muddled impression. . . . By Jove, Madge, you've had a time! I say,
you *have* had a time! "

His eyes, full of a warmth of kindliness she had not
seen for long weeks, scrutinised her face. " I say! " he
repeated, very softly.

All her strength went from her at his tenderness. " Oh,
my dear," she wailed, kneeling at his side, " my dear,
dear! " and still regardful of his leg, she yet contrived to
get herself weeping into his coveted arms.

He regarded her, he held her, he patted her back!
The infinite luxury to her! He'd come back. He'd come
back to her.

" How long has it been? " he asked. " Poor dear!
Poor dear! How long can it have been? "

§ 12

From that hour Trafford mended. He remained clear-
minded, helpful, sustaining. His face healed daily.
Marjorie had had to cut away great fragments of gan-
grenous frozen flesh, and he was clearly destined to have
a huge scar over forehead and cheek, but in that pure,
clear air, once the healing had begun it progressed swiftly.
His leg had set, a little shorter than its fellow and with a
lump in the middle of the shin, but it promised to be a
good serviceable leg none the less. They examined it by
the light of the stove with their heads together, and discussed when it would be wise to try it. How do doctors
tell when a man may stand on his broken leg? She had
a vague impression you must wait six weeks, but she could
not remember why she fixed upon that time.

"It seems a decent interval," said Trafford. "We'll try it."

She had contrived a crutch for him against that momentous experiment, and he sat up in his bunk, pillowed up
by a sack and her rugs, and whittled it smooth, and padded
the fork with the skin of that slaughtered wolverine, poor
victim of hunger!—while she knelt by the stove feeding
it with logs, and gave him an account of their position.

"We're somewhere in the middle of December," she said, "somewhere between the twelfth and the fourteenth, —yes! I'm as out as that!—and I've handled the stores pretty freely. So did that little beast until I got him." She nodded at the skin in his hand. "I don't see myself shooting much now, and so far I've not been able to break the ice to fish. It's too much for me. Even if it isn't too late to fish. This book we've got describes barks and mosses, and that will help, but if we stick here until the birds and things come, we're going to be precious short. We may have to last right into July. I've plans—but it may come to that. We ought to ration all the regular stuff and trust to luck for a feast. The rations!—I don't know what they'll come to."

"Right O," said Trafford, admiring her capable gravity. "Let's ration."

"Marjorie," he asked abruptly, "are you sorry we came?"

Her answer came unhesitatingly. "*No!*"

"Nor I."

He paused. "I've found you out," he said. "Dear, dirty, living thing! . . . You *are* dirty, you know."

"I've found myself," she answered, thinking. "I feel as if I've never loved you until this hut. I suppose I have in my way——"

"Lugano," he suggested. "Don't let's forget good things, Marjorie. Oh! And endless times!"

"Oh, of course! As for *that*——! But now—now you're in my bones. We were just two shallow, pretty, young things—loving. It was sweet, dear—sweet as youth—but not this. Unkempt and weary—then one understands love. I suppose I *am* dirty. Think of it! I've lugged you through the snow till my shoulders chafed and bled. I cried with pain, and kept on lugging—— Oh, my dear! my dear!" He kissed her hair. "I've held you in my arms to keep you from freezing. (I'd have frozen myself first.) We've got to starve, together perhaps before the end. . . . Dear, if I could make you, you should eat me. . . . I'm—I'm beginning to understand. I've had a light. I've begun to understand. I've begun to see what life has been for you, and how I've wasted—wasted."

"*We've* wasted!"

"No," she said, "it was I."

She sat back on the floor and regarded him. "You don't remember things you said—when you were delirious?"

" No," he answered. " What did I say ? "

" Nothing ? "

" Nothing clearly. What did I say ? "

" It doesn't matter. No, indeed. Only you made me
understand. You'd never have told me. You've always
been a little weak with me there. But it's plain to me
why we didn't keep our happiness, why we were estranged.
If we go back alive, we go back—all that settled for good
and all."

" What ? "

" That discord. My dear, I've been a fool, selfish, ill-
trained and greedy. We've both been floundering about,
but I've been the mischief of it. Yes, I've been the
trouble. Oh, it's had to be so. What are we women—half
savages, half pets, unemployed things of greed and desire
—and suddenly we want all the rights and respect of souls !
I've had your life in my hands from the moment we met
together. If I had known. . . . It isn't that we can make
you or guide you—I'm not pretending to be an inspiration
—but—but we can release you. We needn't press upon
you ; we can save you from the instincts and passions
that try to waste you altogether on us. . . . Yes, I'm
beginning to understand. Oh, my child, my husband, my
man ! You talked of your wasted life ! . . . I've been
thinking—since first we left the Mersey. I've begun to see
what it is to be a woman. For the first time in my life.
We're the responsible sex. And we've forgotten it. We
think we've done a wonder if we've borne men into the
world and smiled a little, but indeed we've got to bear them
all our lives. . . . A woman has to be steadier than a man
and more self-sacrificing than a man, because when she
plunges she does more harm than a man. . . . And what
does she achieve if she does plunge ? Nothing—nothing
worth counting. Dresses and carpets, and hangings
and pretty arrangements, excitements and satisfactions
and competition and more excitements. We can't *do*
things. We don't bring things off ! And you, you
Monster ! you Dream ! you want to stick your hand
out of all that is and make something that isn't, begin to
be ! That's the man——"

" Dear old Madge ! " he said, " there's all sorts of women
and all sorts of men."

" Well, our sort of women, then, and our sort of men."

" I doubt even that."

" I don't. I've found my place. I've been making my

master my servant. We women—we've been looting all the good things in the world, and helping nothing. You've carried me on your back until you are loathing life. I've been making you fetch and carry for me, love me, dress me, keep me and my children, minister to my vanities and greeds. . . . No ; let me go on. I'm so penitent, my dear, so penitent I want to kneel down here and marry you all over again, heal up your broken life and begin again." . . .

She paused.

"One doesn't begin again," she said. "But I want to take a new turn. Dear, you're still only a young man ; we've thirty or forty years before us—forty years perhaps or more. . . . What shall we do with our years ? We've loved, we've got children. What remains ? Here we can plan it out, work it out, day after day. What shall we do with our lives and life ? Tell me, make me your partner ; it's you who know, what are we doing with life ? "

§ 13

What are we doing with life ?

That question overtakes a reluctant and fugitive humanity. The Traffords were but two of a great scattered host of people, who, obeying all the urgencies of need and desire, struggling, loving, begetting, enjoying, do nevertheless find themselves at last unsatisfied. They have lived the round of experience, achieved all that living creatures have sought since the beginning of the world—security and gratification and offspring—and they find themselves still strong, unsatiated, with power in their hands and years before them, empty of purpose. What are they to do ?

The world presents such a spectacle of evasion as it has never seen before. Never was there such a boiling over and waste of vital energy. The Sphinx of our opportunity calls for the uttermost powers of heart and brain to read its riddle—the new, astonishing riddle of excessive power. A few give themselves to those honourable adventures that extend the range of man, they explore untravelled countries, climb remote mountains, conduct researches, risk life and limb in the fantastic experiments of flight, and a monstrous outpouring of labour and material goes on in the strenuous preparation for needless and improbable wars. The rest divert themselves with the dwarfish satisfactions of recognised vice, the meagre routine of

pleasure, or still more timidly with sport and games—
those new unscheduled perversions of the soul.

We are afraid of our new selves. The dawn of human
opportunity appals us. Few of us dare look upon this
strange light of freedom and limitless resources that
breaks upon our world.

"Think," said Trafford, "while we sit here in this
dark hut—think of the surplus life that wastes itself in
the world for sheer lack of direction. Away there in
England—I suppose that is westward"—he pointed—
"there are thousands of men going out to-day to shoot.
Think of the beautifully made guns, the perfected ammunition, the excellent clothes, the army of beaters, the carefully preserved woodland, the admirable science of it—
all for that idiot massacre of half-tame birds! Just
because man once had need to be a hunter! Think of
the others again—golfing. Think of the big, elaborate
houses from which they come, the furnishings, the service.
And the women—dressing! Perpetually dressing. *You*,
Marjorie—you've done nothing but dress since we married.
No, let me abuse you, dear! It's insane, you know!
You dress your minds a little to talk amusingly, you
spread your minds out to backgrounds, to households,
picturesque and delightful gardens, nurseries. Those
nurseries. Think of our tremendously cherished and
educated children! And when they grow up, what have
we got for them? A feast of futility." . . .

§ 14

On the evening of the day when Trafford first tried to
stand upon his leg, they talked far into the night. It had
been a great and eventful day for them, full of laughter
and exultation. He had been at first ridiculously afraid ;
he had clung to her almost childishly, and she had held
him about the body with his weight on her strong right
arm and his right arm in her left hand, concealing her own
dread of a collapse under a mask of taunting courage. The
crutch had proved admirable. "It's my silly knees!"
Trafford kept on saying. "The leg's all right, but I get
put out by my silly knees."

They made the day a feast, a dinner of two whole days'
rations and a special soup instead of supper. "The birds
will come," they explained to each other, "ducks and
geese, long before May. May, you know, is the latest."

Marjorie confessed the habit of sharing his pipe was
growing on her. "What shall we do in Tyburnia!" she
said, and left it to the imagination.

"If ever we get back there," he said.

"I don't much fancy kicking a skirt before my shins
again—and I'll be a black, coarse woman down to my
neck at dinner for years to come!" . . .

Then, as he lay back in his bunk and she crammed the
stove with fresh boughs and twigs of balsam that filled
the little space about them with warmth and with a faint,
sweet smell of burning and with flitting red reflections,
he took up a talk about religion they had begun some
days before.

"You see," he said, "I've always believed in Salvation.
I suppose a man's shy of saying so—even to his wife.
But I've always believed more or less distinctly that there
was something up to which a life worked—always. It's
been rather vague, I'll admit. I don't think I've ever
believed in individual salvation. You see, I feel these are
deep things, and the deeper one gets the less individual
one becomes. That's why one thinks of those things in
darkness and loneliness—and finds them hard to tell.
One has an individual voice, or an individual birthmark,
or an individualised old hat, but the soul—the soul's
different. . . . It isn't me talking to you when it comes
to that. . . . This question of what we are doing with life
isn't a question to begin with for you and me as ourselves,
but for you and me as mankind. Am I spinning it too
fine, Madge?"

"No," she said, intent; "go on."

"You see, when we talk rations here, Marjorie, it's
ourselves, but when we talk religion—it's mankind.
You've either got to be Everyman in religion or leave it
alone. That's my idea. It's no more presumptuous to think
for the race than it is for a beggar to pray—though that
means going right up to God and talking to Him. Salvation's a collective thing and a mythical thing—or there
isn't any. Fancy the Almighty and me sitting up and
keeping Eternity together! God and R. A. G. Trafford,
F.R.S.—that's silly. Fancy a man in number seven boots,
and a tailor-made suit in the nineteen-fourteen fashion,
sitting before God! That's caricature. But God and Man!
That's sense, Marjorie." . . .

He stopped and stared at her.

Marjorie sat red-lit, regarding him. "Queer things,

you say ! " she said. " So much of this I've never thought out. I wonder why I've never done so ? . . . Too busy with many things, I suppose. But go on and tell me more of these secrets you've kept from me ! "

" Well, we've got to talk of these things as mankind— or just leave them alone, and shoot pheasants." . . .

" If I could shoot a pheasant now ! " whispered Marjorie, involuntarily.

" And where do we stand ? What do we need—I mean the whole race of us—kings and beggars together ? You know, Marjorie, it's this—it's Understanding. That's what mankind has got to, the realisation that it doesn't understand, that it can't express, that it's purblind. We haven't got eyes for those greater things, but we've got the promise—the intimation of eyes. We've come out of an unsuspecting darkness, brute animal darkness, not into sight, that's been the mistake, but into a feeling of illumination, into a feeling of light shining through our opacity. . . .

" I feel that man has now before all things to know. That's his supreme duty, to feel, realise, see, understand, express himself to the utmost limits of his power."

He sat up, speaking very earnestly to her, and in that flickering light she realised for the first time how thin he had become, how bright and hollow his eyes ; his hair was long over his eyes, and a rough beard flowed down to his chest. " All the religions," he said, " all the philosophies, have pretended to achieve too much. We've no language yet for religious truth or metaphysical truth ; we've no basis yet broad enough and strong enough on which to build. Religion and philosophy have been impudent and quackish—quackish ! They've been like the doctors, who have always pretended they could cure since the beginning of things, cure everything, and to this day even they haven't got more than the beginning of knowledge on which to base a cure. They've lacked humility, they've lacked the honour to say they didn't know ; the priests took things of wood and stone, the philosophers took little odd arrangements of poor battered words, metaphors, analogies, abstractions, and said : ' That's it ! ' Think of their silly old Absolute—*ab-solutus*, an untied parcel. I heard Haldane at the Aristotelian once, go on for an hour —no ! it was longer than an hour—as glib and slick as a well-oiled sausage-machine, about the different sorts of Absolute, and not a soul of us laughed out at him ! The vanity of such profundities! They've no faith, faith in patience, faith to wait for the coming of God. And since we don't know God, since we don't know His will with us, isn't it plain that all our lives should be a search for Him and it? Can anything else matter—after we are free from necessity? That is the work now that is before all mankind, to attempt understanding—by the perpetual fining of thought and the means of expression, by the perpetual extension and refinement of science, by the research that every artist makes for beauty and significance in his art, by the perpetual testing and destruction and rebirth under criticism of all these things, and by a perpetual extension of this intensifying wisdom to more minds and more minds and more, till all men share in it, and share in the making of it. . . . There you have my creed, Marjorie; there you have the very marrow of me." . . .

He became silent.

" Will you go back to your work? " she said abruptly. " Go back to your laboratory? "

He stared at her for a moment without speaking.

" Never," he said at last.

" But," she said, and the word dropped from her like a stone that falls down a well. . . .

" My dear," he said at last, " I've thought of that. But since I left that dear, dusty little laboratory, and all those exquisite subtle things—I've lived. I've left that man seven long years behind me. Some other man must go on—I think some younger man—with the riddles I found to work on then. I've grown—into something different. It isn't how atoms swing with one another, or why they build themselves up so and not so, that matters any more to me. I've got you and all the world in which we live, and a new set of riddles filling my mind, how thought swings about thought, how one man attracts his fellows, how the waves of motive and conviction sweep through a crowd and all the little drifting crystallisations of spirit with spirit and all the repulsions and eddies and difficulties that one can catch in that turbulent confusion. I want to do a new sort of work now altogether. . . . Life has swamped me once, but I don't think it will get me under again ;—I want to study men."

He paused, and she waited with a face aglow.

" I want to go back to watch and think—and I suppose write. I believe I shall write criticism. But everything

that matters is criticism ! . . . I want to get into contact
with the men who are thinking. I don't mean to meet
them necessarily, but to get into the souls of their books.
Every writer who has anything to say, every artist who
matters, is the stronger for every man or woman who
responds to him. That's the great work—the Reality.
I want to become a part of this stuttering attempt to
express, I want at least to resonate, even if I do not help.
. . . And you with me, Marjorie—you with me ! Everything I write I want you to see and think about. I want
you to read as I read. . . . Now after so long, now that,
now that we've begun to talk, you know, to talk again——"

Something stopped his voice. Something choked them
both into silence. He held out a lean hand, and she
shuffled on her knees to take it. . . .

"Don't please make me," she stumbled through her
thoughts, "one of those little parasitic, parroting wives—
don't pretend too much about me—because you want me
with you—— Don't forget a woman isn't a man."

"Old Madge," he said, "you and I have got to march
together. Didn't I love you from the first, from that
time when I was a boy examiner and you were a candidate
girl—because your mind was clear ? "

"And we will go back," she whispered, "with a work——"

"With a purpose," he said.

She disengaged herself from his arm, and sat close to
him upon the floor. "I think I can see what you will
do," she said. She mused. "For the first time I begin
to see things as they may be for us. I begin to see a life
ahead. For the very first time."

Queer ideas came drifting into her head. Suddenly
she cried out sharply in that high note he loved. "Good
heavens ! " she said. "The absurdity ! The infinite
absurdity ! "

"But what ? "

"I might have married Will Magnet—— That's all."

She sprang to her feet. There came a sound of wind
outside, a shifting of snow on the roof, and the door
creaked. "Half-past eleven ! " she exclaimed, looking at
the watch that hung in the light of the stove door. "I
won't want to sleep yet; do you ? I'm going to brew
some tea—make a convivial drink. And then we will go
on talking. It's so good talking to you. So good ! . . .
I've an idea ! Don't you think on this special day, it might
run to a biscuit ? " Her face was keenly anxious. He

nodded. " One biscuit each," she said, trying to rob her
voice of any note of criminality. " Just one, you know,
won't matter."

She hovered for some moments close to the stove before
she went into the arctic corner that contained the tin of
tea. " If we can really live like that ! " she said. " When
we are home again."

" Why not ? " he answered.

She made no answer, but went across for the tea. . . .

He turned his head at the sound of the biscuit tin and
watched her put out the precious discs.

" I shall have another pipe," he proclaimed, with an
agreeable note of excess. " Thank heaven for unstinted
tobacco." . . .

And now Marjorie's mind was teeming with thoughts
of this new conception of a life lived for understanding.
As she went about the preparation of the tea, her vividly
concrete imagination was active with the realisation of
the life they would lead on their return. She could not
see it otherwise than framed in a tall, fine room, a study,
a study in sombre tones, with high, narrow, tall, dignified
bookshelves and rich deep green curtains veiling its
windows. There should be a fireplace of white marble,
very plain and well proportioned, with furnishings of old
brass, and a big desk towards the window beautifully lit
by electric light, with abundant space for papers to lie.
And she wanted some touch of the wilderness about it ;
a skin perhaps. . . .

The tea was still infusing when she had determined
upon an enormous paper-weight of that iridescent Labradorite that had been so astonishing a feature of the Green
River Valley. She would have it polished on one side
only—the other should be rough to show the felspar in its
natural state. . . .

It wasn't that she didn't feel and understand quite
fully the intention and significance of all he had said, but
that in these symbols of texture and equipment her mind
quite naturally clothed itself. And while this room was
coming into anticipatory being in her mind, she was making
the tea very deftly and listening to Trafford's every word.

§ 15

That talk marked an epoch to Marjorie. From that
day forth her imagination began to shape a new, ordered

and purposeful life for Trafford and herself in London, a life not altogether divorced from their former life, but with a faith sustaining it and aims controlling it. She had always known of the breadth and power of his mind, but now as he talked of what he might do, what interests might converge and give results through him, it seemed she really knew him for the first time. In his former researches, so technical and withdrawn, she had seen little of his mind in action : now he was dealing in his own fashion with things she could clearly understand. There were times when his talk affected her like that joy of light one has in emerging into sunshine from a long and tedious cave. He swept things together, flashed unsuspected correlations upon her intelligence, smashed and scattered absurd yet venerated conventions of thought, made undreamt-of courses of action visible in a flare of luminous necessity. And she could follow him and help him. Just as she had hampered him and crippled him, so now she could release him—she fondled that word. She found a preposterous image in her mind that she hid like a disgraceful secret, that she tried to forget, and yet its stupendous, its dreamlike absurdity had something in it that shaped her delight as nothing else could do ; she was, she told herself—hawking with an archangel ! . . .

These were her moods of exaltation. And she was sure she had never loved her man before, that this was indeed her beginning. It was as if she had just found him. . . .

Perhaps, she thought, true lovers keep on finding each other all through their lives.

And he, too, had discovered her. All the host of Marjories he had known, the shining, delightful, seductive, wilful, perplexing aspects that had so filled his life, gave place altogether for a time to this steady-eyed woman, lean and warm-wrapped with a valiant heart and the frost-roughened skin. What a fine, strong, ruddy thing she was ! How glad he was for this wild adventure in the wilderness, if only because it had made him lie among the rocks and think of her and wait for her and despair of her life and God, and at last see her coming back to him, flushed with effort and calling his name to him out of that whirlwind of snow. . . . And there was at least one old memory mixed up with all these new and overmastering impressions, the memory of her clear unhesitating voice as it had stabbed into his life again long years ago, minute and bright in the telephone : " *It's me, you know.   It's Marjorie !* "

Perhaps after all she had not wasted a moment of his life, perhaps every issue between them had been necessary, and it was good altogether to be turned from the study of crystals to the study of men and women. . . .

And now both their minds were Londonward, where all the tides and driftage and currents of human thought still meet and swirl together.   They were full of what they would do when they got back.   Marjorie sketched that study to him—in general terms and without the paper-weight—and began to shape the world she would have about it.   She meant to be his squaw and body-servant first of all, and then—a mother.   Children, she said, are none the worse for being kept a little out of focus. And he was rapidly planning out his approach to the new questions to which he was now to devote his life.   " One wants something to hold the work together," he said, and projected a book.   " One cannot struggle at large for plain statement and copious and free and courageous statement, one needs a positive attack."

He designed a book, which he might write if only for the definition it would give him and with no ultimate publication, which was to be called : *The Limits of Language as a Means of Expression.* . . . It was to be a pragmatist essay, a sustained attempt to undermine the confidence of all that scholasticism and logic-chopping which still lingers like the *sequelæ* of a disease in our University philosophy.   " Those duffers sit in their studies and make a sort of tea of dry old words—and think they're distilling the spirit of wisdom," he said.

He proliferated titles for a time, and settled at last on *From Realism to Reality.*   He wanted to get at that at once ; it fretted him to have to hang in the air, day by day, for want of books to quote and opponents to lance and confute.   And he wanted to see pictures, too, and plays, read novels he had heard of and never read, in order to verify or correct the ideas that were seething in his mind about the qualities of artistic expression.   His thought had come out to a conviction that the line to wider human understandings lies through a huge criticism and cleaning up of the existing methods of formulation, as a preliminary to the wider and freer discussion of those religious and social issues our generation still shrinks from. " It's grotesque," he said, " and utterly true that the sanity and happiness of all the world lies in its habits of generalisation." There was not even paper for him to make notes or provisional drafts of the new work. He hobbled about the camp fretting at these deprivations.

" Marjorie," he said, " we've done our job. Why should we wait here on this frosty shelf outside the world ? My leg's getting sounder—if it wasn't for that feeling of ice in it. Why shouldn't we make another sledge from the other bunk and start down——"

" To Hammond's ? "

" Why not ? "

" But the way ? "

" The valley would guide us. We could do four hours a day before we had to camp. I'm not sure we couldn't try the river. We could drag and carry all our food." . . .

She looked down the wide stretches of the valley. There was the hill they had christened Marjorie Ridge. At least it was familiar. Every night before nightfall if they started there would be a fresh camping-place to seek among the snow-drifts, a great heap of wood to cut to last the night. Suppose his leg gave out—when they were already some days away, so that he could no longer go on or she drag him back to the stores ? Plainly there would be nothing for it then but to lie down and die together. . . .

And a sort of weariness had come to her as a consequence of two months of half-starved days, not perhaps a failure so much as a reluctance of spirit.

" Of course," she said, with a new aspect drifting before her mind, " then—we *could* eat. We *could* feed up before we started. We could feast almost ! "

§ 16

" While you were asleep the other night," Trafford began one day as they sat spinning out their midday meal, " I was thinking how badly I had expressed myself when I talked to you the other day, and what a queer, thin affair I made of the plans I wanted to carry out. As a matter of fact, they're neither queer nor thin, but they are unreal in comparison with the common things of every-day life, hunger, anger, all the immediate desires. They must be. They only begin when those others are at peace. It's hard to set out these things, they're complicated and subtle, and one cannot simplify without falsehood. I don't want to simplify. The world has gone out of its way time after time through simplifications and short cuts. Save us from epigrams ! And when one thinks over what one has said, at a little distance—one wants to go back to it, and say it all again. I seem to be not so much thinking things out as reviving and developing things I've had growing in my mind ever since we met. It's as though an immense reservoir of thought had filled up in my mind at last and was beginning to trickle over and break down the embankment between us. This conflict that has been going on between our life together and my—my intellectual life ; it's only just growing clear in my own mind. Yet it's just as if one turned up a light on something that had always been there. . . .

" It's a most extraordinary thing to think out, Marjorie, that antagonism. Our love has kept us so close together, and always our purposes have been—like that." He spread divergent hands. " I've speculated again and again whether there isn't something incurably antagonistic between women (that's *you* generalised, Marjorie) and men (that's me) directly we pass beyond the conditions of the individualistic struggle. I believe every couple of lovers who've ever married have felt that strain. Yet it's not a difference in kind between us, but degree. The big conflict between us has a parallel in a little internal conflict that goes on ; there's something of man in every woman and a touch of the feminine in every man. But you're nearer as woman to the immediate personal life of sense and reality than I am as man. It's been so ever since the men went hunting and fighting and the women kept hut, tended the children, and gathered roots in the little cultivation close at hand. It's been so perhaps since the female carried and suckled her child and distinguished one male from another. It may be it will always be so. Men were released from that close, continuous touch with physical necessities long before women were. It's only now that women begin to be released. For ages now men have been wandering from field and home and city, over the hills and far away, in search of adventures and fresh ideas and the wells of mystery beyond the edge of the world, but it's only now that the woman comes with them too. Our difference isn't a difference in kind, old Marjorie ; it's the difference between the old adventurer and the new feet upon the trail."

" We've got to come," said Marjorie.

" Oh ! you've got to come. No good to be pioneers

if the race does not follow. The women are the backbone
of the race ; the men are just the individuals. Into this
Labrador and into all the wild and desolate places of
thought and desire, if men come you women have to come
too—and bring the race with you. Some day."

" A long day, mate of my heart."

" Who knows how long or how far ? Aren't you at any
rate here, dear woman of mine ? . . . (*Surely you are here.*)"

He went off at a tangent. " There's all those words
that seem to mean something and then don't seem to mean
anything, that keep shifting to and fro from the deepest
significance to the shallowest of claptrap, Socialism,
Christianity. . . . You know—they aren't anything really,
as yet ; they are something trying to be. . . . Haven't I
said that before, Marjorie ? "

She looked round at him. " You said something like
that when you were delirious," she answered, after a little
pause. " It's one of the ideas that you're struggling with.
You go on, old man, and *talk*. We've months—for repetitions."

" Well, I mean that all these things are seeking after a
sort of co-operation that's greater than our power even
of imaginative realisation ; that's what I mean. The
kingdom of Heaven, the communion of saints, the fellowship of men ; these are things like high peaks far out of
the common life of every day, shining things that madden
certain sorts of men to climb. Certain sorts of us ! I'm
a religious man, I'm a socialistic man. These calls are
more to me than my daily bread. I've got something in
me more generalising than most men. I'm more so than
many other men and most other women. I'm more
socialistic than you. . . .

" You know, Marjorie, I've always felt you're a finer
individual than me, I've never had a doubt of it. You're
more beautiful by far than I, woman for my man. You've
a keener appetite for things, a firmer grip on the substance
of life. I love to see you do things, love to see you move,
love to watch your hands ; you've cleverer hands than
mine by far. . . . And yet—I'm a deeper and bigger
thing than you. I reach up to something you don't reach
up to. . . . You're in life—and I'm a little out of it. I'm
like one of those fish that began to be amphibian, I go
out into something where you don't follow—where you
hardly begin to follow. . . .

" That's the real perplexity between thousands of men
and women. . . .

"It seems to me that the primitive socialism of
Christianity and all the stuff of modern socialism that
matters is really aiming—almost unconsciously, I admit
at times—at one simple end, at the release of the human
spirit from the individualistic struggle——

"You used 'release' the other day, Marjorie? Of
course, I remember. It's queer how I go on talking after
you have understood."

"It was just a flash," said Marjorie. "We have intimations. Neither of us really understands. We're like
people climbing a mountain in a mist, that thins out for
a moment and shows valleys and cities, and then closes
in again, before we can recognise them or make out where
we are."

Trafford thought. "When I talk to you, I've always
felt I mustn't be too vague. And the very essence of
all this is a vague thing, something we shall never come
nearer to in all our lives than to see it as a shadow and a
glittering that escapes again into a mist. . . . And yet it's
everything that matters, everything, the only thing that
matters truly and for ever through the whole range of life.
And we have to serve it with the keenest thought, the
utmost patience, inordinate veracity. . . .

"The practical trouble between your sort and my sort,
Marjorie, is the trouble between faith and realisation.
You demand the outcome. Oh! and I hate to turn aside
and realise. I've had to do it for seven years. Damnable
years! Men of my sort want to understand. We want
to understand, and you ask us to make. We want to understand atoms, ions, molecules, refractions. You ask us to
make rubber and diamonds. I suppose it's right that
incidentally we should make rubber and diamonds.
Finally, I warn you, we will make rubber unnecessary and
diamonds valueless. And again we want to understand
how people react upon one another to produce social consequences, and you ask us to put it at once into a draft
bill for the reform of something or other. I suppose life
lies between us somewhere, we're the two poles of truth
seeking and truth getting; with me alone it would be
nothing but a luminous dream, with you nothing but a
scramble in which sooner or later all the lamps would be
upset. . . . But it's ever too much of a scramble yet,
and ever too little of a dream. All our world over there
is full of the confusion and wreckage of premature realisations. There's no real faith in thought and knowledge

yet. Old necessity has driven men so hard that they still rush with a wild urgency—though she goads no more. Greed and haste, and if, indeed, we seem to have a moment's breathing space, then the Gawdsaker tramples us under."

" My dear ! " cried Marjorie, with a sharp note of amusement. " What *is* a Gawdsaker ? "

" Oh," said Trafford, " haven't you heard that before ? He's the person who gets excited by any deliberate discussion and gets up wringing his hands and screaming, ' For Gawd's sake, let's *do* something *now* ! ' I think they used it first for Pethick Lawrence, that man who did so much to run the old militant suffragettes and burke the proper discussion of woman's future. You know. You used to have 'em in Chelsea—with their hats. Oh! ' Gawdsaking ' is the curse of all progress, the hectic consumption that kills a thousand good beginnings. You see it in small things and in great. You see it in my life ; Gawdsaking turned my life-work to cash and promotions, Gawdsaking—— Look at the way the aviators took to flying for prizes and gate-money, the way pure research is swamped by endowments for technical applications ! Then that poor ghost-giant of an idea the socialists have ; —it's been treated like one of those unborn lambs they kill for the fine skin of it, made into results before ever it was alive. Was there anything more pitiful ? The first great dream and then the last phase ! when your Aunt Plessington and the district visitors took and used it as a synonym for Payment in Kind. . . . It's natural, I suppose, for people to be eager for results, personal and immediate results—the last lesson of life is patience. Naturally they want reality, naturally ! They want the individual life, something to handle and feel and use and live by, something of their very own before they die, and they want it now. But the thing that matters for the race, Marjorie, is a very different thing : it is to get the emerging thought process clear and to keep it clear—and to let those other hungers go. We've got to go back to England on the side of that delay, that arrest of interruption, that detached, observant, synthesising process of the mind, that solvent of difficulties and obsolescent institutions, which is the reality of collective human life. We've got to go back on the side of pure science—literature untrammelled by the preconceptions of the social schemers—art free from the urgency of immediate utility—and a new, a regal, a god-like sincerity in philosophy. And, above all, we've got to stop this

Jackdaw buying of yours, my dear, which is the essence of all that is wrong with the world, this snatching at everything, which loses everything worth having in life, this greedy, confused realisation of our accumulated resources ! You're going to be a non-shopping woman now. You've to come out of Bond Street, you and your kind, like Israel leaving the Egyptian flesh-pots. You're going to be my wife and my mate. . . . Less of this service of things. Investments in comfort, in security, in experience, yes ; but not just spending any more." . . .

He broke off abruptly with : " I want to go back and begin."

" Yes," said Marjorie, " we will go back," and saw minutely and distantly, and yet as clearly and brightly as if she looked into a concave mirror, that tall and dignified study, a very high room indeed, with a man writing before a fine, long-curtained window, and a great lump of rich-glowing Labradorite upon his desk before him holding together an accumulation of written sheets. . . .

She knew exactly the shop in Oxford Street where the stuff for the curtains might be best obtained.

§ 17

One night Marjorie had been sitting musing before the stove for a long time, and suddenly she said : " I wonder if we shall fail ? I wonder if we shall get into a mess again when we are back in London ? . . . As big a mess and as utter a discontent as sent us here." . . .

Trafford was scraping out his pipe, and did not answer for some moments. Then he remarked : " What nonsense ! "

" But we shall," she said. " Everybody fails. To some extent, we are bound to fail. Because indeed nothing is clear ; nothing is a clear issue. . . . You know—I'm just the old Marjorie really in spite of all these resolutions—the spendthrift, the restless, the eager. I'm a born snatcher and shopper. We're just the same people really."

" No," he said, after thought. " You're all Labrador older."

" I always *have* failed," she considered, " when it came to any special temptations, Rag. I can't *stand* not having a thing ! "

He made no answer.

" And you're still the same old Rag, you know," she went on. " Who weakens into kindness if I cry. Who likes me well-dressed. Who couldn't endure to see me poor."

"Not a bit of it. No! I'm a very different Rag with a very different Marjorie. Yes, indeed! Things—are graver. Why!—I'm lame for life—and I've a scar. The very *look* of things is changed. . . ." He stared at her face and said : "You've hidden the looking glass and you think I haven't noted it——"

"It keeps on healing," she interrupted. "And if it comes to that—where's my complexion ? " She laughed. "These are just the superficial aspects of the case."

"Nothing ever heals completely," he said, answering her first sentence, "and nothing ever goes back to the exact place it held before. We *are* different, you sun-bitten, frost-bitten wife of mine." . . .

"Character is character," said Marjorie, coming back to her point. "Don't exaggerate conversion, dear. It's not a bit of good pretending we shan't fall away, both of us. Each in our own manner. We shall. We shall, old man. London is still a tempting and confusing place, and you can't alter people fundamentally, not even by half-freezing and half-starving them. You only alter people fundamentally by killing them and replacing them. I shall be extravagant again and forget again, try as I may, and you will work again and fall away again and forgive me again. You know—— It's just as though we were each of us not one person but a lot of persons, who sometimes meet and shout all together, and then disperse and forget and plot against each other." . . .

"Oh, things will happen again," said Trafford, in her pause. "But they will happen again with a difference—after this. With a difference. That's the good of it all. . . . We've found something here—that makes everything different. . . . We've found each other, too, dear wife."

She thought intently.

"I am afraid," she whispered.

"But what is there to be afraid of ? "

"*Myself.*"

She spoke after a little pause that seemed to hesitate. "At times I wish—oh, passionately !—that I could pray."

"Why don't you ? "

"I don't believe enough—in that. I wish I did."

Trafford thought. "People are always so exacting about prayer," he said.

" Exacting ? "

" You want to pray—and you can't make terms for a thing you want. I used to think I could. I wanted God to come and demonstrate a bit. . . . It's no good, Madge. . . . If God chooses to be silent—you must pray to the silence. If He chooses to live in darkness, you must pray to the night." . . .

" Yes," said Marjorie, " I suppose one must."

She thought. " I suppose in the end one does," she said.

§ 18

Mixed up with this entirely characteristic theology of theirs and their elaborate planning-out of a new life in London were other strands of thought. Queer memories of London and old times together would flash with a peculiar brightness across their contemplation of the infinities and the needs of mankind. Out of nowhere, quite disconnectedly, would come the human, finite : " Do you remember——? "

Two things particularly pressed into their minds. One was the thought of their children, and I do not care to tell how often in the day now they calculated the time in England, and tried to guess to a half mile or so where those young people might be and what they might be doing. " The shops are bright for Christmas now," said Marjorie. " This year Dick was to have had his first fireworks. I wonder if he did ? I wonder if he burnt his dear little funny stumps of fingers ? I hope not."

" Oh, just a little," said Trafford. " I remember how a squib made my glove smoulder and singed me, and how my mother kissed me for taking it like a man. It was the best part of the adventure."

" Dick shall burn his fingers when his mother's home to kiss him. But spare his fingers now, Dadda." . . .

The other topic was food.

It was only after they had been doing it for a week or so that they remarked how steadily they gravitated to reminiscences, suggestions, descriptions, and long discussions of eatables—sound, solid eatables. They told over the particulars of dinners they had imagined altogether forgotten ; neither hosts nor conversations seemed to matter now in the slightest degree, but every item in the menu had its place. They nearly quarrelled one day about hors-d'œuvre. Trafford wanted to dwell on them when Marjorie was eager for the soup.

" It's niggling with food," said Marjorie.

" Oh, but there's no reason," said Trafford, " why you shouldn't take a Lot of hors-d'œuvre. Three or four sardines, and potato salad and a big piece of smoked salmon, and some of that Norwegian herring, and so on, and keep the olives by you to pick at. It's a beginning."

" It's—it's immoral," said Marjorie, " that's what I feel. If one needs a whet to eat, one shouldn't eat. The proper beginning of a dinner is soup—good, hot, *rich* soup. Thick soup—with things in it, vegetables and meat and things. Bits of oxtail."

" Not peas."

" No, not peas. Pea-soup is tiresome. I never knew anything one tired of so soon. I wish we hadn't relied on it so much."

" Thick soup's all very well," said Trafford, " but how about that clear stuff they give you in the little pavement restaurants in Paris ? You know—*Croûte-au-pot*, with lovely great crusts and big leeks and lettuce leaves and so on ! Tremendous aroma of onions, and beautiful little beads of fat ! And being a clear soup, you see what there is. That's—interesting. Twenty-five centimes, Marjorie. Lord ! I'd give a guinea a plate for it. I'd give five pounds for one of those jolly white-metal tureens full— you know, *full*, with little drops all over the outside of it, and the ladle sticking out under the lid."

" Have you ever tasted turtle soup ? "

" Rather. They give it you in the City. The fat's— ripping. But they're rather precious with it, you know. For my own part, I don't think soup should be *doled* out. I always liked the soup we used to get at the Harts's ; but then they never give you enough, you know—not nearly enough."

" About a tablespoonful," said Marjorie. " It's mocking an appetite."

" Still, there's things to follow," said Trafford. . . .

They discussed the proper order of a dinner very carefully. They decided that sorbets and ices were not only unwholesome but nasty. " In London," said Trafford, " one's taste gets—vitiated." . . .

They weighed the merits of French cookery, modern international cookery, and produced alternatives. Trafford became very eloquent about old English food. " Dinners,"

said Trafford, " should be feasting, not the mere satisfaction of a necessity. There should be—*amplitude*. I
remember a recipe for a pie ; I think it was in one of
those books that man Lucas used to compile. If I
remember rightly, it began with : ' Take a swine and hew
it into gobbets.' Gobbets ! That's something like a beginning. It was a big pie with tiers and tiers of things,
and it kept it up all the way in that key. . . . And then
what could be better than prime British-fed roast beef,
reddish, just a shape on the side of underdone, and not too
finely cut ? Mutton can't touch it."
" Beef is the best," she said.
" Then our English cold meat again. What can equal
it ? Such stuff as they give in a good country inn, a huge
joint of beef—you eat from it yourself, you know, as much
as you like—with mustard, pickles, celery, a tankard of
stout, let us say. Pressed beef, such as they'll give you
at the Reform, too, that's good eating for a man. With
chutney, and then old cheese to follow. And boiled beef,
with little carrots and turnips and a dumpling or so. Eh ? "
" Of course," said Marjorie, " one must do justice to a
well-chosen turkey, a *fat* turkey."
" Or a good goose, for the matter of that—with honest,
well-thought-out stuffing. I like the little sausages round
the dish of a turkey, too ; like cherubs they are, round the
feet of a Madonna. . . . There's much to be said for
sausage, Marjorie. It concentrates."
Sausage led to Germany. " I'm not one of those
patriots," he was saying presently, " who run down other
countries by way of glorifying their own. While I was in
Germany I tasted many good things. There's their
Leberwurst ; it's never bad, and, at its best, it's splendid
It's only a fool would reproach Germany with sausage.
Devonshire black-pudding, of course, is the master of any
Blutwurst, but there's all those others on the German side,
Frankfurter, big reddish sausage stuff again with great
crystalline lumps of white fat. And how well they cook
their rich hashes, and the thick gravies they make !
Curious, how much better the cooking of Teutonic peoples
is than the cooking of the South Europeans ! It's as if
one needed a colder climate to brace a cook to his business.
The Frenchman and the Italian trifle and stimulate. It's
as if they'd never met a hungry man. No German would
have thought of soufflé. Ugh ! it's vicious eating. There
much that's fine, though, in Austria and Hungary. I

wish I had travelled in Hungary. Do you remember how
once or twice we've lunched at that Viennese place in
Regent Street, and how they've given us stuffed Paprika,
eh ? "

"That was a good place. I remember there was stewed
beef once with a lot of barley—such *good* barley ! "

"Every country has its glories. One talks of the cookery
of northern countries and then suddenly one thinks of
curry, with lots of rice."

"And lots of chicken ! "

"And lots of hot curry powder, *very* hot. And look
at America ! Here's a people who haven't any of them
been out of Europe for centuries, and yet they have as
different a table as you could well imagine. There's a
kind of fish, planked shad, that they cook on resinous
wood—roast it, I suppose. It's substantial, like nothing
else in the world. And how good, too, with turkey are
sweet potatoes ! Then they have such a multitude of
cereal things ; stuff like their buckwheat cakes, all swimming in golden syrup. And Indian corn, again ! "

"Of course, corn is being Anglicised. I've often given
you corn—latterly, before we came away."

"That sort of separated grain—out of tins. Like
chicken's food ! It's not the real thing. You should eat
corn on the cob—American fashion ! It's fine. I had it
when I was in the States. You know, you take it up in
your hands by both ends—you've seen the cobs ?—and
gnaw."

The craving air of Labrador at a temperature of − 20°
Fahrenheit, and methodically stinted rations, make great
changes in the outward qualities of the mind. "*I'd* like
to do that," said Marjorie.

Her face flushed a little at a guilty thought, her eyes
sparkled. She leant forward and spoke in a confidential
undertone.

"*I'd—I'd like to eat a mutton chop like that*," said
Marjorie.

§ 19

One morning Marjorie broached something she had had
on her mind for several days.

"Old man," she said, "I can't stand it any longer.
I'm going to thaw my scissors and cut your hair. . . .
And then you'll have to trim that beard of yours."

"You'll have to dig out that looking-glass."

" I know," said Marjorie. She looked at him. " You'll
never be a pretty man again," she said. " But there's a
sort of wild splendour. . . . And I love every inch and
scrap of you." . . .

Their eyes met. " We're a thousand deeps now below
the look of things," said Trafford. " We'd love each other
minced."

She broke into that smiling laugh of hers. " Oh ! it
won't come to *that*," she said. " Trust my housekeeping ! "

CHAPTER THE FIFTH

THE TRAIL TO THE SEA

§ 1

ONE astonishing afternoon in January a man came out
of the wilderness to Lonely Hut. He was a French-
Indian half-breed, a trapper up and down the Green River
and across the Height of Land to Seal Lake. He arrived
in a sort of shy silence, and squatted amiably on a log to
thaw. " Much snow," he said, " and little fur."

After he had sat at their fire for an hour and eaten and
drunk, his purpose in coming thawed out. He explained
he had just come on to them to see how they were. He
was, he said, a planter furring ; he had a line of traps,
about a hundred and twenty miles in length. The nearest
trap in his path before he turned northward over the divide
was a good forty miles down the river. He had come on
from there. Just to have a look. His name, he said, was
Louis Napoleon Partington. He had carried a big
pack, a rifle, and a dead marten—they lay beside him—
and out of his shapeless mass of caribou skins and woollen
clothing and wrappings, peeped a genial, oily, brown face,
very dirty, with a strand of blue-black hair across one eye,
irregular teeth in its friendly smile, and little, squeezed-up
eyes.

Conversation developed. There had been doubts of his
linguistic range at first, but he had an understanding
expression, and his English seemed guttural rather than
really bad.

He was told the tremendous story of Trafford's leg ;
was shown it, and felt it ; he interpolated thick and
whistling noises to show how completely he followed their
explanations, and then suddenly he began a speech that

made all his earlier taciturnity seem but the dam of a great
reservoir of mixed and partly incomprehensible English.
He complimented Marjorie so effusively and relentlessly
and shamelessly as to produce a pause when he had done.
" Yes," he said, and nodded to button up the whole. He
sucked his pipe, well satisfied with his eloquence. Trafford
spoke in this silence. " We are coming down," he said.

(" I thought, perhaps——" whispered Louis Napoleon.)

" Yes," said Trafford, " we are coming down with you.
Why not ? We can get a sledge over the snow now ?
It's hard ? I mean a flat sledge—like *this*. See ? Like
this." He got up and dragged Marjorie's old arrangement
into view. " We shall bring all the stuff we can down
with us, grub, blankets—not the tent, it's too bulky ;
we'll leave a lot of the heavy gear."

" You'd have to leave the tent," said Louis Napoleon.

" I *said* leave the tent."

" And you'd have to leave . . . some of those tins."

" Nearly all of them."

" And the ammunition, there ;—except just a little."

" Just enough for the journey down."

" Perhaps a gun ? "

" No, not a gun. Though, after all—well, we'd return
one of the guns. Give it you to bring back here."

" Bring back here ? "

" If you liked."

For some moments Louis Napoleon was intently silent.
When he spoke his voice was guttural with emotion.
" After," he said thoughtfully and paused, and then
resolved to have it over forthwith, " all you leave will be
mine ? Eh ? "

Trafford said that was the idea.

Louis Napoleon's eye brightened, but his face preserved
its Indian calm.

" I will take you right to Hammond's," he said, " where
they have dogs. And then I can come back here. . . ."

§ 2

They had talked out nearly every particular of their
return before they slept that night ; they yarned away
three hours over the first generous meal that any one of
them had eaten for many weeks. Louis Napoleon stayed
in the hut as a matter of course, and reposed with snores
and choking upon Marjorie's sledge and within a yard of

her. It struck her as she lay awake and listened that the
housemaids in Sussex Square would have thought things
a little congested for a lady's bedroom, and then she
reflected that after all it wasn't much worse than a crowded
carriage in an all-night train from Switzerland. She tried
to count how many people there had been in that compartment, and failed. How stuffy that had been—the smell
of cheese and all! And with that, after a dream that she
was whaling and had harpooned a particularly short-
winded whale, she fell very peacefully into oblivion.

Next day was spent in the careful preparation of the
two sledges. They intended to take a full provision for
six weeks, although they reckoned that with good weather
they ought to be down at Hammond's in four.

The day after was Sunday, and Louis Napoleon would
not look at the sledges or packing. Instead he held a
kind of religious service which consisted partly in making
Trafford read aloud out of a very oily old New Testa-
ment he produced, a selected passage from the Book of
Corinthians, and partly in moaning rather than singing
several hymns. He was rather disappointed that they
did not join in with him. In the afternoon he heated
some water, went into the tent with it and it would appear
partially washed his face. In the evening, after they had
supped, he discussed religion, being curious by this time
about their beliefs and procedure.

He spread his mental and spiritual equipment before
them very artlessly. Their isolation and their immense
concentration on each other had made them sensitive to
personal quality, and they listened to the broken English
and the queer tangential starts into new topics of this
dirty mongrel creature with the keenest appreciation of its
quality. It was inconsistent, miscellaneous, simple, honest,
and human. It was as touching as the medley in the
pocket of a dead schoolboy. He was superstitious and
sceptical and sensual and spiritual, and very, very earnest.
The things he believed, even if they were just beliefs
about the weather or drying venison or filling pipes, he
believed with emotion. He flushed as he told them. For
all his intellectual muddle, they felt he knew how to live
honestly and die if need be very finely.

He was more than a little distressed at their apparent
ignorance of the truths of revealed religion as it is taught
in the Moravian schools upon the coast, and indeed it was
manifest that he had had far more careful and infinitely

more sincere religious teaching than either Trafford or
Marjorie. For a time the missionary spirit inspired him,
and then he quite forgot his solicitude for their conversion
in a number of increasingly tall anecdotes about hunters
and fishermen, illustrating at first the extreme dangers
of any departure from a rigid Sabbatarianism, but presently becoming just stories illustrating the uncertainty
of life. Thence he branched off to the general topic of
life upon the coast and the relative advantages of "planter"
and fisherman.

And then with a kindling eye he spoke of women, and
how that some day he would marry. His voice softened,
and he addressed himself more particularly to Marjorie.
He didn't so much introduce the topic of the lady as allow
the destined young woman suddenly to pervade his discourse. She was, it seemed, a servant, an Esquimaux girl
at the Moravian Mission station at Manivikovik. He had
been plighted to her for nine years. He described a
gramophone he had purchased down at Port Dupré and
brought back to her three hundred miles up the coast—it
seemed to Marjorie an odd gift for an Esquimaux maiden
—and he gave his views upon its mechanism. He said
God was with the man who invented the gramophone
" truly." They would have found one a very great relief
to the tediums of their sojourn at Lonely Hut. The
gramophone he had given his betrothed possessed records
of the Rev. Capel Gumm's preaching and of Madame
Melba's singing, a revival hymn called " Sowing the Seed,"
and a comic song—they could not make out his pronun-
ciation of the title—that made you die of laughter. " It
goes gobble, gobble, gobble," he said, with a solemn
appreciative reflection of those distant joys.

" It's good to be jolly at times," he said, with his bright
eyes scanning Marjorie's face a little doubtfully, as if such
ideas were better left for week-day expression.

§ 3

Their return was a very different journey from the
toilsome ascent of the summer. An immense abundance
of snow masked the world, snow that made them regret
acutely they had not equipped themselves with ski. With
ski and a good circulation, a man may go about Labrador
in winter six times more easily than by the canoes and slow
trudging of summer travel. As it was they were glad of

their Canadian snow-shoes. One needs only shelters after
the Alpine Club hut fashion, and all that vast solitary
country would be open in the winter-time. Its shortest
day is no shorter than the shortest day in Cumberland or
Dublin.

This is no place to tell of the beauty and wonder of
snow and ice, the soft contours of gentle slopes, the rippling
of fine snow under a steady wind, the long shadow ridges
of shining powder on the lee of trees and stones and rocks,
and delicate wind streaks over broad surfaces like the
marks of a chisel in marble, the crests and cornices, the
vivid brightness of edges in the sun, the glowing yellowish
light on sunlit surfaces, the long blue shadows, the flush of
sunset and sunrise and the pallid unearthly desolation of
snow beneath the moon. Nor need the broken snow in
woods and amidst tumbled stony slopes be described, nor
the vast soft overhanging crests on every outstanding rock
beside the icebound river, nor the huge stalactites and
stalagmites of green-blue ice below the cliffs, nor trees
burthened and broken by frost and snow, nor snow upon
ice, nor the blue pools at midday upon the surface of the
ice-stream. Across the smooth, wind-swept ice of the open
tarns they would find a growth of ice flowers, six-rayed
and complicated, more abundant and more beautiful than
the Alpine summer flowers.

But the wind was very bitter, and the sun had scarcely
passed its zenith before the thought of fuel and shelter
came back into their minds.

As they approached Partington's tilt, at the point
where his trapping ground turned out of the Green River
gorge, he became greatly obsessed by the thought of his
traps. He began to talk of all that he might find in them,
all he hoped to find, and the " dallars " that might ensue.
They slept the third night, Marjorie within and the two
men under the lee of the little cabin, and Partington was
up and away before dawn to a trap towards the ridge. He
had infected Marjorie and Trafford with a sympathetic
keenness, but when they saw his killing of a marten that
was still alive in its trap, they suddenly conceived a distaste for trapping.

They insisted they must witness no more. They would
wait while he went to a trap. . . .

" Think what he's doing ! " said Trafford, as they sat
together under the lee of a rock waiting for him. " We
imagined this was a free, simple-souled man leading an

unsophisticated life on the very edge of humanity, and really he is as much a dependant of your woman's world, Marjorie, as any sweated seamstress in a Marylebone slum. Lord ! how far those pretty wasteful hands of women reach ! All these poor broken and starving beasts he finds and slaughters are, from the point of view of our world, just furs. Furs ! Poor little snarling unfortunates ! Their pelts will be dressed and prepared because women who have never dreamt of this bleak wilderness desire them. They will get at last into Regent Street shops, and Bond Street shops, and shops in Fifth Avenue and Paris and Berlin, they will make delightful deep muffs, with scent and little bags and powder puffs and all sorts of things tucked away inside, and long wraps for tall women, and jolly little frames of soft fur for pretty faces, and dainty coats and rugs for expensive little babies in Kensington Gardens." . . .

"I wonder," reflected Marjorie, "if I could buy one perhaps ? As a memento."

He looked at her with eyes of quiet amusement.

"Oh ! " she cried, "I didn't mean to ! The old Eve ! "

"The old Adam is with her," said Trafford. "He's wanting to give it her. . . . We don't cease to be human, Madge, you know, because we've got an idea now of just where we are. I wonder which would you like ? I dare say we could arrange it."

"No," said Marjorie, and thought. "It would be jolly," she said. "All the same, you know—and just to show you—I'm not going to let you buy me that fur."

"I'd like to," said Trafford.

"No," said Marjorie, with a decision that was almost fierce. "I mean it. I've got more to do than you in the way of reforming. It's just because always I've let my life be made up of such little things that I mustn't. Indeed I mustn't. Don't make things hard for me."

He looked at her for a moment. "Very well," he said. "But I'd have liked to." . . .

"You're right," he added, five seconds later.

"Oh ! I'm right."

§ 4

One day Louis Napoleon sent them on along the trail while he went up the mountain to a trap among the trees. He rejoined them—not as his custom was, shouting

inaudible conversation for the last hundred yards or so, but
in silence. They wondered at that, and at the one clumsy
gesture that flourished something darkly gray at them.
What had happened to the man? Whatever he had
caught he was hugging it as one hugs a cat, and stroking
it. "Ugh!" he said deeply, drawing near. "Oh!" A
solemn joy irradiated his face, an almost religious ecstasy
found expression.

He had got a silver fox, a beautifully marked silver fox,
the best luck of Labrador! One goes for years without
one, in hope, and when it comes it pays the trapper's
debts, it clears his life—for years!

They tried poor inadequate congratulations. . . .

As they sat about the fire that night a silence came
upon Louis Napoleon. It was manifest that his mind was
preoccupied. He got up, walked about, inspected the
miracle of fur that had happened to him, returned, regarded
them. "M'm," he said, and stroked his chin with his
forefinger. A certain diffidence and yet a certain dignity
of assurance mingled in his manner. It wasn't so much
a doubt of his own correctness as of some possible ignorance
of the finer shades on their part that might embarrass him.
He coughed a curt preface, and intimated he had a request
to make. Behind the Indian calm of his face glowed
tremendous feeling, like the light of a foundry furnace
shining through chinks in the door. He spoke in a small
flat voice, exercising great self-control. His wish, he said,
in view of all that had happened, was a little thing. . . .
This was nearly a perfect day for him, and one thing
only remained. . . . "Well," he said, and hung. "Well,"
said Trafford. He plunged. Just simply this. Would
they give him the brandy-bottle and let him get drunk?
Mr. Grenfell was a good man, a very good man, but he
had made brandy dear—dear beyond the reach of common
men altogether—along the coast. . . .

He explained, dear bundle of clothes and dirt! that
he was always perfectly respectable when he was drunk.

§ 5

It seemed strange to Trafford that now that Marjorie
was going home, a wild impatience to see her children
should possess her. So long as it had been probable that
they would stay out their year in Labrador, that separation
had seemed mainly a sentimental trouble ; now at times

it was like an animal craving. She would talk of them
for hours at a stretch, and when she was not talking he
could see her eyes fixed ahead, and knew that she was
anticipating a meeting. And for the first time it seemed
the idea of possible misadventure troubled her. . . .

They reached Hammond's in one-and-twenty days from
Lonely Hut, three days they had been forced to camp
because of a blizzard, and three because Louis Napoleon
was rigidly Sabbatarian. They parted from him reluctantly, and the next day Hammond's produced its dogs,
twelve stout but extremely hungry dogs, and sent the
Traffords on to the Green River pulp-mills, where there
were good beds and a copious supply of hot water. Thence
they went to Manivikovik, and thence the new Marconi
station sent their inquiries home, inquiries that were
answered next day with matter-of-fact brevity ; " Every-
one well, love from all."

When the operator hurried with that to Marjorie she
received it off-handedly, glanced at it carelessly, asked
him to smoke, remarked that wireless telegraphy was a
wonderful thing, and then, in the midst of some unfinished
commonplace about the temperature, broke down and
wept wildly and uncontrollably. . . .

§ 6

Then came the long, wonderful ride southward day after
day along the coast to Port Dupré, a ride from headland
to headland across the frozen bays behind long teams of
straining, furry dogs, that leapt and yelped as they ran.
Sometimes over the land the brutes shirked and loitered
and called for the whip ; they were a quarrelsome crew to
keep waiting ; but across the sea-ice they went like the
wind, and downhill the komatic chased their waving tails.
The sledges swayed and leapt depressions, and shot
athwart icy stretches. The Traffords, spectacled and
wrapped to their noses, had all the sensations then of
hunting an unknown quarry behind a pack of wolves.
The snow blazed under the sun, out to sea beyond the ice
the water glittered, and it wasn't so much air they breathed
as a sort of joyous hunger.

One day their teams insisted upon racing.

Marjorie's team was the heavier, her driver more skilful,
and her sledge the lighter, and she led in that wild chase
from start to finish, but ever and again Trafford made

wild spurts that brought him almost level. Once, as he
came alongside, she heard him laughing, joyously.

"Marjorie," he shouted, "d'you remember? Old
donkey-cart?"

Her team yawed away, and as he swept near again,
behind his pack of whimpering, straining, furious dogs,
she heard him shouting, "You know, that old cart!
Under the overhanging trees! So thick and green they
met overhead! You know! When you and I had our
first talk together! In the lane. It wasn't so fast as this,
eh?" . . .

§ 7

At Port Dupré they stayed ten days—days that Marjorie
could only make tolerable by knitting absurd garments
for the children (her knitting was atrocious) ; and then one
afternoon they heard the gun of the *Grenfell*, the new
winter steamer from St. John's, signalling as it came in
through the fog, very slowly, from that great wasteful
world of men and women beyond the seaward gray.